PRAISE FOR *HUNTING TIME*

"Deaver pulls the rug out from under your feet so often you'll be sending him your chiropractor bills."
—*Daily Express* (UK)

"Filled with plot twists, survivor skills, shootouts, murders, and an ending you won't see coming."
—*The Denver Post*

"Deaver's plot skills shine out of this tale of treachery and redemption."
—*Daily Mail* (UK)

"A fleet, irresistible tale."
—*Kirkus Reviews*

"The final twists of *Hunting Time* turn it into a masterful adventure."
—*New York Journal of Books*

"The last third of *Hunting Time* is run at breakneck speed, and the finale only seals the deal on Colter's legacy as more than just a mere chaser of rewards."
—Bookreporter.com

"A suspenseful and relentless thriller that (literally) writes its own rules. Not to be missed."
—BookTrib

PRAISE FOR THE COLTER SHAW SERIES

"Jeffery Deaver creates insanely devious plots calculated to make your head explode. . . . [*The Never Game*] dazzles with its crafty twists and turns."
—*The New York Times Book Review*

"Deaver introduces a fascinating new character in the methodical Colter Shaw. Nothing is predictable in the case, and like a curvy mountain road, the twists are intense. Hopefully more stories with Shaw are in the future."
—Associated Press

P9-DNR-811

"[A] superb series launch from Thriller Award winner Deaver. . . . Fans of twisty suspense that pushes the envelope of plausibility without inviting disbelief will be enthralled." —*Publishers Weekly* (starred review)

"Deaver's reputation as a master of the corkscrewing plot is well earned, and fans of the author's Lincoln Rhyme and Kathryn Dance novels will note the same attention to character construction and natural-sounding dialogue here. Colter Shaw seems certain to become an enduring series lead." —*Booklist* (starred review)

"Award-winning author Deaver introduces an engaging new protagonist with staying power. Colter's backstory is fascinating and his persona as much a part of the tale as the crime itself. This is a sure bet for fans of suspense and will find a home with those who like their protagonists to be a central part of the mystery." —*Library Journal*

"As always Deaver gets you in his stealthy grip on page one and then takes you on a wild and inventive ride . . . this time with new star character Colter Shaw. No one in the world does this kind of thing better than Deaver." —Lee Child

"With a twisty plot, riveting characters, and relentless suspense, *The Never Game* fires on every single cylinder. Readers will delight in this compelling new character from one of the finest suspense writers in the field. I always look forward to the new Deaver, but this one tops them all." —Karin Slaughter

"Lightning-fast and loaded with twists, *The Never Game* is a thrill a minute from one of the best. Don't miss it." —Harlan Coben

"Jeffery Deaver is one of our most exciting storytellers, and *The Never Game* pulls off the remarkable feat of intertwining a devilish plot with unforgettable characters, fascinating disquisitions with propulsive action, every element conspiring to make it almost impossible to not turn the page. I absolutely loved it." —Chris Pavone

"Jeffery Deaver knows how to deliver exactly what a reader wants. He has a gift for place and character, and here, the tension ratchets up, page by page, as we follow the exploits of a new hero. Crisply plotted and fraught with danger." —Steve Berry

"Terrific writing, vivid and raw, Deaver grips from the very first line and never lets up. He is, hands-down, one of the finest thriller writers of our time." —Peter James

"*The Never Game* is the very definition of a page-turner." —Ian Rankin

"Grabbing you from the first page, Jeffery Deaver crafts a devilish plot that unfolds with breakneck speed. An excellent start to a new series, Colter Shaw has comfortably nestled onto the bench with Lincoln Rhyme and Kathryn Dance—one of our best literary puppet masters at the end of all their strings." —J.D. Barker

"Jeffery Deaver scores yet again with a fascinating new detective, Colter Shaw, and a plot as full of thrills and twists and turns as you would expect from him. With *The Never Game* you know you are in the hands of a master. But be warned—don't start this too late in the evening, because sleep would be an annoying interruption once you've started reading!" —Peter Robinson

HUNTING TIME

TITLES BY JEFFERY DEAVER

NOVELS
The Colter Shaw Series

Hunting Time

The Final Twist

The Goodbye Man

The Never Game

The Lincoln Rhyme Series

The Watchmaker's Hand

The Midnight Lock

The Cutting Edge

The Burial Hour

The Steel Kiss

The Skin Collector

The Kill Room

The Burning Wire

The Broken Window

The Cold Moon

The Twelfth Card

The Vanished Man

The Stone Monkey

The Empty Chair

The Coffin Dancer

The Bone Collector

The Kathryn Dance Series

Solitude Creek

XO

Roadside Crosses

The Sleeping Doll

The Rune Series

Hard News

Death of a Blue Movie Star

Manhattan Is My Beat

The John Pellam Series

Hell's Kitchen

Bloody River Blues

Shallow Graves

Stand-Alones

The October List

Carte Blanche (A James Bond Novel)

Edge

The Bodies Left Behind

Garden of Beasts

The Blue Nowhere

Speaking in Tongues

The Devil's Teardrop

A Maiden's Grave

Praying for Sleep

The Lesson of Her Death

Mistress of Justice

SHORT FICTION COLLECTIONS

Trouble in Mind

Triple Threat

More Twisted

Twisted

SHORT FICTION INDIVIDUAL STORIES

The Deadline Clock, a Colter Shaw Story

Scheme

A Perfect Plan, a Lincoln Rhyme Story

Cause of Death

Turning Point

Verona

The Debriefing

Ninth and Nowhere

The Second Hostage, a Colter Shaw Story

Captivated, a Colter Shaw Story

The Victims' Club

Surprise Ending

Double Cross

Vows, a Lincoln Rhyme Story

The Deliveryman, a Lincoln Rhyme Story

A Textbook Case

ORIGINAL AUDIO WORKS

The Starling Project, a Radio Play

Stay Tuned

The Intruder

Date Night

EDITOR/CONTRIBUTOR

No Rest for the Dead (Contributor)

Watchlist (Creator/Contributor)

The Chopin Manuscript (Creator/Contributor)

The Copper Bracelet (Creator/Contributor)

Nothing Good Happens After Midnight (Editor/Contributor)

Ice Cold (Co-Editor/Contributor)

A Hot and Sultry Night for Crime (Editor/Contributor)

Books to Die For (Contributor)

The Best American Mystery Stories 2009 (Editor)

HUNTING TIME

A COLTER SHAW NOVEL

JEFFERY DEAVER

G. P. PUTNAM'S SONS
NEW YORK

PUTNAM
— EST. 1838 —

G. P. PUTNAM'S SONS
Publishers Since 1838
An imprint of Penguin Random House LLC
penguinrandomhouse.com

The Library of Congress has catalogued the G. P. Putnam's Sons
hardcover edition as follows:

Names: Deaver, Jeffery, author.
Title: Hunting time / Jeffery Deaver.
Description: New York: G. P. Putnam's Sons, 2022. |
Series: A Colter Shaw Novel; 4
Identifiers: LCCN 2022040283 (print) | LCCN 2022040284 (ebook) |
ISBN 9780593422083 (hardcover) | ISBN 9780593422090 (ebook)
Classification: LCC PS3554.E1755 H86 2022 (print) |
LCC PS3554.E1755 (ebook) | DDC 813/.54—dc23
LC record available at https://lccn.loc.gov/2022040283
LC ebook record available at https://lccn.loc.gov/2022040284

First G. P. Putnam's Sons hardcover edition / November 2022
First G. P. Putnam's Sons premium edition / November 2023
G. P. Putnam's Sons premium edition ISBN: 9780593422106

Printed in the United States of America
1 3 5 7 9 10 8 6 4 2

*To all my friends at the Kastens Hotel Luisenhof,
in Hannover, for their true kindness and generosity
during my recent trip to Germany. Danke Schoen!*

To be human is to be an engineer.

—BILLY VAUGHN KOEN, *Discussion of the Method*

HUNTING
TIME

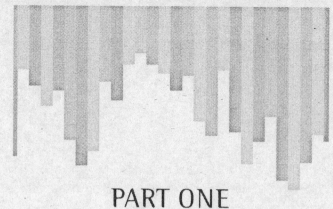

PART ONE

THE POCKET SUN

TUESDAY, SEPTEMBER 20

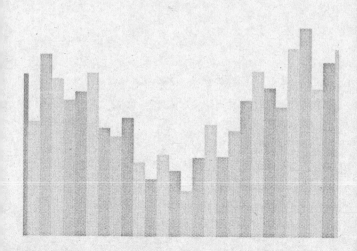

1

The trap was simplicity itself.

And as usual with simple, it worked perfectly.

In the long-abandoned fourth-floor workshop of Welbourne & Sons Fabricators, Colter Shaw moved silently through dusty wooden racks stacked with rusty tanks and drums. Twenty feet ahead, the shelves ended and beyond was a large open area, filled with ancient mahogany worktables, scuffed and stained and gone largely to rot and mold.

Here stood three men, wearing somber business suits, engaged in conversation, offering the animated gestures and the untroubled voices of those who have no idea they're being watched.

Shaw paused and, out of sight behind a row of shelves, withdrew a video camera. It was similar to any you'd pick up on Amazon or at Best Buy, except for one difference: there was no lens in front. Instead the glass eye was a tiny thing mounted on an eighteen-inch flexible stalk. This he bent at a ninety-degree angle and aimed around the side of the storage shelves before hitting RECORD.

After a few minutes, when the men's backs were to him, he stepped out of his hiding place and moved closer, slipping behind the last row of shelves.

Which was when the trap sprung.

His shoe caught the trip wire, which in turn pulled a pin from the supporting leg of the shelf nearest to him, releasing an avalanche of tanks and cans and drums. He rolled forward onto the floor, avoiding the bigger ones, but several slammed onto his shoulders.

The three men spun about. Two were of Middle Eastern appearance—Saudi, Shaw knew. The other was Anglo, as pale as the others were dark. The taller of the Saudis—who went by Rass—held a gun, which he'd drawn quickly when Shaw made his ungainly appearance. They joined the intruder, who was rising from the grainy floor, and studied their catch: an athletic blond man in his thirties, wearing blue jeans, a black T and a leather jacket. Shaw's right hand was gripping his left shoulder. He winced as his fingers kneaded the joint.

Rass picked up the spy camera, looked it over and shut it off. He pocketed the device and Shaw said goodbye to twelve hundred dollars. This was not a priority at the moment.

Ahmad, the other Saudi, sighed. "Well."

The third man, whose name was Paul LeClaire, looked momentarily horrified and then settled into miserable.

Shaw's blue eyes glanced at the collapsed shelf with

disgust and he stepped away from the drums, some of which were leaking sour-smelling chemicals.

Simplicity itself . . .

"Wait!" LeClaire frowned. "I know him! He's working for Mr. Harmon. He's in human resources. I mean, that's what he said. But he was undercover! Shit!" His voice cracked.

Shaw wondered if he was going to cry.

"Police?" Ahmad asked LeClaire.

"I don't know. How would I know?"

"I'm not law," said Shaw. "Private." He turned a stern face to LeClaire. "Hired to find Harmon's Judas."

Ahmad walked to a window and looked out, scanned the alley. "Anyone else?" Directed at Shaw.

"No."

The man then stepped to the front of the workshop, his body language suggesting taut muscles beneath the fine gray suit. He slowly opened the door, looked out, then closed it. He returned to the others. "You," he said to LeClaire. "Check him. Weapons. And whatever's in his pockets."

"Me?"

Ahmad: "*We* weren't followed. You were careless."

"No, I wasn't. Really. I'm sure."

Ahmad lifted a palm: *We're not paying you to whine.*

LeClaire, more dismal by the moment, walked forward. He patted down Shaw cautiously. He was doing a sloppy job and if Shaw had been carrying, which he was not, he would have missed the semiauto Shaw often wore on his hip.

But his uneasy fingers managed to locate and retrieve the contents of Shaw's pockets. He stepped away, clutching the cell phone, cash, a folding knife, a wallet. Deposited them on a dust-covered table.

Shaw continued to knead his shoulder, and Rass tilted his head toward him, silently warning him to be cautious in his movements. Rass's finger was outside the trigger guard of the pistol. In this, he knew what he was doing. On the other hand, the gun, with its mirrored sheen of chrome plating, was showy. Not the sort a true pro would carry.

Never draw attention to your weapon . . .

LeClaire was looking toward an open attaché case. Inside was a gray metal box measuring fourteen inches by ten by two. From it sprouted a half-dozen wires, each a different color. To Shaw he said, "He knows? About me? Mr. Harmon knows?"

Colter Shaw rarely responded to questions whose answers were as obvious as the sky.

And sometimes you didn't answer just to keep the inquirer on edge. The businessman rubbed thumb and index finger together. Both hands. Curiously simultaneous. The misery factor expanded considerably.

Ahmad looked at the phone. "Passcode."

Rass lifted the gun.

One wouldn't be much of a survivalist to get killed over a PIN. Shaw recited the digits.

Ahmad scrolled. "Just says he's coming to the factory to check out a lead. It's sent to a local area code. Others to the same number. He has our names." A look to LeClaire. "All of ours."

"Oh, Christ . . ."

"He's been onto you for a while, Paul." Ahmad scrolled some more, then tossed the phone to a desk. "No immediate risk. The plans still hold. But let's get this over with." He removed a thick envelope from his pocket and handed it to LeClaire, who, not bothering to count his pieces of silver, stuffed it away.

"And him?" LeClaire's strident voice asked.

Ahmad thought for a moment, then gestured Shaw back, against a wall.

Shaw walked to where the man indicated and continued to massage his shoulder. Pain radiated downward, as if pulled by gravity.

Ahmad picked up the wallet and riffled through the contents, then put the billfold in his pocket. "All right. I know who you are, how to find you. But I don't think that troubles you so much." He scanned Shaw, face to feet. "You can take care of yourself. But I *also* have the names of everyone on your in-case-of-emergency list. What you're going to do is tell Harmon you tracked the thief here but by the time you managed to get into the factory we were gone."

LeClaire said, "But he knows it's me!"

Ahmad and Rass seemed as tired of the whimpering as Shaw was.

"Are we clear on everything?"

"Couldn't be clearer." Shaw turned to Paul LeClaire.

"But I have to ask: Aren't you feeling the least bit guilty? There *are* about two million people around the world whose lives you just ruined."

"Shut up."

He really couldn't think up any better retort?

Silence filled the room . . . No, *near* silence, moderated by white noise, unsettling, like the hum of coursing blood in your skull.

Shaw looked over the configuration of where each man stood and he realized that examining the wallet and the in-case-of-emergency threat were tricks—to get him to move to a certain spot in the room, away from the drums that had tumbled to the floor when the trap sprung. Ahmad had no intention of letting him go. He simply didn't want to take the risk of his partner shooting toward canisters that might contain flammable chemicals.

Why not kill him and buy time? The Saudis would be out of the country long before Shaw's body was discovered. And as for LeClaire, he'd done his part, and they couldn't care less what happened to him. He might even be a good fall guy for the murder.

Ahmad's dark eyes turned toward Rass and his shiny pistol.

"Wait," Shaw said harshly. "There's something I—"

2

"You're a lucky SOB, Merritt."

The pale and gaunt prisoner, unshaven, brows knit, looked at the uniformed screw.

The guard glanced at Merritt's balding head, as if just realizing now that the man had more hair when he'd begun serving his sentence than now. What a difference a near year makes.

The men, both tough, both fatigued, faced each other through a half inch of bulletproof glass, a milky sheet as smeared as the walls were scuffed. The business end of eighty-year-old Trevor County Detention had no desire, or reason, to pretty itself up.

Slim, tall Jon Merritt was dressed in a dark suit—the deepest shade of navy blue, good for job interviews and funerals. It was a size too big. A complementing white shirt too, frayed where frays happen. The last time he had worn this outfit was more than ten months ago. In the interim his garb, not of his choosing, had been bright orange.

"You're looking like an ace," the guard said. Larkin was a large Black man whose uniform was much the same shade as Merritt's suit.

"Oh, I just shine, don't I?"

The guard paused, maybe wondering how stinging the sarcasm was meant to be. "Here you go."

Merritt took the envelope that contained his wallet, watch and wedding ring. The ring went into his pocket, the watch onto his wrist. The battery had behaved and the instrument showed the correct time: 9:02 a.m.

Looking through the wallet. The bills—$140—were still there, but the envelope no longer contained the coins he'd had. A credit card and an ATM card were present too. He was surprised.

"I had a phone, a book, paperback. Socks. A pen."

The pen he'd used to jot notes to his attorney at the hearing. It was a nice one, the sort you put a refill in, not threw out.

Larkin looked through more envelopes and a cardboard box. "That's all that's here." He lifted a huge hand. "Stuff disappears. You know."

More important: "And some work I did in the shop. William said I could keep it."

The screw consulted a sheet. "There's a box outside the door. On the rack. You didn't come in with it so you don't gotta sign." He prowled through more paperwork. Found two envelopes, business-size, and pushed them through.

"What's that?"

"Discharge documents. Sign the receipt."

Merritt did and put the envelopes in his pocket fast, feeling that if he read them now, he'd see a mistake. The screw could catch it too and say, sorry, back inside.

"And these." He slid Merritt a small business card. "Your parole officer. Be in touch in twenty-four hours. No excuses." Another card made the short trip. It was a doctor's appointment reminder. It was for eleven today.

"Take care, Merritt. And don't come back."

With not a single word he turned. The lock buzzed and snapped and the thick metal door opened. Merritt walked through it. Beside the door, on the rack Larkin had mentioned, was a cardboard box, about one by two feet, J. MERRITT on the side. He picked it up and walked to the exit gate in the chain-link. The barricade clattered as it crawled sideways.

Then Jon Merritt was outside, on the go-where-you-will sidewalk.

He felt odd, disoriented. Dizzy. This did not last long. It was like the time he and some cop friends went party boat fishing and it took him a little time to find his sea legs.

Then, steadying, he turned south. Inhaling deeply, wondering if the air outside tasted different from the air inside. Couldn't tell.

His feet hurt already. Merritt had enough cash to buy shoes—he wasn't sure if his cards still worked—but it was easier and cheaper to go to the U-Store facility, where his possessions resided.

Supposedly.

The light changed and Merritt started across the asphalt, shoulders slumped, in his tight shoes and baggy, somber suit. On his way to a job interview.

Or a funeral.

3

Wait. There's something I—"

Colter Shaw's words were interrupted by a loud bang from one of the drums that had tumbled to the floor. A huge, dense cloud of yellow gas poured from it and filled the room. In seconds it was impossible to see a foot ahead.

The men began choking.

"Poison!"

"What is it?"

"Some shit from the factory!"

The words dissolved into coughs.

"That man . . . He can't leave here. Stop him. Now!" This was from Ahmad.

Rass couldn't fire, though, not with the lack of visibility.

Shaw crouched, staying under cover of the cloud. He moved in a wide circle.

"I can't see him!"

"There! He's there! Going for the window."

"We're four stories up. Let him jump." Ahmad again.

"No, he's going the other way." Panicky LeClaire's voice was high.

"It's going to kill us! Out. Now!"

Their voices fell into choked shouts and obscenities and then went silent as they pushed toward the door.

Shaw felt his way back through the shelves and to the window by which he'd entered the factory. Choking, he descended the fire escape to a decrepit dock that jutted into the river. He jogged over the uneven wood, dark with creosote and slick with ancient oil, and climbed down into an alley that ran beside the factory from the river to Manufacturers Row.

He walked to the dumpster that sat halfway down the alley and worked on clearing his lungs, hawking, spitting, inhaling deeply. The coughing stopped, but what he was breathing here wasn't much better than the fumes. The air was laced with the acrid off-gases from the wide Kenoah River, its hue jaundice brown. He'd come to know the scent quite well; the distinctive sour perfume hung over much of central Ferrington.

At the dumpster, whose top was open, he scanned around and saw no one nearby. First he lifted out the gray Blackhawk inside-the-belt holster containing his Glock, the model 42, and clipped it in place. Then a thirty-two-ounce bottle of water. He filled his mouth and spit several times. Then he drank down half of what remained and collected his personal effects.

Hand on the grip of his weapon, he looked about once more.

No sign of Rass and his small silver gun, or the other men. Were they searching for him?

Walking to the front of the alley, Shaw noted that the answer was no. The three hurried away from the factory, Ahmad clutching the briefcase. The Saudis climbed into their Mercedes, and LeClaire his Toyota. The vehicles sped off in different directions.

Shaw returned to the dumpster.

Reaching inside, he extracted a backpack and into it he slipped the gray metal box that had been in the attaché case upstairs. He slung the bag over his shoulder and exited the alley onto gloomy Manufacturers Row. He turned right, pulling a phone from the pack and sending several texts.

He then continued his walk toward downtown Ferrington.

Thinking of the trap.

Indeed it was simple and efficient. But it was also one of *Shaw's* making, not one set by the three men in the room.

Hired by a corporate CEO recently to stop the theft of a revolutionary industrial component, which had been designed by the company's most brilliant engineer, Shaw had narrowed the list of suspects to LeClaire. The scrawny, nervous IT man—a compulsive and bad gambler—had arranged to sell the device to the Saudi buyers. Shaw had learned that the transfer was going down in the factory this morning.

While the CEO just wanted the device—known by the acronym S.I.T.—recovered and the identity of the thief revealed, Shaw thought it was a better idea to swap the real one for a fake that contained a GPS tracker, which would reveal its ultimate destination and, ideally, the identity of the buyer.

Shaw's private eye, based in the nation's capital, had found a PI in Ferrington, Lenny Caster. He'd assembled tools, surveillance gear and some other supplies. Then, last night, the two men had rigged the trip wire in the Welbourne & Sons building. Shaw had placed a military-style smoke bomb in one of the oil drums that would fall when the "trap" sprung.

In a van not far away, Caster had been monitoring the entire incident via a bug planted in the workshop. When he heard their code—"Wait. There's something I"—he triggered the bomb, releasing the dense smoke, whose recipe Shaw and his siblings had been taught by their father, obscuring clouds like this one being just another aspect of the art and science of survivalism. Shaw had made the batch himself with potassium chlorate oxidizer, lactose as a fuel and solvent yellow 33, along with a dash of sodium bicarbonate to decrease the temperature of the burn. Trespassing was one thing; arson another.

Once the smoke had filled the room, Shaw had pulled the mock-up of the device from the worktable drawer where he'd hidden it last night and did the swap. He'd then made his way to the window and dropped the real S.I.T. into the dumpster, forty feet below.

Now he was walking through the shadowy, soot-stained brick valley of abandoned factories and ware-houses.

BRISCOW TOOL AND DIE

MARTIN AND SONS IRON WORKS, LTD.

JOHNSON CONTAINERS, INC.

CARBURETOR CORPORATION OF AMERICA

In a quarter mile he broke from that industrial grave-yard into an expanse of huge, weedy lots—twenty or thirty acres of them—where facilities had once stood and were now bulldozed flat and filled with nothing but dis-carded cinder blocks, piles of brick, pipes and the trash that people had tossed over the chain-link. Flyers and sheets of newspapers and shattered Styrofoam cups chased one another in the soft spirally autumn wind.

Shaw had heard redevelopment awaited. His time in Ferrington told him that any glorious makeover would be a long time coming. If ever.

The sidewalk he was on veered right and joined the riverwalk beside the Kenoah.

The trio he'd just scammed would eventually learn that Shaw had made the swap. Would they want revenge against his in-case-of-emergency contacts? That would be time poorly spent. His private eye, Mack McKenzie, had ginned up an identity for him. The slim leather bill-fold LeClaire had relieved him of contained everything

from driver's license to credit cards to grocery store loy-
alty cards (new to Shaw; he'd never used one). Mack had
even photoshopped him into a family portrait. He was
married to a striking Latina; they had two well-scrubbed
and photogenic children.

Shaw assessed a less than one percent chance of Rass
or Ahmad traveling to Anchorage, Alaska, his fictional
home, and even if they did they would not find the fictional Carter Stone and his fictional family.

He looked ahead, at his destination, a ten-story structure, red brick like most other buildings in downtown.
On top was a large sign. The bottom was painted dark
red and the color gradient changed, moving upward until, at the top, the shade was a bright yellow, the color of
the sun on a cloudless day. The words over this backdrop
were:

HARMON ENERGY PRODUCTS
LEADING THE WAY TO A BRIGHTER AND
CLEANER TOMORROW

As he walked, he looked about. Not much reason for
anyone to be in this neighborhood, and it was largely
deserted. Some emaciated teen boys, in hoodies and
loose jeans, leaned against or sat beneath graffitied walls,
maybe hoping to sell some crack or meth or smack, or
buy some. A man of gray pallor and indeterminate age
lounged back, bundled in blankets despite the unsea-
sonal warmth of the day. He sat in front of his homeless
home of cardboard, with a strategic trapezoid of Sheet-

rock for the front door. He hadn't bothered with a begging cup. A sex worker, female in appearance, shared the lethargy of the others, smoking and texting.

No one tried to solicit Colter Shaw, who wore the patina of cop.

Fifty yards up the walk, a tall man with shaggy blond hair was texting as he leaned against the concrete wall, four feet high, that separated the sidewalk from the river. He was facing the water, which was far below street level. There was no bank; the river borders were man-made: walls of cement or the foundations of the buildings.

As he approached the man, Shaw realized two things. He might or might not have actually been texting but he was definitely using the phone for another purpose—a mirror to watch the sidewalk, focusing specifically on Shaw himself.

The other observation was that the man was armed.

Never watch the hip looking for a gun; watch the hands . . .

Shifting the backpack to his left shoulder, unzipping his jacket, Shaw approached. When he was near, the man slipped his phone away, turned and smiled broadly.

"Ah, ah, here is Mr. Colter Shaw!" A mild accent. Russian, Ukrainian, Belarusian. "No need for worries. I have been watching behind you on your fine stroll. No one is following. Even though are three people who might very much like to pay you visit."

4

ever let surprise dull your awareness...

Shaw noted that the street remained unoccupied other than the weary folks he'd just passed.

The Slav was not going for a weapon.

No cars headed purposefully in his direction, ahead or behind.

Only when he assessed minimal threat—less than ten percent—did he turn fully to the man. He had an exceedingly angular face, high cheekbones and a pointed jaw. Curiously, despite the fair hair, his eyes were jet black. Shaw knew that genes could often be fickle.

The man too looked around. "How you like being here in this shithole? But who am I to talk? Where I am coming from, we have many poisoned cities. Thank you, Noble Leader! I been walking around. Is there single place here that *doesn't* stink? I can't find it! Okay, okay, I get to point before I get boring."

The Slav clicked his tongue and his expression was one of admiration. "Smart, smart, what you did, Mr. Colter Shaw. Caught that thief, like mouse in a spring. Just beat me, a hair ahead. I was close on poor, sad Mr. Paul LeClaire. But you were more quick. Your bug was better than my bug." A shrug. "Sometimes happens.

"So, what you do, Mr. Colter Shaw? You swap it for a fake and they not have any idea." He leaned close and Shaw tensed, but the man merely inhaled. "Battlefield smoke . . . Very smart of you, very smart. Arab boys go back home, hook up the S.I.T. and get Chernobyled! Ha! I am loving this."

Shaw asked, "Who's your buyer?"

"Oh, Mr. So and So. Or maybe *Ms.* So and So. What you think, Mr. Colter Shaw?" He grew serious. "You think women screw you over in business world more than men? I think so. Now we talk . . . There is American expression." He gazed over the river. "Talking . . . what? What it is? A bird."

"Nothing to talk about. You know I'm not selling."

"Ah. I remember: talking turkey! How much you make for this job?"

It was twenty thousand dollars.

Marty Harmon was wealthy by Ferrington standards, but his company was a start-up and had yet to make a profit. Since the products he was making were intended mostly to improve Third World living conditions, Shaw had signed on. Also, he liked the challenge of the job.

He said nothing.

"Tell you what I give you. *Fifty* thousand. You want

gold, you want Bitcoin, you want Doge? Mix and match, you want. Even green money. But what bastards want that today?" He frowned. "Rubles? Oh, I make you millionaire with rubles. How about Gazprom stock? Always good." A bright smile, then back to the serious visage. "One. Hundred. Thousand." His index finger rose and fell with each number.

So, his employer was in Moscow, probably, rather than Minsk or Kiev. Given the rubles.

"What's your name?" Shaw asked.

"Name? Name?" A roaring laugh. "My name is John F. Kennedy. No, I am lying. It's Abraham Lincoln. There. That's my name! One fifty. Cannot be more."

"Well, listen, Abe," Shaw said. "It's not for sale."

"I was thinking that would be answer. I was sure. Well, don't worry, no, no." He held his hands up. "No shoot-out at high noon. I know you have gun. I saw, I peeked. A little one—*malen'kiy pistolet*."

Yes, Russian.

The man said, "Okay. *Two* hundred."

So it *could* be more.

"No."

"Fuckish."

Not a word that Shaw was familiar with and in his reward business he'd collected a sizable vocabulary of street terms.

The Slav could see the discussions were winding down. His eyes narrowed. "Too bad. Too bad for you. Lose all that money." He tapped his head. "I'll have to think of something more cleverer."

Delivered not with the tone of threat, though threat it was.

Shaw reciprocated, less subtly. "For your own sake, Abe, don't follow me. We're not alone."

The man's eyes narrowed further, then he looked around. Finally grinned. "Me? Why would I do that? I'm just tourist here! Hey, you see famous Water Clock?"

"No."

"Oh, not to be missed, Mr. Colter Shaw. Not. To. Be. Missed."

Shaw walked past him, continuing up the street, assessing the odds that the Slav would, despite what he'd said, draw his gun and play *High Noon* after all.

He put it around five percent. Abe Lincoln wasn't stupid.

But he *was* desperate.

Fuckish . . .

Okay, maybe ten.

5

At last. His custom-made work shoes . . .

Jon Merritt closed his eyes at the relief of slipping his feet into what he'd worn on the job—when he had a job. Black leather, insets, lace-up. Steel-tipped toes. Occasionally necessary.

He was inside the tiny unit of U-Store, looking over his things, in plastic bins that had been filled haphazardly. Everything just dumped.

Into a backpack bearing the faded logo of a faded pro football team he placed clothing, some toiletries, the cardboard box containing the project from the metal shop—his chosen rehab activity in County.

He continued rag picking. Anything *meaningful*? Anything sentimental?

No.

Here was a trash bag of items from his former job.

And trash bag it literally was, containing in addition a crushed soda can, an empty nail-polish bottle, a year-old slice of hard bread, long past mold. He dug through it and extracted a few things that might come in helpful.

After he pulled down the corrugated metal door, he relocked it and left the facility. Then he bused it across town, head against the glass, feeling the vibrations of the engine and the protest of the suspension on the weather-abused streets. The potholes and cracks were the same as when he went in. Ferrington's infrastructure budget wasn't going to miraculously improve in that short period of time. And even if it had, how much cash would have been siphoned off to flow into officials' pockets?

Quite a bit, Jon Merritt knew very well.

Disembarking and walking three blocks, he entered the small oil-sweet-scented office of the rambling garage.

"Ebb."

The owner blinked and froze. He was a troll of a man, with rolls of flesh below and pelts of hair above. Surprise filled his face. He stepped away from the engine of a large red Peterbilt. The wrench in his hand lowered. "Well. Jon. You're . . ."

Merritt nodded outside. "Didn't do much in the detailing department." The white F-150 pickup was grimy and dusty and the windshield opaque yellow from last spring's pollen. Branches and leaves crowned the hood and roof and lay thick in the bed, where the wind would not have swept them away.

Merritt believed they'd talked about storing the truck

inside the garage, though he wasn't positive. He'd been drunk when the conversation occurred. It was the day of his sentencing.

Maybe Ebb believed, or hoped, Merritt would die inside and somehow he could keep the truck. Only 154,000 miles on the odometer. Nothing.

The man took in Merritt's unsmiling face. He was somewhat afraid now, knowing why Merritt had gone to prison. "Really, Jon. I'd known, she woulda been spic-and-span . . ." A new tack: "You're paid up for two more years. I'll get you a refund check. Pronto. Gimme an address."

"Don't have one. Where's the hose?"

"I'd help you out, but Tom Ehrlich needs his rig."

"Hose?" Merritt had learned long ago that a soft voice is scarier than loud.

"Sure, Jon. There, outside. You want soap and polish? You give me a day, I'll have her like new."

"Keys."

Merritt took the offered chain.

When the Ford was clean enough so as not to draw attention, he fired up the engine. It knocked but was no knockier than it had been a year ago.

He sped into the street and cruised for fifteen minutes, pulling to the curb near an electronics store. Inside he bought a burner phone. Getting one set up wasn't as easy as it seemed in the movies. He knew this from his prior life. Yes, you could buy one without a credit card or a real address. But an email was necessary. The clerk, a beefy kid with impressive, meaningless tats, helped him out, and they got the thing activated.

Sitting in the driver's seat, he stared at the phone for a long time. He placed a call. He heard three ascending tones, then the announcement that the number was no longer in service.

Not surprising, considering that the woman whose number it once had been was his ex-wife, the complaining witness—that is, victim—in the case that led to his arrest for attempted murder and assault with a deadly, resulting in, as the indictment reported with a drama you didn't expect in legal pleadings, "grievous bodily harm."

6

As he approached Harmon Energy Products' campus, Colter Shaw looked back at the riverwalk.

No sign of Abe Lincoln.

A dark gray Mercedes Metris was approaching. The van pulled to the curb and out climbed a slim man in a black jacket, collar turned up, and black slacks. The outfit had many pockets, as tactical attire often did. The man was of a skin shade only slightly lighter than the clothing and his head was shaved. His wing-tip shoes were polished to dark mirrors.

Shaw stopped and nodded to Lenny Caster, the private eye who'd helped with the trap.

"Lenny."

"Colter. Went okay?"

"Aside from my visitor."

Caster had been tailing Shaw from the factory in case

the three men had learned of the switch and returned for him.

We're not alone . . .

Shaw continued, "Could you make him?"

Caster nodded. "Got some good pictures. Sent them to Mack."

The woman had some excellent facial recognition experts she could call on.

The man pulled out his phone. He read from the text: "'Sergei Lemerov. Former GRU.'"

Russian military intelligence.

"In the country on a B-1 temporary. Kicked out of Germany for dirty tricks ops. Believed to have been involved in the assassination of an oligarch in London and an activist in Belarus."

He looked up. "Couldn't find his travel particulars. Maybe private, maybe government."

Shaw said, "His best was two hundred K."

"Peanuts," said Caster.

Government shenanigans came with shoestring budgets. With any commercial competitor wishing to buy the stolen S.I.T., $200K would have been a starting point.

"Mack said she'll try to keep track of him. Anything she finds she'll send directly to you and Marty."

"I'll brief him. Our trio?" A nod back to the factory.

He called up an app on his phone. "The Saudis're going north on Fifty-five. Probably to Granton Exec airport. They'll have a G7 or something overseas fueled up. LeClaire started for home, then turned south. He's on the beltway now." Caster had put GPS trackers in the wheel wells of the men's cars.

The men shook hands. "Good working with you, Lenny. You ever get out of town? Could use some help from time to time."

Caster said, "I stay close to home. Born and bred here. Coach my son's basketball and daughter's soccer. But, for a day or two? I could swing it. And I have a feeling whatever you'd have going on, it'd be . . . interesting. Keep me in mind."

"I'll do that."

"Oh, and by the by? Mack said the oligarch and the activist that Lemerov killed? They were poisoned with polonium. That's not a fun way to go. Until you're well out of town, Colter, I wouldn't drink anything that doesn't come in a bottle that you don't open yourself."

7

Jon Merritt was leaving the Trevor County Medical Services building, following his appointment.

A nondescript place in a nondescript part of Ferrington.

The building needed a peel and scrub. It could have been a slightly better-off cousin of the prison, only ringed by chain-link, not razor wire.

The building was home to maybe forty physicians of many different specialties. You could get treated for every ailment under the sun, from cloudy eyes to painful guts to broken bones to wrinkles, if you considered wrinkles an ailment.

He glanced at the list of offices and he noted one of the larger signs.

FERRINGTON PSYCHIATRIC CLINIC

He was thinking of a particular physician he'd been seeing recently. Recalling their first session.

The frumpy doctor, about forty, is in a brown suit. No tie. That must be in a manual somewhere. Strangulation risk. His shoes are laceless slip-ons. His hair is similar to his patient's—that is, blondish and not abundant, to put it kindly.

There is a smell about him. Merritt can't quite place it. In his chair, across from Merritt's, Dr. Evans sits forward. He has explained that he will always remain outside Merritt's "sphere of personness."

This is a psychological thing, it seems, intended to demonstrate that the physician is attentive to the patient but doesn't make him uncomfortable.

Sphere of personness . . .

Merritt would simply say "his space." But then, he doesn't have the medical degree.

The distance between the two is also a security measure, considering what many of Dr. Evans's patients are here for.

Murder.

Attempted murder.

Grievous bodily harm . . .

The room bears little resemblance to a traditional therapist's digs. No couch, no armchair, no box of Kleenex, no diplomas, no framed pictures or posters carefully picked to cause the patients no offense.

The doctor is jotting notes on a tablet, not with a pen or pencil. Apparently there was an incident a few years ago—though, luckily, the ER doc up the hall managed to save one of the psychiatrist's eyes.

A wireless panic button sits on the table next to Dr. Evans's chair. It's not red. Merritt has wondered how many demons descend if the doc pushes it.

Has he ever?

"Let's just chat, shall we, Jon?" *The man is only half here. Distracted.*

And what is that smell?

Merritt is all smiles and cooperation. "Sure, I guess. About what?"

"Anything that comes to mind. How you're feeling about being here."

Did he really ask that?

But again the smile.

"Your childhood."

"Oh, sure."

Just wanting the minutes to go by quickly, he begins to ramble about growing up in Ferrington. Telling stories good and stories bad and stories traumatic and stories affirming. Some are even true.

He's careful about what he says, though. Dr. Evans, of the curious scent, may be sharper than he seems and is looking for tells, like a carny mind reader, that will lead him to a secret about Jon Merritt that Jon Merritt does not want him to know.

Merritt thinks of the secret simply as the "Truth" about him. With a capital T.

As he talks, staying far, far from the Truth, he notices that the doctor's gaze strays around the room, often ending up on the window. The thick glass opens onto the yard. But it's a prison; there is no view.

Merritt wonders if the doctor's inattention is due to the fact that he is wrestling obsessively with diagnoses and treatment plans in order to cure his prisoner-patients.

Or if the man doesn't give a shit about them and is daydreaming of hearing out housewives from the Garden District, who might be depressed or tightly wound, but never sociopathic and homicidal.

Jon Merritt now left the medical center behind and moved through the parking lot in a taut lope. He was six foot two inches but tended to walk stooped over, which made him appear to be a predatory animal. He climbed into his big Ford and in twenty minutes he was slicing through a commercial row south of downtown.

This was a neighborhood familiar to him. He'd spent plenty of hours on these streets. Here you could get the nails tipping your fingers and toes polished to gems, your car repaired, your hair extended, your baldness covered. You could buy electronics, toys, sundries, pay-as-you-go phones, used furniture, appliances big and appliances small, all off-brand and cheap and with short life spans.

You could also rent a girl or boy or combination of both for an hour or two, transactions that Merritt was also familiar with.

He cruised up the street toward the Kenoah until he came to the River View Motel. Ferrington spawned lodgings like this—one-story structures of pastel shades, well overdue for new paint, some bulbs of the neon signage dark, the parking lots weedy. The vending machines were bulletproof.

The motel did have what the name promised—a few

rooms at least and the lobby looked onto a patchy city park that descended to the water. The appeal, though, was another matter and depended largely on whether or not you had a sense of smell.

Merritt checked in, left his belongings in the dim box of a room, closed the curtains and turned on the TV, suggesting occupancy. He stepped outside, hung the DO NOT DISTURB sign on the knob and walked to a convenience store he'd passed on the drive here. He picked up some toiletries, two Italian subs, some soda, some barbecue chips.

Then on to the most important destination: the ABC store.

He walked into the place, which, like all liquor stores he'd ever been in—and that was many, many—was filled with a sweet aroma. Was that from the occasional broken bottle? Or maybe something about the paste used to affix the labels to the bottles? The cartons possibly.

Merritt's gut did a happy twist when he smelled that smell and saw the rows and rows of bottles.

His friends.

It was Bulleit bourbon he selected, a fifth. The clerk, a skinny man of indeterminate race, seemed briefly surprised. In this neighborhood, most purchases would be what the bulk of the inventory consisted of: pints, half-pints and miniatures. Also, it would've been months since anyone had shelled out for a premium like this.

The last time he'd drunk any Bulleit was the day of his sentencing. His lawyer had not been pleased he'd shown up in court drunk. Nor had the judge.

On the way back to the motel, he was distracted by motion to his left. He paused to watch a long barge, faded green, rusty, being pushed west by a mule of a tug. It was loaded with shipping containers, baby-blue Maersks being the most common. Ferrington was now only a blip, a mile marker on the trip to and from points east and points west. Once, the town had received dozens of vessels a day, workers emptying them of certain types of cargo and loading them with others. Mostly it was iron ingots arriving and finished metal products leaving. The name of the town itself, every schoolchild here had learned, came from the atomic symbol for iron, Fe.

The barge plowed out of sight and Merritt returned to his room. He chained the door and wedged a chair under the knob. This was a notoriously popular break-in locale. He got the AC running. He set his deli purchases and the bourbon on the bedside table. He rolled onto the bed and ate his late lunch hungrily, alternating bites and gulps.

Leaning back, eyes closed, he felt his gut churn.

Maybe not a good idea, packing in the food and drink.

The sensation, which had been building, struck.

Merritt rose fast and walked into the john, where, dropping to his knees, he puked aggressively.

Rinsing his mouth, he walked back to bed, lying flat this time. After some moments he sat up and pulled the backpack close and extracted the envelopes the guard had given him.

One was the discharge order itself. Nothing of interest. Lots of "don'ts" and legalese. He opened the second envelope and withdrew four sheets of paper, stapled together. He read them carefully and slipped them back into the envelope, which he returned to the backpack.

Jon Merritt drained his glass, did the suggesting-occupancy trick again and stepped outside, making sure the door locked properly. He pulled his phone from his pocket and placed a call, surprised that he still remembered the number.

8

Four days earlier . . .

have a problem. A serious one. I need help."

The man was short and broad, his hair brown and curly. He wore a tie-less blue dress shirt, sleeves rolled, and tan slacks. A checkered sport coat, black and white, was hung, without hanger, on a hook behind the door of the office that he and Colter Shaw sat in. His shoes were bright orange sneakers.

In the few minutes Shaw had known him, fortyish Marty Harmon had proved to be cherubic, edgy and focused as a laser gunsight, shifting seamlessly from one mode to another.

They faced each other across a battered, file-covered desk.

"You're like a private eye?"

Shaw told him about his reward business.

Harmon offered an interested grunt. "Never heard of that."

Colter Shaw in fact was here not in the role as a practitioner of that trade, but to consider taking on a for-hire job. A friend—Tom Pepper, a former FBI agent—had called him, explaining that the assistant special agent in charge of a Midwestern field office hadn't been able to take on a case. Pepper had asked, was he interested?

With no good reward jobs beckoning, Shaw had thought, why not?

Harmon now rose and walked to a whiteboard. Began drawing. "First, background."

The lecture began and Shaw listened with interest. He was learning about something he had not previously known: that there was such a thing as miniature nuclear power plants.

They were officially known as SMRs, or "small modular reactors."

The adjective was a bit misleading, as the average SMR weighed in at about sixty tons, it seemed. Still, they were prefabricated and could be shipped intact to their destinations, making them essentially portable.

Harmon Energy Products' version was known by the clever trade name the Pocket Sun.

In bold strokes he continued his artwork. Shaw gathered it was a cross section of one of these.

He was in an armchair that had seen better days. The springs were shot and the leather was cracked and worn where elbows and butts would wear. There was a couch too, half covered with papers and objects—metal parts, wires, solid-state boards. This was not the glitzy office of a Silicon Valley start-up, but the functional operating suite of a hardworking businessman heading up a no-nonsense Midwestern manufacturing company.

The only decorations here were a picture of the man and his dark-haired wife in her mid-forties and a large posted periodic table of the elements. On the bottom row one of these substances had been enclosed by a bright red drawing of a heart. It was the letter *U*.

Uranium.

The poster had been signed by scores of people, presumably employees. It would mark some significant event in the company's history.

There were no diplomas or certificates or industry awards on the walls, which might offer a glimpse into the CEO's bio. Shaw had, though, had his PI run a basic backgrounder. Harmon had an engineering degree from a lower state university and had founded, run and sold several other companies—of the low-tech sort. Energy, mostly. Some infrastructure. He steered clear of the press, once telling a reporter he didn't have time for that "stuff," appending a harsh modifier to the word. Still, Mack found a few articles, which depicted him as a workaholic and an uncompromising innovator and businessman. He himself owned a dozen patents for engineering devices, whose purposes Shaw could not figure out from Mack's report.

As he drew on the board, Harmon continued his TED Talk. "So, Mr. Shaw, imagine! With our SMRs, developing countries can have dependable refrigeration, lighting, phones . . . And computers! The internet. Healthcare. There're some sub-Saharan people're living in the nineteenth century, and Pocket Suns can bring them into the modern era. Prejudice and idiotic ideas—about race, AIDS, Covid, STDs—only exist in the vacuum of ignorance. Give people energy, and they'll have not only lighting, but enlightenment."

A line from a sales pitch, but not a bad one.

"Now," Harmon said, turning away from the board. "To the problem. There's a little-talked-about concern in the nuclear energy world: that someone'll steal nuclear fuel and weaponize it. It's known as 'proliferation.' Pretty sanitized term, no?"

Because SMRs like Pocket Suns were often installed in countries with fewer safeguards and security staff, there was a risk someone would strip out the fuel or even steal the unit as a whole.

The nuclear material in the Pocket Suns was the same as in most reactors—U-235, enriched to around five percent, the level that met government approval. Harmon said, "To make a bomb with that kind of enrichment, you'd need the amount of fuel roughly the size of a full-grown elephant. But if you enrich to forty-five percent, then all you'd need is thirty-six kilos to make a bomb. That's the size of a German shepherd.

"See this." After scratching his upturned nose, he indicated his diagram, which looked like a bell jar, inside of which were clusters of thin vertical pipes. At the bottom of each was a small box. It was to one of these that he now pointed. "This's the S.I.T., or 'security intervention trigger.' My most brilliant engineer came up with the idea. If someone moves a Pocket Sun without authorization or tries to break into the fuel compartment, the S.I.T. blows the uranium pellets into dust and floods them with a substance I've invented, a mesoporous nano material. It binds with the uranium and makes it useless in weapons. No other SMR manufacturer has anything like it."

The cherub suddenly vanished; his other side—the angry side—emerged.

He leaned slightly forward and pointed a blunt finger for emphasis. "We do spot inventories. A few days ago the auditors found components'd gone missing, along with some mesoporous material. Somebody here is making an S.I.T. He's—or she's—going to sell it to a competitor. They have to be stopped. Agent Pepper said this's the sort of thing you could do. Twenty thousand if you catch him and recover the trigger, Mr. Shaw. I'll pay expenses too."

Shaw considered what he was hearing. "You think it's going overseas. If it were a U.S. competitor you could just sue for theft of trade secrets and patent infringement. Get a good lawyer and you could probably close them down."

For a time, after college, Shaw had worked in a law office in California. He liked the challenge of the law, though he decided that however mentally stimulating the profession was, office jobs were a poor fit for someone known as the Restless Man.

Harmon said, "Exactly right. I know my competitors in the States. It's not them. Look, we're a small company, running on fumes. The S.I.T. is one of the few things that differentiates us. It's a huge selling point. Somebody else gets it, undercuts our price, we're gone. And I'm the only manufacturer who's planning installs in the Third World. And, okay, let's be grown-ups. I want to make some change myself. Too many people apologizing for capitalism. Bullshit. I make profits, I sink them into the next big thing, employing workers, making products that people . . ." He stopped himself and waved his hand, as if swatting away a hovering lecture.

"Tom Pepper told me the local FBI can't handle it."

A grimace. "Backlogged. And the Ferrington PD? They've cut staff by fifty percent. I even said I'd contribute a shitload to the benevolent fund. But they can't keep up with drugs, homicides and domestics. A missing gadget's not even on their radar."

Shaw said, "I'll take the job."

The man strode forward and, though diminutive, delivered a powerful handshake.

Harmon returned to his desk and made two brief calls, summoning people.

No more than five seconds passed before his door opened and a tall woman walked inside. Her long black hair was tied back with a blue scarf, which matched the shade of her studious eyeglasses. High cheekbones, generous lips. She wore a tailored suit. Shaw wondered if she'd been a fashion model.

Harmon introduced Shaw to his assistant, Marianne Keller. "Mr. Shaw's going to be helping us with the trigger."

"Ah, good, Marty." Her face bloomed with relief. Shaw supposed that a company like this fostered a sense of family. A betrayal stung them all.

"Anything he needs for expenses, carte blanche." Then he frowned. "Okay with no private jets?"

"Off the table," Shaw assured him.

"Yessir," Keller said. Shaw handed her a card containing only his name and current burner phone number. And he took down her direct line on the back of another.

As she left, someone else entered. As tall as Keller, this woman was blond, hair braided carefully and affixed behind her head. She too had an alluring face. Her build was athletic, and he wouldn't be surprised if she ran marathons.

Sonja Nilsson, it seemed, was head of Harmon Energy security.

"Mr. Shaw," she said, also shaking his hand firmly. "Good to meet you."

He expected an accent and he got one, though it placed her not in Stockholm but within a hundred miles of Birmingham, Alabama.

"Colter," he said.

Nilsson offered, "Marty told me he was talking to you. I looked you up. Rewards for a living?"

"Like a private eye who doesn't bill unless he delivers."

She sat perfectly upright and moved her hands and arms economically. She held a tablet but didn't fiddle with it. She wore a complex analog watch and no jewelry other than a ring on the index finger of her right hand. It seemed to be a serpent. He couldn't tell for certain. Shaw made another deduction: she was a veteran. And that she'd seen combat. The eyes—a rare green shade—were completely calm.

Nilsson said, "I've gone as far as I can, looking for the thief. Nothing. We need a fresh take."

Shaw now opened a notebook, 5 by 7 inches. From his jacket he removed his fountain pen, a Delta Titanio Galassia, black with three orange rings toward the nib. He knew some might think in this day and age using an instrument like this was pretentious. But Shaw took lengthy notes during the course of his rewards jobs, and a fine pen like this—it was not inexpensive—was kinder to his hand than ballpoints. It was also simply a pleasure to write with.

As she described what had happened in detail, he jotted notes in his perfect handwriting, the lines horizontal on the unruled paper. This was a skill that had not been taught to him but simply passed down from his father. Both were calligraphers and artists.

When he felt he had enough to get started, he said, "I want to see employees' RFID log-ins and log-outs. And security tapes."

Nilsson said, "I've already pulled that together."

They rose and shook hands once again, Shaw nodding away the effusive thanks and hoping a businessman's hug would not be forthcoming.

9

Sonja Nilsson's office, curiously, was bigger and contained better furniture than her CEO's. Good art on the walls too. Landscape photos mostly. He wondered if she'd shot them herself.

They sat on a couch before a long glass coffee table, on which were neat stacks of manila file folders.

Together, they reviewed employee records and the data from digital key entry and exit points, Shaw taking occasional notes. She lifted a seventeen-inch laptop onto the files, booted it up and logged on with both fingerprint and password. On this she called up surveillance tapes of the corridors where the S.I.T. components had been stored. Even though they fast-forwarded the tapes, this took a solid hour.

When they'd finished, Shaw said, "Again."

It was halfway through the second viewing that Shaw spotted the fly.

He scrubbed back and examined the scene again.

"Look."

He pointed to a video of the corridor leading to the facility where the S.I.T. components were stored. No one was seen entering or leaving the place between the closing time of 5:30 and the start of business at 8:00 the next morning.

He froze a frame and pointed to the insect on the wall.

"Okay. Got the little critter," she drawled.

"Now look at the next day."

He ran that tape to the time he recalled.

The same fly landed in the same place.

"Well, damn." The latter word was two syllables.

Somebody had gotten to the security videos and replaced them with one downloaded earlier. For two evenings, the thief would have had unobserved access to the storage facility.

Whoever did that had tech skills and Shaw was sure the thief had erased entry logs into the burgled offices. They also would have altered RFID information about entering and leaving the building itself.

"That's hard hacking," Shaw said. "Let's focus on your IT people."

Shaw came up with an idea for an undercover op. Marianne Keller arranged interviews between those in IT and an outside consultant hired by Harmon to consider opening an IT facility on the West Coast. For the gig, Shaw—in the role of Carter Stone—had donned the one business suit hanging in his Winnebago and a pair of glasses with non-magnifying lenses.

"I look corporate enough?" he asked Nilsson.

She replied, "Middle manager all the way."

He sat in a bare office, yellow pad before him, and the employees filed in one by one. Shaw didn't begin the discussion with the corporate move but let his purpose hang vaguely over them for five or so minutes as he asked about their career history at the company, where they'd worked before, if they had any complaints. Only when he sensed suspicion rising did he mention the move. He jotted their response, thanked them and then called in the next employee.

All the while he'd been gauging each man's or woman's reaction.

One was notably uncomfortable, his body language easy to read: guilt and worry. Shaw put him at ease right away, shifting to the relocation story. Paul LeClaire soon relaxed. Shaw stayed true to the role and, with a good businessman smile and a good businessman handshake, sent him off.

He called Nilsson. "We've got him. Now we need to find the trigger."

She said, "Surveillance."

"Right."

Over the next couple of days they tailed LeClaire and listened to his public conversations and read his emails, as his employment contract allowed. The phone was issued by the company, but while they could geotrack it, they could not eavesdrop.

Shaw and Nilsson followed him to meetings with two men at a motel outside of town. Using a Big Ear microphone they picked up the men's names: Ahmad and Rass, Saudi businessmen, brokers in the energy field. They learned too about the handover time and location: an abandoned factory on the Kenoah River.

Sonja Nilsson and he had taken their findings to Harmon, who was as dismayed as he was angry. "Paul? Really? We've been nothing but generous to him . . . Damn. Well, we've got a name, and you've got evidence. Now the FBI and police *have* to get involved."

"Are you sure you want that?" Shaw had asked.

"What do you mean?"

Nilsson said, "Colter and I were talking."

Shaw took over and offered the plan. "I think we should swap out the real S.I.T. for a fake one with a GPS chip in it."

Nilsson added, "We let the exchange happen, then track the fake S.I.T. and find out who the buyer ultimately is."

Harmon's eyes had narrowed as he considered this— the sniper-focused mode. "Good. Put it together. I want his goddamn head."

Shaw rose and stepped toward the door, trying to remember the formula for battlefield smoke.

10

Present day

We had another bidder."

It was a half hour after he'd left Lenny Caster, following the encounter with Lemerov, aka Abe Lincoln. Shaw was once again with Marty Harmon in the man's modest office.

They were sitting in front of the cluttered coffee table. The Swedish Alabaman security head, Sonja Nilsson, was here as well. Today in a silver jacket, black skirt, white blouse, small pearls.

The elfin man rubbed his frizzy hair and frowned. "Go on, Colter."

"A Russian." He explained about the attempted preemptive offer.

"How did he find you?" Nilsson asked.

"He was running surveillance too." Shaw then told them what Lenny and Mack had discovered about the man.

Nilsson said, "GRU? Soviet apparatus . . . He could surface again. Phoenix from the ashes. They do that."

Shaw said, "He got rebuffed. If he's freelance, he might move on. If he's on payroll, the failure won't sit well with his bosses. That means he'll try again."

Nilsson nodded. Her blond tresses were down, cascading over her shoulders and ending in a severe cut about twelve inches below the nape. Shaw had noticed that her nostrils had flared slightly when she'd joined them. She knew about the camo smoke he'd concocted but now her face registered familiarity with the scent, which supported his deduction about her time in the military.

Shaw glanced at the S.I.T. "Check it. We need to make sure it's real."

"You mean the prick might be a double agent or something? Selling the Saudis a fake? And then the real one to someone else?"

Nilsson lifted an eyebrow. "Foolish. But he's got those debts. The gambling."

Harmon rose and walked to his desk. Among the clutter he found an electric screwdriver and undid the dozen tiny Phillips-head screws and removed the housing. He examined the guts. "It's real." The CEO set the unit aside.

He asked how Shaw would like the check made out and Shaw said to himself. Harmon wrote it, tore it from the book and handed it to him. "You should get yourself a corporation. Limited liability. You know, legally, a good idea."

He believed he had one. He'd have to find out. Shaw took the check, stashed it in his wallet, next to another one he'd received for a reward job from a month ago. He'd forgotten to deposit it.

Shaw glanced Nilsson's way. And what was with those eyes? So intensely green. Contact lenses? He'd been trying to decide.

"Now. LeClaire. What do we do? Call the prosecutor? Write out affidavits? And I want a civil suit too. Let's break him."

But Shaw said, "Might have a better idea. You have a payroll office here?"

"We do," Harmon said.

"I need a thousand singles and four hundred-dollar bills. Temporarily."

"Done. What for?" With a nose scratch, Harmon leaned in. His cherubic look gave way to the focused one.

"I'm going to find LeClaire and offer to buy the S.I.T. back. I'll flash what looks like a hundred K."

Harmon said, "But it's already on that private jet. Halfway to Mexico or the Caribbean by now."

Nilsson, though, was smiling. She got it. "Ah, but that'll convince him and his buyers that it's the real item. Maybe there was some splinter of doubt that Colter swapped it out when the smoke bomb went off."

"What if LeClaire accepts?"

"He won't." Shaw and Nilsson said this simultaneously.

Harmon muttered, "And *then* jail?"

Nilsson said, "I don't think we want a trial, Marty. Details of the technology'll come out."

Shaw said, "Trade secrets aren't very secret once you get into court."

Nilsson said, "And let's not telegraph to customers we had a security breach."

"I suppose," he griped. This remedy clearly went against Harmon's take-no-prisoners philosophy.

Shaw said, "Fire him. And then don't do anything. He'll keep waiting for the police to come knocking. Every time he hears a siren or sees a dark sedan parked nearby he'll have a very bad day."

This was a good second-place alternative and Harmon was laughing. "Love it! The other-shoe punishment!" He turned to Nilsson. "Why don't we hire Colter? Put him on our security staff?"

She looked Shaw's way with a smile. "I wouldn't mind that." A brief pause. "But I don't think it's the sort of job that would appeal."

"Not for me."

"What? You don't love our beautiful burg?" Harmon glanced out the window at the dun cityscape. The river, its shade yellowish-gray from this angle, was prominent. Disintegrating cardboard boxes, driftwood, trash and dead fish floated downstream.

His face once again grew dark. "Yesterday? Another half dozen in the hospital, half of them kids."

Shaw said, "How's the cleanup coming?"

Harmon scoffed. "Slow, slow, slow . . . The city and

county're bankrupt. We have to go begging to the state and feds for help. Prying money out of their hands takes forever."

Nilsson said, "And what *is* allocated to the cleanup? A lot's unaccounted for. Millions are missing. And who knows where it went. Contractors, city councilmen, the state capital? Washington?"

Her boss said, "A reporter for a local TV station was investigating and . . ." He shook his head. "Died in a car crash. I'd do air quotes but I don't do air quotes."

"Contract hit?"

"Who knows. Probably. There wasn't much of an investigation, I heard." A sour laugh. "Ferrington had a lovely tradition of corruption even before the water issue."

Nilsson said, "If it doesn't get cleaned up soon Marty's going to lose his shirt."

Harmon, it seemed, was distributing free water to those in the affected part of Ferrington, which was a wide swath of the city.

He made a call on the intercom and a moment later his willowy assistant, Marianne Keller, appeared. "Yes, Marty?"

"Authorize disbursement of cash. Colter and Sonja'll tell you the amount and denominations."

"I'll get the paperwork." Her eyes took in the trigger and they glowed. "You got it back."

Family . . .

"Mr. Shaw pulled a switcheroo . . ."

She smiled his way.

Harmon and Shaw shook hands, and this time the CEO did come in for a bear hug. He stepped back and frowned. "You really should think about that job offer. Good pay. Pension plan. And all the bottled water you can drink."

11

The round man, in a navy suit and open shirt, was evenly tanned, a healthy color. His thick, swept-back hair was a shade that nestled between red and blond.

He looked up from his lunch, which was meatloaf or chopped steak, sitting on a solid white plate decorated with blue stripes, concentric, near the rim.

Eyeing Merritt carefully, he said, "Ah, Jon. Sit. Sit down."

Merritt joined Dominic Ryan at the chrome-trimmed table in a dim corner of the Ferrington City Diner off Manufacturers Row. He looked around the large, dark, breezy room. The walls, painted green, bore faded murals of muscled, thick-legged and broad-necked laborers, wearing overalls and fedoras, en route to their jobs.

The diner had been a popular feeding trough for working people when there *were* working people in this part of town. Then, it had been packed and noisy and boisterous. Men (and only men) in suits and men in overalls talked and gestured and laughed and argued and ate piled-high plates of food before heading back to the office or floor.

Now there were exactly four people inside, in addition to Ryan and Merritt. One was a large man in jeans and a black leather jacket, sitting with his back to the wall. A magazine was before him, but his eyes had been on Merritt as he entered. He now returned to the periodical.

Ryan sent a glance across the room and a waitress walked up to them. She asked, "Can I get you anything?"

"Coffee. Black."

"Anything else? We got specials."

"No."

When she was gone Ryan said, "You okay, Jon?" The brown eyes scanned him closely.

Merritt muttered, "You know County. No sun in the yard. Food's crap. Who wants to eat?" He absently tapped the inside pocket of his windbreaker, where sat the envelope containing ten thousand dollars he'd just withdrawn from a nearby branch of his bank. It was over the IRS reporting limit, but he didn't care. He wasn't a terrorist and he wasn't a money launderer. Those weren't things he'd been convicted for. There was more if he needed it. As part of the divorce, his ex had agreed to split their savings account. He wasn't surprised all the money was there. She was perfectly capable of screwing him but not that way.

A nod of thanks to the waitress as she set down the

cup. He took it and sipped. Didn't really want any. But he was testing his gut. After a moment he concluded: no, it wasn't going to come up again. He added sugar. Another test. Same result.

Ryan had more of his meal, cutting it with his fork. "I eat meat at lunch. At home, at night, June watches the fat." He tapped his gut. Round, yes, but Merritt wouldn't've worried about it. "Sometimes it's just a salad. For dinner. You can believe it? And dressing? Low fat."

Ryan glanced Merritt's way, subtly. The rambling meant he was treading lightly. He'd seen Merritt out of control. Blood had spilled.

And this caution was coming from one of the most ruthless mob bosses in Ferrington's history.

The man's freckled face concentrated on the plate over the course of several bites, washed down with sips from his half-empty pint glass. Bass ale, Merritt could tell from the aroma.

He looked off again and he was not wholly present. He was thinking of—no, was *seeing*—the words he'd just read on the last sheet in the second envelope Larkin, the big guard, had given him: letters addressed to the discharge board. Three recommended his release. The last one did not.

My ex-husband is a brutal and sadistic man.
Throughout the marriage I was constantly in
fear for my and my daughter's physical safety
and emotional health. Our daughter has been in
therapy for years. Only through regularly

*meeting with a psychologist is she able to cope
with the trauma she has experienced throughout
her life thanks to my husband—thankfully now
"ex."*

*He puts on a charming façade. Do NOT let
him fool you. My therapist said he is a classic
sociopath. Friendly when he wants to be, but
cruel underneath.*

But three to one.

And he was free.

After a couple more bites, Ryan brought him back.
"Jon?"

"You ever come here as a kid?"

"Here? Sure. You?"

Merritt didn't say anything for a moment. Then:
"With my old man, ten, twelve times." He was staring at
the mural. "Lunch break. He was at Briscow."

"The tool place?"

A nod.

Those lunches were at a time when Jon was the star on
the high school baseball team. He hadn't wanted to
come, never knew what his father might do or say, even
in public: bully and insult. But the man had insisted, and
if Jon had said no, things definitely would've been bad.
So he rolled the dice and went. Usually it was okay. A
little bullying, a little sarcasm. Not terrible.

When offers from the pro teams, even bush league,
never materialized, the lunch invitations from his father
stopped. And he didn't have to worry about it anymore.

Merritt sipped coffee. The waitress came by and refilled

the cup. He waited until she was across the room, then eased close to the Irishman. "I need two things, Dom."

"If I can help you out." Given who Merritt was, this qualification was required. But appended delicately, so as not to light any fuses.

"A piece. Not fancy. Wheel gun's fine."

Ryan didn't ask if he was sure. Everybody knew that for a con who'd just been released, possession of a firearm was suicide: the fastest way to get processed back inside— the fastest way, short of using it, of course.

"When?"

"Now."

Ryan's brow furrowed. He nodded to himself and sent a text. The response was nearly instantaneous. "Twenty minutes. Out back. Expect a frisk for a wire. It'll be energetic."

"Fine."

"And the second thing?" Ryan asked.

Merritt was seeing more of his ex's letter. The last paragraph, in particular.

There are things about Jon that I know, that he does not want to come to light. This was, I'm sure, one of the reasons for his attempt to kill me. I had hoped to be able to relocate with my daughter before he was released, as I know our lives are still in danger. A release now would not give me the chance to finish important projects at work and move.

*Please, honor the terms of the plea
arrangement, and keep him in prison for the
entire time of his sentence.*

*Respectfully,
Allison Parker*

Just below her name were two thick black lines of redaction. The redactor, however, had done a fast job of it.
Holding the letter up to the light, you could just make
out a street address. It would be her new house, whose
location she would have gone to great lengths to keep
secret from him.

"The second thing . . ." Merritt was leaning closer yet.
"Special services."

Ryan had a parcel of pink meat halfway to his mouth.
The fork returned to the plate, fully loaded.

In the shadowy world of these two men, the phrase
didn't mean elite military units, or concierge treatment
of VIP guests in posh hotels. The "services" referred to
all things involving for-hire murder—from tracking
down the target, to turning the living into the dead, to
disposing of the resulting work product in clever ways so
that the body was never found. Which was, Jon Merritt
knew very well, a task far more difficult than, at first
blush, it seemed.

12

Wearing a yellow plastic apron, the man stood in the middle of his workshop.

He'd pulled the latex gloves off to read the text he'd just received. Now he slipped the phone away and eyed the end table.

It was a functional piece, no particular era, about two by two feet, thirty inches high, the beaded trim around the top being the only fillip.

"Dawndue . . ." came the sound from his thin lips, the fabricated word a habit, an affectation. He uttered it the way someone might whistle or hum. He was often unaware of doing this. One woman he dated had asked if he was a bird-watcher and the sound was that of a dove.

Moll Frain was a big man, with broad shoulders and a thick neck. He was, in effect, a column. A slim paintbrush looked silly in his blunt hands. His face was pocked but not extensively. Sometimes you couldn't even see it.

He was today in what he wore frequently: black dress slacks and a white shirt, both of which the smock protected from paint.

Moll was a native Ferringtonian, born here, the son of laborers in one of the ironworks, father on the line, mother in bookkeeping.

He was infinitely grateful that he'd found within him some talent that sent him on a different career path from that of his parents.

Eyeing the table again.

The temptation was to continue, enhance some more. And more after that. But he'd learned to resist. Once you were done, you were done, and—in your heart—you knew it.

The table was made of machine-cut pine, but now, in its transformed state, it was something more: the legs were white marble, streaked with veins of black. The top appeared to be copper aged to green.

Such was the magic of faux finishing. Turning something into what it was not. The large, airy workshop behind his modest house contained fifteen pieces, some drying, some dry. Others were in their dull mass-marketed state, awaiting his magic touch.

Moll's favorite was a chair sitting near the wall. It was constructed of aluminum. He'd painted it to resemble wood. He liked the irony. This piece he would never sell.

He washed his brushes in turpentine—he used only righteous oil paints, not acrylic—and sealed the cans tight with a rubber mallet.

He hung the smock on a hook, then returned to his

living room. He pulled on a suit jacket and knotted a deep blue tie around his neck. He looked at his watch. It was time to go.

Come on, man. Come on.

Glancing past the timepiece at his wrist, he examined his ruddy skin. It was worse. He was having an allergic reaction to something—his arms, neck, legs and chest were red and burned and itched. He hadn't noticed the condition right away because he was an outdoorsman and had a late-season sunburn. But this was something different. It was spreading.

The decor of his bungalow was pale green, the same shade as the exterior siding. The color in here was more vibrant; the windows were curtained and no sun intruded. The outside clapboard was bleached pale. While he produced a piece of furniture or picture frame once a week or so, he had yet to paint the exterior of his dwelling.

The place felt empty today.

He was thinking, as he often had recently, that at this age, forty-three, he should settle down, be serious about it, get a woman.

That's what his mother had written him in emails . . . while she still knew what a computer was.

And what writing was.

Settle down . . .

Well, he wasn't *that* old. Not nowadays. He'd get it worked out.

"Dawndue," came the quiet birdcall. He sprayed Benadryl on the rash on his left arm.

The doorbell rang.

"Open!"

Desmond Sawicki walked inside, slight and skinny as Moll was large and thick. Another difference between them: Moll always wore a suit, while his occasional partner preferred casual. Today, a tan windbreaker like a golfer might wear on a cool spring day, dark slacks. They both had abundant hair. Moll's was brown, Desmond's dirty blond and longish and slicked back with lotion. Hand cream, Moll believed. The thirty-eight-year-old might have been an aging surfer, if Ferrington had not been a thousand miles from the nearest wave.

"You alone?" Desmond asked, looking around.

"I am."

Desmond seemed to want more but Moll did not accommodate.

"Where you been?" Moll asked. A gloss of irritation. "We're late."

"Had to finish something."

Probably involved a woman. Desmond had this habit.

"Any food?" He walked into the kitchen.

"No time. The job. Got to move."

"Coffee at least?"

"To go."

Desmond returned, sipping brew as beige as his jacket. Moll smelled cigarette. He himself had never smoked but he'd heard it was very addictive.

"What is with that?" Desmond said, eyeing the man's red skin. "It's still there."

"It will get looked at." He didn't want to talk about the crimson flesh either.

They walked out the door to Moll's Ford Transit, as convenient a vehicle as Detroit had ever created.

As they climbed inside he noticed Desmond was frowning, thoughtful. He was muttering, "I don't know."

Was he troubled about today's job?

Desmond was fine killing a meth cooker, an Oxy dealer, a whistleblower, a witness about to turn evidence—those were all in a day's work. But Moll wasn't sure if he had ever killed an innocent female. Was this going to be a problem? He had to find out. Right up front.

"So. What's with the mope?" Moll asked.

"I don't know," the man repeated and gave a shrug. "Afterward, fried chicken? Or Chinese? I just can't decide."

Moll considered. "Barbecue. That new rib place on Castle Drive."

Desmond brightened considerably. "Oh, yeah. Good call."

13

"There."

Colter Shaw nodded out the window of Nilsson's burgundy Range Rover. He was indicating Coz-EE-Suites, a pleasant-enough motel on the outskirts of Ferrington.

The tracker that Lenny Caster had stuck in the wheel well of Paul LeClaire's Toyota had led the pair here. Probably believing police were surrounding his home, the IT man was on the run.

The device had led them only to this wing of the motel, but his room number was easy to deduce. His car sat in front of room 104, the only occupied one on this wing.

"Didn't think to park around back?" Shaw mused.

Nilsson said, "Good at stealing parts from his employer. Not so good at tradecraft."

"You a former officer?" he asked.

The job title in this context would mean CIA.

She said, "No. But I worked with Langley some."

That she didn't give the name of her former employer made Shaw wonder if she'd ever crossed paths with his brother. Russell too worked for some anonymous government security agency. But now was not the time for it's-a-small-world conversations.

She steered around the corner and parked.

Nilsson said, "You're carrying."

He nodded. Like Abe Lincoln, she'd noticed this too. But it was an easy deduction by a pro. Shaw, for his part, had seen that she too was armed. Inside the waistband, like his. No woman in this line of work ever carried her weapon in a purse.

"Odds that *he* is?" she asked.

Shaw considered. "Ten percent. When everything was going down in the factory, he wanted to climb under a desk till it was over."

A smile crossed her face.

"How do you want to handle it?"

He said, "We'll get his hands up—in case of that ten percent—and let him see the money out the window. He'll say no. We make him stay at attention. I collect the cash. Then we leave." He looked at her. "And have lunch."

"I like that plan."

Shaw took the attaché case holding the fake hundred thousand and set it in front of the window for him to see. He pulled out his phone and called the hotel, then asked for room 104. The clerk said they needed a name to connect to a room. He shared this with Nilsson, who said, "Probably not using his real one. But give it a shot."

"Paul LeClaire."

"Yessir, I'll connect you."

Nilsson muttered, "Oh, brother . . ."

After eight rings: "Um, hello?"

Shaw said in a stern voice, "Paul, you have two options. If you hang up on me, a SWAT team'll be in your room in five minutes. Or you can hear me out."

"Who—"

"Two options."

"I . . . Okay. I'm listening." The familiar whimpering grew more pronounced.

"We met today at the factory."

"You! If I come out you'll kill me."

"Paul. Open the drapes and window. And keep your hands where we can see them."

"Do it now," Nilsson called.

After a brief pause the curtain parted. LeClaire stood, a deer in headlights, staring out the window into the parking lot. His hands raised, like a stickup victim in an old Western. He wore the same clothing he had on earlier. His white shirt was stained from the yellow smoke. Shaw approached. He examined the room. It appeared clear.

Shaw then explained the offer to buy back the S.I.T.

In a quivering voice the man said, "I don't know anything about it."

Shaw sighed. "Paul . . . Mr. Harmon wants it back."

There was no answer for that. "I . . ."

"That's a hundred thousand dollars. No questions asked."

"I . . ." The pronoun stretched out this time. Quite lengthy.

"It's out of the country, isn't it?"

"Maybe. I don't know."

Which was enough of an answer for Shaw.

His eyes met Nilsson's and she nodded. LeClaire, and the others, now had confirmation they'd gotten the real S.I.T.

She kept her hand near her weapon while Shaw stepped forward and collected the attaché case.

As they walked toward her Range Rover, LeClaire shouted, "Wait! Can I move now? Can I lower my hands?"

Disconnecting the call, Shaw said to Nilsson, "So how about that lunch?"

14

Don't think about the damn thing, she told herself. Allison Parker, doing the ungainly and adored butterfly stroke, finished her laps and climbed from the backyard pool. She'd done a mile today.

Do. Not. Think.

The forty-two-year-old brunette, tall and in taut athletic shape, was wearing a blue Speedo one-piece. She pulled off the matching swim cap and snagged a towel. The cap helped but wasn't a tight seal. Her hair, long and curly, dripped, tickling. This she blotted first, and then dried the rest of her body.

Don't think . . .

Swimming occasionally came with a memory: of another pool, the one in the backyard of the house she'd recently sold. Their marital home. *Former* marital home. She could picture the lapping water, the comforting blue tiles, the stonework of the deck, the mismatched metal and plastic furniture on the stone patio.

But those images were overshadowed by what she'd been thinking of today, while trying not to. The white cement sculpture, a shallow three-dimensional relief in the wall of the rinse-off shower beside the pool.

A seahorse.

The creatures can be comical or eerie or sensuous. The one at their old house was supposed to be the last of those, smoothly curved and with a seductive eye.

Don't think . . . But think she did.

She sees the snowflakes falling delicately, landing on the creature's head and back and tail. Flakes melting. It appears to be crying.

Mid-November. The family is in the kitchen. Parker is thinking of Christmas baskets and baking. Jon and Hannah are working on a school project.

But then he rises and, with that damn look in his eyes, says he has to go out. He won't be long.

"No, please," she says. Not a woman who begs, she is begging now.

The night has been good. It doesn't need to go bad.

Parker brought herself out of the memory and finished blotting, hung the towel on a rack, to dry in the sun, pale though it was. She wrapped a glaring-yellow SpongeBob SquarePants towel around her, stepped into her orange flip-flops.

Her hair drooped, stringy. Center parted, it ended at her shoulders.

She glanced at her reflection in the glass patio door.

This's quite the look. She laughed. She untucked the towel, rearranged it. The cartoon character's wide gaping eyes had exactly covered her breasts.

Then into the small house, ranch-style, three bedrooms. It was nondescript to the point of being invisible, built to rent, not own.

The clear autumn day was warm, but the AC was going full blast, as Hannah had set it, hardly necessary. Maybe if the girl didn't wear sweats all day, she wouldn't have to push the boundaries of the electric bill.

But some battles you fought, some you didn't.

Allison Parker would never waste parenting capital on the trivial.

The sixteen-year-old sat on the brown leather living room couch. She had a pretty, round face, framed by shoulder-length center-parted hair; she was her father's blond. Currently a red streak dominated the right side. She was huddled, lost in her phone, texting. Her feet were bare. She'd been painting her toenails—a deep mahogany—and had apparently been interrupted by a vital message.

Six piggies down, four to go.

"You've got math," Parker said.

"I did it."

"All of it?"

Fingers moving on the phone's keypad, fast as startled hummingbirds. "Yeah."

Parker finger-combed her curls. "Let me see."

A pause. "Maybe there's a little more."

"Hannah." Her voice was stern. The deceptions had been coming more frequently lately. Small, but a lie is a lie.

A sigh. "All right. I'll do it."

"Thank you." Parker glanced at the coffee table, where the assignment sheets sat.

She'd let the girl take a mental health day. After the incident last November, her daughter had had to cope with three traumas: a mother who'd been badly injured, a father jailed for the crime and life under a microscope at school. (Every student would have known about the incident a half hour after it happened. Thank you, social media—though Parker supposed that fifty years ago, word would have spread almost as quickly via analog phone calls. And before that? Telegraph and twice-daily newspapers. Nothing can stop the spread of a good, horrific story.)

Hannah was certainly improving, but there were bad days. How much of this was because of the incident and how much because of teenageness, though, was impossible to tell.

Without looking up from her toes, Hannah said, "The smell's still there."

The landlord had painted the house before they moved in and, yes, whatever he'd used had off-gassed an unpleasant sweetness.

"Won't be long till we get our Greenstone." A reference to the fortress the girl, at ten, had loved hearing her mother describe as she read a fantasy book aloud before bed every night. She'd gotten the Greenstone Lego set one Christmas, to her breathless delight.

Now Hannah gave no response. She fielded another text. Eyes down, she said, "Windows?"

Prone to paranoia and exceedingly security conscious, Parker kept the windows closed and locked at all times. This would be why the girl had the AC cranked up, of course. A bit of passive-aggressive sniping?

Probably.

Parker inhaled. She thought it was better. "We'll air it out on Saturday."

The girl sent another text.

"Hannah. Phone down. Now."

With a tint of exasperation the girl complied.

Parker slid the assignments in front of her daughter, who scooted closer to the coffee table. Her mother scanned them. There were five problems still to do for class. Five out of seven. So not exactly just "a little more."

Parker tapped problem 2.

Find the domain of function $f(x) = \dfrac{x - 1}{4 - x^2}$.

Her daughter glanced down and then returned to polishing a nail.

"Hannah," Parker said. Usually her mother referred to the girl in the light, truncated form of her name. The full two syllables contained a hint of warning.

Without looking up, the girl recited, "The domain's the intersection of two sets." She lifted a pen and wrote the answer in fast, careless script:

The first set is $x \leq 1$. The second is $-2 < x < 2$. The answer's $1 \leq x < 2$.

Her mother blinked and gave a soft laugh. "That's right."

Hannah's expression said: obviously.

Parker raised her hand, five-high. The girl grimaced and returned an unenthusiastic tap.

Lord . . .

Parker was hardly surprised at the speed of the correct answer. The girl's brilliance had been obvious for years. It just mystified her that she made the calculations so effortlessly, while Parker herself labored to arrive at the finish line.

So why did the girl have so little interest in a subject she was so good at, while preferring the arts: photography, drawing and writing?

"Get the rest of them done."

"Okay." A pause. "I was texting Kyle?"

"Were you?" Something was brewing. Parker measured responses. "How is he?"

"Cool. He says you're pretty."

"That's very sweet."

Another glance at a question. Hannah jotted more numbers, letters and symbols on the homework sheet. This answer too was right. The girl said, "He's going to the mall tomorrow. He's got to pick up a present for his brother."

Hannah was clearly asking if she could join him. Students as young as thirteen or fourteen pseudo-dated— really just hanging out together, more flirtatious than anything, and in theory Parker had no problem with her daughter doing so. But her mother's swelling unease usually kicked in and derailed plans.

Parker warned her daughter about the level of crime in the tough, under-policed city of Ferrington, which was certainly true.

But she didn't tell her the full truth.

About how much risk they both might be in because of her ex.

And so she kept the girl close.

But now, as a reward for her tackling the homework, she said, "I think that'll work out."

In response to the tacit question: Can I go too?

"Yeah?"

"Yeah. Finish up. Pizza for dinner?"

A bright smile.

She'd use the meal to learn more about Kyle. She'd met him twice and he seemed nice. She wanted to know more.

Shivering, she headed into her bedroom to change into jeans and, what else, given the temperature? A sweatshirt.

On the way to her dresser she glanced at her phone, lying faceup on the bed.

She stopped in mid-stride, feeling her heart ratchet up.

Eleven missed calls.

Parker listened to the first message.

"Oh, Christ . . ."

15

Packing.

Fast.

Careless.

In jeans, a gray sweatshirt and a quilted baby-blue vest, Allison Parker was tossing random clothes into a large gym bag and backpack with shaking hands, her muscles weak. "Two years early? Letting him out?" Spoken aloud or to herself? She didn't know.

Hannah was in her room, slowly debating what to put into her own luggage.

"Just the basics! Get going."

"Jesus, Mom. Chill."

Her phone sounded with a noisy rock song she'd loaded because her daughter liked it. Her lawyer, David Stein, was calling back. Her quivering hands nearly dropped it. She plugged in earbuds and continued filling the suitcase. She stepped farther into her bedroom so her daughter couldn't hear her side of the conversation.

"How did it happen?" she asked.

"I don't know. You ask me, he worked them. He did one of his slick songs and dances." He fell silent a moment. Then said in a voice even more somber: "Listen to me, Allison. There's something else you need to know." A pause, as if working up his courage. "After he got out, a couple of cons—prisoners—went to a guard. They said Jon had told them when he got out, he wants to find you." Decibels dropped as he continued. "He wants to find you and kill you."

Allison Parker lowered her head.

"Of course he does . . ."

Maybe whispered, maybe thought.

"What, Alli? I didn't hear you."

So, whispered.

She was thinking. So, here it was: the moment she'd dreaded, the moment she'd thought she could dodge forever. And the plans she'd made for disappearing with Hannah to a new life, somewhere far away, before he was released, were useless.

Of course he does . . .

She asked, "Do they know where he is?"

"No. He has twenty-four hours to register with his parole officer, with an address. He hasn't. I talked to a detective at FPD. After what those cons told them, there'll be officers looking for him."

What to take? Jeans, sweats, underwear, socks,

perfume . . . Wait, perfume? She set it back on the dresser, choosing Tampax and Advil instead.

"We're leaving town."

"You should. Where?"

"I don't know. I'm not telling anybody. I'll call from the road. Only your landline. I don't trust mobiles."

Paranoia was the unreasonable concern about an imaginary threat. The danger Jon Merritt presented was real.

"Alli—"

She disconnected, staring at a drawing Hannah had done at age ten. A watercolor on white construction paper. A unicorn, its coat the spectrum of a rainbow.

This musing lasted only seconds. The past had arrived. She would now make sure she and her daughter had a future.

Parker shoved the door open and walked into the hallway, gripping the bag and backpack firmly.

The girl was sitting on her bed, beside a half-filled gym bag. Inside were only her computer and a few articles of clothing. She was texting.

"No, no."

The girl glanced her way.

In a low voice, as steady as her hands were now, Parker said, "Phone away. Finish. I fucking mean it."

"Language!"

"I don't have time for that. Pack."

The girl shot an exasperated look her mother's way, then rose, slipped her phone into her right rear pocket. She started sifting through drawers. Parker stepped quickly into Hannah's room and filled her bag and back-pack with random clothes and toiletries.

"Wait. I want to take—"

"No." This word was a growl.

Parker hurried into the kitchen and looked out into the backyard, half expecting her ex to come charging out of the bushes, holding a baseball bat or axe.

She loaded the electronics into a Whole Foods reusable bag—phone and computer chargers and cords, her Dell laptop, a seventeen-inch model, a Wi-Fi router, battery packs.

"Where are we going?" the girl whined. "You said I could go to the mall!"

"Your bags. Now. We're leaving."

She reluctantly picked them up. "So Dad's out of jail? So what?"

Of course he does . . .

They had just walked out the front door when the girl stopped and ran back into the house.

"Hannah!" Parker called. "No!"

"I can't," came the girl's voice.

"What?"

"My iPad. I'm not going anywhere without it!"

16

I n the backyard of his ex-wife's house on Maple View, Jon Merritt was making his way through the brush toward the back door.

He tensed and crouched as he heard an engine roar.

His ex's SUV raced over the curb and skidded around the corner onto Cross County Highway, heading west.

Goddamn.

He began sprinting back to his truck, which he'd parked three blocks away, just to be safe. As he ran, he pressed his hand against the grip of the pistol so it didn't fly from his belt. In the garbage-decorated alley behind the Ferrington City Diner, Ryan's man had, yes, conducted a vigorous frisk for wires. Unnecessarily rough, but Merritt was more offended that a battered two-hundred-dollar gun was priced at seven, no negotiation.

Supply and demand . . .

Gasping, he continued along the sidewalk, dodging a

homeless man, as he watched her 4Runner. It was closer than he'd expected. He could catch them.

Had she seen him? Or had somebody called her with the news he was free?

The run hurt, muscles and lungs. He was out of shape. You might lift weights in prison but you don't get aerobics. Nobody runs.

Breathing hard, gasping, he got to the Ford and leapt into the driver's seat, shoved the key into the ignition and started the engine.

As long as he wasn't lit up for speeding they were in his grasp. Any cops nearby? Probably not. Random traffic patrols were not budget-strapped Ferrington's strong suit. Anyway, sometimes you just had to take a chance.

Into gear, spinning the wheel and slamming down the accelerator.

The big truck bolted forward.

And began to stagger.

Thump, thump, thump, thump . . .

He braked hard, dropped the transmission into park and, shoving the door open, stepped out onto the asphalt.

For Christ's sake . . .

He closed his eyes in disgust and fury. She could've gone east or west but chose west and spotted the truck. She had let the air out of the right front tire. It was completely flat.

He gazed up Cross County to where the battered asphalt disappeared into the hills. She was already out of sight.

Merritt lowered his head to the driver's-side window.

After a full minute of letting the anger pass, he pulled out his phone. He composed a text saying that plans had changed—Allison had fled and he needed help finding her. He'd get back soon with specifics. He would pay. A lot.

The response, affirmative, came back in a matter of seconds.

Merritt looked west, into the afternoon sun. Where are you going? he thought. Where the hell . . . ?

He was startled when a voice intruded. "Hey, mister, need a hand?" The question came from a middle-aged man. He was in a casual jacket and slacks. Apparently just out for a stroll on a gentle fall afternoon.

Merritt was inclined to say no, the fewer people who could place him here the better. But the guy had already seen him and Merritt was pressed by urgency. "You don't mind getting your hands dirty. Always hard to lift up the spare and get it on the lugs."

The man took his jacket off and rested it on a nearby hedge. "Don't I know it? They give you a jack for the car; they oughta give you a jack for the tire."

Merritt said, "Now, there's an invention for you."

The men walked to the back of the truck and the neighbor unwound the spare while Merritt got the jack and the tools from the compartment in the bed.

He fitted the device to the bracket on the undercarriage while the neighbor wheeled the spare up. He surveyed Merritt, who was energetically working the jack handle. "You're in some hurry there, sir."

Merritt scowled. "Just going to pay a visit to my wife

and daughter. Who I haven't seen for a long time. I've been away. And *this* happens."

"Isn't that always the way? But we'll get you back on the road fast as we can. You must miss 'em."

"You don't know the half of it," Merritt said, breathing in gasps as he pumped.

And under his frantic hands, the two-ton vehicle rose slowly into the air like a ghost leaving a recently deceased body.

17

There it is. Our most famous attraction. Get out your Polaroid."

Sonja Nilsson slowed the Range Rover and pointed. They were downtown on the road that paralleled the Kenoah. Across the river was a tall brick building not unlike the others here. Mounted on the portion of the building's foundation just above the surface was a ten-foot-diameter clock, in art deco style. The face and hands, frozen at ten until two, were the green of aged copper and the brown of rust.

"The Ferrington Water Clock. That building, it was the Carnegie Iron Works. The CEO—no, not *that* Carnegie—wanted a public relations gimmick. His radiators and car parts weren't sexy enough to get traction. So he had it commissioned. It ran on the river's current. People'd come from all over the state to see it and get pictures of themselves with the clock in the background."

"When did it stop? And I've got the ten-to-two part."

She laughed. "Long time after Carnegie did. The city kept it going, but money dried up. Probably twenty years ago. The hands: people call them the 'Angel Wings.'"

The SUV accelerated fast, then turned away from the river at the next intersection. She told him she had a pub in mind she thought he might like.

She was wearing aviator shades. He'd tried to get a look at her eyes. He really wanted to know if the color was from genes or from plastic.

After some silence he asked a common silence-breaking question. "How'd you end up here?"

"Now, that is a long story. I'll trim." Her voice, enwrapped in that lovely Southern accent, was low. The word *sultry* came to mind. "I wanted to—yes, see the world—so I joined up. Did a couple tours in Hawaii and California. Met a boy, also from Birmingham. After our hitches, we went home, got married. Yeah, 'hitched!' That didn't work out . . . Not his fault. I'm a tough person to live with."

The confession amused him. It seemed almost like a warning.

"I wanted to stay in security. A job recruiter told me about an opening at Harmon Energy. I liked the product, liked Marty's mission—helping save the poor. So. Here I am. Sorry you asked, aren't you?"

"Think you trimmed just right."

A car passed at speed—and she was well over the limit. The Acura SUV had tinted windows. A problem?

Nilsson said, "It's good." Her eyes had been following

the car's trajectory too. "Any threat would have presented by now."

More miles rolled by: brown and flat. Shaw had grown up surrounded by mountains.

"When my friend Tom called about the job, I thought 'Ferrington' was familiar. Something in the news. Crime, I think."

"The corruption cases Marty was talking about?"

"No, violent."

"Oh, the Street Cleaner? Serial killer."

"That's it."

"Few years ago, somebody was shooting street people—a homeless guy, tweakers, a woman in the sex trade. Mostly around Manufacturers Row."

Shaw remembered those people he'd seen around the riverwalk, after the S.I.T. operation.

She added, "Still an open case. Whoever it was, was smart. Cleaned up afterward. You ever work a case with a psycho?"

Shaw called them "jobs" not "cases" but felt no need to explain. "Once. Killed four women. Brilliant. Medical student. The police caught him but he got away. Vanished completely. After a month, the county posted a reward."

"You found him?"

"I did."

"How?"

"Staked out plastic surgeons."

She gave a laugh. "Smart."

Shaw's eyes were drawn to a gaudy yellow billboard.

BRAXTON HEADLEY LAW FIRM
SPECIALISTS IN TOXIN-POISONING CLAIMS.
DO YOU HAVE CANCER, EMPHYSEMA OR
OTHER ILLNESSES?? YOU MAY BE ENTITLED
TO MONEY. CALL NOW!

It was one of a dozen lawyers' signs decorating the highway.

Another sign was:

UNITED DEFENSE INTERNATIONAL, INC.
FERRINGTON ADVANCED TACTICAL
SYSTEMS FACILITY BE A PART OF YOUR
COUNTRY'S FUTURE! NOW HIRING. ALL
SHIFTS.

Someone had climbed to the bottom of the billboard and spray-painted:

ASSHAT!!!

She noticed his gaze.

"Kick in the teeth," she said.

"How's that?"

"Ferrington survived the downturns. You catch that, Colter?"

"Plural."

"Yep. The city was the iron capital of the Midwest a hundred and fifty years ago."

The Range Rover was automatic but she used the steering-wheel paddles, which was manual transmission light, not real shifting. Still, it was more fun than just using your right foot and it let you tach into the red.

"Ferrington was never a pretty city. But it was grand. It was alive. It had more factories and rail yards than any city in the state. The hotels were as fancy as anything in Memphis or St. Louis."

"But then," Shaw said.

"But then. Iron was out and steel was in. That meant Gary and Pittsburgh and New Jersey were the new meccas of industry. And after that, China and Japan. Recently things started to look up. Some outfits saw cheap real estate and bought up some of the old buildings— Marty's company, a chipmaker, and there's a government contractor makes some parts or another for the Defense Department, nobody knows what. Amazon was considering a distribution center on Route Eighty-four. That got everybody excited. Things were looking up."

"And the tooth kick?"

"The water. Nobody knew how polluted the old factory sites were. When they cleared acreage for the redevelopments, it unearthed the toxins. The Kenoah's worse than the Ohio, the Tennessee and the Ward Cove."

"What's it polluted with?"

"Quite a cocktail. Coal tars, heavy metals, aromatic hydrocarbons, MTBE."

Shaw shook his head.

"Methyl tert-butyl ether. Never heard of it either, but all you have to do is read the *Daily Herald* for the past six months and you'll learn enough to get a degree in chemistry.

"And the companies looking our way were reading all about it too. Like that billboard? United Defense? They were going to be hiring fifteen hundred people on two campuses. Now it's on hold, and probably not going to go through. Same with American Household Products. That hire was going to be eight hundred."

Hence: *Asshat . . .*

"They going to reassess when the cleanup's done?"

Nilsson said, "It's not like washing cars, you know: goes in dirty and comes out all buffed and shiny. It's a slow process. CEOs don't want to gamble their shareholders' money—and their own bonuses—that the same thing won't happen next year. Here we are."

She skidded the SUV to an abrupt stop in a gravel parking lot in front of Mitchell's. The pub and attached inn were both rustic and quaint, with dark wood siding and forest-green trim on windows and doors. A flagstone path snaked lazily to the entrance.

Nice place, Shaw reflected. An objective assessment; he was not one for atmosphere. As long as there was a local beer on tap and something substantial to eat— burger or steak—the place would do. Also, he hoped for relative quiet.

After they both did subtle security scans of the area around them, Nilsson and Shaw walked to the door. He was encouraged to see a sign.

WE SERVE IRON TOWN IPA.

In his travels Colter Shaw liked to sample local brews.

That satisfied his first wish, and the second was likely to be granted too, judging from the smell of grilling meat.

They climbed the three stone steps to the porch that fronted the inn, and as they did, their shoulders brushed. They shared a glance. Shaw was reaching for the door handle when Nilsson's phone chimed. She carried two. This was an iPhone. The other was larger and more complex, maybe satellite. Nilsson read the text.

Her lips tightened.

"It's Marty. I have to go into the office." She looked up. "He asked for you too."

18

"hat was mean."

Piloting the 4Runner west from Ferrington at just over the limit, Allison Parker glanced at her daughter, who sat knees up, in the front seat, looking at her computer.

"What?"

"Daddy's tire."

Parker turned back to the road.

As they'd hurried away from the house, without the iPad, Parker had skidded onto Cross County Highway and sped up, but then—to her horror—she had seen a white Ford F-150 parked curbside and empty. She braked hard. Yes, it was Jon's—she knew the dings and scrapes. Looking around, she didn't see him. He'd be at the house about three blocks away. She had only minutes. "Stay here," she'd ordered. "Do not get out."

Parker had jogged to the truck, looked in the bed for

something she could slash the tires with. Nothing. So she'd unscrewed the air nozzle cap and with a twig bled the air out of the right front. Thought about the left but decided it was too risky to stay longer.

After five or so miles she had made another fast stop, scattering gravel and flattened cans on the shoulder. Glancing continually in the rearview mirror, she had sent emails to her mother and Marty Harmon, telling them what had happened and that she and Hannah were leaving. She'd be in touch when it was safe. She left a message with David that he'd been to the house—a violation of the restraining order. He could now be arrested.

Finally she responded to her daughter's earlier comment. "I didn't do it to be mean. I did it to keep us safe."

"Safe?"

Parker was not prepared to tell Hannah that her father's intent was to kill her. She said softly, "Hannah, please. You know his tantrums, all the times he lost control? How mad he was at me for pressing charges? If he's drinking again, and I'm sure he is—"

"You don't fucking know that!"

Parker did not, of course, go to "Language!"

"He could make a scene. He could hurt somebody, even if he doesn't mean to. Or hurt himself. He can't legally be on our property. He could get into a fight with the police."

"Maybe he was just coming by to apologize."

Oh, sure, Parker thought in her most cynical silent voice.

She glanced at the Dell in her daughter's lap.

Parker had the only router, so the girl wasn't on-line . . . Or was she?

She might've bought a pay-as-you-go Wi-Fi with her allowance.

"Are you online?"

"What? No."

"Turn your screen."

"Seriously?"

"Your screen. I want to see you're in airplane mode."

"How could I get online? You won't let me have a jetpack. Like everybody else."

She defiantly turned the computer and for a moment Parker thought she was going to pitch the Dell into her face. Oh, the girl had definitely inherited some of her father's disposition.

She squinted. It was just GIMP, a photo-editing pro-gram like Photoshop.

"I'm sorry. But we need to take charge of this."

"You're, like, totally overthinking. *You're* the one who said he's two different people."

True, she had. Though she'd told Hannah this to leave a portion of the good memories of past years intact. She had not added that multiple personalities were also a defining quality of sociopaths.

She'd meant when he was drinking, but she had also wondered if, even when he was sober, the dark side could eventually come to predominate, and the generous and reasonable persona vanish.

Could a brain's nature be fundamentally and perma-nently changed?

Why not? It could be done with real wiring and capacitors; why not with neurons and synapses?

Finally Hannah broke the silence. "Where are we going?"

"I'm thinking about that."

Parker had yet to work out a destination. Immediate escape had been her priority. Now she drove along the Cross County, old warehouses and developments giving way to grazing land and razored cornfields and dense forests. At Route 55, miles west of Ferrington, she made a sharp turn south, left, and drove five miles to the small town of Carter Grove, where strip malls and a multiplex and a dusty golf course defined civilization.

She parked in one of these malls now, in front of a nail salon. She said sternly, "Wait here. Do not get out of the car."

The girl gave her a look.

"Hannah."

"All right."

Parker snagged a logo-free blue baseball cap from the backseat, tugged it on. She climbed out and, carrying her large brown leather Coach purse, walked around the corner to First Federal Bank. She returned less than ten minutes later, dropping the purse on the floor of the backseat.

Leaving this mall, she pulled into another, anchored by a Target. This time she insisted Hannah come with her. They went inside and Parker bought a burner phone. The clerk, a skinny boy, shot a flirt at Hannah, who vaporized him with a look.

Turning to mom, he said, "The phone, it's tricky, kinda. I'll set it up, you like."

It wouldn't be tricky at all but he could use *his* computer to activate the device. She wanted to keep all their existing devices offline.

Fifteen minutes later, they were in the car once more. She started the engine and her eyes went to the Toyota's navigation screen.

"Is there a way to shut it off?"

The girl's perplexed look was wildly exaggerated. She only shrugged.

Parker tapped the touch screen a few times but didn't see a way to disconnect it from the satellite. That probably involved going into the dash.

She asked Hannah, "There's a bus station in Herndon, right?"

"Bus?"

But Parker remembered that there was. Downtown. She put the SUV in gear and steered back onto Route 55, scattering gravel as, this time, they drove north.

Hannah muttered, "I don't want to take a bus. They're gross. Jesus, Mom, what? You think he can track the car? He doesn't have superpowers."

Except that, yes, Jon Merritt did.

Her ex-husband had been a decorated and popular Ferrington Police Department detective, sixteen years on the force. He still had plenty of friends at FPD, men who didn't give a shit about a drinking problem and an arrest for spousal assault. (*A desent wife would have got him help you bitch!* read one anonymous email she'd received.) It wasn't impossible that he'd appeal to these friends, on the QT, to peek at server information and highway cameras to track her.

And even more troubling were the contacts he'd made on the *other* side of the law. She knew that as a cop, Jon had cut deals with some of the most dangerous organized crime bosses in and around Ferrington. Maybe at this very moment he was calling in a favor: Help me hunt down my ex . . .

And if that didn't give him the superpowers of a Marvel Comics character, it came damn close.

19

Shaw and Sonja Nilsson walked into the same office they had been in not two hours earlier.

Marty Harmon gestured to the couch.

At the moment he was all edge and sniper. The humor was gone.

The two of them sat and Harmon eased forward in his chair. "LeClaire?"

Nilsson said, "Did just what we thought. Didn't take the money. Probably called the buyers right after we left to tell them that they have the real trigger."

Or that's what he did when he lowered his arms, which was undoubtedly somewhat after Shaw and Nilsson's departure.

Harmon said, "I talked to our tech department. The GPS is still dark. They're monitoring it."

The fake S.I.T.'s tracker was on a timer so as not to be detected on planes. Many passengers didn't know that pilots could tell if someone was trying to use a mobile phone on an aircraft.

But it was clear that LeClaire was not the first thing on his mind. He absently rubbed a thick finger against the side of his pug nose. "Something's come up. The engineer who developed the S.I.T.?"

Shaw nodded. "We interviewed her. Allison . . ."

"Parker."

The clear-eyed brunette, furious that her "baby" had been stolen, had been helpful in running through procedures for securing the components and the mesoporous nano material.

It was the woman Harmon had described as "brilliant."

"Alli was married to an abusive husband. Jon Merritt. About a year ago he tried to kill her. Put her in the hospital. Got three years in prison. Only he was released early—this morning. Alli sent me an email saying she was going into hiding, with her daughter. She wouldn't say where. She probably was terrified he'd find out."

"She thinks she's in danger?" Shaw asked.

"Oh, she is. Her lawyer told me she knows something about Jon, his past, something that he didn't want to get out. And that may have been why he wanted to kill her in the first place."

"What?"

"David didn't know." Harmon's fists balled up. "But if there was any doubt, get this, just after he's released, a couple of prisoners go to a supervisor. Merritt told them first thing he was going to do when he got out was kill her. Merritt was completely calm about it. Like talking about a game. They said it looked like he didn't care what happened to him. Maybe murder-suicide, killing their girl too."

Nilsson shook her head, frowning.

"How'd the prison miss that?" Shaw asked.

Harmon scoffed. "I don't think they take a poll of fellow prisoners in deciding to release somebody or not. And why didn't the board or the prison shrink pick it up? I've met Merritt. He can be charming, funny, your best friend. He played the staff."

Nilsson said, "I think I met him. A party here. Christmas. Caused a scene. Bad one. It got physical. Somebody was hurt."

"Has he done anything illegal yet?" Shaw asked.

"Violated a restraining order."

"Misdemeanor. But there'd be a technical warrant. Police have a stakeout on her house, right?"

"No. FPD staffing, remember? Part of the reason I hired you. And probably another reason the board didn't ask too many questions. The system's always cut Merritt some slack. He was a cop, a *revered* cop. A hero. He was almost killed saving his partner's life." The scowl was broad. "And there's some bullshit feeling that Alli was too fast to press charges. Should've gotten him some help instead."

Nilsson muttered, "Seriously? Patting the little lady on the head, saying, oh, it wasn't so bad."

"Merritt?" Shaw asked. "Any possible connection to the theft of the S.I.T.?"

Harmon's shoulders fell. "First thing I thought of when I heard about what he had in mind. But I can't see it. If he even *heard* of the S.I.T., it would've been over a year ago. And he was in prison when LeClaire was contacted by our friends.

"Now, Mr. Shaw . . . Colter. I'm in a real bind here." His sniper eyes were trained on Shaw's. "Alli's a friend. I've known her for years. But—okay, you've guessed it— I need her. She's my senior engineer. She's developing another product that's got to be finished before we can launch. And there'll be others after that."

His muscles were taut and veins that had been invisible rose and darkened. "I called the FBI again and they don't have jurisdiction, unless he crosses state lines. And we know how much the police are going to help.

"I don't have anywhere else to turn." A pause. "You do this for a living—finding people. Will you? Find Alli and Hannah and keep them safe until he's back in prison?"

Shaw was thinking of his meeting with the woman, whose mind danced from idea to idea regarding the logistics of how a thief might make off with the components— a session interrupted at one point when her mobile buzzed and a smile appeared. She'd said, "Excuse me. It's my daughter. I have to take this." And had answered.

Shaw said, "Let me get my notebook and pen."

20

The helpful neighbor had refused the twenty that Jon Merritt had offered for assisting with the tire, saying, "No, sir, no, sir, thank you for the offer but it's the Christian thing to do. Pay it forward. Put it in the plate at church."

He'd be assuming that Merritt attended; any man that didn't cuss at a flat tire had to be religious.

The instant he put the tools away Merritt had jumped into the truck and taken off in the direction Allison had vanished.

He was now fifteen miles out of Ferrington. Moving quickly at exactly the magic—that is, safe—six miles over the limit. The road he was on, Cross County Highway, had few motels, he knew from his days on the force, when he worked Vice and was obsessed with ridding the city of sex trade and drugs. He doubted she'd stay this close to home anyway. Maybe Monroe or Pickford, but even those seemed unlikely. She'd go for distance.

And she wouldn't fly. She'd know that he still had connections and maybe one of them could pull flight manifests. She'd want anonymity. And that meant escaping by car, bus or train. No, train was unlikely; there was freight service in Ferrington but no passenger trains for a hundred miles.

So, car or bus.

He continued on 55 to Herndon, which had the only bus depot nearby.

It was an old mill town, now devoted to outlet malls, healthcare and auto sales and repair. The depot was in the center of town, a neighborhood badly in need of a face-lift that would never happen. Merritt circled the terminal in his truck. In the back lot sat a half-dozen coaches, idling as diesel exhaust perfumed the air. There was a large parking area for cars contiguous to the bus tarmac. His ex's 4Runner wasn't here.

Pausing at an intersection, he ignored the horn of the driver behind him and looked up and down the street. He turned left, cutting off another car and earning a finger. About two hundred yards along the broad commercial avenue he pulled into a Walmart lot. He cruised the rows. After hitting them all, he steered into the back lot. Here, two dozen vehicles sat in the shade under a thick overhang of oak boughs.

One of them was her Toyota. Empty of people, empty of luggage.

The SUV had been left within walking distance of the bus depot.

He returned to the truck, fired it up and skidded back onto the highway, this time scoring two horns. A few minutes later he was at the station. A street dweller approached Merritt, hand out. The responding look seared the man and he turned and walked away fast, muttering.

Inside, a half-dozen waiting passengers sat on formfitting benches, talking and reading texts and playing games on their phones. He walked to the counter.

"Afternoon," he said to the clerk, a heavyset man of dark complexion, wearing a light blue suit and red tie, white shirt. Merritt flashed his expired police ID and a fake badge that years ago he'd taken off a meth dealer posing as a federal agent. These had been in the U-Store, the bag his ex had dumped unceremoniously into a bin. Along with the trash.

He tucked them away immediately.

"Yes, Officer?"

Merritt displayed a picture of his ex and daughter. "Did these two individuals buy tickets in the last hour?"

The clerk's eyes gave a flash of recognition.

Nobody read body language better than Detective First Jon Merritt.

"Hold on a second, sir." The man's eyes dropped to a screen and he typed.

Was he calling up sales records? Or security footage? There were several cameras here.

The clerk continued to type, then stopped, and a

moment later they were joined by another man. Also Black, also in a suit. His name was Titus Jones, according to the plate on his lapel, and an additional line indicated he was the general manager.

"Sir, you're police?"

No backing up now. "That's right."

"And you're looking for those individuals in connection with an investigation?"

"Parental kidnapping."

"I see. Well, we can't give out any passenger information without a warrant."

"I understand. I just happened to follow a lead here and stopped in. Thought maybe you could help me out, so I don't have to go to the magistrate." He smiled.

Jon Merritt could be the master of charm when he needed to be.

Jones said, "Mr. Randall here said you displayed an ID card. Who're you with? Mr. Randall missed it."

Merritt noticed an armed security guard in the corner, looking his way.

"Ferrington PD."

"Let me take a look at that again. Maybe I'll make a call and we can circumvent the warrant process."

A pause. Tension rose. So did Merritt's anger. He controlled it. Just.

"You know, Mr. Jones, it's probably best to follow procedures. I'll get started on that paperwork right now, back in the office."

As he walked to the door, he snagged a timetable.

Once in the cab of his truck, he sat back, calculating. She left her house at 2:50. Given that she would drive only slightly over the limit—like he'd done—she could be at the terminal at 3:45 if she came straight here. But he didn't think this was the case. She'd had no warning that he was out of County. So she'd fled with only the basics. He guessed she'd stopped for money and—what he would have bought if he'd been in her shoes—a burner phone.

So add a half hour. He opened the timetable. What buses left around 4:15? There were two. One terminated in Detroit, the other St. Louis. The Michigan-bound bus was a local, making perhaps three dozen stops along the way. St. Louis was almost an express. It stopped at only four cities before it reached its destination.

Detroit . . . St. Louis . . .

Merritt stretched.

He thought back to a case years ago. He'd been working Narc and had been constantly stymied by a ruthless meth user, who was not your typical tweaker. He was brilliant. After robbing and killing a wealthy couple, the wiry skel vanished and no one could find him. This drove Merritt to rage. Finally, he forced himself to calm. He had to think not like the hunter, but like the prey. A week later Merritt kicked in the door of a cheap apartment in South Ferrington and with no little amount of satisfaction shot the man to death. He had, in effect, *become* the tweaker and realized, in a burst of inspired thought, where he'd gone.

Now his mind tried to get inside his ex's. Oh, his thinking wasn't nearly as sharp as it had been once. Could he do it?

Reciting to himself:

Detroit, St. Louis, Detroit, St. Louis . . .

21

Funny how men—some men—can have this dark side. You don't see it. They keep it hidden. Completely camouflaged. Then it's like a snake striking." Fingers snapped. "*That's* Jon Merritt."

Allison Parker's mother, Ruth, was in Denver, speaking via Zoom to Harmon, Shaw and Nilsson, who had volunteered to help, an addition Shaw didn't mind at all.

The CEO was behind his desk. The other two were on the couch again. When they'd sat their knees had touched and both moved away slightly. They now faced a large monitor on the wall.

Her hair long and brindle-brown and gray, Mrs. Parker was dressed in a dark red-plaid suit, a white blouse. She was in a den or study. Books filled the background. Many were about decoration and interior design.

"Hidden for years," she continued. "Hid the drinking too. Until he didn't care."

Nilsson stared at the screen unemotionally but he believed her eyes flickered at this comment. Shaw wondered if the ex she'd referred to had behaved this way as well.

Mrs. Parker wore a stern gaze. "What kind of man hurts a woman? A husband cheats and you find out. It's terrible." She paused for a sliver of a second. "But it's not physical. What Jon did to her last November . . ." Her eyelids dipped briefly.

Shaw supposed the laundry list of familial grievances was long, but to him it was irrelevant. They needed to start their search for mother and daughter now.

Harmon had introduced Shaw as a "personal protection expert"—which, in a way, he was. Mrs. Parker accepted this without asking more.

Shaw opened his notebook and turned to a fresh right-hand page, leaving behind his account of the S.I.T. theft, and uncapped the fountain pen. "Her emails? What did they say exactly?"

They were similar, telling each recipient about Merritt's release and how she and Hannah were going away until he was caught for violating the restraining order and returned to prison. She was concerned he'd use the contacts he'd made as a cop to find her, and so they were staying off all social media and not using their phones or email any longer.

"Are you both sure they came from her?"

"How do you mean?" Harmon asked.

Sonja Nilsson: "It's her email address and server?"

They both said that it was.

Shaw asked, "And language, punctuation?"

The two seemed perplexed.

Nilsson said, "We're worried that Merritt sent it himself."

"You mean he might've hurt her already?" Harmon asked, alarmed.

But Ruth said, "No, it was Alli, I'm positive. Her phrasing, you know. And she signed 'OXOX,' backward from normal. It was a joke just between us. Jon wouldn't know that."

Harmon scanned the email he'd received. "Yes, it sounds like her, the way she writes her memos and emails."

Nilsson asked, "You emailed back?"

They both had, but she hadn't responded.

Shaw asked, "Does Allison see her father?"

The woman's fractured marital status was an easy deduction from her earlier comments.

"Once a year maybe. Not involved. Never was."

Though, cheater that he had been, he'd never hit his wife.

"So she wouldn't go stay with him?"

A laugh was the response.

"Any siblings?"

"No, Alli was an only child."

Taking notes, Shaw pressed on the matter of friends. Success in the reward business—or in tracking in general—relies on people. Web history and car tags and video cams can be helpful but there's nothing like a human for a source of information. Even if someone lies and swears the missing soul has gone east, if you read people carefully enough, you know he's headed west.

Ruth thought for a moment and recited the names of several people her daughter had mentioned to her. The information was sketchy. She had no addresses or phone numbers and wasn't even certain of the last names. Harmon could only offer a few; he and Parker did not socialize much, he explained.

Nilsson asked, "How about any favorite places she might go? Places that her ex wouldn't know about?"

Her mother looked ceilingward. "She didn't take vacations much."

Harmon gave a wan smile. "It was hard to pry her out of the office."

Shaw asked, "When she did go, any geographic preference? Mountains or forests, beach?"

"We didn't do outdoors much when she was young. Resorts mostly. Recently? They never went to the beach that I heard about. Disney and Universal, places like that, with Hannah."

Shaw asked, "Any phobias or aversions to any particular types of transportation or places?"

"You mean, does she get seasick?"

"Or carsick. Anything that might limit the distance she'd travel."

"No, nothing like that," Ruth said. "She and Hannah and I drove to some of the Summit ski areas two years ago. No issues, either of them."

Shaw looked at Harmon, who shook his head. "Can't help you there."

"You think she'd know how to go off the grid?"

Ruth told them, "I know she and Jon and Hannah

went camping some." In a wry voice she added, "But that hasn't been for a while; last I checked there weren't a lot of bars in the woods. As for living in a tent and catching her own fish? No, that's not Alli. She's not one of those survivalist weirdos."

Shaw kept the smile at bay. "Would she be armed?"

"No, no. She hated Jon keeping his gun in the house. Because of his drinking. And with what happened last November, she wouldn't have anything to do with a gun."

Shaw said, "If we're lucky she'll check email. Both of you send her a message asking her to call me or Sonja. She'll remember me from the S.I.T. investigation."

He recited the digits.

Both Harmon and Parker's mother typed.

"Done," she said.

Harmon asked, "What're the odds she'll read it?"

Colter Shaw, a man of assessing percentage likelihood in all aspects of his life, knew that sometimes there were simply too many variables and too few facts available to allow you to assign a number.

It was Nilsson who answered. "All we can do is hope."

As good an appraisal as any.

"You'll tell me how it's going?" Ruth asked in a soft voice.

Harmon said, "Absolutely. Colter and Sonja'll keep me posted, and I'll let you know."

"Thank you."

Nilsson asked, "Mrs. Parker, why do you think she stayed with him?"

After a moment: "You hear that question a lot. Why do abused women stay with their men? Out of fear, I guess. Fear of loneliness . . ." She looked away. "And even when they work up the courage, and do the right thing, the brave thing, and walk away, they have to ask, is the empty house worth it? Sometimes the answer's yes, sometimes the answer's no."

22

Mother and daughter were speeding north, once again on rough-and-ready Route 55.

Not on a bus, or in her SUV. But in a late-model Kia sedan that she'd just rented.

Jon Merritt was a dangerous drunk but he had been a damn good detective. She bet that he'd guess she was so paranoid that she'd abandon her car and take an untraceable bus, buying tickets with cash.

That made sense.

But a bus did not fit into her own plan for escape. A Greyhound or Trailways would not take her where she wanted to go.

Where she *had* to go.

A place where she would be safe.

Yes, she had pulled into the depot lot, bought two tickets to St. Louis, making a minor scene when she complained that her change was wrong so the clerk would remember her. She'd grinned ruefully and apologized for mixing up the bills herself. She and Hannah had left and driven the Toyota to a nearby shopping center, which is exactly what somebody escaping from a smart, dangerous ex would do—not leaving it in the bus terminal lot.

Then, amid Hannah's grumbling, they had walked a half mile to the car rental agency, lugging suitcases, gym bags and backpacks. She'd used her company credit card, which could ultimately be traced to her, but doing so would take some digging. Her engineering projects were made up of untold layers of subsystems and interfaces. Intimidating to many, these complications were simply part of a day's work for Allison Parker and her mind had no problem juggling and sorting them.

She had planned that Jon would find the car, coerce a bus ticket clerk to give up their destination—maybe using an old badge of his—and then would hit the bus terminals on the way to St. Louis, figuring they'd get off before they reached the city with the famed arch. He would try to pick up the trail there.

As she figured, doing that would expose him to security cameras and raise suspicion. If she was lucky, he'd be spotted and arrested within twenty-four hours.

Allison Parker's profession was engineering. She addressed her professional tasks systematically. She was, Marty Harmon had said about her, maybe the most goal-oriented and efficient person he'd ever met. She'd actually blushed when he'd said those words at an award ceremony.

"But Allison brings something more to the table. Her creativity."

She had blushed again.

For this quality she had an idol to thank: the famed Billy Koen, the engineering professor at the University of Texas at Austin.

She had read his landmark book *Discussion of the Method* a dozen times. It was the bible for approaching an engineering challenge. He wrote:

The engineering method is the use of heuristics to cause the best change in a poorly understood situation with the available resources.

The heuristic method was a problem-solving technique that didn't pretend to be perfect: like trial and error, educated guessing.

The point was that you could rarely find the perfect solution to a problem. You started out, trying this and that, and slowly arrived at an answer that was sufficient.

It was through heuristics that she had invented the S.I.T. trigger and a unique fuel containment vessel for the Pocket Suns.

And Koen had suggested that "engineering" was far broader than its industrial or scientific definition. We are all engineers, he said, in every aspect of our lives.

It was this method that she'd used to come up with a plan to escape her ex-husband.

Several solutions had coalesced in her mind. She analyzed, established priorities, tested out models and the consequences of each.

Discarding, discarding, coming up with yet another. Discarding again.

Finally, she believed she had the best solution, under the circumstances.

Not perfect. Further refinements would be required.

But it was a start.

Now they sped north on 55, she sipping coffee that was burnt tasting but doctored with hazelnut creamer, and Hannah a Diet Pepsi. Her daughter thought she was heavy but she absolutely was not. The concern, though, did not rise to the troubling levels Parker read about on her school's website or saw on TV regarding girls' body image on Instagram and other social media sites.

Parker scanned the landscape. Economic downturn and the pollution in the Kenoah had stabbed the industrial heart of Ferrington. But the world no longer had use for those early twentieth-century giants, and here you could find more than a few smaller warehouses and fabricators. There'd be a long stretch of blackness, then a corrugated single-story structure would flash into sight before they plunged again into wasteland.

On the radio was a Top 40 station. The gold sedan had SiriusXM, but Parker didn't mention this to her daughter. She stuck with FM. She knew for a fact that one could trace a car via its entertainment system, and satellite left more of a record than terrestrial. She'd learned this not from her cop husband but a true crime show.

Hannah was studying the car's dash. Parker expected her to complain that it didn't have as many amenities as the Toyota, which it didn't.

But the girl surprised her by smiling and whispering, "Sweet."

"You like it?"

The girl was looking coy. "Kind of *me*, you know."

Parker smiled too. At sixteen, soon to have her driver's license, the girl had been planting seeds about what kind of car her mother would buy her.

"What color can I get?"

It would depend on what was for sale at CarMax or Carvana or the local used car lot at a reasonable price. But, not wanting to endanger the minor détente between them, Parker said, "I'm sure it'll come in any color you want. Short of puce. Or amaranth."

"What?" Hannah was frowning. "That's not real."

"Yes, it is. Kind of red-pink. Comes from amaranth flowers." She shot her daughter an enthusiastic look. "Oh, wait! I know! What you need is a car that's coquelicot."

Hannah was giggling.

"Wait!" Parker whispered, laughing herself. "Gamboge . . ."

"Fake, fake, fake!"

"Real, real, real!" Parker was going to say look it up but remembered, just in time, that she'd forbidden the girl from going online.

Hannah was unable to speak for the laughing and Parker's heart was near to bursting with happiness.

They each ate a Hostess crumb donut, the particles tumbling down their chests and into their laps. After a moment, several sips later, the girl grew serious. "I'd want red or yellow. They're hot."

Parker didn't know about the hot but she wouldn't object to the hues. They were more visible at night and in bad weather.

She also knew that those two colors were more often targeted by the police than any other. A thought that led to Jon and chilled some of the joy.

It was 6:24, according to her new phone. They would stop soon, a small non-chain motel. She'd pay cash. She could have driven on to her final destination tonight—another two hours. But her plan was to make sure that her ex didn't guess where she might be headed.

If after two days, Jon hadn't shown up, they'd continue north, to what she was thinking of as her "safe house."

If he hadn't been rearrested by then.

Where was he now?

What did he happen to be thinking at this moment?

How drunk was he?

How furious was he that he hadn't caught her at the rental house?

Don't. Think. About. It.

And as if that were a magic incantation, an image of the seahorse appeared.

So did a taste-memory, metallic, from the blood in her mouth.

Her sobbing.

Why are you doing this to me?

The impact of the pistol cracking her cheekbone.

The—

"What?" Hannah asked.

Parker turned to her.

"You got all weird looking."

"Nothing. Just thinking where we'll stop for the night."

Hannah continued to gaze at her for a moment.

The deceptions have been coming more frequently lately. Small, but a lie is a lie . . .

On either side of the road were forests of black trees and fields of dying grass and of corn and wheat stubble. The mile markers appeared and vanished. She thought of calculus, whose name came from the Latin word for "little pebble," and referred to the practice in ancient Rome of using small stones to measure distances. Of all the mathematical disciplines, Allison Parker loved this one the most and she used it daily in her job.

Hannah was less animated now; she would have sensed her mother's mood. Parker accelerated slightly along the deserted two-lane highway. The sun was gone. Clouds were low in the fragrant autumn evening and moved fast, a continuous blanket. Wind tugged leaves from branches and swirled them downward, where they swirled yet again in the vehicle's turbulent wake.

"It's spooky," the girl said.

It was.

"I'm tired. How much farther?"

Allison Parker didn't have an answer for that. All she knew was that every mile she put between the two of them and Jon Merritt felt like a gift.

23

The detective was young, with short-cut hair that clung close to his scalp, not unlike Shaw's, though brown. He wore black slacks and a blue shirt, and a red-and-black tie hung down from the open collar, a look that Shaw never understood.

Dunfry Kemp's physique was triangular and his muscled arms tested the cotton of his shirt. He'd been a wrestler, Shaw's sport in college.

Presently on the phone, he glanced up with a blink as Shaw sat down in the only free chair. The other two were filled with paperwork. His nod of greeting was a burdened one.

Kemp's office was on the Ferrington Police Department's second floor, along a lengthy corridor devoted, signs explained, to Investigations and to Administration. The cubicle, though, might have been a storeroom. Stacked on his desk and against the green walls and on the brown carpet and on two-thirds of the chairs were battered folders, manila and brown accordions. Must have been two hundred. Piles of loose papers too. A whiteboard was on the wall—it was a flowchart about the investigation into the Street Cleaner serial killer, the faces of the victims.

Kemp disconnected and asked, "And it's . . . ?"

A woman in a blue uniform brought in two more folders. Kemp eyed them with dismay.

"Colter Shaw."

"You work for Marty Harmon. Security?"

It was close enough.

"That's right."

"And this's about . . . ?"

Another bee buzzed into the office and deposited yet more folders. No wonder the kid was having trouble finishing sentences. A whisper: "Oh, man."

Shaw picked up the narrative. "I'm trying to locate Jon Merritt's wife and daughter. I understand you caught the case."

Kemp looked at Shaw out of the corner of his eye. Nothing deceptive about this. It seemed to be just his natural angle of gaze. "Fact is, being honest, I normally wouldn't talk to a civilian, but the captain said it's for Mr. Harmon. And I don't know if you know but he's sort of saving the city."

"The water."

"Yessir. But fact is there *is* no case really. Jon just *talked* about hurting her."

"Killing her," Shaw corrected and noted that the detective had used Merritt's given name.

"But he was lawfully discharged and didn't commit any overt acts. That's the key word. Overt."

"Then you don't know about violating the restraining order. He was at her house."

Tapping his large fingers on a large file, he gave a tempered frown. "I heard that from her lawyer, Mr. Stein. But he couldn't say for sure Jon was within a thousand feet of the house. And she wasn't home."

"So there's no warrant?"

"No. And we don't really do anything about violations like that. Not even sure the order's enforceable if she wasn't home."

"It is," Shaw said. He couldn't stop himself from saying: "Is this because it's Jon Merritt?"

His silence was a yes. But his expressed answer was to gaze around the room, inviting Shaw to join him. "Like you can see, sir. We've got to prioritize. I've got rapes and homicides and drug cases I'm running. I've caught part of a cold serial killer case. And an arson."

"All accounts, Detective, he's a sociopath. Like your serial killer. One of the cons said he talked about a murder-suicide. I hope you understand how at risk they could be."

"I do, sir."

Shaw said, "I called the prison. I wanted to talk to his therapist. No one's gotten back to me."

Kemp said, "So, they're stonewalling because they didn't investigate him good enough before the discharge." He then stopped speaking, thinking he might not want to share this aloud, obvious though it was.

The huge shoulders rose and fell. "Fact is, psychiatrists won't talk anyway. The privilege, you know."

Shaw said, "Doctor-patient privilege fails if the patient tells the doctor he intends to hurt someone."

"Well, I guess he hasn't. Or we would've heard and that'd be in the file. Which it isn't."

"Would you call County?"

Kemp hesitated a moment and said he would.

Shaw wondered why he felt the urge to thank a law enforcer for merely doing his job.

"And you'll put in paperwork for a restraining order violation warrant?"

"I'll get to it."

Someone approached in the corridor and Kemp looked toward his doorway with a grimace. But the officer passed on, without a look.

"And get Allison's and Hannah's names on a missing persons bulletin?"

Another sideways glance. "Well. How long they been missing?"

"Officer . . ." Shaw said nothing for a moment. "I'm trying to keep Allison and Hannah safe."

Personalizing them by using their names. A trick he used in the reward business when speaking to reluctant witnesses.

"And I guarantee Merritt *will* try to kill them."

Kemp looked at the wall of files. "Fact is, a missing persons report wouldn't raise an eyebrow. Nobody looks at it. But one thing I could do . . ." A nod to himself. "Put it out as flight of material witnesses." No sideways glance now. He looked straight into Shaw's eyes. "That'll get some attention. Maybe. Can't say for sure."

"Thank you, Detective. You find them, would you call me? I don't want them in one of your safe houses."

He laughed. "Safe house. Yeah, right."

A budgetary issue, Shaw supposed.

Then Shaw's eyes dropped to the brown accordion folder. The faded white tape on the side read: *Merritt. 399407.*

"Can I look at that?"

Kemp hesitated. Shaw knew the request was over the line. But he just looked back into the man's dark eyes.

One of the massive hands slid it forward.

He opened the file and flipped through the contents, which included the investigation and disposition of the aggravated battery from last year. He didn't think there would be anything helpful in his search for the woman and girl now. He just wanted to see what had happened in the attack.

Colter Shaw was no stranger to violence. He had witnessed it, experienced it and caused it. But the pictures taken of Allison Parker's face were tough to see. The skin had been cleaned of blood, but there were many dark brown stains on her collar and, if you looked closely, her hair. Most troubling was the damaged symmetry of her face. Merritt had slammed his service pistol into her cheek and cracked it, altering the tectonic plate of the bone.

Equally troubling were the tears, distorting the perfect lenses of her eyes.

He closed the file and pushed it back. He fished a card

from his jeans pocket and handed it to the detective. It went not into a drawer but on a spot beside his computer keyboard.

He thanked Kemp again and rose, leaving him to his massive array of files.

Had the meeting been helpful or not?

His answer was: only twenty percent.

Still, sometimes the least likely approaches worked to sterling advantage. So you pursued them anyway.

Fact is.

24

N o bus.

That hadn't happened.

Jon Merritt was at a McDonald's, the intersection of Cross County and Route 55, absently watching customers come and go.

No bus. His ex had rented a car. He was ninety-five percent positive.

Detroit, St. Louis . . .

Neither.

She was just like the tweaker he'd killed, coming up with a plan meant to fool everybody.

She'd bought tickets—he knew that from the clerk's expression—and left the Toyota sort of but not really hidden, and then hiked away from the terminal to one of the nearby car rental agencies. He debated going inside but he decided he'd pushed his fake cop stuff too far. The bus clerk already might have called someone at FPD.

He had parked the truck butt-in, to have a good view

of any approaching threat. This was habit. Jon Merritt had made plenty of enemies in his prior life, all the way from those in crack houses to the county building—and beyond. Enemies who would want him dead out of vengeance or, perhaps, for some other reason. Ironic, he now thought. From the early days of their marriage he'd warned Allison to be vigilant and defensive. She surely would be assuming that same attitude to evade *him* now.

A bite of burger, a sip of soda. Okay, think . . .

She's driving. First, how far tonight, and how far tomorrow? And which direction?

It was getting late. He guessed the perimeter would be about a hundred miles from home. She'd stop somewhere in that circle.

As for direction, she'd started north; he assumed she'd keep going that way and Route 55 was the most efficient choice.

Something was in that direction, something that offered protection.

What was it?

Where would a fleeing wife flee to?

Some options came to mind.

Her friends. Likelihood? Not much. He knew most of the people she was close to. Knew too their addresses, or could easily find them. She wouldn't put them at risk.

Her mother. Likelihood: not much. Oh, they might take 55 to I-70, then west. But Ruth was over a thousand miles away, a long and risky trek. They'd be exposed on those roads. Too easy to pull alongside and shoot through windows.

Camping out. Likelihood: so-so. As a family, they'd been to a dozen campgrounds. It wasn't truly roughing it, but Allison knew how to put up tents and cook on camping stoves. The factor gravitating against it was Hannah. At age eight, she'd been delighted. His gut told him the sixteen-year-old that she'd become would veto the outdoors.

A motel in the boonies. Likelihood: high.

A women's shelter. Likelihood: high. Several times, when he'd been on a bender and had trashed the house, she and Hannah had fled to one. She'd possibly do the same now. It would be a smart call. Most of them had armed guards, usually off-duty cops.

Friends of hers that he didn't know. Likelihood: high. This would include people from the office—from which he'd been effectively banned, after several incidents.

Of the three most likely he decided the shelter and unknown friends were the best to pursue. The motel was good in theory but would be nearly impossible to find. Dom Ryan was helping but his contacts were mostly in the beehives of government. Allison would find a non-chain hotel and check in under a fake name, paying cash.

So: shelter or friends.

He ate some burger, drank some soda, debating.

Well, time was critical. He couldn't do both. He came to a decision. He himself would try to track down any unknown friends. As for the shelter, he'd delegate that job. It was, after all, his money he was spending.

25

oll leaned back in the driver's seat of the Transit, watching an optical illusion, four car tires cemented at a forty-five-degree angle, revolving around a vertical pole. They seemed to spin magically.

It was hypnotic.

He and Desmond were in a strip mall parking lot a block and a half from Allison Parker's rental house on Maple View, where they'd been for hours, after Merritt's wife and daughter had fled.

The job was on hold as they awaited further instructions.

Which might be incoming at the moment; his phone hummed with a text. He read it, muttered, "'Bout time."

"And?"

He tucked his phone away. "Merritt thinks they might've gone to a shelter. We're supposed to check them out."

"A . . . Oh, for battered women."

"What were you thinking? Tornado?"

Desmond asked, "Why there?"

"She was in one. She might go back. Makes sense . . . Dawndue."

The verbal tic could be cheerful. It could also be a minor obscenity.

Neither man was happy that the ex and daughter were on the road.

"That wasn't very bright of Merritt, spooking them."

Moll happened to be thinking to his sometimes partner: *Or you could've gotten to my place on time, and we could have kept the ladies company at their place until Merritt arrived.* He didn't say this, though. What was the point? A moody Desmond was an irritating Desmond.

Moll went online on his iPhone and checked addresses of shelters in the city. He picked the closest one that was north of Ferrington—the direction Merritt had said they were headed. He put the Transit in gear and pulled onto the road.

Desmond was examining a willow branch, bright green, about eighteen inches long. It was fresh and damp and cut smooth at both ends. He began tapping it with the handle of his open SOG locking-blade knife.

The *thonk, thonk, thonk* might be a bother to some but Moll kind of liked it.

"What's *he* doing?"

"Merritt? Following up some other lead."

Thonk, thonk.

Desmond's face foretold another gripe.

"This was supposed to be in-out, fast, and then barbecue. I was fantasizing ribs. How long's it going to be now? I've got business, you know." Desmond laundered money through a used car lot he owned. He knew what he was doing. Where else in the world were 1998 Subarus going for $250K?

Moll had projects too. While he enjoyed faux painting, his special services job found him the go-to man for disposing of bodies—ones that either he and Desmond, or other clients, had made. Presently he needed to complete an assignment involving one Edgar Barth, a potential whistleblower, who was cold and stiff and swathed in a tarp, tucked into a cabin in Ralston. The idea was that Edgar would be deposited someplace unfindable on the way to Akron, where Moll would deliver a painted settee. He'd planned on leaving late this afternoon.

But now . . .

His neck and hands complained and he sprayed Benadryl once more. Better.

Desmond examined the willow branch carefully. He put it down and took out his phone. Moll noted that he was looking at the texts about the job, specifically the pictures of Allison Parker and her daughter.

They had memorized what the females looked like. It made sense to be absolutely sure of your target. When you're after woodcock you don't want to take an out-of-season quail by mistake.

Moll noted the glint in Desmond's eyes as he scanned the whole-body shot of Allison Parker.

The man had this habit . . .

Moll said, "No."

Desmond swapped phone for willow branch. He shrugged. "A man can dream, can't he?"

And began the *thonk, thonk, thonk* once more.

26

Allison Parker was looking over the unfortunate beds in unfortunate room 306 of the Sunny Acres motel, whose bold pink vacancy sign had been a beacon in the spooky night and beckoned them in for shelter.

The place was shabby and worn, the window cracked, the frame and gutters in need of paint. The view was the parking lot and a chain-link fence, whose mesh was fitted with slats to block out the view of Buddy's Salvage.

So, it's come to this, she thought.

"Here?" Hannah asked.

The girl's dismay was the exact opposite of her happy reaction to the rental car.

The walls, painted white, needed another coat. Blond, scarred, tired furniture. Industrial dark blue carpet, just the shade to camouflage stains, though it was largely un-successful in its mission. A two-socket lamp with one bulb. Two double beds, not even queens. The scent was of musty air and powerhouse cleanser.

"It'll do for now."

The girl gave another exaggerated sigh.

"We're on an adventure."

This had once brought a smile to the girl's face— when she was younger and the family was about to embark on a drive to the zoo, a theme park, a camping trip.

Now no such reaction.

Parker didn't even consider mentioning Greenstone, the mythical castle of their bedtime reading pleasure. How distant were those days . . .

"'For now'?" Hannah asked, her voice edgy. "How long is that?"

"Not long."

Now a sigh of a different order.

They finished bringing in their bags.

Parker got the AC going. The room wasn't that hot but she wanted to cover up the sticky noise of traffic on Route 92, trucks mostly. This she found both intrusive and, for some reason, depressing.

She was going to unpack completely. Organized to the extreme, Allison Parker always did this when she traveled, never happy living out of suitcases. But it occurred to her Hannah would deduce that "for now" might extend longer than the girl hoped.

Still, as Hannah scrolled through the basic cable stations, Parker risked scrutiny and got the toiletries assembled in the bathroom and some clothes hung in the closet. The Keurig coffee maker, on the desk, seemed in working order and there were pods that she guessed had distant expiration dates, if any. The creamer was of the powdered variety. She was stabbed by a memory—not long after she and Jon had been married and they were having his lieutenant from FPD over for dinner. She'd realized there was no milk for the cake she was going to bake. It was important to her to make a nice meal but it would have taken too long to hit the store for a quart.

Parker told Jon she had an idea—and concocted a cup of "milk" by mixing warm water and Coffee mate.

At dinner the supervisor's wife had eaten the confection and had a second sliver. Then she had asked for the recipe, wondering aloud what made it so special. Parker and Merritt had shared a smile. "There's a secret ingredient," she'd said.

With this memory, she was suddenly overwhelmed and tears pricked. She glanced at Hannah to see if the girl caught it. She did not and Parker wiped fast.

For dinner: Burger King (Hannah's the meatless selection). They heated the sandwiches and onion rings in the microwave that she thought about scrubbing but gave up worrying about.

Hannah seemed to enjoy her meal, splurging, for a change, with a vanilla milkshake.

To Parker everything was merely fuel.

U-235 came spontaneously to mind.

She gathered up the empty bags and wrappers and stuffed them in the too-small trash container.

"Go take a shower."

"Mom . . ."

"And your teeth."

"I didn't bring any . . ."

Parker handed her daughter an unopened box of Crest and a sealed brush.

The girl sighed once more, but this exhalation fell into the off-the-shelf mother-daughter-nighttime-routine playbook.

All good.

The instant the door closed Parker dug through her purse and extracted a black envelope, about twelve inches by three and quite thick. It was made of a polycarbonate material and was fireproof. Even temperatures over two thousand degrees would have no effect on the contents.

When she'd cashed the check at First Federal Bank in Carter Grove after fleeing from Jon that afternoon, she had gone straight to her safety deposit box—hers alone, unknown to anyone else—and removed the envelope and stashed it in her purse. She'd taken the Coach, rather than her usual leather bag. It would be a curious choice for a simple check-cashing errand but the girl had not noticed.

A glance at the door, an ear to the shower. Then Parker lifted the Velcro-sealed flap with a loud tearing noise and pulled open the zipper. Inside were scores of documents and a thumb drive. She plugged the storage device into her laptop's USB port and, after opening an encrypted container on her drive, selected thirty files—text and JPG photos—and copied them to the drive. When the bar hit one hundred percent, she tugged it out. She then wrote a note on the top document, jotting quickly in her careless hand. Then the papers and USB went back into the formidable envelope.

After sealing it up once more, she rose and, checking that the water was still streaming, she stepped outside and hurried to the car.

There she slipped the envelope into the glove compartment and closed it.

She returned to the room, locked the door and sat back on the bed, sipping Diet Coke. Her heart was pounding and her breath came hard. Slowly, eyes on a TV show she wasn't watching, Allison Parker began to calm.

Much of the peace, she realized, came from her confidence that the contents of her secret envelope would be safe from fire, flood and any other disaster, except—she couldn't help but think—nuclear ones.

27

Colter Shaw was sitting in an unoccupied office in the security division of Harmon Energy Products' Building One.

His high-tech ergonomic chair was before a glass-topped desk, on which sat a computer, presently snoozing, and his notebook and pen. He flipped through the pages, reading his handwriting. Sonja Nilsson was playing private eye, canvassing employees who knew Parker, and she had been feeding him facts as to their possible leads, of which there were not many.

> *Jon Merritt, 42, ex-husband of Allison Parker,*
> *42. Released from Trevor County Detention,*
> *early discharge. Serving 36 months for assault*
> *and battery with a deadly weapon causing*
> *grievous bodily harm. Parker told police that*
> *Merritt said he intended to murder her. As*

*part of plea bargain, the state dropped the
attempted murder charge.*

Merritt was career law enforcement. Started as
rookie, sixteen years ago, Vice, Street Crimes,
Narcotics, promoted to detective ten years
ago, working corruption and organized
crime mostly. Was decorated. No complaints
regarding performance until about three
years ago.

After Merritt's release, information arose that
he had told other cons in County that when he
was released he was going to find Allison and
kill her.

Merritt has history of opioid and alcohol abuse.
In the years before his arrest, police were
dispatched to marital home dozens of times,
no arrests made. Merritt sporadically attended various 12-step programs. Unsuccess-
ful. Had not attended for a year prior to
assault that led to his arrest.

Merritt and Parker have one child, Hannah. 16.

Allison is senior nuclear engineer at Harmon
Energy Products. Has national security
clearance. Invented S.I.T. trigger (prototype
stolen but recovered) and a fuel rod transportation vessel, key to the company's product, a
small modular reactor, trade named the
Pocket Sun.

Motive for wanting to kill Allison unknown.
Possibly revenge. Possibly worried that she

*knew things about him he wouldn't want
brought to light. Might have been motive for
initial assault in November of last year. No one
interviewed knew what these facts might be.*

Merritt characterized as classic sociopath.
*Charming and highly functioning on one
side, rageful and homicidal on the other.*

Discharge order invalidated and warrant
*issued for his arrest for violation of restrain-
ing order by trespassing on her property
today. Ferrington PD considers this a minor
infraction, and is not aggressively investigating, due to workforce shortage and Merritt's
past favorable history in the department.*

Merritt's name and the make and tag of his
*vehicle are on the countywide wire. He drives
a white Ford F-150 pickup, tag JKT345.
Unknown if he has other vehicle.*

Merritt's whereabouts not known.

Her lawyer, David Stein, does not know where
Allison and Hannah are.

Emails to Marty Harmon and Ruth Parker, her
*mother, sent from her phone, give no indica-
tion of where she might be going.*

Profile of Allison Parker re: possible whereabouts.
*Generally prefers inland, that is, camping,
to beaches. Has rudimentary outdoor
skills, sufficient for survival in temperate
weather like at present.*

*No physical conditions affecting travel
    (true for daughter too).
In good health, athletic, swimmer.
Driving a gray Toyota 4Runner, tag
    RTD478.
Probably unarmed.*

*Ferrington PD detective Dunfry Kemp is
    running the investigation but is making
    little effort to find Merritt. His name and
    vehicle are on countywide wire. So are Allison
    and Hannah. No field detectives assigned to
    a search for either.*

*All of Allison's and Hannah's known social
    media sites closed down. Allison's phone is no
    longer active. Email accounts might be
    active, but she's not responding to messages
    sent by Harmon or her mother.*

*Sonja Nilsson interviewing Alli Parker's
    coworkers. None have suggested where she
    might have gone. Still more subjects to
    contact. Parker has no relatives in the area.*

*Jon Merritt's mother lives in Kansas; father is
    deceased. Mother reported that she's heard
    nothing from her son or Alli Parker, with
    whom she was on terms that were friendly, if
    distant.*

He read through his notes twice. It was enough background.

The Restless Man was restless.

Shaw rose and walked to Sonja Nilsson's office. She was on the second of her two phones, the off-brand one. Her conversation seemed serious.

She looked up.

He told her, "Going out. Back in an hour or two."

She nodded and turned her full attention back to the call.

Shaw fished the motorcycle keys from his pocket and walked to the elevator, past some colorful renderings of Pocket Suns. Bright yellow lines radiated outward from the dome of the units, reminding Shaw of nothing so much as the beams emanating from the heads of Christian martyrs in medieval paintings as they were about to meet their ends.

28

He parked on Cross County again—no risk of her deflating any tires now—and made his way along the same route he'd taken earlier in the day, through the woods behind her house.

Jon Merritt assessed the place: Nice enough. Small. A pool, of course. She *had* to have her pool.

He pictured the seahorse . . .

The snow . . .

Spattered with her crimson blood.

Then he dumped the memories and slipped up to the back door.

The lucky SOB got lucky once again.

His ex and daughter had left so fast they'd forgotten to lock the door and set the alarm. The light on the unit glowed green. He stepped inside. He was going to go from room to room to close the drapes but his wife had conveniently done so. Still paranoid, it seemed.

Cartons sat stacked in neat rows against the wall, each one carefully labeled—unlike at the U-Store facility, where she'd tossed things into the containers helter-skelter. A third bedroom was packed floor to crown molding with boxes and racks of clothing.

She'd unpacked only the necessities. Where was she planning on moving permanently? Out into the country? Another state? Her job was important to her but there were other miniature reactor companies. Some had tried to steal her away, he recalled.

Sparse, yes, a residence for a transitional life. Still, she'd built some comfort; the house was homey lite. Cut flowers, real ones, exploded from a half-dozen clear glass vases. Macy's oriental rugs covered the laminate floors. Pictures on the walls. Every relative was represented but him. She'd done what the Soviet dictators did. Purge.

The ransacking began.

His ex's bedroom was also her office.

Her laptop was gone, and her desktop locked. He found an old phone that he remembered, a Nokia flip. He recalled it was her second phone—and one she hadn't told him about—because it was for work, she claimed. One morning a year and a half ago, he woke up, still drunk, alone in their bed and found that he'd thrown the mobile across the room. The device was unharmed. The mirror was shattered. He powered it on now; it was no longer active.

Squatting, Merritt began rifling through her desk, pulling out drawers and dumping the contents on the floor. Looking for diaries, notebooks, address books, envelopes with handwritten return addresses, business and greeting cards, receipts, Post-it notes, bills, credit card statements, flyers . . .

Jon Merritt knew very well that a case might be closed thanks to the smallest of jottings. If he found something that might be helpful he didn't read it carefully now but shoved it into his backpack; he didn't want to spend any more time here than was necessary. A police visit was unlikely but not impossible.

Digging, digging, sorting, discarding, stuffing . . .

God, there was a lot of crap, much of it for work: schematics, diagrams, spreadsheets and long, complicated reports. He didn't remember her bringing home this much when they lived together. There was a policy against taking most documents out of the office.

Once the desk was depleted, it was on to the bedside tables, the dresser, vanity, closets. A search of those yielded only marginal prizes. In the end he hefted the backpack onto his shoulder and estimated he'd collected a good five or six pounds of Allison Parker's Personal Life.

Now on to his daughter's room, though he didn't think he'd have much luck there. For one thing, it would be his ex who had their destination in mind, not Hannah. Also, a typical teen, the girl kept *her* existence mostly digital. No diary, no address book, no Post-its. Some doodlings on class assignments. A pink scrap of torn paper that said *Kyle is crushing on you. I am serious!!* There were two other references to the kid, who Merritt had never heard of.

Were Kyle's parents among those unknown friends they might stay with?

Merritt was flipping through a thick stack of poetry, photos and school assignments when he heard the rattle of a motorcycle outside. The engine gunned and stopped. He stuffed the papers into his backpack and peered out.

In the front yard was a trim man, in his thirties, resting a helmet on the seat of a Yamaha dirt bike. He was in a brown leather jacket, black jeans and black shoes. The jacket wasn't zipped and Merritt believe he saw the butt of a pistol on his right hip, back and low. It was nestled in a gray inside-the-belt holster.

Who the hell was this?

Jon Merritt walked to the kitchen, opened the garage door and stepped inside, drawing his own weapon.

A two-hundred-dollar gun that had cost seven.

29

Following the agreeable voice of the GPS girl, Moll pulled into the parking lot in front of the one-story building. It was white clapboard, with black-trim windows.

The modest sign above the door read:

SAFE AWAY

This was the third women's shelter on the list. Allison Parker had had no connection with the one north of the city—which had been the most likely one, given the direction of her flight. The second was in Bakersville, the seediest part of Ferrington, and no one there knew Allison.

"Better be it." Moll snagged an envelope, 8½ by 11, white. And stepped out of the Transit.

He was almost certain Allison Parker and her daughter

weren't here, since it was south of Ferrington. But she might've headed north, then circled back. Merritt had said she'd definitely spent some time in one of the shelters, and Moll's hope was to find somebody she had become friendly with, somebody she might have spoken to *after* she fled. Maybe they'd even recommended another shelter in a different county. Nothing wrong with putting some miles between her and any threat.

Moll pushed the intercom button.

"Yes?" A woman's voice floated out from the speaker below the camera. She seemed stern.

"Hi, delivery." Moll was as professional as he could be. He held up the envelope. "Need a signature."

The probing eye would see a man in a suit and tie. A white man. Made a difference, sad to say. The door lock buzzed, and he entered, thinking: careless of them.

The front office was paneled with cheap wood and was obviously a DIY job, with mispatched alignment and sloppy joints. Behind a scuffed desk sat a woman of around thirty-five in a white blouse and dark skirt. She had long brunette hair, ponytail strangled by two scrunchies or whatever they were called. One near her head and the other near the end of the tail.

She was not alone. A large dark-skinned man, wearing a security guard's blue uniform, sat in the corner. He eyed Moll and went back to texting. He was armed.

With as pleasant an expression as a hulk of a man can muster, Moll displayed the envelope on which a label was pasted. He said, "Copy of a revised restraining order for

Ms. Allison Parker." He was going to pretend to hesitate and look at the name on the envelope. But that might be overacting. "The sheriff's out serving Merritt now. If he can find him."

"Allison?"

Moll's bad day improved considerably with this. She hadn't asked, "Who?" She knew Merritt's ex.

"That's right. She's in residence here, isn't she?"

The woman was then frowning as she glanced at the envelope, maybe expecting him to show her the contents, which wasn't going to happen, since they were ten sheets of blank computer printer paper. Her response was "No."

Moll now took on the same confused expression she was projecting. "The clerk of the court said she was in a shelter. I just assumed it was this one, since the paperwork said she was here before."

"That's right. But she's not now. You better check with the magistrate's office."

"Has she talked to you recently about possibly coming in?"

It was not a question a process server would ask. She looked him over. Was there suspicion?

"Can I ask, why didn't you just call first?"

Good question.

A shrug. "I was in the area on another delivery. Thanks for your help. You have a good evening now."

The woman nodded and, fortunately for Moll, turned back to the screen, which gave him the chance to memorize her chest. For future reference.

Desmond had a problem. Moll had control. But he was, after all, a man.

Outside, he climbed into the driver's seat. "The receptionist? She knows her."

"Did she say anything we can use?"

Moll said, "Not yet. She will."

30

Colter Shaw's father, Ashton, had a rule: *Never break the law.*

Though the final word in that sentence was subject to some interpretation.

There were laws and then there were *laws*, and occasionally survival required you to redefine the concept of legal prohibitions.

You could also get good mileage out of the concept of affirmative defense: Your Honor, yes, I broke the law, but I did it to save a life. Nearly-a-lawyer Shaw had become very familiar with this concept in the reward business.

So he didn't think twice about pushing open the unlocked back door of Allison Parker's rental house on Maple View.

Besides, if the cops weren't energized enough to track down an intended wife-killer, Shaw's crime of trespass would not appear as the faintest blip on their radar.

He stepped into the dark kitchen and remained still, hand on his pistol, scanning what he could see from here: dining area, a portion of the living room, the pantry.

Listening.

The creaks of a settling house. The tap of branches and skittering of leaves; the breeze had picked up.

He needed light, but not until he cleared the small one-story house.

Room by room.

Shaw, who'd drawn his pistol, moved through the kitchen, the living room, a tiny bedroom in the back, a large bedroom in the front of the house and a smaller one across the hall. Bathrooms, clear. Closets, clear. No basement to search.

This left only the garage, the door to which was in the kitchen.

Instinct told him to crouch as he pulled the door open and lifted his gun.

He found himself aiming at a shadowy space, filled with sealed boxes and furniture and other items awaiting their final home.

No movement.

He needed to check behind the cartons, a good hiding space, if Merritt was in fact here. The odds were that he was not, but the consequence if that slim chance proved to be the case would not be good.

Shaw could only search behind the boxes by walking around the stacks.

Making him a perfect target.

And so he picked another option: with his left hand

he shoved the top row of cartons into the space behind them, keeping the Glock pointed toward where an attacker would emerge.

One by one, they fell with varying types and levels of noise. China and glassware were not his priorities, but nothing seemed to shatter.

This took less than a minute. He circled around and confirmed no one was here.

When he finished, he returned to the kitchen, locked the door and began turning on lights. He walked from room to room, looking for anything that might tell him where Allison had gone.

It didn't take long to see that this would probably be futile. The bedroom in the back was empty, except for a few storage boxes, which were sealed. As for the other two, it looked like a tornado had swept through them. Of course they'd been in a hurry to leave, but this was not the result of fast, careless packing. The rooms had been tossed, and by somebody who knew what they were doing—an ex-cop, for instance. Drawers had been removed and inverted, as Merritt would have looked for anything taped underneath. The contents of the desk, dresser and bedside tables were in different piles on the carpeted floor. Shaw could just about tell where Merritt had sat to sort through what he'd gathered.

The same was true about the daughter's room.

Anything helpful would be gone.

He doused the lights and stepped outside, then walked to a neighbor's house. The home was dark, except for one interior light, dim, and he was not surprised there was no answer when he rang the bell. The residence on the other side was well lit and occupied. The woman who answered nodded pleasantly to a smiling Shaw—his expression of choice for getting information from strangers. He told her he was a friend of Allison's mother's, a not wholly deceptive statement, and had some things to give her. She was supposed to be home but she wasn't answering the door.

"You know when they'll be back?"

"Oh, I couldn't tell you. I haven't seen them today. Matter of fact, they keep to themselves mostly. The mother and girl. Always seemed suspicious. Not social at all. I left cupcakes, and she mailed me a note. I thought she'd come over in person."

Shaw thanked her and returned to the street in front of the house and walked to the intersection of Maple View and Cross County, a four-lane thoroughfare. Sitting on the sidewalk in the middle of the block was a man in dusty rumpled clothing. A sign beside him informed passersby he was out of work and a veteran.

Shaw approached. He dropped a ten into a cardboard box, in which sat a few coins.

"Bless you." Spoken with an understandable hint of wariness, since Shaw was not walking on after the donation.

"Got a question." He displayed pictures of Allison and Hannah on his phone. "These two, they're missing. You seen them today?"

He frowned, tilted his head.

A twenty made its way into the box.

"Yeah, they left, fast, hours ago. Her SUV ran the

stop sign. A driver gave her the finger. She just kept go-ing fast, till she got to the truck."

"What truck?"

"White pickup. Was about there." He pointed.

"Ford F-150?"

He shrugged.

"You said she stopped?"

The man chuckled. "Yep. Let the air out of a tire. Then kept going. Bat outta hell."

There were skid marks where she'd gunned the en-gine.

"How soon after she left did the driver of the truck come back?"

"Oh, right after. Dangerous-looking guy. Pale, spooky. Ghoulish. Don't hear that word much, do you?"

Shaw pulled out his phone and showed a mug shot of Merritt.

"Yeah, him."

"What'd he do after he got the spare on?"

"Drove off after her."

"You have a phone?"

"I got a phone."

Shaw dug into his pocket and peeled off a hundred in twenties. Into the box they went.

"My, oh, my."

Shaw also dropped a card with his burner numbers on it; only that, no name. "Give me your number."

He glanced up cautiously. "You gonna sell it to a tele-marketer?" Then grinned. He recited the number and Shaw loaded it into his phone.

"You see that white pickup around the house, call me."

"I will."

Shaw turned to leave.

"But he won't be back."

Facing the man again. "How do you know?"

"You spooked him good."

"What do you mean?"

"You pull up on that motorcycle of yours and not three minutes later he's climbing out that window." He pointed to the garage. "He runs to the pickup and, this time, goes east." Tugging a lengthy eyebrow. "Can I still have the hundred?"

Shaw sprinted to the Yamaha, fired up the engine and skidded into the street.

Two miles later, having passed scores of arteries major and minor, which would have taken Merritt anywhere through the warren that was this part of Ferrington, he braked sharply to a stop, lifted his phone and composed a text to Sonja Nilsson.

Just before he hit SEND he received one.

From her.

Both messages said largely the same thing.

31

Jon Merritt parked the F-150 in one of the many vacant lots near the river, off Manufacturers Row.

There had been no point in engaging the guy on the motorcycle.

Muscle.

But working for who?

A big question. But he didn't waste time speculating. He had to move. So far his only crimes—*known* crimes—were violating a restraining order and trespassing. Soon this would change, of course, and even the Hero of Beacon Hill would no longer be immune from pursuit.

But for now, he had a certain period of grace.

He climbed from the truck's cab. Some crack and meth heads, scrawny men and a few women, sat or stood on the riverwalk, eyeing him. They were twitchy and desperate and hoping he could hook them up. Or, if not, he might have something they could relieve him of, which in turn they could barter for a hit. Two men rose unsteadily and approached. He displayed the gun and they turned and vanished, as if the wind had blown them on their way. Just like the bum at the bus depot.

People like these were mosquitoes. All it took was a slap, and they were gone.

Merritt walked west toward the Fourth Street Bridge. The city's paint jobs had been haphazard, both the original sickly green and more recent darker versions of a similar hue. Much rust too. He crossed on the sidewalk, which was edged with a ten-foot chain-link barrier. The fencing had been added some years ago after the bridge had become a popular site for suicides. This was curious since the distance from bridge to water was about fifty feet. You couldn't work up lethal velocity in that distance. The deaths—mostly laid-off workers—came from drowning.

Merritt had run some of these cases as a rookie. He thought if he ever wanted to take his life it would be by firearm, not the suffocation of drowning, especially in this toxic soup.

The autumn moon was a disk camouflaged by haze—some smoke, some pollution. This was Ferrington. Better than when Merritt was a teenager, his father working in one of the plants that spewed whatever it was the towers spewed. He'd heard it was just heated air; the poisons were treated into nothingness within the factory. That was a lie, of course.

Across the river was a faded billboard.

FERRINGTON MAKES, THE WORLD TAKES.

Beneath the slogan was painted a parade of industrial items. Merritt had no idea what exactly they were. Metal parts, tubes, tanks, boxes, controllers. Ferrington was not known for consumer products.

Merritt came to a commercial strip on Fourth, most of the offices dark, but he passed a storefront that was still inhabited. He stepped into an alleyway across the street and checked his gun. Soon this office too went dark. A short man in his forties but with prematurely gray hair stepped outside. He was in a suit and a short overcoat and carrying a briefcase. He locked the door and walked north, his gait a waddle. Merritt stepped from the alley and followed, twenty feet behind him.

They covered a block in tandem, when he heard a car bleat and saw the lights flash their brief inanimate welcome. Merritt moved in quickly.

The man climbed into the driver's seat and slammed the door. Before he started the engine, Merritt approached and rapped on the window. He stood tall so his face wasn't visible and held his police ID against the glass.

The window came down.

"Officer, can I—"

Instantly Merritt reached in, pressed the passenger-side lock and ripped the door open, pulling out his pistol. He dropped into the seat and swung the gun into the face of David Stein, Allison's lawyer.

The man's shoulders slumped and he shook his head. "Jon, Christ."

"Shh." Merritt rolled the window up.

"What's this getting you? Just a shitload of trouble. I never did anything to you."

Merritt shivered in rage at those words.

Stein backed down. "I'm sorry, Jon. I was just doing—"

"Shh." Merritt pulled on his seatbelt. He said, "Keep yours off, start the car and drive where I tell you."

"Jon—"

"Straight. Left on Monroe."

Grimacing in disgust, the lawyer did as told.

Merritt cocked the gun, drawing a gasp from the lawyer, and rested the muzzle against his neck.

This message was: *Drive slowly.* He didn't need to add that the road surfaces of Ferrington were in such sad shape that any kind of heroic maneuver would in all likelihood not end well for him.

32

At 11 p.m. . . .

The receptionist stepped out the front door of the Safe Away shelter.

The dark-haired woman was slimmer than Moll remembered, though just as top heavy. He could tell because her black leather jacket was close-fitting.

She walked away from the door and lit a cigarette, the smoke vanishing fast on this cool windy night. Hiking a gym bag higher on her shoulder she made a cell phone call and had a conversation.

There were four cars parked in the lot. Moll wondered which was hers. He hoped it was the white Camry, easier to follow.

The plan was simple. They'd force her off the road, grab her, and get her into the Transit. Then they'd park in the shadows and get to work. Did she know where Allison Parker had gone?

She'd say either yes or no.

Moll could tell if she was being honest, either way.

"Would you hang up the damn phone and move," Desmond muttered, eyes on her.

They couldn't do anything until she got to her car and left.

The woman just puffed and talked, puffed and talked.

"Check out her—"

"—belt," Moll said. "I saw it."

The reference was to a canister of pepper spray.

Victims fighting back was always a risk, ranging from karate to spray to firearms, but never insurmountable. Just something you took into account and handled.

The woman nodded and swayed, as if ending a conversation and mentally moving on from the caller.

At last.

Then Desmond stiffened. "Shit."

He'd been looking in the side-view mirror. Moll did the same and saw the cruiser—a county deputy's vehicle—moving slowly toward the Transit.

Both men instinctively slipped the guns into compartments under the front seats. They looked like built-in DVD players. Moll had made them himself.

Moll and Desmond remained calm. They hadn't been drinking and there was no evident blood on the bed of the van. Luminol would reveal some traces of Edgar's blood, but using those fancy lights would require a warrant or probable cause.

They'd pulled over simply to make a phone call and

send some texts. Distracted driving is one of the leading causes of traffic deaths, I heard, Officer. My friend and I are always careful.

But the car cruised past, the deputy paying them no mind. He pulled up to the front of the clinic, and the receptionist disconnected her call, ground out the cigarette and climbed into the front seat. She and the deputy exchanged a ten-years-married kiss.

The man put the car in gear and they drove off.

"Well." Moll grunted. He sent a text delivering the bad news. Tonight, at least, the shelter was a dead end. He tucked the phone away.

They retrieved their guns.

Moll pulled slowly onto the state route and headed back toward his house in Ferrington.

Desmond pulled out the willow branch and began fiddling with it, tapping it again with his black knife.

Moll thought about poor Edgar, becoming less human every hour. He *had* to get to Ralston and take care of it. By now it would be VapoRub in the nose to handle the stench. Though the sawing would be easier.

Tomorrow. Please tomorrow. Let's get this finished.

He was tired . . . and hungry. Chain burgers, not fine barbecue, had figured in the day's calories.

Desmond was sighting down the branch. "You had no problem with the banker's wife."

This again?

"No, the job is a hit. Pure and simple. Your dick cannot figure in this picture. And that wife? You got to her before I even knew what you were up to. And we had to burn the cabin after. For the evidence."

Thonk, thonk, thonk . . . More pounding on the willow branch. This part of the project took a long time, Moll knew.

Moll looked Desmond over. "You *do* understand that just by sitting there, you've left enough clues to earn a one-way ticket to Harper Maximum. Imagine what you'd leave if you unzipped."

Desmond tilted his head, reflecting. "Rest assured, friend, I will refrain from having carnal knowledge with the vehicle. Tempted though I am."

The man could occasionally display a sense of humor.

"Go to one of your truck stops."

Desmond scoffed. "There? Half those girls didn't start life as Betty or Sally."

"What do you care who you put it in?"

"I'm just saying."

Where the hell did the man get his hormones?

An incoming text. Moll read it, glancing between the screen and the road.

"Merritt had a talk with her lawyer. It did not pan out."

"Shit. That could've been a good lead."

Desmond seemed to get tired of playing with the branch. He put it away, the knife too. "What about that guy, Motorcycle Man?"

"What about him?"

"I mean, he's got a gun, he breaks into her house. Who knows what he'll do?"

Moll considered this. "The way I look at it: he is both helpful and a problem."

"Uh-huh." Desmond's I'm-not-in-the-mood look emerged. "And that means what?"

"If he leads us to her, that is helpful. Once he does, *then* he is a problem."

33

At 11 p.m. . . .

Allison Parker was standing at the window of Sunny Acres, lifting aside the curtain to gaze at Route 92.

She wondered why she bothered to do this. How could she possibly identify a threat? The headlights that zipped past could belong to a station wagon driven by a nun on her way to a nun convention. Or to a Ford F-150, driven by a man who used his superpowers to find her, against all odds.

Then he would park, suss out the room they were in and . . .

Stop it, she told herself.

And began the mantra. Don't. Think. About. It.

Hannah had grown moody once more. She was staring at her computer screen, typing fast. Her silence was like a splinter, black, deep in the skin.

"You have to stay in airplane mode," Parker said. There was no way to shut off internet service in only one room. She'd asked the clerk.

The girl snapped, "I am. Want to see?" She was angry.

"No, honey. I believe you."

Five more minutes of silence, then Hannah closed the lid of the laptop and set it on the nightstand. Saying nothing, she pulled her sweatpants off. She wore navy-blue boxers underneath. The girl climbed under the comforter and rolled onto her side, away from her mother.

Parker sat in the motel's excuse for an office chair and closed her eyes. After five minutes she roused herself to stand and walked into the bathroom and tended to her nighttime routine. She looked out the window once more. A glance toward the golden Kia, holding its magic envelope. Then she shut the light out and she too lay down in bed, tugging the sheet and blanket around her.

Listening to the now sporadic traffic.

Nuns?

Or her ex?

More memories. These of her daughter.

Hannah at five. Disney for the first time, the Florida palms swaying, the heat, the 4 p.m. downpour, lasting exactly fifteen minutes. Goofy scared her to tears.

At seven, her face glowing as she sat under the Christmas tree and ripped open the package containing the American Girl doll.

At ten, returning shyly from school, clutching an envelope from the principal. As the girl ate her after-school snack of mozzarella sticks and Goldfish, Parker tore it open, worried that her daughter had gotten into trouble. Later that night, she and Jon framed the Certificate of Mathematics Achievement, for getting the highest score in the history of Benjamin Harris School.

At twelve, her face glowing as she sat under the Christmas tree and ripped open the BB gun her father had bought and wrapped himself. Parker was unsure about the gift, which Jon hadn't told her about. Still, she smiled at Hannah's happy enthusiasm as the girl plinked away at empty Sprite cans that tumbled into the snow, where they lay green and contrasty in the monotone December morn.

At thirteen, asking her mother about girls kissing girls. Casually. Like she was asking: Would it rain today? Her carefully constructed answer, which had been composed about a year earlier, was simple and contained not a hint of judgment. A month later the girl was "dating," that is, hanging with, none other than Luke Shepherd, yes, that's the one, the school's star quarterback.

At fourteen, watching with cautious eyes her father weaving through the living room, stumbling over a chair and struggling to get up.

At fifteen, racked by uncontrolled sobs, flinging herself at her parents as Jon, inches from Parker's face, screamed obscenities and accusations. He was numb to his daughter's grip, trying to pull him away. Oblivious too to his wife's cries of "Stop it, stop it, stop it!"

And then, November of last year, sitting on her bed, lost in texting and whatever music was coursing loudly and directly into her brain through the Beats headphones, while the bloody drama unfolded under the seahorse outside.

Sleep wasn't happening. Parker rolled onto her back, staring at the popcorned ceiling. A faint pink glow from the sign out front made it into the room. She wished she could shut it off, superstitiously thinking it might somehow tell Jon Merritt where they were.

Motion from the other bed. Hannah had stirred. She was sleeping the way she used to when she and Jon would check in during the night: on her side, hugging a second pillow.

"Love you, Han."

A moment later, she heard the girl's voice. Though distorted, layered into the girl's soft breathing and muted by institutional cotton, the words could very well have been a reciprocating "Love you too."

For the next fifteen minutes, until sleep unspooled within her, she tried to analyze the meaning—not of the words themselves, if they were in fact what she hoped— but of the tone with which her daughter had spoken them: sincere, a space filler, an obligation, an attempt to keep an enemy at bay, sardonic? Allison Parker, the engineer mother, approached this question as if she were facing a mathematical problem that was aggressively difficult, involving limits and sine waves and integrals and differentials and sequences and variables . . .

But her analytical skills failed her, and the only conclusion she could draw was that the calculus of the heart was both infinitely complex and absurdly simple and, therefore, wholly insoluble.

34

At 11 p.m. . . .

Jon Merritt was sitting propped up in bed.

Outside, he heard the lonesome horn of a tug pulling or pushing barges on the Kenoah.

Beside him were the whisky bottle, a soda can, the remains of one of the sandwiches from earlier and hundreds upon hundreds of pieces of intelligence that he'd collected from his ex's home.

He was angry.

The lawyer had been unhelpful, tearfully reporting that he knew nothing about her whereabouts. In the end, Merritt believed him.

Under other circumstances he might have felt bad for what happened to the unfortunate man—and what his family would be going through. Not tonight.

No luck with Attorney Stein.

No luck at the women's shelters either.

So, it was down to doing what detectives did: excavating.

Post-its, scraps of paper, cards, clippings, annotated pages ripped from engineering journals, reports about Hannah from teachers.

His only hope at this point was to find that person who was a friend of his wife's but a stranger to him.

Nothing, nothing, nothing . . .

He downed the contents of the plastic glass, so thin it nearly cracked under his grip. He poured some more. He drank.

Back to the task . . .

Slips of paper passed under his bleary eyes on their way to the discard pile.

This put him in mind of running his big corruption case. Poring over page after page of financial documents, real estate, corporate contracts and filings, checks, accounting books, Excel spreadsheets, and so much more.

And then . . .

At last he had found a gold nugget. No, *platinum*. The lead that took him to Beacon Hill, and to what he'd found hidden in the sewer pipe that went nowhere.

And eventually what happened after.

He sipped from the fragile glass.

His eyes closed.

The smell.

It's tuna, Merritt has recognized. His sessions with Dr. Evans are at 1 p.m. and he supposes that a tuna salad sandwich is what the shrink looks forward to at lunch: an oasis in the desert of dangerous crazies.

Today the doctor is wearing two hats: shrink plus voca-tion counsellor. "You'll need to get into a program when you're out."

"Oh, I will. I'll probably be in one forever. I like them."
Jon the Charmer *is back. Always when in the shrink's room.*

"And then a job. You won't be able to be a policeman anymore."

The reminder, obvious, infuriates him. He says in an enthusiastic voice, though, "I've been thinking about that, Doctor. I've got a lot of options."

"I've seen reports from the staff. They've said your work in the metal shop is exemplary . . ." He then pauses, perhaps thinking that the big word is too much for a con.

Merritt had graduated from college before the academy but gives no clue as to the resentful anger. "I enjoy working with my hands. It's kind of a gift. You?" He puts on a face of genuine curiosity.

"No." The doctor doesn't like to answer questions about his life outside the four corners.

"I put myself through college working the line at Hen-derson Fabrications."

One of the few companies on Manufacturers Row still operating, if not thriving.

Dr. Evans stares at the tablet. Merritt isn't sure if he's reading it or not. Zoning out seems to be a mainstay of his practice. He can be counted on to do this several times a session.

Obsessively wrestling with his prisoner-patients' mental health?

Daydreaming of the cares of housewives?

Or thinking of tuna sandwiches?

He flutters back to this dimension and looks at Merritt. "The report I got, Jon. That con from C. He jumped you. You didn't fight back."

"Oh, I wouldn't want to do that, Doctor." A laugh. "Nothing good would come of it. That'd be a sure way to really get my ass kicked."

Oh, it was close. For an instant Merritt was seared by the rage. And though he isn't a big man any longer, he could still have snapped the neck of the wiry tweaker, crazed because he couldn't get product and somehow, in his decayed mind, associating Merritt with that absence.

But he'd stepped back and taken the blows.

What choice was there? He wanted to get out. Fighting would keep him in.

So he dropped to the wet concrete and covered his head. He could take a beating like a man—

Take the blows.

Take the belt.

The belt . . .

And suddenly, he's surprised to realize that just this once he doesn't want to deceive the doctor. "Hey, you know, there's something I'm thinking of. This time I was nineteen."

The doctor is looking his way, nodding.

"I was working overtime for money for school and I got home after second shift and my father had this tantrum. He thought I'd been out, crowning around. That's what he called it when you screwed around with girls, smoking, having a beer. 'Crowning.' I told him I put in for overtime.

For the shift differential. But he didn't believe me. And, okay, I'm nineteen, remember? He stands up and starts to take his belt off and—"

"Oh, say, Jon. I see our time is up. That sounds like something we should explore." He flips the tablet screen, queuing up the next hopeless patient.

Merritt is furious. His anger is fundamental. In his soul. But he lets it go and smiles and says, "Sure thing, Doctor. See you next week."

And as he leaves he's thinking it was probably a good idea to end it there. If he'd continued down that road the façade of charm might have cracked and certain facts might have spilled out.

Among them the capital-T Truth: that the agreeable patient with the 1 p.m. slot is in fact a murderer. And he's not talking attempt. The real thing.

Now, in a cell of a different sort, the River View Motel, Jon Merritt shut the light out, nearly knocking the flimsy thing over. He set the alarm on his phone and lay back in bed. Not washing up, not peeing, not brushing his teeth.

All he was thinking at the moment was that he hoped to hear another cry of horn from a tug or a riverboat. It was something superstitious. The more horns, the luckier the lucky man would be.

Over the next few minutes he collected two, one loud, one barely audible, and then sleep took him.

35

At 11 p.m. . . .

Colter Shaw was back in another windowless office within the security department of Harmon Energy Products.

He was not alone. Sonja Nilsson sat beside him at a long desk on which were dozens of computer monitors and keyboards.

Shaw was on the phone with Detective Dunfry Kemp.

Never antagonize law enforcers . . .

But it was hard to keep the frustration from his voice. "Well, Detective, all respect. Now it's overt. He was inside the house. He tossed it, looking for where Allison's gone."

"You saw him?"

"I saw the mess he made. And a homeless man saw him leave. I've got the number."

"A homeless man has a phone?"

"You want it?"

A pause. "And you were in the house yourself, Mr. Shaw?"

"State Penal Code 224.655. It's an affirmative defense when one enters upon a premises without permission to save the life of others."

"You looked that up."

"I did."

"Before or after you broke in? Never mind."

"Detective, this takes it up a notch. Gets some gold shields assigned."

Or maybe puts it on the desk of somebody who's not too lazy to do it?

No, that was unfair, given the walls of files. Still . . .

Nilsson was looking at him. He shook his head.

Shaw remained silent. There was no better prod than this. Quiet beats repeating the question a dozen times for getting a response. "Fact is, it's still a misdemeanor."

Again, not a word.

A sigh. "I'll get it to the powers that be."

He inhaled long. "Anything you can do, Detective. Much appreciated."

He disconnected.

"Almost useless," he muttered. "It's like Merritt's walking around in body armor."

"So, back to the digital legwork," Nilsson said.

Her text message, the one that he had read when he pulled over on Cross County Highway, had said:

No luck here. Let's check cams.

The one he'd been about to send:

Too many haystacks. Can we get intersection
camera access?

Nilsson explained that the city of Ferrington might be down a number of human law enforcers but in some compensation city hall had invested in an above-average municipal video surveillance system.

"Not inexpensive, but cheaper than bodies and no insurance or pension payments."

The system was enhanced by access to some private cameras—in retail stores and service stations whose owners volunteered them.

Being the famed benefactor of the city, Harmon made calls and had gotten the okay for Nilsson, and therefore Shaw, to log in to the consolidated system.

This room contained dozens of monitors and they were now searching footage for Allison Parker's Toyota 4Runner and her ex-husband's Ford F-150 pickup.

They had started with the fact she fled west on Cross County Highway.

Shaw had called up a map of North Ferrington. Nilsson leaned close, beside him. He detected a flowery scent. Then concentrated again on the grid. Cross County was intersected by many streets and roads. But near Ferrington, they were closed neighborhoods with no way out.

She gestured toward it. "Maybe she knows someone there."

"Possible. Ten percent, I'd say. I think she'll keep going. Put as much distance between Ferrington and herself as possible."

"Agreed."

They'd then sat down, where they were now, and begun to review footage along Cross County starting from the approximate time she would have fled.

Shaw believed he had a hit of a 4Runner, the color of hers, turning south on 55. There was a truck behind the turning vehicle, though, partially obscuring the view. The tag was not visible at all.

Nilsson peered at the images. "Could be. Anybody inside you can see?"

No. Glare and grain.

Shaw switched to cameras along 55 south, while Nilsson continued to scan for Merritt's pickup, both west— the first time he'd fled her house—and east, after he'd escaped during Shaw's visit.

"May have her," he said.

About a half hour after she'd turned south, a 4Runner pulled quickly from a shopping center parking lot and sped north on 55. If it had been hers that they'd seen turning south, she'd been in Carter Grove briefly. When the vehicle arrived at Cross County, it kept going north. "It's her." The intersection camera had caught a clear image of her tag. "Where would that take her, going that way?"

"Chicago; Detroit; Indianapolis; International Falls; Red Lake, Ontario, where I used to fish with my father. Look at this."

Shaw eased close to her, their shoulders brushing, like they had at the failed attempt to have lunch. She was playing video from the camera closer to downtown, pointed west on Cross County. It was capturing a cityscape, stores, apartments, a car repair garage. A white pickup was driving toward the camera. The time stamp indicated it was not long after Merritt's second visit to the rental. It turned right, south, and vanished. She rewound it.

"If this were a sci-fi movie," she offered, "I'd say, 'Enhance, enhance,' and we'd get the make, model and eye color of the driver."

Interesting she said that. And he wondered again about the green hue.

"It's definitely a 150," he said.

"Yes, but is it *his*?" Nilsson wondered. This state did not require a front license plate.

"The street he turned on?"

"Miller. Leads downtown." She sighed. "It's a warren. We'd need a dozen sets of eyes and two or three solid days to scan them all."

"Let's focus on finding Allison and Hannah. She's headed north on Fifty-five. Cameras there?"

She looked over a list the FPD had provided. "No city or county ones past Cross County. Some private ones." Her long fingers, nails dark, typed fast. "Six we can access. We have to log on. Here's the IPs and passwords. You take the top three; I'll get the others." She set a sheet of paper before him.

He concentrated on his monitor, logged in to the first camera he'd drawn—at a gas station. It offered only a partial view of the road. The image was grainy and colors washed out. He had to scrub slowly and pause at each passing vehicle to study it. Fifty-five was a major road; traffic was heavy.

He glanced beside him. Nilsson was in an identical posture. She was frowning in concentration—as, he supposed, he had been too.

Returning to scrubbing, Shaw asked, "Any train stations, bus depots, rental cars in that direction?"

"No trains, but there's a bus terminal in Herndon. Three car rental places. And dealerships that probably rent cars too."

"Buses're always good. Cash and no ID. Rental car possibly, which leaves a record. But I'd say that's a chance she'd take."

Nilsson asked, "What do you think, warrant for Hertz or Avis or whoever? Look at their vids?"

Shaw said, "They'd fight it, on these facts. Same with the bus company."

After five minutes of silence, other than the clatter of keys, Shaw asked, "What'd you fish for?"

Not missing a beat: "Pike and bass mostly. Some muskie."

Shaw's mother, Mary Dove, was the primary hunter in the family. The best with a long gun. Colter was next. But everyone fished. Shaw remembered assembling tackle and going out with one or both parents, sometimes a sibling, early—in cold blue-black dawn. Each would take up a different position on a promontory around what Dorion, his sister, had named Egg Lake, for the obvious reason. By 7 a.m. they would have their take for the week.

In the Compound it wasn't catch and release. It was catch and eat.

Never toy with animals. They aren't there for your amusement . . .

"You?"

He told her he didn't fish much now. "But growing up, we were a self-sufficient family."

"Okay. That requires some keep going."

Where to start?

Shaw gave the nutshell version. How his father, Ashton, and mother, both esteemed academicians, fled the San Francisco Bay Area when Shaw was six, his brother twelve, their sister three, for the property in the Sierra Nevadas.

"Fled?"

"Ashton was into conspiracy theories, only his turned out not to be fictional. He found something that threatened some very powerful people. So he taught himself and us survival skills."

"These people? They came for you?"

"That's right. My father didn't make it."

"Oh, I'm sorry." She then glanced his way with an expression he deduced meant: And was the matter ever resolved?

"I took care of things."

She seemed like a woman who would herself be inclined to take care of things too.

"My mother still lives in the cabin. My sister runs a disaster preparedness and emergency response company on the East Coast. My brother works for the government."

"Yep. That's a story and some change."

"Long answer to a question about fish."

They returned to their frustratingly slow task.

Each scrubbed through two of their allocated videos without finding any image of her SUV. This meant either she'd turned off, or it had been hidden from the camera by traffic.

Shaw and Nilsson started on their last cameras. Shaw's showed a grainy, low-def and dark image of a gas station pump. You could see a short stretch of 55 on the far side of the apron.

After a few minutes she said, "Noticed. You haven't taken or made any calls since you've been here."

He had an idea where the inquiry was headed.

"No."

And, sure enough:

"You're not married."

He thought of Margot, as close as he'd come.

"No. You said you'd been."

"That's right." She shrugged. "But a waste-of-time decision. Not an oh-shit decision. You seeing anybody now?"

He thought of Victoria.

"Sometimes."

He explained how he and the woman—a security specialist herself—occasionally saw each other, if they had jobs in the same area. "Couple of times a year."

"That's not seeing someone," she said, and the keys clattered.

He said, "You *have* been making calls. The other phone of yours."

She laughed. "Believe me. Nobody I date."

Silence for a moment.

Neither of them typed.

Colter Shaw swiveled toward her. Looked into those verdant eyes and the gaze in return contained a message. He gripped her by the shoulders and kissed her. Hard. She reciprocated, and then rose. He did too, sending his chair wheeling sharply into another workstation.

For a short moment the two were as still as statues, eyes locked. They kissed again. Nilsson's hands slid to the small of his back and this put the two of them firmly together.

His own right palm slid down her spine, stopping just below the narrow horizontal strap. He too pressed hard.

He felt her breasts against his chest, was embraced by the ambiguous, seductive aura of flowers.

Her eyes closed, then his.

They kissed harder, their mouths hungry.

Her hands went to his cheeks. He took her right and kissed the finger that was enclosed by the serpent ring. She ran the black-tipped nail around his lips.

He looked past her, at the couch against the wall.

He noted a lock on the door and the absence of video cameras in the room—ironic considering what they were doing here.

Her eyes were making the same transit. Her gaze ended at the couch and she turned back and nodded.

They both started toward it, his arm round her waist.

And as they did, Shaw happened to glance to his left. He saw the frozen video image of Route 55. No cars were depicted, no trucks, no hitchhikers. Just the business end of a gas station with a quick mart across the road.

An establishment that Allison Parker might have pulled into sometime that afternoon and, when buying a soda or chips, might have asked the clerk a question about any nearby motels that were decent, or made a comment from which their final destination could be deduced.

He turned to Nilsson, who, he found, was staring at the same screen.

Their eyes met once more, a different gaze this time. He smiled. For Nilsson's part, she gave a wistful laugh. Another long kiss and they retired to their respective workstations, each hitting PLAY at exactly the same moment.

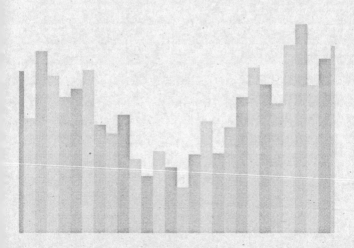

PART TWO

HIDE AND SEEK

WEDNESDAY, SEPTEMBER 21

36

t was good for me. How was it for you?"

The hour was 6:30 a.m. and Sonja Nilsson was sitting on the edge of the couch in the monitor room, braiding her hair.

Colter Shaw sat up straight, wondering when the pain in his back would vanish. "I've had better."

Her smile was both demure and seductive, not an easy combination.

At around two that morning, exhausted from examining videos, they'd decided they needed to surrender to sleep. Shaw insisted Nilsson take the couch. He locked the wheels of two office chairs, put them face-to-face and sat, resting his feet on the opposite one. He crossed his arms, tilted his head forward and slipped under almost immediately. This was a helpful talent for a survivalist, though one that could not be taught. He was simply lucky in his ability to doze anywhere, anytime.

The marathon viewing sessions of the night before had been only a modest success.

Shaw's third camera—the low-def one at the service station—had caught Allison Parker's SUV speeding north on 55, three miles south of Herndon, the home of the bus terminal and rental car agencies.

Just past that sighting Parker had crossed into Marshall County, where Ferrington's guardian angel Marty Harmon had no clout when it came to government officials opening up traffic cams. Shaw had left a message for beleaguered Detective Kemp to see if he could access any videos up there. But the man had not called back. The odds he would? Ten percent, tops. If there was any good news in this it was that they also hadn't spotted Merritt's truck going north on 55 in pursuit.

Stretching, Nilsson said, "HEP is the land of overnighters. There's a shower on every floor. Toothbrushes. Shave kits."

Shaw's beard grew in dark and coarse, curiously the opposite of what crowned his head. Facial hair didn't bother him but it did make him look sinister, and considering what lay ahead today he'd take advantage of a razor.

"Next steps?" she asked, making coffee from a Keurig in the corner. She lifted an eyebrow and he nodded.

"I'll talk to friends outside of the office. You keep going with employees?"

She nodded and handed him the cup. He snagged a creamer from a bowl and poured it in. Let it self-stir.

"Bathroom?"

"I'll show you."

They walked out together, Nilsson pointing toward the restroom.

They offered silent nods in farewell. She continued to the elevator and Shaw stepped into the bathroom. He locked the door behind him. He sipped coffee and set the cup down on a ledge. The bright, clean room, of blue tile, was well stocked for the hardworking. Plenty of towels and individually wrapped packets of soap, shampoo, toothbrushes and paste and the shaving kits.

He stripped, stepped into the shower and stood under the hottest water he could stand, then the coldest. The Winnebago was downstairs, in the lot, but didn't have water pressure or temperature like this; he always took advantage of landline pipes when he could. He toweled off, dressed and shaved.

In the monitor room once more, he collected his backpack, which contained his computer, phone and notebook. The Glock had remained affixed to his belt constantly, even when he'd slept.

On the ground floor, he carded out and stepped into a damp, still morning. Either he was getting used to the scent of the Kenoah or the off-gassing was milder today. Maybe the cleanup was finally having some effect.

In the camper, he changed into clean jeans, a navy polo shirt and a gray sport coat. Outside, he tugged on his helmet and muscled the two-hundred-pound Yamaha off the rack on the back of the vehicle, where he had—out of habit—affixed it once again after returning from Allison's. He swung on, fired up and typed into GPS the first address on his list of Allison Parker's friends. He memorized the route and skidded out of the lot.

In the reward business he always called on interviewees in person if he could; a phone call could be terminated with a mere tap of a finger.

Riding through progressively nicer neighborhoods, he arrived at the stately white split-level in twelve minutes. There was a low-end Mercedes in the driveway. He motored past and parked around the block and left the helmet. Bikers, even those dressed like CEOs of computer start-ups, will often be ignored when knocking on doors.

He rang the bell and stepped back.

A blond woman of about forty opened the wooden door but left the screen closed. Shaw suspected it was locked.

"Ms. Holmes?"

"That's right." She scanned him carefully.

"My name's Colter Shaw. Alli Parker's mother suggested I talk to you."

A child—a boy of about five—wandered up and stared. Holmes turned him around and said, "Go play."

Back to Shaw. "Alli's mother? Why?"

"Alli's ex-husband, Jon, was released from prison yesterday. And her mother's worried she might be in danger."

The woman's eyes widened. "What?"

The surprise was genuine. This deflated the potential value of the lead significantly; she hadn't heard from Parker in the past two days. Still, she might know of other friends or of getaway spots the woman might head to.

"She and her daughter've disappeared. I'm trying to find them and make sure they're all right." He knew the answer but asked anyway. "Have you heard from her in the past few days? Or know where she might've gone?"

Holmes's eyes narrowed considerably. "And, again, who are you?"

"I'm in security. You can call Alli's mother or her boss at Harmon Energy if you want confirmation."

"I only met her mother a few times. And I don't know her boss. Isn't this something for the police?"

"They're investigating. But Mrs. Parker thinks they're not doing enough. So, any thoughts where she might be? We know she was headed north out of Ferrington. Friends or inns or hotels in that direction she might've mentioned?"

Now she was looking behind him, scanning the street, her face a mask of worry. "No, I don't know anything. Please leave." Her voice was desperate, her eyes imploring. A whisper: "He could've followed you here. He could think I'm helping you."

"No, he didn't. I'm sure."

The woman asked bluntly, "You know where he is?"

"No, but—"

"Then he *could* have followed you. What Jon did to her! Did you see her face?"

Shaw knew her tone and could see where the conversation was going: into a brick wall. He pulled a card from his jacket pocket. It bore his name and burner phone number.

"Call me if you think of anything. And if Alli calls you, have her check her email. There's one from her mother she should read."

He slid the card under the screen door.

Odds it was destined for the trash in thirty seconds?

Eighty percent.

In the reward business, Colter Shaw had learned that one of the largest demographic groups in the world is the Uninvolved.

"I have to go now," Holmes said, and the door closed. She hadn't picked up the card.

He heard the deadbolt and the chain secure the door, then walked back to the bike and fired it up.

He put to use the second name and address, but the meeting was a virtual rerun.

As was the next. There was no occupant at the fifth house—or at least no occupant willing to open the door to a stranger.

At the next locations he found friends more sympathetic than the others. But those he spoke with said they knew nothing helpful, and he sensed they were being honest.

When he ran out of individuals he had addresses for, he turned to the phone list. Sitting on the Yamaha in a Walmart parking lot, his notebook balanced on the gas tank, he made the calls. Four of the six picked up. There was an element of suspicion on their part, though mentioning Ruth Parker's name allayed this to some extent.

No one had any idea where Allison might have gone. One, a man who was a former neighbor, volunteered that Jon Merritt was unstable and dangerous. He'd gotten drunk at a block party and fought with a guest over a perceived slight.

"Man is a damn bully."

He'd left messages for the two he hadn't been able to reach and wondered if he should call again.

But then decided: no, no. This was pointless. He was doing this wrong.

Allison Parker, the brilliant engineer, would be brilliant as a fugitive too.

She would have thought out her escape carefully and wouldn't confide in or seek the help of anyone her ex knew about or could easily find—someone he and Nilsson could easily identify too.

She'd run only to someone or someplace that Merritt would know nothing about.

The strip mall where he sat happened to be on a rise; the street was Humphrey Mountain Road, though that was an exaggeration. The geologic formation jutted from the otherwise flat earth here no more than a hundred feet. Still he could see the flat landscape for twenty miles in all directions. To the north, the industrial heart of Ferrington rose like red-brick tombstones along the sad Kenoah. East, west and south were densely clustered suburbs that ended abruptly, at lines of field and forest that vanished to the Midwest horizon, muted by a gray haze.

Tell me, Allison. Tell me.

Where are you going?

Like all mathematical problems, her methodology of escape would be laughably obvious to her.

And a mystery to most everyone else.

It was then that his phone hummed. He glanced at the screen.

Possible lead re: your request this morning. Motel in Ferrington. Should have name and address in 15 or 20.

This information came not from a local source but from many miles away.

Mack McKenzie.

His private eye was working her magic.

37

Jon Merritt lay in the rickety, creaking bed.

He squinted as the sun blasted through the torn curtain of the motel window and ignited a thousand dust motes that were parading slowly in the still air.

The Bulleit bottle had left a mark on his side, as he'd slept partially atop it. This put him in mind of his father, who on more than one occasion had fallen asleep with a bottle propped up next to him in his green Naugahyde armchair while watching sports. He would return home, announce, "Time to fire the sunset gun," and pour his first of the night. Once, he woke in the morning, still in the chair, enraged that the bottle had emptied its contents into his lap. This somehow was Jon's fault. Out came the belt.

Rolling upright, then out of bed, Merritt now struggled to the bathroom.

Puking? He waited.

No.

Thank you . . .

He showered then dressed, slipped his gun into one windbreaker pocket, loose shells into another and gathered up the half of Allison's papers and notes that he hadn't reviewed last night and stuffed them into the backpack.

He stepped outside into the tidal wave of sun.

At the convenience store Merritt bought a breakfast burrito and a black coffee and walked to the small park overlooking the river. Well, not so fragrant here, but it was good to be outside.

Merritt ate his breakfast. Tentatively at first, then with gusto. No nausea now. He sipped the coffee and then eased back and closed his eyes, bathed with a warmth that went beyond the excited electrons of the sunlight bearing down on him.

He allowed himself this sensation for only a few minutes, though.

Back to the task at hand.

He pulled out his phone, replenished the minutes, and went to the internet. He scanned once more for Allison's and Hannah's names on social media and found nothing active.

Slipping the phone away, he turned to the documents from his ex's house. On top were Hannah's assignments, poetry and selfies. Another Post-it about Kyle. Some with dates and initials. He flipped through the photos. Were one or two taken at an inn, a campground, a friend's house they might have fled to? No. Just moody pictures taken by a moody adolescent. He read through her poems until he realized there was nothing helpful there either.

He turned to the stack of Allison's papers. After five minutes he found something that snagged his attention.

It was an envelope addressed to Allison, postmarked a month ago. It bore a return address he didn't recognize. Inside was a greeting card. On the front was a watercolor of two butterflies hovering over a daisy. He read the inked message inside.

Ah, good, the detective within him thought. Very good.

He slipped this into his windbreaker pocket, rose and adjusted the gun on his hip. He then started back to his motel room.

He found himself thinking of the picture on the front of the card the woman had sent Allison, the delicate watercolor. The flitting insects.

Merritt remembered, long ago, seeing a TV special about butterflies. The commentator had said that, yes, they were beautiful, they possessed the navigation skills of GPS, they had the energy and wherewithal to migrate hundreds of miles.

There was another fact about the creatures that few people knew, and that Jon Merritt had found amusing: in addition to those nearly miraculous skills, butterflies were also ruthless and aggressive cannibals.

38

Colter Shaw sat in an armchair upholstered sometime in a prior decade, if not century. Comfortable, though, he had to admit.

He was in a small room, in a small motel, not far from the Kenoah. This was the address that Mack McKenzie had uncovered for him.

The view was of a parking lot. Two homeless—men, he believed—slept against a warehouse wall. A woman in the sex trade smoked and eyed passersby.

Shaw thought of the Street Cleaner, the serial killer. These would be prime targets.

Did the man feel that it was less immoral to kill the marginalized?

Or did morality not enter into the equation at all? Maybe he killed for amusement or lust or out of boredom.

Shaw turned his attention back to the place, noting evidence of a weapon.

Ammunition, but not the firearm itself.

Very little personal was here. Shaw was itinerate. He was on the road most of the year. Yet, the Winnebago contained artifacts that connected him with family. A photo of the Compound, preserves his mother had put up, photos of the children on hikes, Ashton holding the trout he'd caught not with rod and reel but with a simple line and hook he'd made himself, paintings that Dorion's two daughters had done for him, documents his father had sent that had launched Shaw on the quest to find the people who had killed the man.

He glanced again at the papers he'd riffled through when he'd first gotten inside. Like the bullets, they were evidence of impending murder.

A text hummed and he read it.

He replaced what he'd found exactly in the order he'd discovered the items. He then rose and stepped into the corner of the room. He reached to his right hip and drew the black Glock. Held it firmly.

There was only a faint click when the key card slipped into and out of the lock slot. The door swung open slowly and the man walked inside, eyes on his phone.

When the door closed, Shaw said calmly, "You're targeted. Don't move."

Leggy Sergei Lemerov stopped.

Did his shoulders sag slightly? Shaw wasn't sure.

"Mr. Colter Shaw."

"Drop the phone. Raise your hands."

"Maybe I am talking to beautiful woman. That will make her unhappy."

Shaw was silent.

Never banter . . .

The Russian muttered, "Ah, all right."

The Apple bounced when it hit the carpeted floor.

"Turn."

He did and the dots of black eyes in the angular face looked Shaw up and down.

"With your right hand, thumb and forefinger, remove the gun." Lemerov was predominantly left-handed, he could tell, but the Russian military teaches ambidextrous shooting.

With no inclination for heroics, he went through the prescribed routine. The weapon ended up on the armchair Shaw had just been sitting on. Shaw tossed a zip tie to him. He grimaced but pulled the band on. He didn't play the looseness game. They efficiently secured his wrists.

Shaw indicated a chair and the man sat, tossed his head to get a stray shock of long blond hair from his eyes.

The Russian did not seem particularly troubled. Shaw was a reward-seeker and a troubleshooter for Harmon Energy. There was no risk that Lemerov would be taken into an alley and treated the way the GRU disposed of *its* prisoners.

Shaw glanced at the papers he'd been through earlier. Maps, photos of himself and of the Winnebago, notes, names and addresses he did not recognize. Shaw had taken time with them, looking specifically for any reference to Allison Parker. It wasn't logical that Lemerov knew of her personally, but it was her brainchild he wanted. And Shaw had to make certain that there was indeed no connection between Jon Merritt's mission and the S.I.T.

And there was not.

He now said to the Russian, "All of your homework. You have a destination plan. And I'm the traveler."

A faint frown. Lemerov would be curious how Shaw had come to know the euphemisms used by Russian security services for a targeted kill. He had learned this from his brother, who swam in the current of intelligence.

He recovered. A smile. "What you talking? Everything you say is news to me. All that?" A nod at the paperwork. "Just about surveillancing you, when you went looking for that S.I.T."

Shaw didn't reply that the pictures were taken *after* the scam with Ahmad, Rass and LeClaire.

Yes, this might have to do with Marty Harmon's reactor trigger, but if so, it was a *future* plan to steal it. Shaw would have to be eliminated; the message would be clear to Harmon: There'll be consequences if we don't get the device.

Then too this might be personal. Maybe Lemerov was just a very sore loser.

"Who ordered it? Be better if you tell me."

"Ha, Mr. Colter Shaw, truth? Okay. Truth? Just wanted scare you. So you take bargaining serious. Nobody hurt a hair on head. Come on, come on, let's us get back to turkey talking . . . You are not made of money. I can line your pockets. We can do accounts, we can do

offshore. Bring in the experts. We have insurance, guar-
antees in place, so you safe, family safe. No more that."
A nod at the paperwork, the plan to get Shaw to his
"destination."

Shaw frowned. "How do I know your money's good?
Who'd write the check?"

"A rich friend."

"That doesn't answer my question."

"He likes secrecy. Or *she* likes secrecy."

"You've got to have a handler."

"Why?"

"You don't sound like you come from Boston or Atlanta."

"Oh, maybe I am born in the U.S.A. Maybe my handler is Bruce Springsteen! Two hundred fifty thousand.
A quarter million! Buy you lots of anything."

"Tell me who."

Instantly the man changed. His face contorted and his
voice was a snarl. "Fuck Abe Lincoln. No fun and cute
anymore. You don't help, I come back and visit you. Middle of night. I will say, 'Hello, Mr. Colter Shaw' and that
will be all you hear. Maybe when you with your woman.
Surprise, surprise, and goodbye to both of you." His
wild gaze danced around the room, twitchy, if eyes could
twitch. Like Jon Merritt, perhaps, Lemerov sported a
borderline personality.

And, true to his diagnosis, the cheerful side of Lemerov returned, so quickly the transformation was eerie.
"But what will come of this today? Your little clever
scheme? What? I wonder." He was as calm as could be.

"Here is what happens, your police people come and take me away. I spend hour or two in jail, meet interesting friends. Have a Coca-Cola. Then lawyer comes and I leave. How is that? Because I have friends here, oh, in the state capital. What do you think of that? I call them, they call someone else, I finish my Coca-Cola and I'm out." He affected a pout. "We have to start all over again. Waste of time. Two hundred fifty thousand? All you do is walk *into* HEP, walk *out* with trigger and you a rich man." His grin was conspiratorial.

Shaw knew there were places where a quarter million made you rich. Not even Ferrington was one of them.

A knock sounded.

Shaw walked to the door, keeping the gun aimed at Lemerov's torso—in a moment of mania he could charge them; his hands were bound but they were in front of him and could still punch and strangle.

"Yes?"

"Customs and Border Protection," came a husky woman's voice.

The captive's smile vanished.

He was being arrested by the *feds*. Whoever he'd paid off in state government would have no sway. Shaw had called his friend Tom Pepper, who arranged for the takedown with CBP.

A large man and a large woman stepped into the room, both in dark blue uniforms. Three other agents stood in the hallway. They too were not small.

"Colter," the woman said.

"Agent Gillespie," Shaw offered, then nodded to the

man, dark complected, muscled and broad. "Agent Stahl."

They looked over Lemerov. Gillespie, blond hair in a ponytail, nodded to her partner, who walked forward and, while the woman kept her hand near her gun, cut off the zip and cuffed the Russian, hands behind his back. The agent then frisked him and removed his wallet and passport, money, a long locking-blade knife, which Gillespie glanced at with raised eyebrows.

"You can't do this! I didn't commit no crime!"

She picked up his passport and took a picture of the front page.

"Now, Mr. Lemerov, Mr. Shaw swore out an affidavit that he observed you in possession of a firearm. The one right there?"

Shaw nodded.

"He's lying!"

"There are photos of you with the weapon, attached to the affidavit."

Lenny Caster was quite the artist with the Canon.

Stahl pulled on latex gloves, unloaded the weapon, locked it open and then read the serial number to Gillespie, who typed into her phone.

A moment later: "Sir, you're in possession of a stolen firearm."

"No, no! I bought legally. Private sale. I know about Second Amendment."

"So you admit you purchased the gun."

Maybe he was thinking he should have said "found." He licked his lips.

"Apart from the gun's status, do you have a valid hunting permit or sports participation certificate?"

Silence again.

"Well, sir, then you don't meet the requirements of 27 Code of Federal Regulations Section 178.97, regarding nonimmigrant aliens possessing firearms." She read him his Miranda rights.

"I want lawyer."

And his Coca-Cola, Shaw couldn't help but think.

"You'll have one." Stahl placed the Russian's possessions in evidence bags.

They led him toward the door, each gripping one arm.

He called over his shoulder, "You like boxing? I like boxing. You never know how end. Seem all wonderful, round one and round two. Then, bang, and there's knockout.

"So. One and two to you. But don't pat back too fast, Mr. Colter Shaw. More rounds to come. More rounds to come . . ."

39

Allison Parker let the hot shower stream course over her body.

The Sunny Acres motel was a dive but offered two advantages. One, the clerk was willing to forgo ID when an attractive businesswoman, accompanied by her daughter, explained with chagrin—and a handful of cash—that she'd left her billfold at a restaurant on 55, presently closed.

And, two, the water heater was top notch.

She rested her head against the blue tile.

Blue as the wall of the shower rinse-off by the pool, the wall on which the comical or eerie or sensuous white plaster seahorse reared in profile.

It's November of last year, the fifteenth.

Parker is sitting with coffee, in the kitchen, staring out at the snow, the covered pool. The flakes descend in bright flares through the spotlight that shines over the pool. She stares at the tiny white fireworks. It's a placid scene and she usually thinks how the blanket of snow covering the backyard is "heartwarming." She laughs sometimes when she has those contradictory thoughts. Tonight she is only anxious.

Hannah has abandoned the history class project she and Jon were working on earlier, before he rose abruptly and drove off into the night. The girl has gone to bed. It's eleven. On the glass-topped table, behind Parker, are pieces of metal and plastic, soldering iron and glue gun. She doesn't know what the project is supposed to be; it was a daddaughter thing.

Was . . .

Parker will have to write a note for Ms. Talbott about an extension.

A sip of coffee. Zero taste for it.

Her heart pounds as she hears a thunk from outside, faint but man-made—not the sound of the occasional branch surrendering to the weight of the wet snow.

Walking to a front window, she draws aside the curtain and peers out. Yes, Jon's truck has overrun the driveway and decked the big blue recycling bin.

She hoped, and yes, prayed, that he simply went for a head-clearing drive.

And now reflects on her searing naivete.

She walks into the living room, stopping to look in on Hannah. Yes, she's gone to bed but not to sleep. She's lying back, Beats headset on, staring at her phone, her face illuminated weirdly blue. It's time for lights-out but Parker lets it go. She also thinks it's a good idea to be deaf to any spousal exchanges this evening, and hopes, contrary to wise parenting, the volume is up nice and fucking high.

Locking the front door, she returns to the kitchen and turns on the light to the side porch. If she's lucky, he'll follow the path of least resistance: around the side of the house, through the gate and aim for the kitchen.

Upon intercepting Jon, she will guide him into the bedroom. Maybe a shower, more likely just a fully clothed landing on the bed. Or the floor. It's carpeted. Once, he collapsed on the driveway and once on the garage concrete, waking with nothing worse than a muscle ache. Apparently in their altered state, drunks often fall soft and limber.

The front doorknob turns, once, then again. He doesn't pound. She sees his form moving through the snow in the direction she'd hoped, drawn by the lights. A back entrance will get him straight to bed without going past Hannah's room. Had he come in through the front he might stick his head in to see her and ramble or puke.

Another thud, then a crash. He's bypassed the garage— the code usually defeats him—and he's tripped over the garbage.

She moves quickly now. Any more noise and, if Hannah has de-headphoned, she'll come out to investigate. And that will be difficult—for Parker herself. Hannah tends to be sad about her father and mad at her mother.

Now through the sliding patio doors. The cold stings and she thinks about a sweater, but it's too late. Jon's weaving through the pool fence gate and along the patio. He's fallen somewhere and there's a gash on his head. The blood is dark and crusted.

She walks to him.

"Don't start," he mutters.

"You're hurt."

"You don't care. You never care."

You can't counter word for word, thought for thought. It doesn't work that way.

The best course is to distract and deflect.

His hair is wild, his clothes disheveled. He rages, "Did you call him tonight?"

"Be careful. There's ice."

"Oh, be careful," he mocks. He seems to think of better words to sling, but then they sail away.

The scent of the whisky is powerful. Jon once told her that he could tell how much a driver had had to drink by the scent. He could predict the Breathalyzer result with uncanny accuracy.

They are standing in the drift gathering on the pool deck beside the seahorse relief. She shivers as the flares of snowflakes dot her head. It's twenty degrees, Alexa has reported.

"Where is she?" He stares through the door at the table, where sit Hannah's notebook and parts for the history project. "What were you saying to her tonight? Turning her against me. You do that!"

"Jon, please. Just stop." She says these words instinctively. They will have zero effect. Like always. He doesn't hear them. So what is the point? But she can't help herself.

He stumbles to the back of the garage and pukes.

If only it could purge his system. But it never does, of course. That's not how the physiology works.

He stumbles back. "I know what you do. I know what you've told people about me. I've heard. You go to those parties and I know what you say. What you really think of me. You think I don't know?" He frowns. "You think I don't know what you've told her about me? She—" He hesitates, as if he's forgotten his own daughter's name. "I'm going to tell her. She deserves—"

Parker grabs his arm. He turns with a frenzied glare.

And five minutes later, the longest minutes of her life, Allison Parker is lying on her back, sobbing, in a drift of delicate snow—white spattered with red. The seahorse is bleeding too. She is pressing the flaps of skin torn from her face above her cracked cheek.

"Why are you doing this to me? Why . . . ?"

Allison Parker now stepped out of the shower in room 306 of the Sunny Acres Motor Lodge.

The shower stall as blue as the wall the seahorse rose from.

Tears mix with the hot steam.

And she told herself sternly what she had just that morning. A half-dozen times.

Don't think about it.

Drying herself. A towel turbaned around her hair. Another enwrapping her body.

Thinking of the SpongeBob boob towel.

The calculus problems that her genius daughter nailed.

The plans for pizza and learning about Kyle.

The final moments before the world exploded.

Was it yesterday, or ten years ago? Or a hundred?

She stepped into the chill room. She'd left Hannah snoozing but the girl was up now, channel surfing.

How would her mood be?

Warming Parker's heart, Hannah smiled. "Hey!"

"Morning, sleepyhead."

Parker noted that the chain was off the door.

"You went out?"

"Just the front office. For breakfast. They don't have any here."

Parker hadn't expected Sunny Acres to offer up gourmet fare, though she'd hoped they could score coffee, tea and pastry.

"But the clerk? He said there's this diner up the road. It's, like, famous. And they deliver." She handed her mother a menu and announced, "I want waffles."

40

Moll undid his tie and opened his shirt. He navigated the Benadryl up under the cloth and blasted his shoulders, which were the itchier parts today.

The burning migrated. Neck and arms yesterday. Chest a few days ago. What the hell was it, and how did it happen?

He felt some relief thanks to the miracle substance.

"Allergy's getting worse?"

"Just will not go away," he told Desmond.

Moll had asked himself the where-did-it-come-from question a number of times. He finally believed he'd hit upon the answer. He had had a job six weeks or so ago—killing a truck driver. The man had done something he shouldn't do or was going to say something he shouldn't say or had pissed off the wrong man, and he had to go. Good money. Desmond was busy so Moll handled it solo. He'd killed the man where he was working on his truck, which was stuck in a tributary to the Kenoah. He'd dragged the body out and then schlepped it miles away to an industrial site, long abandoned, for disposal. Either it was the Kenoah or the reservoir where he sank the corpse that was polluted with some really bad crap. One of the two had to be the source. He never had the problem until then. He resolved to be more careful about the sites he picked in the future. Then reminded himself to also check with his paint supplier.

The men, coffee cartons in hand, were in the front seats of the Transit. Desmond had put down the willow branch and was on his computer, online, searching for mama bear and baby bear.

Merritt was looking for them too. Nobody was having any luck.

Moll sighed. "Hurry up and wait."

"What?" Desmond asked.

"That's what they said in the Army."

"You weren't Army."

Moll said, "My dad. 'Hurry up and wait.' You bust your ass, you get somewhere, then you just hang. Funny, I do not mind hanging tight in a blind, waiting for duck or elk."

"Or hog."

"Or hog." Moll sipped. "But this is getting obnoxious. Too long, too long."

"Hurry up and wait." Desmond smiled at the sentence, as if he'd found a shiny quarter on the sidewalk.

More coffee. Moll whispered, "Dawndue . . ."

Desmond asked, "So. You really think Merritt's crazy?"

"Oh, I would say yes. Certifiable."

"I never knew what that meant. Who certifies you crazy?"

Moll considered this. "Probably the government. They must have a mental department."

Desmond scoffed. "Somebody on state payroll, our taxes, with nothing better to do than say, 'Sane, insane.' Stamp their file. Put 'em in a padded cell or let 'em go. Next." *Thonk, thonk.* "So, the wife? What exactly's the scoop him wanting her dead so bad?"

"She pressed charges. Went from a cop with a cushy deal to detention. Ruined his life. She did not stand by her man," Moll said.

"That's a song, right?"

"I think. And there is something else. The story is she has something on him he doesn't want out."

"Women." *Thonk, thonk.*

VapoRub would not do it, Moll decided. He'd need a mask and oxygen for Edgar's surgery up in Ralston. He had a tank somewhere. Maybe—

"Holy shit." Desmond sat up straight. He was staring at the computer screen.

"What?"

"Look." The man swung the laptop toward him.

A picture on Instagram.

Moll said, "Cannot be."

But it was.

Desmond added, "We can be there in twenty. Let's get psycho boy there."

Moll was about to ask who he meant, then realized: certifiable Jon Merritt.

41

"olter."

It was Marty Harmon's voice and Shaw could hear dismay.

"Yes?"

"Merritt got Alli's lawyer."

Shaw, at the dining table in the Winnebago, set down the cup of coffee he'd just brewed. He had yet to sip.

The CEO explained that the man had not arrived home last night. His car was found abandoned in a park beside the river, a mile from his office.

"Details?"

"I don't know. God. Dave was a friend of mine too. We were Rotary Club together."

Did Merritt torture him, then kill him when the man could reveal nothing about Allison's whereabouts?

"How'd you hear?"

"Police called, asking if I'd heard from Alli, if she had any information about it."

"I'll talk to them."

After the men disconnected, Shaw called the main FPD number, dropped the CEO's name and three minutes later he was on the line with Dunfry Kemp.

"Detective. It's Colter Shaw."

"Yessir." The voice was burdened. Because of this call or had more files arrived in the night?

"I understand that Ms. Parker's lawyer has disappeared."

A moment of debate. Then: "You'll keep this to yourself."

Meaning from the press.

"Yes."

"Security video in a storefront on Fourth Street showed a man, dark windbreaker—what Merritt was wearing earlier in the day—getting into Mr. Stein's car. Had a gun. Then it drove off. The car was found abandoned by the Kenoah about six this morning."

"So he's armed." Adding quite the complication. "Any sign of a struggle? Blood?"

"I don't know at this time."

"Have you talked to anyone in his office? They see anything?"

"His paralegal-slash-secretary. She never heard from him after she went home about five."

"Can I speak to her?"

Kemp's cooperation wouldn't extend there. "She

doesn't know anything. Anyway, she's taking a few days off. She's scared of Merritt."

"I left you a message about video cameras in Marshall County."

"Oh, yessir. I called them. Haven't heard back." The detective covered the mouthpiece and Shaw heard him speaking in muffled tones with someone else.

Shaw said, "So. This's a felony investigation now."

"It is. We have some patrol officers searching the area where his car was found."

"You assign Homicide detectives?"

"It's Major Cases here, and we will be."

Shaw was tired of this. "You haven't yet?"

"No. But those two patrol officers? They're veterans. They ran a canvass on Fourth Street, then moved on to the river."

"You have their report?"

"Not at this time." Now the voice was not only burdened but resistant.

"You'll call me if there're any developments, won't you, Detective Kemp?"

"I have your card right here, Mr. Shaw."

They disconnected.

Useless.

Shaw tried the cooling coffee. One sip before his phone hummed again.

"Mack."

"Get to your computer," his PI instructed.

He pulled the unit toward him and powered up, his router too.

After a lengthy thirty seconds he said, "I'm on."

"Check your email."

The first message was from her. Attached was a screen-shot of an Instagram photo. The image was a selfie: a smiling Hannah Merritt, in stocking cap and sweatshirt, gazing at the camera.

The time stamp was about forty minutes ago.

"I thought all their social media was closed down."

"It was. And it probably took the girl sixty seconds to make a new account."

Looking over the picture he said, "The background."

"Exactly."

That edge rose within him, what he felt when he was after deer or elk and had spotted fresh tracks left by what would be dinners for the next week. Or uncovering the first solid clue that led to a kidnap victim.

Shaw studied the image closely. You could see a town water tower, painted blue—to make it slightly less of an eyesore. There were five letters visible: *HILLS*.

Mack said, "In your part of the state, north of Ferrington, it has to be Thompson Hills. I pulled Google Earth shots. The picture was probably taken in the back parking lot of the Sunny Acres Motor Lodge. It's not a chain. Allison could pay cash and give a fake name. Claim she's on the run from an abusive spouse or lost her ID. A clerk'd bend the rules."

Shaw typed the motel's name into GPS.

He was twenty-seven minutes away.

42

oom 306 of Sunny Acres was claustrophobic and funky smelling. Yet, Allison Parker thought, the ladies were making a pretty good go of it. The fragile peace that had emerged this morning was enduring.

The food was on its way. A Disney sitcom glowed from the big-screen TV, one of those that was mostly for kids but had been seeded with somewhat more sophisticated humor for parents forced to oversee.

Parker's heuristic plan was to stay here for two days and if Jon wasn't caught by then they'd continue north to their safe house. She texted the owner now, and received back:

Ready and waiting. Keep me posted. Take
care . . .

While they ate, she checked the news on her phone. Nothing about Jon.

She called her lawyer to see if he had learned anything. No answer. She didn't leave the burner's number and said she'd call him back. She was irritated that she hadn't heard from him. He was supposed to be her lifeline to status reports.

Parker opened her laptop and reviewed the deck she was working on. She could be humorous in front of a crowd and always articulate and organized. Marty often tapped her to give presentations to investors and potential customers. Small modular reactors were as complex as equipment got and Parker was known to have the gift of translating the impossibly complicated to layperson understandable.

Would Jon's escape affect her appearance at the meeting next week?

God, if he wasn't captured by then . . .

On the TV, the Disney happily-ever-after ending faded to the credits.

She noted Hannah looking over her shoulder at her mother's computer. No teen on earth could resist a screen.

"Dope," the girl said. "Graphics rock."

Parker moved the mouse pointer over a blue dot on the side of the reactor depicted on the slide filling the screen.

"That's your thing, the Futvee!"

Parker nodded. Like the S.I.T. the F.T.V.—"fuel transport vessel"—was her brainchild, a proprietary device that contributed to making Pocket Suns unique, and more marketable than most SMRs. Traditionally uranium fuel rods had to be carefully loaded into the core and, when spent, removed just as carefully, all by experts. The trip from the enrichment facility and to disposal sites was always risky. Parker's Futvee was a self-contained pod that could be mounted and dismounted by any worker and was virtually impervious to damage.

The phone rang. Parker hesitated and then picked it up.

No need to worry. The food had arrived. She walked to the lobby to pay the delivery boy.

In the room once more, she set out, on the bed, the waffles, bacon for Mom, red and blue berries. Real whipped cream and fake syrup. Under the circumstances, the girl's concern about her weight remained largely on the distant horizon.

There was a coffee for each of them.

Passing her daughter a plastic plate, she glanced at a slide of the S.I.T. trigger. "Hey, want to hear a story? An employee stole one of these. He was a spy. He was going to sell it to a competitor."

"Stole? No way."

"Yes way." She smiled. "Mr. Harmon called me yesterday morning and told me somebody he hired recovered it."

"The guy who stole it, he was in your department?"

"No. He was IT."

"Computer people," Hannah said. "Can't friggin' trust 'em. Look at *The Matrix* . . . Did you know him?"

"No. He was in Building Five."

"The new one." Hannah knew the company almost as well as her mother did. Parker often arranged for the girl to come hang in her office after school. Before November 15 this was to keep her from being home with a drunk, temperamental father. Afterward, it simply made the paranoid mother feel more comfortable her daughter was nearby.

"What happened? The prick got arrested?"

Parker let the language go. "I don't know." Not adding that she didn't have a chance to follow up with Marty about the spy's fate because just after the S.I.T. was recovered, she and Hannah had had to flee.

"Can't say your mother has a dull job, huh?" Impulsively she squeezed the girl's hand and, after a nearly unbearable moment—will she reciprocate or not?—Hannah scooted close and threw her arms around her mother's shoulders, buried her head against the woman's neck.

Parker held her tightly and fought to keep the tears at bay.

43

"There." Moll, in the front seat of the van, was pointing at the Thompson Hills water tower.

The thing stood out like a blue-and-silver spaceship lording over the stubby fields and low brown buildings of yet another lost mill town.

Desmond squinted it out. "So, the kid was there, in the back, when she took the shot." He was looking at the lot behind the Sunny Acres motel.

"That sign is like to blind you." Moll was referring to the big, pink vacancy sign. If you got close, he supposed, you could probably hear it sizzle.

They drove through the lot, in a slow U around the grungy motel. They knew the woman would no longer have the 4Runner; she'd rented something, make and model unknown.

"We check out every car?" Desmond asked. "Figure which one's theirs. Take them when they come out."

Moll shook his head. "What would they leave in the

car that would identify them? They would take everything into the room. I say we just go in, have a conversation with the clerk."

"Fine by me. Where's Merritt?"

"Not far," Moll said.

"We don't wait for him?"

"Not necessary. We get the girls in the van, pacify them a little and go somewhere to wait for him."

"In the van," Desmond repeated slowly and gave a thoughtful smile that Moll found disturbing in the extreme.

Ski masks and gloves.

These were uncomfortable. But they had no choice. All motels, even the unfortunate Sunny Acres, had video cameras nowadays. They'd try for the hard drive but there was that damn thing called the cloud.

They walked fast into the lobby, guns up, ready to shoot. This was the world of concealed carry. Moll always assumed everyone over fifteen was armed.

"Oh, Lord," the chubby clerk said, his face and bald head burning red. His hands shot up. When he spoke it was a single long sentence. "Take the money but there isn't much we're mostly credit card you can understand I'll give you my ATM the PIN is 8899 take it all . . ."

Desmond's punch to the face was quite satisfying to Moll.

"No, no, no!" The man's hands came away bloody. He stared. The color seemed as troubling as the pain.

"Guest. Allison Parker and her daughter. Checked in yesterday."

"That name I don't know it nobody here like that name, sir, really I mean it we're a small place and my mother and I are doing the best—"

Now Moll slugged him. The jaw. He yelped.

"You know who we mean."

"Room three oh six, sir, three oh six."

They escorted the miserable man into the office. "I don't know anything about you I didn't see your faces of course you've got those masks on and I wasn't looking at your clothes or height or anything and I've got a terrible memory anyway everybody knows that and—"

Moll made a fist and the man shut up and squinted, turning his head away.

"Security camera hard drive."

The man nodded toward a black box, holding a 3½-inch drive. Moll ripped it from the desktop and pocketed the unit.

Desmond zip-tied him and Moll found some packing tape, which he used to wrap his mouth. They left him on the floor to spend time in the company of the misery of signing the death warrants of two of his guests.

They started down the hall that led to the rooms, past the ice, past the vending machines. The corridor ended at a wall with a picture of the Eiffel Tower. Why that? Moll could not figure. To the right were rooms 301–319. The two men walked quickly that way.

As they approached 306, the door opposite opened and an elderly couple stepped out, both in leisure suits, hers pink, and blue for him. On the man's head was a gray herringbone Greek fisherman cap. They stopped about as quickly as you would expect.

"Oh, my," the woman whispered.

Moll glanced to Desmond, who said, "Hey there, folks, let's go inside for a minute." He ushered them back in and the door closed.

He emerged only three minutes later. "He called me an a-hole. Wouldn't even say 'ass.' I don't like people like that."

The men walked to 306. Moll bent close to the wood, listening. He could hear a TV program playing. He sniffed. "Coffee and bacon."

Having been in the business of making bodies and hiding them for some years, Moll had learned a half-dozen ways to get through doors. He'd taught himself lock picking and he became pretty good at the art. But then hotels started to go with electronic locks and key cards, which was as irritating as the discovery of DNA.

But there was a technique that was tried and true.

He glanced at Desmond, who nodded. Moll stepped back, took a deep breath, which for some reason seemed to help, and drove his size-twelve foot into the wood just below the lock with all the force of his solid right leg behind it.

44

Colter Shaw steered his Winnebago over the cracked asphalt of the Sunny Acres motel's parking lot, off Route 92.

Even in broad blaring daylight there would be nothing sunny about the place, given the trash-filled grassland encircling it. Small industrial facilities were the view to each side, if you could see over the green-slatted chain-link. In the back was tall grass, from which rusty appliances and machinery rose like cautious soldiers, awaiting a skirmish.

In the distance was the telltale water tower.

He checked his Glock 42. The slim gun contained six rounds in the magazine and one in the chamber. He sometimes carried an extra mag—always left hip, as his father had taught. Sometimes two. Today, he clipped both, each in its own leather holster, on the sinister side of his belt. He untucked his black knit shirt to make sure the weapon was covered; it tended to be visible underneath the leather jacket when he bent or turned.

In a rare moment of verse, his father would recite the rule:

Never reveal when you're supposed to conceal . . .

Hand near the weapon, he moved fast toward the motel office, scanning for Merritt's pickup or Parker's 4Runner. Neither vehicle was here, though he was sure she'd swapped her wheels for something else. Was one of these others theirs? There were some sedans, some SUVs, a white Ford Transit, two tractor-trailers. Many had out-of-state plates, but one could still be a rental of Parker's; the companies were forever moving cars here and there.

Inside, no one was behind the counter.

He rang the clerk's bell. No response to the ding.

He drew his weapon and started up the hallway, knocked on the door to the office.

A grunting voice responded.

A thud.

Shaw pushed inside, gun up, holding it two-handed. There he found the clerk, zip-tied and gagged, thrashing frantically, trying to free himself. The round man, whose face and shirt and hands were covered in damp blood, panicked even more when he saw Shaw and the gun and tried to scrabble away, as if there were a hiding place in a twelve-by-twelve box of a room.

He yanked the tape off.

"Ow, Jesus."

"When was he here?"

"I'm bleeding."

"When?"

"Five minutes."

"He armed?"

"They both were."

"Both?"

"Two of them."

Two? What was this about? Merritt and someone else? Or men working with him?

"Describe them, fast."

He hesitated.

"Now!" Shaw growled.

"A big guy in a suit, one in a tan jacket. He was skinnier. Masked. Guns. Big guns. They were going to kill me!"

"What room?"

"They—"

"I'm not asking again."

"Three oh six."

Shaw flicked open his locking-blade knife and sawed through the zip. "Call the police."

Gun in hand, Shaw moved fast along the Lysol-scented hallway. The door to the room had been kicked in. He moved in slowly, gun low and tight to his right side.

Never extend a handgun out in front of you when entering a blind doorway . . .

Then, inside, keeping low, pivoting, aiming at every site of concealment.

All the doors were open, bathroom, closet. The place

was vacant. The remains of breakfast were scattered over the bed and floor. Articles of clothing and toiletries too.

A children's cartoon was on the flat-screen TV.

Shaw returned to the office.

"And?" The clerk's voice quivered.

Shaw said, "Nobody's there. The two men and the guests in three oh six? You see any of them leave?"

"No, sir. They were going to kill me!"

No, they weren't. Or they would have.

The clerk nodded at the phone. "I called the sheriff. They're on the way."

"What were the men driving?"

"I don't know. They just, you know, were here, with their guns."

Shaw looked out the greasy window. The boxy Ford van was gone. "Any guests drive a white Transit?"

"Not that they put down when they registered."

Eighty percent that was their ride.

"Security tape," Shaw said.

"They took the hard drive."

"What county are we in? Marshall?"

"Yessir."

Shaw jogged outside. He put it at ninety percent that the responding law, in a different county from Ferrington, would have little sympathy for Jon Merritt—at least not now, after killing Allison's lawyer and breaking in here. Still, he didn't want to count on the burdensome protocols of law enforcers. He'd go after them himself on his Yamaha. They had a head start, but not much of one. He could catch them easily.

Though, which way?

Probably back toward 55, the main north–south high-way.

But only probably. If he chose wrong, he'd lose them entirely.

He tucked his gun away. He noted a family—husband, wife, two teenage boys—packing up their SUV. He asked if they'd seen a white Transit leave the parking lot. He was prepared to say the driver left his phone in the office and he wanted to get it to him—leaving it to the family to work on the improbabilities of that.

No fiction was necessary. The husband said they'd like to help but they hadn't seen the vehicle. The wife nodded a confirmation. Shaw believed them.

Then, looking for other guests, his eyes strayed to his camper. He walked toward it, mouth tightening as he got to the rear.

No high-speed pursuits after all.

Both tires of the motorbike had been slashed.

And, for good measure, so was one of the Winneba-go's.

45

*A*h. Here we go.

Detective Jon Merritt is crouching beside some unfinished sewer drains in a construction site—half built out and abandoned, as there are no supplies and equipment anywhere near. The sky is clear on this late autumn afternoon, the temperature unusually warm. The scent of mud and decaying leaves is strong.

He has just leveraged a cinder block aside with a piece of rebar and is training a flashlight into the twelve-inch pipe that would have gone to the city sewer system but now goes nowhere.

Looking around. He doesn't see anyone. But there are kids on skateboards nearby. He knows this from the rushing clatter of the wheels on concrete. Hannah tried it for a while. Broke her wrist and that was that.

Merritt's partner, Danny Avery, is canvassing nearby buildings to see if they can describe the workers who were here, any names on pickups, bulldozers or cement trucks, if any limousines were parked in front of the site.

Merritt has records that show that pouring this foundation and putting in a few pipes—the going-nowhere kind—cost the city two point seven million dollars. For a job that was worth thirty thousand. Tops.

The detective peers into the sewer pipe, his tactical flashlight turning the dark visible. He sees rubble.

Where there's no reason for rubble to be.

He pulls on latex gloves and digs through the muck and stone and dirt.

His radio, on his hip, clatters, startling him.

"Detective 244, come in."

He turns the volume of the Motorola down with his left hand, the one that is unmucky.

"This is 244, Central."

"You're in Beacon Hill?"

"Affirmative."

What was this?

"Reports of shots fired, 8248 Homewood."

It's a block away, less. He wonders why he didn't hear the gunfire. But much of the construction in Beacon Hill is early twentieth-century stone and brick. Built to survive winters here, built to last.

"History of domestics. Owner is Harvey Trimble, convictions for possession. Held on suspicion of battery, released."

I'm busy, he thinks. But he mutters, "Copy. Where's Tac?"

"Fifteen out."

The Ferrington SWAT team was good but spread out like a half pat of butter on a whole piece of toast, a captain had once said—to groans in the watch room.

"There're kids in the house, Jon. Neighbor heard screaming."

"Shit. We're responding. Over."

"'K. I'll advise Tac you may be inside."

It's now that Merritt moves one more piece of rubble and sees what he's been looking for: several letter-size envelopes, thick ones. He pulls them out and slips them into his jacket pocket. Spends sixty seconds looking for more. None.

He stands and shouts, "Danny, got a 10-71 up the street. We gotta go."

The stocky detective, thick brown hair, which matches his suit, joins Merritt, who's at the car and popping open the trunk.

"What? Shit. You hear that?"

Two shots. Maybe a scream.

They have no armament other than their sidearms. Some detectives keep M4 assault rifles in the trunk but Merritt and Danny don't. Glock 17s will have to do.

They shed their suit jackets, Merritt making sure the envelopes don't fall out. Then they're strapping on the body armor.

His partner, nervous, says, "The hell is Tac?"

"About fifteen out."

"Jesus Christ. The city isn't that big."

Merritt laughs. "You want to live forever?"

Avery slows, eyes down.

A joke too far.

He recalls that the detective, seven years younger than Merritt, has never been in a firefight, has never drawn his weapon anywhere but on the range.

"Hey, Danny. It's cool. The shooter's a tweaker. He's gone on his own product. We'll be on him before he even sees us."

Another shot.

Another scream.

The detectives begin the short jog to the squat brick house.

Colter Shaw returned to the corridor where room 306 was located.

He found an elderly couple in colorful jogging outfits, peering out the front door of their room across the hall. They saw Shaw—no ski mask, pistol on his hip, close-cropped hair—and made the common assumption. "Officer?"

Shaw nodded. "You see what happened?"

They were oddly calm, considering.

The wife: "These two men, bullies, thugs. One of them was in here. He said not to say anything. Threatened us."

Husband: "But we got one up on them."

Which meant what? Shaw wondered.

He gestured for them to continue.

They explained how the men were walking up the corridor, when the couple opened the door. One herded them into the room, took their phones and ripped the landline cord out, then threatened them and warned them to stay in the room and keep quiet.

"Very rude," the wife added.

"Then we heard them kick the door down. The one that woman and girl were staying in."

"Did the men take them out of the room?"

"No. They ran off before those a-holes got here. Five, ten minutes."

"Stanley," she warned.

Ah, so they'd gotten away . . .

The wife added, "The woman was shouting at the girl. Mad, real mad. 'How could you?' Something like that. And the girl was shouting back. They just threw some things in their car and drove off."

"Bat out of hell."

"What model car?"

"Kia," the husband said. "Just like her cousin drives."

"Just like Bett's. Only gold."

"Wish I'd bought one of them."

"You see which way they went?"

"We could see which way they *didn't* go—right, east. That's the only view we got from here."

A left turn would take them back to 55, though the highway the motel sat on, Route 92, was a major artery and would get her ultimately all the way to the West Coast.

The wife continued, "That man, the one in here. He threatened us. Looked at his license. Memorized the address."

The husband said with a laugh, "But it's a year old! I never got around to changing it after we moved. Joke's on them."

The one-up-on-them part—a variation on the same tactic that Undercover Shaw had used with Ahmad in the warehouse yesterday morning.

Shaw thanked them and returned to the office, where the clerk was manipulating his nose.

"It's not broken. Don't play with it." Shaw pulled out his phone and scrolled to the most recently dialed number.

46

"Don't say a word."

Allison Parker was speeding west on Route 92.

"You were spying on me." Hannah tried to sound indignant and wronged. The words rolled out, though, laced with fear.

Parker muttered, "Don't. Go. There."

The girl sat in the passenger seat, hugging her knees. Her stocking cap was unevenly tugged over her head and her gray coat was on the floor. She would have been looking at her phone under other circumstances. Not now, of course. The Samsung was in Parker's pocket, where it would remain.

Her heart pounding, she looked in the rearview mirror. Expecting Jon's truck to be following.

Not yet. But he could have come close to finding them.

Thanks to Hannah.

Just after the heartwarming embrace, as they were about to eat, Parker had glanced down at the girl's phone, which was not only no longer in airplane mode but was open to an Instagram account. Not her old one. But @HannahMer-maid447788.

According to the time stamp she'd posted the selfie, taken in the back of the motel, when Parker was in the shower. So her errand was about more than just scoring a breakfast menu.

The picture was an uncharacteristically smiling face, behind which was the water tower with part of the name of a nearby town visible. Thompson Hills. It would take anyone with half a brain and access to Google no time at all to figure out where they were.

Parker had barked a scream and leapt up, scattering food, spilling coffee.

"We're leaving. Now!"

"What?"

She had shut off and pocketed her daughter's phone.

"Hey, that's mine."

Parker flung their computers and some clothes into their bags.

"What's wrong?" the girl had wailed. "I don't want to leave!"

She had gripped Hannah by the arm. "Now." The word was an enraged shout.

There would have been something about her mother's unhinged expression that rattled the girl. She didn't nod, didn't say a word, just grabbed the luggage and pushed out the door, ahead of Parker. Their bags were not even fully zipped up. Toiletries and a half-dozen articles of clothing were left behind. Another silly Disney show was on a TV screen too big for the room.

Now Parker pushed the accelerator hard and hit seventy-six in a seventy zone, wishing to do ninety, but she could not risk getting pulled over.

She muttered, "Did it not occur to you that he's checking social media? That he could scan for 'Hannah'? And 'Mer'? How stupid could you be?"

They drove in silence. The girl was staring defiantly out the window.

About five miles from the motel, Parker skidded to a stop on the shoulder. She reached into her pocket and pulled out the girl's phone. Hannah lunged for it and her mother lifted an arm to block her. It was the first painful contact between the two of them since a two-year-old Hannah punched her in the lip reaching for her necklace.

"Stop it!" Parker raged and her daughter sat back, fuming. Parker knew the PIN and soon the phone was live. She flipped through the apps. No Facebook or Twitter. Just the new Instagram.

"Password."

When the girl didn't answer immediately, she asked again, in a threatening tone.

The girl gave it to her. Parker deleted the account and tapped the phone to sleep in airplane mode once more.

"Christ."

She now skidded back onto the asphalt and sped up. Her daughter was not, of course, careless at all. What she'd done was calculated. She *wanted* her father to know where they were. She knew he was checking for their names. So she'd left him what was, in effect, a coded message: Come and find us, without saying so specifically.

Deniability.

"Your father wants to hurt me. Do you understand?"

"You don't—"

"Do you understand?"

"You don't know him. Why do I have to keep telling you that?" Hannah was now sobbing. What was the most painful component of her sorrow? Her mother's anger or the loss of a digital device?

Another few miles streaked by. Parker began to calm.

And she realized that this was her own fault. The overprotective mother had kept the girl far from the legal proceedings following November 15. She'd done the same yesterday, not sharing Jon's true mission.

"Han, I wasn't honest with you. I didn't tell you everything."

The girl continued to stare out the window.

"I didn't tell you everything that David found out. I said I was worried he'd make a scene. It's more than that. Worse. Your father wants to hurt me. He told some prisoners before he left he was going to find me." A deep breath. "He wants to kill me."

"Bullshit. He'd never do that."

"He's not who you think he is."

Hannah shot back with: "And how would you know? You sent him to prison, just threw him away. And that was it. You never visited him!"

No, she hadn't. She couldn't. Nor had she let Hannah.

That was not going to happen. This had been an open wound in their relationship. One of them.

"You dumped him there and went on to something else."

Parker felt her heart beat faster yet. If that were possible. "What?"

"Don't you have anything to say?"

More silence. The car edged up over eighty. She eased off the gas.

"I'm sorry, Han. I know it's hard to hear. It breaks my heart. I made a judgment. I had to press charges. It was time for somebody to stand up to him. And now I'm going to keep you safe. Whatever I need to do. And that's the way it is. We need to be together on this. I need your help."

The girl scoffed.

Parker reached out and set a hand on the girl's leg.

"Don't touch me, bitch."

Parker stared ahead at the ribbon of highway they coursed along, like so many others around here in need of the blessing of new asphalt. Tears of a very different type from those just a few hours ago formed in her eyes.

Her daughter leaned as far away as she could and reached instinctively for her rear hip, before recalling that the phone was no longer in attendance. She crossed her arms and looked blankly at farmworkers burning the residue from a recent corn harvest, the low orange flames sending pale, aromatic smoke rising uneasily into the air.

47

Jon Merritt parked his pickup in a shady portion of a public park in northwest Ferrington.

Few people were present. Some joggers lost in the zone. Some businesspeople striding decisively, heads tilted sideways or down, concentrating on their phones. Some teens—dressed the sweatshirty way that Hannah dressed—walked or hung out in clusters or did their fine acrobatics on gravity-defying skateboards.

He'd learned that his ex and daughter had been staying at a place called the Sunny Acres in Marshall County. He'd been on his way there when he got the news they'd vanished. Maybe their trail would be picked up again, but until then he himself would search elsewhere for their whereabouts. He had braked hard, spun his truck into a wide, lawn-destroying U-turn and, ignoring the horns, sped south.

And now it was:

Butterfly time . . .

Theodore Roosevelt Park was lush, one of the few urban spaces whose lawns, arboretums, planting beds, ponds and stream were kept up. Benches painted, graffiti scrubbed. Parks elsewhere got hardly a dollar for maintenance. But this was the Garden District, the poshest of 'hoods in Ferrington, and though that was a low bar, the area was really quite nice. Merritt didn't know it well; FPD made few calls here. A doctor was collared for skimming opioids. There was the occasional break-in or Mercedes-jacking. One business partner shot another—and the case wound up on the cable series *When the Rich Murder*. The producer had interviewed Jon and his partner.

Not Danny. A different partner.

Before Danny.

He shut the engine off, climbed out and started toward the address handwritten neatly—and conveniently—in the upper left-hand corner of the envelope that contained the cannibalistic-insect greeting card.

The sender was Dorella Muñoz Elizondo, who his ex would have met within the past year. Merritt didn't know her, hadn't heard the distinctive name. Yes, there'd been blackouts, but he would have remembered Alli's friends.

It was possible Allison could have confided in her. She might've given Dorella her new phone number. Dom Ryan was helping him in the search. If Merritt could find the number, Ryan could get a location out of a greedy or intimidated underling at her mobile service provider.

Dorella lived in the heart of the ritzy Garden District.

Merritt recalled the inscription in the butterfly card, penned by Dorella to his ex.

Sometimes the love for new friends can be as deep and enduring as the ones we've known since childhood. Hang in there, Alli, you'll get through this . . .

He supposed he could search her house for anything that might relate to his wife. But he really hoped she was home. He'd make sure she shared everything she knew about her.

Walking with purpose, he strode to the gate in the picket fence and unlatched it. He stepped through, closed it behind him and continued to the house.

Glancing up, he saw the door open, and out stepped a tall, handsome woman, wearing what was called, he believed, a sundress. Yellow, frilly, thick straps. A hem not far below the knees. She carried a watering can and paused en route to a half-dozen opulent pots. Her glance toward him was of curiosity but more friendly than frown.

"Can I help you?"

"Good morning. Dorella Elizondo?"

She nodded a pleasant greeting. "That's right."

He walked to the bottom step, no farther. He held up his old badge, tucked it away. Then, using his best canvassing voice, confident but friendly: "I'm Detective White, Ferrington Police. I'm trying to locate Allison Parker and her daughter. We understand you're friends. Have you heard from her in the past couple of days?"

"Oh, my," she whispered, her face troubled. "Is Alli all right?"

"I'm sorry to say they've been missing since last night. Her husband was released from prison yesterday and violated a restraining order. We think they've fled. We'd like to find them, get them into protective custody until he's recaptured."

Lines furrowed her carefully dusted brow. "Alli told me he was abusive. Missing? Do you think he . . . hurt her? And Hannah?"

"No reason to believe that at this time. We're just trying to find her." A placid voice. Jon Merritt knew the rule: always stay calm when talking with victims, witnesses and the suspects themselves. The voice of Jon the Charmer-Detective.

"Well, Detective, we haven't been in touch for a week or so, I guess."

"You have any thoughts about where she might've gone? Outside of Ferrington? We heard she was headed north."

"North?" the woman mused and set down the watering can, which seemed heavy. "I remember Alli mentioned someplace she was interested in going to. She thought maybe we could go together. Her daughter too. It's a spa. Ladies' weekend, you know. Near Spartanburg."

The town, a quaint tourist attraction, was northeast, nearly two hours from Ferrington. A good place for his ex and daughter to hide.

"I think I've got the address."

"Appreciate that."

"Of course."

She walked inside.

A few minutes later, he heard Dorella's voice. "Found it!"

A lead, at last.

He saw her approaching through the screen.

As the door swung open she said in an amused voice, "I'm just curious, Jon. Did you really think Alli never showed me your picture?"

She calmly leveled the shotgun and fired one round into Merritt's right thigh, racked the gun, then parked another center mass in his belly.

48

P rivate eye?"

"No," Shaw said. "Not licensed. I'm a security consultant."

The county deputy, about Shaw's age, was writing in her notebook. She was blond—the shade slightly darker than Nilsson's, he found himself thinking. The thick strands were pulled tight into a severe bun, as women cops often wore it. Her face was angular, her hips narrow. A shadow of a tat peeked from her left blouse cuff.

"I'm helping to find the woman and her daughter who were here. The FPD're underwater."

She took this in with a knowing nod, though she said nothing critical about LEA in a different jurisdiction.

"The name on the material witness wire. Allison Parker."

Well, overworked Detective Kemp was true to his word.

The radio clattered. "No warrants. CCP's good."

"Roger," she said into the Motorola mic speaker attached to the left shoulder of her blouse. She handed back his license and concealed carry permit. On her chest was a name tag, DEP. KRISTI DONAHUE.

They were in the parking lot of the Sunny Acres motel. Her cruiser sat beside the Winnebago, and two more official cars were in the parking lot. One was printed with CRIME SCENE. An ambulance was near the front door. The medics were inside, tending to the clerk. Who, Shaw had assessed, needed little tending.

An audience of a dozen stood outside, this scenario probably being more interesting than most of what Thompson Hills had to offer.

Shaw's documents had been validated but the deputy wasn't completely at ease yet. The situation was, of course, a complicated one. "And her husband broke out of detention and is after her?"

"No, he was released. Just after that, they found out he wants her dead. He's probably killed her lawyer and's still hunting for her." He nodded to the motel. "Those two're working with him. Triggermen, I guess."

"Hired muscle? To tag an ex?" Her voice lifted high.

"It's not your typical domestic."

"I would say. I heard about Merritt. He was a good cop years ago, closed some big cases. Vice, OC, corruption. Then it all went south. Drugs, drinking. I've seen what that shit can do."

From the radio: words through the static. "Hey, Kristi."

"Go ahead, Marv."

"Scrubbed the traffic cam like you said. A gold Kia—
it's a rental, name of Harmon Energy—went west on
Ninety-two. Turned north on Fifty-five."

"Any sightings of Merritt's truck?" Shaw asked. He'd
told himself to keep the frustration from his voice. At
this, he was only partially successful.

Silence.

Donahue said, "He's okay, Marv."

"No F-150s."

The deputy said to Shaw, "No cameras north on Fifty-
five or Eighty-four till Millton. That's with two 'L's.'
Because it used to be.

"And the Transit?" she asked into the Motorola. "Any
sightings?"

"Caught a white van. Couldn't tell the make. Continued west on Ninety-two, past Fifty-five. This was, oh, I'd
guess about three minutes after the Kia."

"Thanks Marv. Out."

"'K."

She examined the tires. "You were going to go after
them."

He nodded.

"Only for the purpose of getting the tag numbers,"
she asked pointedly.

"That's right, Deputy."

She kept her eyes on his face for a moment. Then,
"You have spares?"

"Not enough for the bike. But one for the camper.
Jack won't work on this." He nodded to the soggy ground
beneath the Winnebago. Worried that Merritt was closing

in, he'd braked to a stop half on the lawn. He'd called several service stations for a tow truck to lift the rear so he could change the tire. Only one had been interested, even after he offered two hundred dollars in cash as a need-to-move-fast bonus. It wouldn't arrive for more than an hour.

Deputy Donahue walked to the Yamaha and ran a hand over it. Her look was both admiring and curious.

Shaw asked a question he knew the answer to. "You ride?"

Donahue paused a moment. Then: "Harley." Perhaps a smile. Hard to tell. "My ex liked to show me off at biker bars. And that meant H-D. He was surprised when my lawyer told him he could have the pickup, but the bike was mine . . . or else he'd have a world of trouble to deal with. I can set you up with a dealer's got a good supply of tires."

"No time now."

Donahue asked, "So. Security?"

He explained about the reward business.

"Well, that's a new one on me." She gave a smile. "Maybe you should stick around. With county budgets shot to hell, might be cheaper to pay you a reward to find the perp, 'stead of adding personnel. You could pick up some change, sir."

"Colter's fine. Or Colt."

"Colt," she said.

"If I head back this way, I could use the number of that repair shop."

"Sure. Call me." She handed him a card. He gave her

one of his. "And if we get any reports on those vehicles, I'll let you know."

Which is when the Range Rover skidded to a fast stop in the mouth of the motel lot. As the dust cloud settled, Sonja Nilsson rolled down the front-seat passenger-side window and gave a smile. She was the one he'd called when he tapped the most-recently-dialed button on his mobile.

Deputy Kristi Donahue glanced at Nilsson, then lifted an eyebrow to Shaw. "Hey, good luck, travelin' man."

49

J on Merritt grunted as he tried to sit up, his belly
and leg throbbing, the pain radiating outward.

Nonlethal slugs—usually a metal core covered
with rubber—fired from a twelve gauge strike the body
with huge force. They are meant for crowd control, but
they also can break bones and rupture organs and blind.
And they've been known to kill.

He took stock. Nothing broken, no internal ruptures.
Not yet.

Dorella stepped closer, racking another shell.

Merritt knew that there was a protocol for using a
shotgun for defense. You loaded rubber slugs last in the
tube—to fire first—then, if that didn't do the trick, there
came skin-breaking bird shot, and finally lethal double-
ought or lead slugs. Dorella clearly knew her way around
weapons and he suspected something more painful, if
not deadly, would soon be coming his way.

As he struggled to his feet, doubled over in pain, he drew his pistol and fired.

She fled back into the house.

Merritt staggered to his truck.

Though partially deafened by the shots, he could just make out in the distance the sound of approaching emergency vehicles. Sirens and get-out-of-the-way bleats. The cars were about a mile away, he guessed. And the very fact he could hear them at all meant that they were bursting through intersections fast.

He swung open the door of the truck and, after steeling himself a moment, climbed into the cab, groaning with pain.

Keys out, engine on.

Then he was speeding away from the curb, tires squealing and smoking. He wasn't sure which direction the squad cars were coming from—sounds can deceive, especially to numbed ears—but he supposed the respondings would assume he'd be heading for the interstate or major state routes. But, no. He vanished into the maze of Garden District side streets.

The strategy was correct. He saw not a single black and white in pursuit.

Merritt powered through the red light, drawing yet more middle fingers and horns. He heard a collision.

Then Auburn Road presented a lengthy straightaway. He shoved the pedal down, and when he hit the first "traffic calming" hump in the road—at about seventy—he was surprised that the heavy truck actually caught air.

Mobile Eight One to Central."

"Go ahead, Eight One."

"I'm 10-23 at Frederickson and Sycamore. Suspect's 150's off the road. He missed a turn. He crashed."

"Roger. Injury?"

"Don't know yet. Looks bad. Send a bus."

"Roger, Eight One. Be advised. Subject is armed. Wanted in connection with assault with a deadly just now and a homicide."

"Roger."

Jesus, thought the slim, shaved-headed young officer, whose name was Peter Nagle. Jon Merritt had killed somebody? He hadn't seen that on the wire. Nagle was uneasy. The dog had caught the school bus and wasn't sure what to do with it. The white pickup was sitting in a ditch, axle deep. It wasn't going anywhere.

He couldn't see Merritt clearly. The man was keeping low in the cab and seemed to be looking around, considering options. There was only one, if he wanted to keep running: climbing out the passenger door and shooting his way past Nagle.

Lord . . .

"Any other units?"

There was a pause. "Not in the vicinity. Nearest is answering a call on Chesterton. Can be there in ten, twelve."

Welcome to Ferrington PD.

Nagle eyed the cab again. Yes, the former detective

was the Hero of Beacon Hill. This Jon Merritt, though, was somebody very different.

"Eight One to Dispatch. Further to that homicide?"

"His ex-wife's lawyer."

Jesus.

Nagle was new to the force—eighteen months—but he'd run a dozen domestics. Sanity went out the window when love, or its corpse, was involved.

"Eight One, you there?"

"Roger that. Proceeding to subject now. I am."

Wondering what the last sentence meant.

"And weapon is confirmed?" he asked uneasily.

"Affirmative, Eight One."

"Roger."

Well, he knew his job. He had to clear the cab and disarm Merritt.

Not only for his and everyone else's safety, but for his own reputation. He could hear: What were you doing, kid, just standing there with your thumb up your ass? You didn't even *try* to collar him?

He crouched behind his open door and drew his Glock. Nagle peered through the window. Glare. Not much to see other than the former cop's silhouette. No sign of his hands.

He thought of the fiancée he'd proposed to just one week ago at their favorite Outback. He'd rested the black Zales ring box on a napkin in the center of the restaurant's signature Bloomin' Onion.

Oh, Kelli . . .

Well, muscle up some balls. Crouching, Nagle pointed

the weapon at the outline of the cop's head. When the window didn't come down he felt more confident. Aiming, two-handed, keeping low, he stepped from cover and slowly approached.

"Jon Merritt! Put your hands out the window. If you do not show your hands you will be fired upon!"

This line came not from training but a thriller novel he'd been listening to on speed-trap duty on Old Davie Road. Sounded good, though, and it was probably what real cops said because the author had been with the NYPD.

No response.

"Merritt! Let me see your hands!"

Moving close, Glock up, he slipped his finger from outside the trigger guard to in. Still no clear view of Merritt, but he saw his own reflection in the window. With his left hand he gripped the door handle. If it was locked, he'd just retreat and wait. He'd done his duty.

Please let it be locked.

It wasn't.

Nagle yanked the door open all the way and dropped immediately to his knees like doing squats at the gym, praying that when Merritt shot, he would hit the armored plate and not flesh.

The young officer blinked and lowered the gun.

He couldn't imagine how the teenager, a gangly boy in an AC/DC sweatshirt and with a panicked expression on his pimply face, had managed to curl up into such a tiny ball that his entire body fit perfectly on the passenger-side floor.

50

They finally would sit down to a meal.

Though it would have to be a brief one.

Sonja Nilsson had motored east along Route 92 to this diner, a mile from the Sunny Acres motel.

Shaw wanted a briefing as to how her canvass among employees of HEP was going; he would give her details of the assault at the motel.

Could this be done over the phone?

Of course.

But . . . why not meet in person, as long as he had time to kill while the Winnebago was being repaired?

They climbed from the Range Rover, Shaw noting that she had changed. She now wore a black pleated-skirt business suit and a black silk blouse. The jacket fit closely and had been tailored to add a bulge on her right hip, slightly back, the exact place where Shaw wore his Glock.

Her blond tresses were down and shimmered in the muted sunlight as they danced in the hay-scented breeze.

She radared the surrounding. Shaw did too. He saw neither lead nor threat.

The diner was the only living structure in the immediate vicinity. The other buildings were long abandoned, some in a partial or full state of collapse. A rusted sign with the silhouette of a green dinosaur swung back and forth before a long-closed gas station. What was the brand? Shaw couldn't recall. From ages ago.

Shaped like an Airstream trailer, gleaming even in the shade, the diner was an architect's fantasy. Inside, all the seating surfaces were covered with red Naugahyde. The floor was gray linoleum, the counters abundantly armed with chrome condiment racks: you would never want for salt or pepper or ketchup or mustard in the Route 66 Diner, the name apparently deriving from an old TV show; black-and-white production stills and headshots were mounted everywhere.

At the register, Nilsson pointed to a booth in the back and a waitress said, "Sure thing," and led them to it.

Shaw usually sat facing the front.

Never present your back to the enemy . . .

But Nilsson took that spot. He didn't mind; she seemed just as watchful as he was.

A cheerful, pink-uniformed waitress, inked on the forearm with a bared-tooth tiger, took their order— BLTs for both, coffee for Shaw, tea for Nilsson.

"The attack?" she asked.

"Two of them, armed. Wore ski masks. I don't think

Merritt was one of them. On the video at the lawyer's car he was wearing a dark windbreaker. These two were in a black suit and tie, and a tan jacket. Looks like he's hired a pair of triggermen."

"Pros?" She frowned.

The beverages arrived. Shaw added milk to his, Nilsson lemon.

Shaw said, "He probably used a contact from his cop days. Somebody with a crew."

"He really wants her dead. I know reason goes out the window with domestics, and that's part of it. But it smells like there's more. Maybe—"

Shaw completed her thought: "What Marty was talking about earlier. She's got something on him he doesn't want to get out."

She lifted the tea, inhaled the steam. "You know, Colter, I was thinking. Those two, at the motel? There was a hit downtown. A month ago. Whistleblower for a state agency. Another corruption thing—dipping into cleanup funds. A witness said the perps were two white males and one was in a black suit. They got away in a white van. There was a third perp, a driver. Not identified. You know what the two at the motel were driving?"

"White van—a Ford Transit."

She said, "I wonder how many Transits there are."

"Eight million since it was introduced. Most of them are white."

"You know that from your reward business?"

"Just looked it up online. That deputy back at the motel—"

Nilsson asked, "Oh, the pretty one?"

Shaw came back with "Was she?"

Drawing a wry smile.

"She's got it out on the wire. We're in Marshall County, but it'll go to all surrounding. And Allison's in a gold Kia sedan now. Sheriff's office's looking for that too."

The food came and they ate. Shaw understood the popularity of the diner. The sandwich was excellent. *Crisp* would have figured prominently in a review, applying it to the entire dish: bacon, lettuce, tomato and toast.

Nilsson gazed around. She was then aware he was watching her face and turned her attention back. "Classic. Feels like we're in a Quentin Tarantino movie. He gets a lot of mileage out of diners."

Shaw had started to watch one of the director's films with Margot, years ago. He couldn't remember the title but seemed to recall that, yes, there'd been a big scene in a diner. The two of them never finished the film, though not because of cinematic flaws. Something had intruded. Afterward, they'd been too tired to fire up the DVD player again.

"Any word about the lawyer?" Shaw asked.

"Still missing, presumed dead. The Kenoah's a popular burial ground. FPD has divers but nobody wants to go in. They draw straws. They're running a grid search near his car. Any idea which direction Allison went from the motel?"

"A camera got her on Fifty-five, north. The Transit kept going west on Ninety-two. Assuming she's not bound for Canada, what's around here, where she could go to ground?"

"Not much. No motels until you get north of Millton. Mostly forest and field. Marshland. A few residences: vacation places. Cabins and trailer parks. Has some bad pockets."

"Meth?"

"That. A couple militias, survivalists . . . Not your kind."

"One thing for certain. The girl's not going to be posting any more helpful selfies."

"Nope, that phone of hers is history. Mom ate it."

Shaw said, "At the company? Your canvass didn't turn up any leads."

This wasn't a question. Otherwise he would have heard.

"I've talked to a couple dozen employees. Marianne Keller—his assistant, remember?"

Shaw nodded.

"She's helping out. But no luck. Nobody we've talked to knew Allison very well. She kept to herself. Worked long hours. May have been embarrassed—those times her ex showed up at the office drunk."

Shaw didn't think it was likely that Allison had confided to a fellow worker where she was going. He gave that twenty percent. If she didn't tell her boss or mother where, why would she tell a coworker? Shaw was convinced she was running to someplace, or someone, her ex-husband knew nothing about. Still with so few other leads, why not pursue it?

Which was a reward-seeker's mantra.

They ate in silence for a moment.

He said, "You can tell me if you want."

She looked back from the front window.

He continued, "Checking horizons. Vantage points for sniper nests. A second phone—encrypted, I'm thinking—you have serious conversations on. Paying attention to unattended packages."

"You're quite the observant one," she said. After a moment: "Okay. I'm not Sonja and I'm not Nilsson."

This part was a surprise, though he supposed it shouldn't have been.

"You're on a list."

"I'm on a list. I never talk about it. But now, after last night."

The kiss, he assumed she meant.

"How big's the risk?"

"Not high. I'm not invisible, but with a new name, new look, it's manageable. If you saw my Army ID, you'd see a brunette who weighed forty pounds more than I do now."

But with or without green eyes?

"Hardest part of the new identity is staying skinny when I'm a born foodie." She gave a laugh and ate a few of the chips that nestled against the other half of her sandwich.

"Confession?"

He nodded.

"Most of my bio was fiction. No hubby. Never was. They give you a cover story, you stick to your cover story."

"So no San Diego or Hawaii. Where in the Middle East? Can you say?"

"No. But I can tell you it was a high-value target. The shit had lots of followers. Was going to light some fuses. I took care of it. I was extracted. All was good. For a while. Then came Thomasleaks."

So that was it. A contractor with access to Pentagon files stole and published a trove of operational documents, which included personal information on intelligence officers, U.S. soldiers, contractors and foreign assets. Shaw hadn't followed the story closely but he recalled that three locals in Syria were killed after they'd been outed, and a dozen covert officers had had to leave their posts—quickly. There were others on various kill lists.

"They call it a fatwa. Tony Soprano'd just say 'hit.' Same difference. So, fair warning: last night you kissed a marked woman."

"I wondered what made it so good." Shaw looked over her pensive face. "So why Ferrington?"

"My handler gave me a couple of options for safe-house cities. Ferrington was close enough to home to see family regularly, far enough away from the old me to keep off the grid."

Silence between them. Another kiss loomed, but this time it was interrupted by Shaw's humming phone. The screen showed a local number. He answered.

"Mr. Shaw?" the man's voice asked.

"Yes."

"Your camper's ready."

Shaw said, "Thanks. I'll be there in ten." He disconnected, told Nilsson, then turned and waved for the check.

"Good news," she said. "You're back on the road."

Marred only by the fact that he had nowhere to go.

51

Fooling them had been easy.

Because the cops weren't thinking like he was. They were reacting.

Not being creative.

After his NASCAR race to flee from shotgun-lady Dorella Muñoz Elizondo, Jon Merritt had not sped to any highways, but instead lessened pressure on the accelerator and steered to nearby John Adams High. He parked behind the gym and examined his wounds. The bruises and welts from the rubber slugs were dark and gaudy but he could function. Merritt climbed from the vehicle, leaving the engine running and the window open. Then he'd walked away, trying to assume a normal gait, into the neighborhood of frame houses and postage-stamp yards.

The school had been on his beat when he was just starting out at FPD. The place was now populated by the same gangs and unaffiliated shits as most institutions of lower learning—kids who could be counted on to get into trouble, for no reason other than they wanted to get into trouble.

And a favorite sport was helping themselves to someone else's vehicle.

Technically, to be convicted of grand theft auto—a category of larceny—you needed the *intent* to permanently deprive the owner of the car. This was sometimes hard to prove, so you'd charge the perps with the offense of joyriding, which was basically borrowing the car and planning to return it after you'd driven the vehicle to hell and back.

Jon Merritt didn't care what the teenager would be written up for. A gangbanger would chop it for parts. Somebody else would want to see what an F-150 could do off road. Yet another would just want to cruise around until he found a good place to make out, or more, on a threadbare blanket in the bed.

Merritt was just leaving the grounds when he saw it go down. The Ford had sat, running, for merely one minute, when a skinny kid with a bad complexion and a ratty sweatshirt, emblazoned with the logo of a long-ago rock group, walked past. He paused, looked up and down the parking lot, and in a flash was inside and skidding across, then out of, the lot.

Now, head down, Merritt hiked the backpack higher on his shoulder and continued to limp along the sidewalk under the rows of elm. Now that he had a moment of peace, he looked at his phone and examined his texts.

After escaping from Sunny Acres, his ex and daughter had disappeared once more. There were no clues to their whereabouts.

He sighed in anger.

This meant that he'd have to start plowing once more through the litter he'd picked up in her house. How much paper remained?

A thousand sheets and scraps.

But first he needed wheels.

He walked for another six endless blocks, when he noted an elderly woman parking her shiny dark blue Buick, an older model, in the driveway of a modest house. She climbed out, took a bag of groceries from the backseat and headed up the walk.

No one coming out to help her. So she lived alone, or at least was by herself at the moment.

Odds of dogs? At her age and frail state, any canines would be little yappers, not rotties or pit bulls.

Sidewalks deserted, the street was free of vehicles.

She walked to the front door. Drawing his gun, he followed.

He stepped silently into the living room, which hummed with the white noise of the modest HVAC system. He smelled lavender and lemon and some cleanser. Ah; it was ammonia. He recalled a case from years ago, a house not unlike this one. A wife had tried to kill her husband by mixing ammonia with other household chemicals, making a dangerous gas. She'd knocked him out then, as if he'd fallen, hit his head on the corner of the counter. She then poured the lethal potion on the floor.

He remembered being impressed with her ingenuity—up to the point she neglected to dispose of the hammer she'd brained him with. Her fingerprints and his blood got her thirty years.

Merritt's eyes took in a collection of tiny figurines. Animals mostly. White porcelain. Very meticulously crafted. He particularly liked the elephant.

He made his way silently toward the kitchen, where the woman was humming a pleasant tune. It was familiar, from a Broadway show, but for the life of him Jon Merritt couldn't place it.

52

Standing at the massive raw-oak front door of the large contempo house, Allison Parker rang the chime. Melodic tones, three of them, sounded from inside, reminding her of the note made by running a moist finger around the rim of a glass.

The angular, glassy place was impressive and she nearly asked Hannah what she thought of it. Then remembered she was mad at the girl.

Bitch . . .

Footsteps, a shadow. The slab of wood swung open and Frank Villaine was filling the doorway, looking down at mother and daughter. He was smiling. The man was very much as she remembered: huge, bearlike, bearded, brown hair thick and with a few gray strands, but no more than when they'd known each other years ago.

"Well, hello."

"Frank," Parker said and they embraced. The same cologne, after all these years. "This is Hannah. Mr. Villaine."

His was a broad smile; the girl's muted. No physical contact. Hannah was cautious. Understandable. He was a stranger and he towered. And, then too, their life had descended into nightmare.

"Come on in." Frank picked up their bags and ushered them inside, looking out over the hundred-yard driveway that led here from an unpaved country road. His eye squinted slightly and this was probably the look he affected when scouting for game. His permanent residence was in Chicago. This was his getaway home and hunting lodge.

He closed and locked the door and directed them through a large living area and into the kitchen, which like in many homes seemed the heart of the place. He moved slowly by nature, not physical limitation. He'd been working and the island, of dark green marble, was strewn with engineering diagrams, charts, graphs, notes. Two computers sat open.

The interior of the house featured walls of bird's-eye maple and plank floors and oak doors that swung on and latched with wrought iron fixtures. Wide windows, curtains open, looked out on rolling hills to the east and, opposite, the imposing forest that dominated this portion of the state.

Only now did she notice that a rifle sat muzzle-up behind the door.

He'd been fully apprised of the Jon Merritt situation.

"I don't know what to say, Frank." She sloughed her jacket and he took it and hung it on a peg by the back door. Hannah kept hers on—as if ready to make a fast exit. Parker continued, "I racked my brain to think of somebody Jon didn't know . . . And somebody who'd be crazy enough to let us stay for a day or two."

"As long as you like."

"It won't be long. They *have* to be close to catching him."

Did Hannah glare at this? Possibly.

"I checked the news," he said, "there's nothing about it. And I didn't call the police or prison to find out."

She'd asked him not to, only to monitor the press. "Thank you. He's still got his connections."

She was afraid someone at the FPD or detention would see the number, trace it to Frank and eventually here.

"My lawyer's monitoring it. I've called but he hasn't gotten back to me."

"I'll show you your rooms."

"Hannah and I can share."

"I'm your Airbnb. Whatever you like."

Hannah said, "Maybe if you've got, like, another one." Her polite smile was utterly fake.

He glanced to Parker, who gave a shallow nod, deciding it was probably a good idea to give the girl some space. Good for herself too. Her fury about the selfie ebbed and flowed. Yes, she hadn't been honest about the risk her father posed, but the girl had blatantly ignored her instructions. Not acceptable.

Carrying their bags and backpacks as if they were pillows, Frank led them down a long dark corridor.

"Here you go." He nodded to two bedrooms, next to each other. They were spacious, each with its own bath. The sheets on the beds seemed new and at the feet rested neatly folded towels. Parker took the first one they came to, Hannah the next.

"Han," Parker said, standing in the girl's doorway, "take your jacket off. Wash up."

The girl took her backpack from Frank and dropped it onto the bed, then pulled out her computer, opened the lid.

"Han?"

"I will."

Frank set Parker's bags inside her room. He said, "I'll be in the kitchen."

A whispered "Thank you," and a firm hug.

She stepped into her bathroom and scrubbed her hands and face. She looked pale and haggard and if anyone needed makeup, she did. But she didn't bother. Then too most of the jars and bottles and tubes were on the floor of the Sunny Acres motel. Her hair was a mess. She finger-smoothed the curls, and let it go at that.

Returning to the kitchen, she found Frank at the back door, once again scanning slowly. His shoulders were raised slightly. It brought back a memory of a time they'd camped. A cold September in the mountains. One morning they'd both gazed out over a stunning dawn. She'd been swept away by the beauty of the light on dewy foliage. He had been entranced with a 10-point buck.

She now asked, "You have open internet?"

"Open? Oh. No, the router's passcoded. I'll give it to you."

"I don't need it. Can Hannah get the code?"

"It's on the router. There."

The black box sat in the corner.

"Can you hide it?"

He moved the device to a closet and closed the door. "Why?"

"Hannah doesn't get how much we're in danger. I'm afraid she'll post something." Her heart clenched. "She already did. Jon could have found where we were staying. She was trying to tell him where we were."

He frowned. "Why on earth would she do that?"

Parker's eyes too now scanned the property. "She wants her father. Well, the father she remembers from the old days. Thinks he'll apologize and we'll be a happy family again. She doesn't see who he is now." A shrug. "She's happy to forgive. And thinks I should too."

There was much more to say, almost too much.

But Allison Parker let it go at that, though she added, "I'm sure he's drinking again." She continued to stare out on the expanse of grass and scrub. "That's a match and gasoline."

"Well, you'll be safe here. It's a fortress. There're druggies, meth, in this part of the county. Jon can't get in once I seal it up. I've got a central station panic button. And then . . ." He nodded to the dark corner where the rifle sat. She knew he was quite the shot.

"Really, only a day or two. If they don't get him by

day after tomorrow, I'm going to Indianapolis. One of my old roommates lives there. I've never mentioned her to Jon."

And then it was time—past time—for the subject of Jon Merritt to go away.

She studied him with a faint smile. "You seeing anyone these days?" Frank had been a widower for years. They had dated after his wife passed away.

"Nothing serious. Too old for that nonsense."

She scoffed.

"Well, too busy."

"That's more like it." She shook her head. "Sixty-hour weeks, I'll bet. Like me."

"The modular reactors. That's exciting work. What're yours called again? Interesting name, right?"

"Pocket Suns."

"That's clever. You in production yet?"

"Next year. And how are Frank Junior and Ella?"

"West Coast and East respectively. Ella's turning me into a grandfather."

"Oh, Frank! When?"

"Couple of months. I arrange my own lecture schedule. So I see them both quite a bit. Frankie's got a partner now, going on three years. Thom's a computer whiz. We talk math till Frankie falls asleep."

"Happy for you."

His eyes dropped. "I haven't been in touch. I should've called."

She held up a hand. "I'm just as guilty. Life moves on."

"How about I get some lunch going?"

She gave a sour laugh. "That'd be great. Breakfast ended a little quicker than we'd planned."

He put a large pot of water on to boil and got some fresh pasta and a bowl of cooked bacon from the fridge.

Parker said, "Sorry. Hannah's a vegetarian."

The strips went back.

"Cheese?"

Parker shook her head. "I don't know. The rules change all the time. Maybe today it's zucchini only."

Frank called, "Hey, young lady. How's cheese pasta suit you?"

There was no answer.

"Hannah, can you hear us?"

"Yeah."

"Answer Mr. Villaine. Is cheese okay for lunch?"

"I'm not hungry."

"Hannah!"

"I'm not hungry, thank you."

Parker lifted her palms and Frank gave a laugh. His children had been teens once too. "Give her cheese. She'll eat it."

Frank asked, "What do you do at Harmon?"

"I just finished up a stint as anti-terror girl. Now I'm garbage girl."

"Okay."

She explained about the S.I.T. trigger and her current project: the fuel rod pods. "Like changing batteries—the difference being batteries won't kill you if you come within twenty feet of them."

"Your idea?"

"It was."

"You like nuclear work?"

"Who wouldn't?" A beat of a pause, then: "We're leading the way to a brighter and cleaner tomorrow."

He was clearly amused.

"Ah, just because it's a slogan doesn't mean it's not true. And I believe in what Marty wants to do in developing countries. You're mostly green, right? Wind and solar?"

"A hundred percent."

"We'll see where it goes," she told him. "Lot of thinking that nuclear isn't green at all. That debate's going to heat up."

"To critical mass?"

She laughed.

Parker didn't add that she not only believed in nuclear power but she found the science particularly comforting, because of its certainty. You could rely on the immutable words of Einstein: energy and mass are interchangeable, $E=MC^2$. All else in life might be in shambles but the formulas and equations she spent time with daily never betrayed, never lied.

"Hannah, come on in here." She didn't add: Be social.

Again, no response.

"I'll go get her."

Frank said in a soft voice, "This must've been hell for her. She can stay there if she wants."

"No. She should sit down with us." Parker rose and walked into the girl's room. She found her sitting on the bed with her computer. But her eyes were out the immaculate windows.

The fields were autumn sparse and dun colored, but the trees beyond were spectacular in their radiant spectrum, interspersed with rich green pine.

It would be nearly impossible for someone at the forest line to look into the rooms, but the exposure troubled Parker and she walked to the window and lowered the blinds. She wondered if Hannah would object. She didn't.

Parker leaned back against the dresser, crossed her arms. "Okay, Han. I was mad about your selfie. You were mad I got mad. And I was wrong not to tell you the risk. I should've done that. Let's put it behind us."

No answer.

Trying to keep a parental edge from her voice, she borrowed Frank's word. "I know this's hell, honey. But it's not going to last forever." Then tried a hapless cliché: "And it's only going to get worse if we don't pull together."

The girl didn't even roll her eyes at the trite words.

Parker tried again. "Please. What's all this about?"

"Nothing."

Which was the hardest single word your child could utter. It could mean the literal definition. Or it could mean the opposite: everything. Or any one of a million stops in between.

And you, the person who desperately wanted to know the answer, left wholly in the dark.

"Please. Talk to me."

Then startling her, the girl blurted angrily: "I don't want to stay here. In this house. I want to go."

"Why?"

Her eyes shot defiantly toward her mother's. She nodded toward the kitchen. "He's the one you cheated on Daddy with, right? Go ahead. Just admit it!"

The girl slammed her computer shut and turned away.

53

Mrs. Butler's Buick was as pristine a car as Merritt had ever seen.

Even the steering wheel had been polished. It was slick. He smelled Pledge.

He piloted the car into a shopping mall parking lot and drove to the far side, where dozens of modest vehicles rested. It was the spot where employees of the stores were told to park, freeing up spaces closer in for paying customers. Very little traffic—vehicular or foot—here.

Head back, pressing into the padded rest. Eyes on the textured ceiling.

He wanted to sleep. He was exhausted and groggy and in gobs of pain from the rubber shells, the second one of which had slammed into muscles still sore from the puking. But no time now. His anger was growing and growing, making him nearly as nauseous as he'd been earlier.

Get to it.

He sat up and opened the backpack. It was full. He'd brought all of his possessions from the River View. He'd checked in by paying cash, but there was still a chance he'd be recognized. Better to find someplace else.

He dug through the bag, set the whisky bottle beside him and some clothes, then lifted out the trove of remaining documents he'd taken from Allison's rental home.

It took a half hour and he was nearly to the bottom and growing more discouraged and therefore angrier, when he stopped, studying a printout of an email. He set this on the dash and continued through the rest of the stack. Nothing else.

The one email would have to do. He read it again.

He went online and looked up the name in the "From" line. He found plenty of references but no addresses.

He then sent a text to Dom Ryan asking him to use his contacts to see if there was a nearby address associated with the name.

The mobster replied right away that he'd check. Of course he would. The money clock was running.

The email was a curious one. It was an interoffice email, dating to when Allison worked for a different company ages ago.

The missive was brief.

Hey there, Alli!

Euler's Identity has been called the most beautiful of formulae.

$$e^{i\pi} + 1 = 0$$

I know *another* identity that'll give Euler a run for his money . . .

Apparently the sender, his ex's coworker Frank Villaine, wasn't too much of a geek to have a romantic side.

54

"Tell me what you're talking about."

The girl's rounded jaw was set. Her eyes red. "You think I was fucking deaf? I heard your fights. He said he knew all about you. You were cheating on him! Everybody in the neighborhood could've heard."

Some did, yes.

"Go on," Parker whispered, finding a calm center. Somehow.

Hannah's whisper was vicious. "Dad said he knew all about you. The affair. It was him, right? Frank!" Her eyes were filling with tears. "You cheated on him. He found out. That's why he started drinking! You ruined his life!"

So this was behind her comment during their fight earlier.

You dumped him there and went on to something else . . .

Tears in her own eyes now, Parker tried to grip her daughter's forearms, but the girl pulled roughly away.

"No, no, no, honey! When you heard that, he was drunk, wasn't he? Rambling, sometimes incoherent?"

"So? It doesn't make it a lie."

"Not a lie, no. But he believed things that just weren't true. He'd forget the day of the week. He called me Judy—his old girlfriend. He called you Abby."

Parker never knew where that name came from.

"Remember that party? Fourth of July at Hank and Patty's. Your father got into a fight with Mr. Simms because he was sure he was saying things behind his back. He got paranoid and mean. Jesus, Han. Think about it: When would I have time for an affair? Sixty-hour weeks. Home the rest of the time."

"Why would he make it up?"

"Because he got paranoid and delusional and angry. He wasn't in his right mind. I never—"

"Don't lie to me!"

"She's not lying, Hannah." Frank was standing in the doorway. His round, kind face was cast down at her. The girl looked up, clearly shaken that someone else had heard the exchange.

"Can I come in?"

When she didn't answer he entered anyway, but only a few feet.

"I'm sorry. I heard what you were saying. I just wanted to tell you about your mom and me."

What a calm voice, what kind eyes . . .

Hannah was frowning toward him but she gave a shallow nod. Wiped tears.

"Your mother and I used to date. Years and years ago.

Before she met your father. Only for a few months. Then it was over with."

Parker said earnestly, "Han, cheating? No, that wasn't *us*. I had my faults. Your father had his. But that? No, never."

What was the point? In fast memory, flaring spontaneously, she was picturing the last time Jon and she had made love, which wasn't that long before he was arrested for assault.

It had been so nice. It always was. Consuming. And it was yet one more thing she regretted saying goodbye to when she'd pressed charges.

This memory killed her.

What she'd told her daughter was one hundred percent true. Oh, there were flaws in the Merritt-Parker marriage, but infidelity was not one of them.

"All the things he said when he was drunk? Nonsense and mean. And half of it didn't make sense in the first place. He lit candles on a waffle for your birthday—six months early. And got mad at you when the tablecloth caught fire. He said why didn't you thank him for the dog he bought you? What dog? There never was a dog. He accused me of banging up the new car—when it was him. His reality was different."

Hannah was wiping tears on her sleeve. Her mother plucked a tissue from a box printed with gaudy orange daisies.

Don't go away, she begged silently. Stay with me.

Hannah took the slip of Kleenex and wiped.

For the tenth, the twentieth, time in the past two days, she found herself touching her cheek, the skin just above the crack, long healed, the ridge prominent as a mountain, despite the doctor's reassurance that that could not be.

Parker took her daughter's hands. "They'll find him, they'll get him some help in prison." And added spontaneously, "The help I should have gotten him last year."

This was what the girl needed to hear. She nodded.

Emotions roiled within Parker. Oh, her daughter believed her about the infidelity. She was pretty sure on that. But this, of course, was not the end of the story. For the time being, though, the angst and anger were sidelined.

It was time for strategic withdrawal.

"I'm starving." She looked at her daughter. "Mr. Vill—"

"No, make it Frank."

"Frank's going to make some lunch for us."

"Okay."

"You go on," Parker said. "I'll be there in a minute."

The girl blew her nose and pitched out the tissue. She pulled her jacket off, tossed it on the bed and followed Frank into the hallway. Parker stepped into the bathroom and leaned, hands on the vanity, head down, wiping her own tears.

From the moment they'd met in the research department of Midwest Particle Technology she'd been comfortable with him. He was kind and funny. And he was as smart as she was, smarter in some disciplines.

They had both understood at exactly the same moment that there wasn't enough chemistry to make them a couple—the sort of chemistry that sparks a true connection.

Chemistry . . .

That flare, that gut twist she'd never experienced with Frank but was front and center the first time she'd met boyish Jon Merritt at a Halloween party. She'd been wearing a Chicago Bears T-shirt with a large price tag on it, he'd been wearing a dark blue police uniform. They made eye contact and he walked up. "Okay," he said, eyeing the outfit. "I give."

"I'm a state of the union," she replied.

Without missing a beat, he'd said, "New Jersey. Wow."

"And you're what? A cop from some TV show?"

"No, I'm a cop from a cop shop. Ferrington PD. I was too lazy to come up with a costume."

"So," she said, smiling coyly, "that means the handcuffs're real."

They'd talked the entire night. Well, most of the night. The two had ended up in his small bachelor apartment, where the chemistry continued into the early hours of the morning . . .

Now, in an instant, consumed with rage, breathing impossibly fast, Parker drew back her fist and aimed for the center of the mirror, two feet in front of her, not caring what shattered, what sliced.

She heard "Mom?"

The girl was calling from the hallway.

A deep breath. Two.

"What, honey?"

"I'm cold. Where's my gray sweatshirt?"

Parker's shoulders slumped. "I think it's in my gym bag. Let's take a look."

55

They sat in the white Transit, Moll behind the wheel, tapping it with his long thick fingers.

They were in a 7-Eleven parking lot, having finished a late lunch—from cellophane wrappers. The long-awaited barbecue was still on hold.

They'd driven twenty miles west on Route 92 from the Sunny Acres motel, to put distance between themselves and any law, pausing only to pitch the motel's security hard drive into a creek. They'd then flipped a mental coin and decided to keep north, though avoiding the cameras at the intersection of Routes 55 and 92. They'd join the former well into Marshall County.

Merritt had a lead and they were now waiting to see if it panned out.

Hurry up and wait . . .

As he sprayed his neck, Moll glanced at the passenger seat, where Desmond continued to work on the willow branch.

It was an interesting thing, this hobby of his. You pounded the branch until the bark was loose enough to work off. Then you cut a notch—called, for some reason, a fipple—in a three-inch plug of the wood and slid it back on the hollow tube of bark, the end result being a musical flute.

Desmond now set his SOG knife down and lifted the green instrument to his lips. He played, producing a soothing, resonant tone. He stopped and continued to refine the instrument with the blade. Then he played some more.

These flutes lasted only a week at most. Once the willow dried out it was useless. It turned back into a branch. This at first seemed like a waste of time to Moll, but then he realized: What in life lasted very long?

Forty-three years or a week . . . Both were nothing. Finger snaps of time.

Desmond played some more notes. It was a tune Moll didn't remember but it had something to do with one of the rebellions in Ireland, fighting the British for independence. A girlfriend had once turned Moll on to the idea of reincarnation and he sort of believed it. He had suggested Desmond might have been a rebel in a former life.

The man had considered this and liked the idea. He asked Moll who he thought he'd been. Maybe Jack the Ripper.

But Moll had seen some movies and TV shows and he had said no. Jack had killed for lust and was sloppy. Moll killed for money and was organized and neat. Making bodies was, to him, like painting faux furniture.

It was all art. No difference.

Desmond cocked his head. "So? Jean?"

Moll hesitated a moment. "Gone."

"Oh, you didn't say."

"It just happened."

"I'm sorry about that, man. She seemed okay." Desmond played a riff, then cut a glance to the side. "She *gone* gone?"

Took Moll a moment. "What? No, no. Of course not."

Though it wasn't an unreasonable question.

Desmond was happy finding satisfaction at truck stops. Moll wanted something more with a woman. The settling-down part that his mother used to mention. He could nearly picture the future. He would hunt and work and paint furniture and return home to help her, whoever she might be, fix up the house, go to county fairs, prepare dinners and eat them not in the driver's seat of a Ford van but at a real dining room table. He'd help her with the dishes and pick a good wine. He was determined to teach himself the subject.

Jean, a voluptuous brunette who'd been a manager at Huxley's Pub, had been the sort who might fit the bill.

But she was also smart and observant, which defined the dilemma. Smart and observant people had the potential to be significant liabilities in his line of work.

Why do you have to deliver the furniture yourself? You could ship it.

Did you cut yourself? Is that blood in the van?

Et cetera.

So, a conundrum.

He would get it worked out someday. Meanwhile he liked painting. He liked making bodies and liked finding creative ways for them to go away forever.

Someday . . .

Desmond asked, "She still in the area? Jean?"

Moll said, "She moved back to Dubuque."

"That's a funny name." Desmond shrugged. "But I'm one to talk. Mine you don't hear much."

Moll offered an indistinct grunt. Thank you, Mother and Father, so very much. They'd believed she was delivering a girl, to be named Molly, after a relative. Oh, damn. It's a boy. Let's improvise. He recalled when a classmate said, "Hey, isn't 'moll' what they called some slut, you know, a gangster's whore?"

The kid was out of school for the rest of the semester, after being injured in a freak accident whose nature he simply could not recall. And no one ever made fun of Moll's name again.

Moll's phone hummed. He read the words and smiled. "Dawndue."

"What?"

"Merritt found somebody. We've got an address." He started the engine and typed on the GPS screen. The men buckled up. Moll said, "And speaking of weird names? His is Villaine. Spelled different, but like a bad guy in a movie."

"Okay," Desmond conceded. "He wins."

56

Allison Parker and Hannah joined Frank, who was clearing the island, moving his computers and documents to a cluttered desk in the corner of the kitchen.

Frank asked, "Soda? Coke? I have diet. Not that you need it."

The girl came close to smiling. "Yeah, diet."

He got one for her.

"That's the biggest refrigerator I've ever seen."

Frank lifted an eyebrow to Parker and picked up a bottle of red Italian wine. He'd be thinking that after Jon's problem she would abstain. She didn't drink much but wanted some now, needed some. She nodded.

He opened the bottle and filled two glasses. They sipped.

Frank was heating tomato sauce on the six-burner stove. It simmered, bubbling gently. To Hannah he said, nodding toward the stove, "In Italy they don't call this sauce. It's gravy."

"Smells cool. Why'd you guys break up?"

No one did non sequiturs like teenagers.

Parker said, "I moved to a different company, Marty's."

"And I went to Chicago. We both decided long distance wouldn't work. Besides I'm not sure how compatible we would've been. I'd've forced her to go traipsing through the woods to go, quote, 'shopping' for dinner."

"Instead of doing it the right way: Whole Foods."

Hannah offered a fraction of a smile.

The water was at a rolling boil and he eased fresh fettuccine into the pot. "Well, the feast's almost done. Hannah, any chance you could help me set the table?"

"Where's the stuff?"

"Over there." He pointed to a massive mahogany buffet at the far end of the kitchen.

"Everything's big here." She was looking at a dining room table that would seat sixteen or eighteen people.

"We'll eat there." He nodded at a round kitchen table near the island. He moved aside engineering diagrams. "I like this better. The rest of the house? It's like an interior designer cave. You two eat in the kitchen much?"

"Yeah, usually. Our dining room's too dark. We're renting and we can't put in new fixtures." A glance at her mother. "Or paint."

The girl'd been taught home manners and in a few minutes had plates, place mats, silver and napkins properly arranged on the glass-top table.

Frank mixed the sauce in the pasta and removed some grated cheese from the refrigerator. Then from the big oven came a loaf of Italian bread, its crust crisp and alluring. He pulled a mitt onto his left hand and used a serrated knife to cut slices. These went into a bowl. He removed a salad from the fridge and took several different dressings from a door rack.

Together, the three of them moved everything to the table.

He took one seat and pointed to those next to him, Parker on the left and Hannah to the right.

She realized then why he wanted to eat here and why he wanted to take the seat he had. So he would have an unobstructed view of the long driveway and the dirt road that ran in front of the house.

She studied it too, and expanded her glance to take in the long rifle in the corner by the door.

Then told herself: Relax. Jon couldn't possibly know about this place.

They began to eat. Conversation meandered, from the energy industry, to climate change, to politics, to the scenery, to life out in the country, to Hannah's school, to her uncanny ability to solve math problems. Parker supposed she'd want to talk about her passion—her selfies project—but had the good sense to keep mum on *that* topic.

When they were nearly finished, Frank froze, glass halfway to his mouth. He set it down.

"I want you two to go into the parlor." His voice was commanding, far different from his laconic tone.

Hannah looked up in alarm. "What?"

Parker rose. "Han, we'll do what Frank says."

"Go on. Now."

Parker and her daughter stepped into the dim room, dominated by an eerie elk head.

"Mom?"

"Shh."

She caught glimpses of Frank walking from the kitchen to a gun case. Opening a drawer.

Then she too heard the noise that would have alerted him, a snap.

She walked to a window and gasped.

The figure was pushing through the tall brush that bordered the side of the house.

"Frank!" she called. "Outside!"

57

Your mother and Marty Harmon hired me to find you," Colter Shaw said to Allison Parker.

When he'd arrived at Villaine's property, outside the small town of Greenville, Shaw hadn't known if the Twins—as he called the pair of hired thugs from Sunny Acres—had gotten here before him. So he had parked on a side road and hiked in through the woods. He'd surveyed the house and then done a quick and silent surveillance. When it was clear there were no hostiles inside—Parker, Hannah and Frank Villaine were eating lunch—he'd walked from the side yard to the front, rung the bell, stepped back and kept his hands in plain sight.

Villaine had greeted him with a pistol. Parker had barked an astonished gasp and said, "No, no, Frank. It's okay. I've met him. He recovered a reactor part that was stolen from the company." To Hannah she added, "He's the one I told you about."

Now that identities had been verified, Shaw pulled out his phone. Parker eyed it warily. "Could Jon track it?"

"It's a burner I haven't used before. And I don't think a Verizon or Sprint technician'll risk going to jail for an ex-cop."

She considered this and reluctantly nodded. Shaw called Marty Harmon.

"Colter."

"I'm with them both."

A sighing voice: "Oh, God. And they're okay?"

"They are."

"Merritt's still at large. The police don't have any leads. Is there anything I can do?"

"Not at this point. I can't talk now. I just wanted to let you know. Call Ruth."

"Of course."

"I'll call when we're someplace safe."

"Colter—" The man's voice broke. "Thank you." He disconnected.

Frank asked, "You're a private eye?"

"Like that."

"How did you find me?"

Shaw said, "Marianne Keller—"

To Frank, Parker said, "My boss's assistant."

"She was helping Marty's head of security track down people you might've been close to in the past but Jon probably wouldn't know. Frank's name came up. He lived north—the direction you'd been driving. I thought it was a sixty percent chance or so you'd come here."

Frank asked Parker, "But what's the danger? Jon doesn't know about me."

"Maybe not. But he ransacked your house. Would there be anything there with Frank's name and address?"

She closed her eyes briefly. "I don't think so but maybe. Oh, Frank, I'm so sorry . . ."

Shaw continued, "We have to assume he and his two men know about it. They could be on their way here now."

"What men?" Parker asked.

"I don't know who they are. But the way they operated they're probably pros, muscle. From some crew—a gang. Maybe they were hired by your husband or they owed him from when he was a cop and he called in a marker. They're helping him find you."

"Oh, no," the woman whispered.

Frank: "You mean, like hitmen?"

Shaw nodded.

"Mom!" A gasp. Hannah's eyes opened wide.

"They attacked the clerk in Sunny Acres and found your room. You left just before they got there."

At this news Hannah looked away. She'd be thinking of her infamous selfie.

"Oh, Alli," Frank whispered.

"The clerk?" she whispered.

"He's okay."

Hannah asked, "Was my dad with them? At the motel?"

"I don't think so. They probably split up, to have a better chance of finding you." Shaw looked at Parker. "If you've been offline, then you don't know about your lawyer."

"David?"

"He's missing. Presumed dead. The police think Jon was trying to find your location from him."

Tears flowed now. She covered her face with her hands. "Oh, God, what a nightmare . . ."

There'd been enough talk. Shaw said, "We've been here too long. We need to leave now."

"Where?" Parker asked.

"I know somewhere," Frank said. "A fishing lodge on Timberwolf Lake. A friend of mine owns it. He's out of town. There's no connection to me, and it's way out in the woods. Impossible to find."

"Good," Shaw said.

Parker said to Frank, "You come too."

"I will. You go ahead. Let me get this place battened down. The shutters and doors. It's break-in proof and there's a central station alarm, if they try." He gave Shaw the address of the lake house.

Shaw was then aware that Hannah was looking at him, her face a curious mix of defiance and caution. He smiled to put her at ease and said, "It's Hannah, right?"

She nodded. He didn't extend his hand. But she did and he shook the warm, dry palm.

He said, "It's going to be okay."

She regarded him with an expression that was eerily adult and seemed to ask, How on earth could you possibly know?

58

Placid.

The lodge that Frank Villaine had sent them to, a modest beige clapboard structure, was on a lake that, in this breezeless valley, was flat as a piece of glass. Surrounding the oblong body of water were a thousand trees, ten thousand, some clothed in vibrant color, some green, some brown, some dead and gray. The spiky skyline was inverted on the mirror surface of the water.

It would be a fine place to fish. Cold, clear, expansive.

He thought of Sonja Nilsson.

We took pike and bass mostly. Some muskie . . .

Shaw pulled the Winnebago to a spot behind the house and killed the engine. He climbed out. Inhaling deeply. Smelling, almost tasting, air rich with leaf and mud and water and decaying vegetation.

Parker and Hannah, in the gold Kia, arrived a moment later. She parked beside the camper. Shaw gestured for them to wait. He walked to the front door and punched in the key code Villaine had given him. The lock clicked and, hand near his weapon, he pushed the door open.

In a few minutes he'd cleared the homey three-bedroom place and walked onto the porch to join the other two. They carried their belongings inside. There wasn't much: a shopping bag, backpacks and gym bags.

They all stepped inside and Shaw closed the door.

Hannah wasn't feeling well; the last few miles of the road from Route 84 meandered in sharp curves. She walked to the couch, whose cushion covers featured a Native American design in red and black, and dropped onto it, her head back.

"It'll pass," her mother said.

"No, it won't. I'm going to puke." She moaned, with a touch of teenage drama.

It *would* pass, but there were a few more debilitating conditions than nausea. Shaw didn't want her to feel bad, of course, but he also needed them both aware and present. No distractions. This was a good safe house. But they weren't invisible.

Shaw walked into the kitchen and looked through the cabinets. He found what he was looking for and dumped some powdered ginger into a pan, added water and boiled the concoction for a few minutes. He strained it through a coffee filter into a mug and dumped in two generous spoonfuls of sugar, then stirred. He handed it to the girl.

She stared uncertainly. "Um, thanks. But . . ."

"Try it."

The girl took a tentative sip. Then another.

Shaw left her and joined Parker, who had returned to the porch, looking out over the field. He walked to the back, collected his own backpack from the camper and returned. The lot was about seven or eight acres of grass and sedge, in which grew a few solitary oaks and hawthorns and maples. About two hundred yards from the house was a row of trees running parallel to the road that had led them here.

"Can be a good defensible position," he said.

Parker gave a brief laugh. "You sound like we're soldiers."

"Here." Shaw dug into his backpack and took out a gray plastic pistol case. He opened it and removed a Colt Python. This model, a .357 magnum, was considered the finest revolver ever made. It was competition accurate, and its mechanism operated as smoothly as a fine timepiece's. This particular one had been given to a young Colter Shaw by his father. It was the same weapon that he'd used to drive an armed intruder off the family's Compound.

He'd been thirteen.

Shaw offered it to her.

Parker shook her head.

"Take it. Put it in your waistband. It's a revolver. It won't go off by accident."

"No."

He said firmly, "I might need you to use it."

In a voice equally stern: "Then you'll have to think of something else."

Hannah interrupted the argument, if that's what the exchange was. "It worked." Her eyes were on the gun as Shaw slipped it into his own back waistband.

The girl added, "It's butter beer out of Harry Potter. Or what I imagine it tasted like."

Shaw said, "We're going to make this place safer. The odds're with us, but even a one percent chance of being attacked means you prepare."

Parker asked, "What do we do?"

"I'll make an early defense system at the main entry points. The driveway and the lake."

"The lake?" Parker frowned. "How could they come that way?"

Her daughter made the point Shaw had been about to. "We passed a Walmart. They sell boats."

Shaw asked the two of them, "Can you cover the windows? Sheets, towels, whatever you can find." He was nodding at the rustic landscape posters mounted on the walls. "There'll probably be a toolbox somewhere, with a hammer and nails. It has to be dark. Use two or three layers if you have to."

Hannah looked around. "How long're we going to be here?"

"No way of knowing," Shaw said. "I've got food and water in the camper. That'll last us a week."

Hannah said enthusiastically, "Oh, there's a fire pit. We can cook out."

Shaw said, "No. Too telltale."

"How about now? Sun's out."

"You can smell smoke miles away. We'll microwave."

"There could still be smoke." Hannah was looking at her mother, who confessed to Shaw, "I'm not much of a cook."

She and her daughter both laughed.

Parker stepped away and began going through closets and kitchen cabinets. She found a small yellow plastic toolbox. She carried it to the dining room table, removed a hammer and a box of picture-hanging brads. The woman set off in search of blankets.

Shaw eyed the contemporary structure. To Hannah he said, "My father was a survivalist."

Frowning, she seemed to be debating. Then finally asked, "But aren't they weird? Like . . . Well, you know, racists?"

"Some, yes, but he wasn't like that." Shaw explained briefly about Ashton and the Compound. He then said, "The two fundamental rules of survival are never be without a means of escape, and never be without access to a weapon. So. The first. Escape? What do you think?"

Looking around. "Back door—to the deck. The front door, front windows. Side windows."

"What's best?"

She seemed to sense she was being tested but didn't mind. In fact, she seemed to enjoy the challenge.

"Side," she said firmly. "You could jump out and run there." She pointed to the tall yellow and green brush, which was close to the house. "Good place to hide."

"That's right."

"But the windows don't open." She glanced around and her eyes settled on the fireplace. "We have to break them out with that thing, the poker."

"No. It's too thin. That'd leave shards on the bottom." Shaw was nodding to the kitchen. "See those cast-iron skillets?" They were hanging from a rack above the island. He walked into the kitchen and returned with two large iron frying pans. These he set under the windows Hannah had indicated. "We can break the glass with them and pound the bottom of the frame to crush the spikes."

"The guy owns this place?" the girl said with a frown. "He's not going to be, like, totally happy. You know, breaking his windows, nailing up his blankets."

"We'll pay him back."

Allison Parker walked into the dining room bearing an armful of linens. She dumped them on a couch and surveyed the windows, then opened the packet of brads.

Shaw said, "I'm going to get our security system up outside."

"Can I help you, Mr. Shaw?"

He glanced at Parker, who nodded.

Shaw asked her for the remote for the rental. She handed it to him.

He said to Hannah, "Let's get to work."

59

She'd heard from him.

Colter Shaw had called and said that the search had paid off. Alli and Hannah were safe.

Sonja Nilsson had asked if he wanted any help. He'd told her no; they would be on the run. It would be better to remain in Ferrington and continue to follow up on leads there. He'd hesitated a moment before answering, though. This told her he'd considered her offer.

She concurred with his decision. It was a good idea. A wise idea.

But after what had happened to her, and now feeling crosshairs on her back, Nilsson knew that sometimes you didn't feel like doing what was good and wise.

You felt like doing something for yourself.

Still, she could be patient. The memory of the kiss remained, the memory of the contours of their bodies fitting together.

She was presently in her Range Rover, driving through the Garden District of Ferrington. She had canvassed around Dorella Muñoz Elizondo's house, trying to find someone who had seen Merritt around the time he'd received a rubber-slug welcome from the woman.

No luck there.

She was now approaching John Adams High. The young man who'd boosted Merritt's bait truck was a student here and she hoped a teacher or fellow student might have seen him—and, ideally, seen what his new wheels were.

As often happened, her mind went to her "situation," as she thought of it.

Crosshairs . . .

The shot that had killed the target was not distant: eight hundred yards. Nor was it difficult. The day was windless and dry (moisture lumps the air and makes bullets do strange things on their route to kill). A soft pull, a hard recoil and two seconds later, the man stiffened as if under an electric current and dropped, the man who tortured his prisoners, who married children—yes, plural—who mesmerized a cult of foolish, unquestioning and dangerous followers.

An easy day's work.

And, pre-internet, that would have been that. She'd have gone to other jobs, then retired, started work for a contractor. She might actually *have* married a man like the fictional sort in the tale she'd originally spun to Colter Shaw. Only kinder, nicer. Maybe someone who was a little like him.

But, that was not to be: thank you World Wide Fucking Web . . .

Which gave Michael Dean Thomas the opportunity to publish the thousands of pages of files he'd stolen from the Pentagon. Endless bureaucratic prose, dense and dull and remarkable for only one thing: its betrayal of hundreds of hardworking, patriotic individuals.

You just kissed a marked woman . . .

The Pentagon and other national intelligence officials sent her TARs—"threat appraisal reports." They said virtually nothing, in effect: "Might be someone on your trail, might not. Just be careful."

She couldn't blame them. Five hundred people had been put at risk by the traitor's leaks.

The traitor who, as last reported, was living in a beachfront villa on the coast of Venezuela, probably using the extradition notices sent to officials there from U.S. law enforcement to start the fire in his barbecue pit to cook dinner.

Nilsson now parked the SUV in the lot where the kid had reported he'd jacked Merritt's pickup truck. She climbed from the vehicle, closed the door and locked it. She adjusted the Glock 43 on her hip. The nine-millimeter model. She believed Shaw had the same. Or possibly the 42, which fired the slightly smaller .380 slug.

She made the rounds, knocking on doors, displaying her private investigator's license and Merritt's picture, and telling those who answered she was looking into a suspicious individual who had been hanging around the school.

True, in the way that truth can wear several coats.

Everyone was happy to talk to her—who didn't want to round up all the perverts?—though men spent more time talking to her than the women did. The reason for this was obvious. But the six-foot Nilsson, who'd done a bit of modeling in college, wasn't troubled. As somebody had once said of advertising: sex sells.

However long the discussion, though, no one could provide anything useful.

Then it was time to get back to the office. There she would check with the police, get a status update for the Jon Merritt manhunt. She would also attend to a dozen other matters. Security for a nuclear reactor manufacturer wasn't put on hold simply because of one employee's abusive husband.

Or for a manufacturer that had been the victim of an attempted robbery of a vital component by two different thieves in the same few days.

As she approached the Range Rover, Sonja Nilsson pulled her phone from her side pocket, paused and typed on the screen.

She'd barely finished doing so when the improvised explosive device erupted in a ragged shape of orange flame and launched shrapnel in a thousand different directions.

60

Shaw and Hannah were in the Kia, driving slowly through the field to a stand of trees beside the lake. They were off the driveway and the car rocked gently on the soft soil.

Hannah pulled off her stocking cap. He was surprised she had long hair. He'd thought it would be cropped. The dark blond strands, streaked with red coloring, were pulled back in a ponytail, bound with a black tie.

When they were about forty yards from the entranceway to the property—a gate in a post-and-rail fence—Shaw steered right and nosed the car into a stand of pine and scrub near the lakeshore. He shut the engine off and climbed out. Hannah joined him.

Slinging the backpack over his shoulder, he walked toward the gate. She followed.

They hiked through the field of low vegetation, yellow and pale green; it had not rained for some weeks. Grasshoppers and leafhoppers and stinkbugs danced away from their legs in fast streaks.

"Ick. I hate bugs."

"Those are insects," Shaw said, recalling his father's lesson on the distinction. "Bugs are a type of insect."

"Like, all bugs are insects but not all insects are bugs."

"That's it."

She'd be wondering why the entomological distinction was important but now was not the time for a lesson in the value of precision in survivalism. Toxic versus nutritional. While *Hemiptera*, true bugs, could destroy plants, none were dangerous to humans. Nine types were edible.

They arrived at the gate. The girl swatted a mosquito.

Shaw stepped into the woods bordering the property, looked down and ripped from the ground several floss flower plants. He tore off the leaves and handed them to her. "It's got coumarin in it. Crush it and rub it on."

She smelled it, wrinkled her nose. "Bet it doesn't taste as good as ginger."

"Doesn't," Shaw said. "And it'll *make* you puke."

He withdrew the car remote and pressed LOCK. The horn beeped. Good. He'd been concerned about the distance. There are ways to increase the range of a car remote—press it against a bottle of sports drink or your head or add a piece of metal to the antenna—but there was no need for that here.

He picked up a long flat piece of bark and studied the ground until he found a small round pebble. From his backpack he took a roll of electrician's tape. With this he secured the pebble against the panic button, and the remote itself he taped to the bark. He set this, remote side down, in one of the tire tracks in the driveway.

She laughed. "So when the car drives over it, the alarm goes off." She seemed delighted at the idea. "This's so dope."

"Try it."

She stepped on the bark and the Kia alarm blared.

"It worked!"

Shaw quickly picked up the bark and pressed the LOCK button, which shut the alarm off. He replaced it on the ground and scattered some leaves to hide it further.

The two began hiking back to the cabin.

"You learn that from your father?"

"Yes, and no. Not the remote specifically. But he taught us to improvise."

"Like, who's 'us'?"

"I have a brother and sister."

He explained about Russell—to the extent he could. Much of the man's government security work was so secret even Shaw didn't know his employer. Hannah was particularly interested to hear about Dorion, who had a degree in engineering. "Like your mother. She's got a disaster response company. Hurricanes, oil spills."

"You have any kids?" Hannah asked suddenly.

"No."

Hannah watched more insects shoot out of their way. "Mom wants me to be an engineer and scientist." She shrugged. "I'm good at math. She says I'm a prodigy. I don't know. Maybe. But I solve a calculus problem, and it's right and I'm like, okay, so? What I really really like's writing—poetry, mostly—and taking pictures." She was frowning. "I'd do a series here except Mom took my phone. I did something stupid."

"The picture of the water tower you posted."

"Yeah."

Shaw said, "Look at it this way: you hadn't posted it, I might not've found you."

"I guess."

"What would you do a selfie of here?"

She looked around. "Most of it's boring. Nature? Ugh." She squinted. "I know, I'd take one of you. You'd be in the background. Looking at the lake or the forest—checking for a place where there could be somebody dangerous. It'd be just your back. Dark, a silhouette."

As they walked through the grass, she was looking at the lake. "Timber wolf? Are they around here?"

"Could be. They're rare."

"Are they dangerous?"

"Usually they avoid humans."

"But not always."

"No."

"You have your guns. If we're attacked, you can shoot it."

Shaw shook his head. "Don't want to do that."

"Why?"

"We're in *its* territory. *We're* the interlopers."

"The what?"

"We're the ones trespassing. If they see you, you don't need to shoot. Just stand as tall as you can, open your jacket to make yourself look bigger. Don't turn your back, just keep eye contact. Never run. If his tail goes up and his hackles rise . . ."

"What's hackles?"

"The hairs on the back of its coat. If they go up and he's growling, you growl back. Show him that you're too much trouble to attack."

"Have you ever done that?"

"A couple of times."

"No shit."

They were nearly to the cabin.

"Just one more alarm and we're good."

61

FPD had a bomb squad. Of sorts.

It amounted to two officers, a robot that didn't work very well and a dog that did.

The latter two were intended only to *find* IEDs and were useless for the post-blast analysis work. It was up to the pair of lean men in their thirties, former military, to try to piece together what had happened.

So far they had learned that the device was made of some type of plastic explosive that had been surrounded by a layer of nails and Sheetrock screws.

The whole parking lot was cordoned off in a trapezoid shape of yellow tape. In it sat an ambulance and fire trucks and police cars. The flashing red, blue and white befit a carnival. Around the perimeter spectators watched, most recording the scene on their phones.

"We're not sure about the detonator," the taller of the two said.

Sonja Nilsson said, "Remote."

"Not a timer?"

She didn't bother to ask how a timed device might have worked here. The bomber would not have known when she'd return to the Range Rover. He'd had to lie in wait—which in this state made the offense attempted *capital* murder. Death penalty.

"And a shielded detonator with a dedicated frequency. So a kid playing with a drone wouldn't set it off prematurely."

They both looked at her, clearly wondering how she knew this. She might have told them it was because she had made one or two IEDs herself.

"We'll look for the parts," the smaller one said.

"You were lucky, Ms. Nilsson."

No, luck had nothing to do with it. Vigilance did. One of her security habits was to do just what Colter had observed of her: looking not only for potential shooters but for potentially threatening objects. And so when she was approaching the SUV to head back to the office, she noticed something present that had not been there when she left the vehicle: an eighteen-inch length of terra-cotta drainpipe sitting against the curb by the driver's side of the Range Rover.

The bomber would have seen the transit of her eyes and her body language and understood that she'd spotted it. When she stopped and pulled her phone out of her pocket, he'd decided there was nothing to do but to detonate it, hoping she was close enough that some of the projectiles would hit.

None did.

As she summoned police she'd done a fast search of the area, keeping her hand on her weapon. He would have to have been nearby. But she'd spotted no one fleeing.

An FPD detective joined her and the bomb squad officers. He was a large man with a notable sunburn that could only have come from a recent beach vacation. He verified that she was unhurt, then his eyes slowly scanned the site. She told him about one possible actor: someone connected to the Russian who wanted the S.I.T. trigger. There was also the possibility that the fanatics from her former life had found her. But this she would share only with her Army handler. She didn't want to take down her cover just yet.

He jotted down her narrative. Then she showed him where she'd searched for the bomber—the likely places where he'd waited for her. The detective then sent two patrol officers, all the FPD could muster, to continue the canvass.

She glanced at the Range Rover. A dozen pieces of the wicked shrapnel had pierced the door of the vehicle. She would have died if she hadn't noticed the device.

Crosshairs . . .

"Crime Scene'll need it for a while," the detective said.

"Understood."

She couldn't drive it off anyway. Only one tire remained inflated. She would arrange for a rental.

She'd call Shaw too and let him know.

First, though, she needed something else. She told the detective and the bomb squad men, "I want an expedited chemical analysis of the explosive."

They regarded one another, the problem being she was, after all, civilian. There'd be rules.

She broke the silence with: "I was almost blown up."

The bomb people deferred to the senior officer. The detective said, "All respect, what good's that going to do you?"

Nilsson fixed him with a cool look. "Because once I know the percentage of cyclotrimethylenetrinitramine in the explosive, I'll know where it was made."

Russia or the Middle East.

He blinked and glanced at the taller of the bomb squad men, who offered a she's-right nod. A bit of a smile too.

"Give me your email and I'll make sure you get it."

"ASAP."

"Yes, ma'am."

62

ike, what is it exactly you do, Mr. Shaw?"

"People post rewards. You've seen them."

A nod. "For missing kids and things."

"And the police post them for criminals they can't find. Escaped prisoners. I see an announcement and I try to find who's missing."

"And you're a bodyguard too?"

"Sometimes."

"You know how to fight?"

"A few things."

"Could you teach me? Like karate?"

"I don't do that. It takes a lot of time to master martial arts. Too much. I'm hardly ever in a fight and when I am it's a type of wrestling. Called grappling."

"I got sent to detention for fighting."

"What happened?"

"This girl, she was trash-talking to a trans friend of

mine. And I'm like, 'Bitch, back off.' And she got in my face and it just happened. I was so frigging mad I was screaming and we were fighting and everything. Kicking, rolling around. She was bigger than me." A shrug. "I guess she won. But she lost some hair. Got a bloody nose. I told the safety officer what she said about my friend. And he was like he didn't care. And the principal said I should've told the sensitivity counsellor about it, and the school could've handled it." She scoffed. "Sensitivity counsellor. Bullshit."

For homeschooled Colter Shaw, this was a staff position new to him.

He said, "Some advice?"

She frowned. "One of your father's rules: Never fight somebody who weighs fifty pounds more than you?"

Shaw smiled. "'Never engage unless you have to.'"

"'Engage'?"

"Engage your enemy. Fight. You weren't going to change . . . What was her name?"

"Brittany."

"You weren't going to change Brittany's mind. She was a bigot. What was the point?"

"She was a bitch was the point."

"Fighting won't make her less of a bitch."

Hannah thought for a minute. "Okay, what was the point? It felt good."

"Fighting's not about feeling good. Take that out of the equation. Let's say you've *got* to engage. Brittany was going to *hurt* your friend, bad. You have to stop it. Then remember the next rule: 'If you have to engage, never fight from emotion.'"

"What's that mean?"

"You're not happy, sad, scared . . . definitely not mad. Distorts your tactical decisions."

Hannah was absorbing every word.

Shaw asked, "Your fight? How long did it last?"

"Forever." Hannah looked at the lake as a duck came in for a landing. Ungainly on land, but how elegant in air and on water. "I guess really? Five minutes. I don't know."

"It should've been over in twenty seconds. Her on the ground, breath knocked out of her. You without a scratch."

"Dope . . . How?"

"You move fast. Surprise. A feint."

"Fainting?"

"No." He spelled the word. "A fake move. As if you're going to hit her. She gets ready to block it but you drop to a crouch, wrap your arms around her thigh and just stand up. Legs are a lot stronger than arms. She goes down on her back, breath knocked out of her. You put an elbow in her solar plexus." He pointed it out on his own torso. "Elbow. Not a knee. That could kill."

"Oh, cool! Show me. Pretend I'm Brittany!" The girl turned and went into a fighting position.

Shaw gave a laugh and kept on walking. Hannah caught up.

He said, "The next alarm. The lake."

"Fifty-nine, ninety-nine on sale."

"What?"

"The Walmart boat. How come your father's rules are always, like, 'Never do this, never do that'?"

"He thought it made more of an impression. My brother called him the King of Never."

They came to the shoreline.

"So, what's the alarm?"

He told her, "We run fishing line through the grass about eight inches off the ground along the back of the property. Then we balance a box of kitchen pans on a plank or branch and tie the line to it. They trip the wire, the box falls and we hear."

"Can I do it?"

He handed her the spool of forty-pound-test he'd taken from the house and they walked to the tree he'd indicated.

"Your father taught you all this?"

"Yes."

"When you were my age?"

"Little younger."

When he was Hannah's age, Colter used what his father had taught him and rappelled a hundred feet off the top of Echo Ridge to where the man—his dad—lay, in the hope that he could save him. A futile hope, as it turned out.

"Tie it there."

She started to but he stopped her. "No, this way." He tied an anchor hitch, making sure she understood how to bind one. Then they walked along the shoreline, Hannah unspooling as they went.

Hannah looked over the property. "They could still

come through the woods." She was pointing to the dense forest to the right of the cabin as you faced the front.

"No defense is perfect. The point is to hunt time."

"Hunt time?"

"My father. You know the expression 'buying time'? He thought that was too mild. He said, 'Survival is about *hunting* time—grabbing enough to assess the risk, enough to come up with a plan to defeat it or escape from it, enough to shelter in place until help arrives.'"

He looked at the woods. "They could come that way. But I put it at thirty percent. It'd mean circling around the property and hiking through forest. It's almost a thousand yards. And it'd take a whole day for us to rig a line there. Too far."

"You always do that, Mr. Shaw? Make percentages?"

"I do."

"How come?"

"My father, again. You look at every possibility and assign a percentage likelihood of success. What's the percentage of surviving a blizzard by sheltering in place versus hiking out? What's the percentage I can free-climb this rock face when there're no cracks to pound in a safety line piton?"

"You rock climb?"

"A hobby."

"No way! We have a climbing wall at school." She lifted the fishing line away from a sapling it had become stuck on. After a moment she said, "You could do percentages with boyfriends too, right?"

Shaw frowned.

She continued, "Like, there's this guy you like, but he's only like ten percent into you. You should forget it and look for a ninety percent."

"Is there somebody you know who's coming in at ten?"

"I don't know. Maybe this guy Kyle. He's a boarder."

"Snow?"

"No. Well, I don't know. Maybe. I mean skateboarder. Mom's all, 'Tell me about him, what do his parents do, maybe when you're at the mall hanging with him, I can come by . . .' Jesus." She tugged at her ponytail. "It's like we ignore the ninety percent ones and go for the ten percent, even if it's a bad friggin' idea."

Amen to that.

They continued along the shoreline. Shaw broke the silence. "Something you should read. I think you'd like it."

"Yeah?"

"An essay. *Self-Reliance*. Ralph Waldo Emerson."

"Who was he?"

"Philosopher from the eighteen hundreds. A lecturer, poet, activist. An abolitionist."

"We studied that. Antislavery. What's the book about?"

"It's about being yourself, a nonconformist, not relying on anyone else, or anything else. Not being swayed by other people's opinions unless you respect them. My father gave me a copy. Think you'd like it."

"Can I download it?"

"Probably. But it's better to have a printed copy."

Hannah pulled down a stand of tall milkweed and continued stringing the alarm line.

"That's good," he told her.

She nodded but appeared distracted.

"Mr. Shaw . . . can I ask a question?"

A glance her way. Hannah's eyes were wide and there was something conspiratorial about her smile. "Will you teach me how to shoot?"

63

D ad got me a BB gun when I was twelve. I was good!" She nodded toward his waistband. "Your father's rules—never be without a weapon, right?"

"Don't need one. You're with me."

"But *I* don't have anything."

"Guns take lots of training."

"I know how they work. I've seen all the *Mission: Impossible*s . . . Just kidding! *You* can train me."

"Your mother doesn't like guns."

"I'm here *because* of my mother." Hannah said this in an even voice that once again was laced with an adult edge.

Shaw debated, then drew the revolver from his waistband. It was an elegant weapon, the six-inch barrel and the receiver richly blued, the grip splendid mahogany.

The girl stared.

He pressed the catch and swung out the cylinder. He

emptied the six blunt .357 rounds into his palm and
pocketed them.

Closing the cylinder with a sharp click, he ignored her
outstretched hand, which she lowered.

"Colter, listen to me."

"Okay, Ash."

*The children are encouraged to call their parents by
their given names. This draws curious looks from friends
and family but is in keeping with the philosophy of self-
reliance encouraged by Ashton and Mary Dove.*

*Colter is ten years old. This is a milestone year, he will
later learn. It is the firearms age in the Shaw family. He
and his father are alone, standing behind the cabin in the
Compound.*

"This is a revolver because . . . the cylinder revolves." *The
wiry man with a bushy beard and wild hair spins it with a
satisfying series of clicks.* "It's also called a wheel gun."

"All right."

*Ashton opens the cylinder and displays the empty cham-
bers.*

"Is the gun loaded?"

"No, sir."

"Yes, it is."

*The boy looks from the cylinder, which is as empty as
empty can be, to his father's stern face.*

"Never assume a weapon is unloaded. Even if you see it
with your two eyes, then close it up yourself, it's still loaded.
You understand?"

Not exactly, but: "Yessir."

"What's the rule?"

"*Never assume a weapon is unloaded.*"

Colter wants to take the gun and start pulling the trigger and shooting. He will learn he is a long way off from that.

"*There is nothing on earth more serious than a firearm. It is not a toy, it is not a tool, it is not a curiosity. It is in a category all its own. A gun exists for one purpose only. To take a life.*"

The boy nods.

"*Now. You never draw it unless you intend to use it. Repeat that.*"

Colter is mesmerized by the solemnity of the moment. He does as told.

"*Never point it anywhere but at your target or a safe place, and that's down, never in the air. Some people disagree but a bullet in the ground is a bullet in the ground. One in the air could hit a schoolyard.*"

"*Target or down.*"

"*Never fire it unless you have a clear target. You never fire blind.*"

More repetitions from the concentrating boy.

"*You never shoot to wound. You shoot to kill. You shoot to take another life. So you don't draw your weapon unless you're prepared to do that. And, therefore, you never use a gun unless there is no other option for your survival. Repeat that.*"

"*You never shoot to wound. You—*"

"—shoot to kill," Hannah said. "And, therefore, you never use a gun unless there is no other option for your survival."

"Good. Again. All the rules."

She repeated everything. Word perfect.

And held his eyes, never looking away.

He pointed the muzzle toward the ground and pulled the trigger several times. "This's double action."

She was listening attentively, frowning, studying.

"The hammer's down. You pull the trigger. Draws the hammer back and when it's all the way back it releases and hits the cartridge." He did this again. "It takes more effort that way and because of that it's less accurate."

She'd been watching. "Yeah, the end moves around."

"The end. The muzzle. So if you can, you fire single action. You pull the hammer back until it clicks. That's called cocking. Then when you pull the trigger the muzzle doesn't move so much."

He illustrated this too.

"I want to try it."

He didn't belabor the rules.

Never sell your students short . . .

He handed her the gun.

"It's heavy."

"Forty-two ounces."

Math prodigy Hannah came back with "Two pounds, ten ounces."

"Dry fire it."

"Dry fire. Oh, without bullets. Even though it *is* loaded."

"Go ahead."

She aimed at the lake.

"Why don't you want to shoot there?" he asked.

She considered this. "Because the bullets could bounce off the water?"

"Ricochet. Down, a safe place."

Hannah targeted where he'd indicated.

"Double action first."

She frowned in concentration, aimed and tugged the trigger.

Click.

She smiled.

He didn't. "Too fast. You jerked. You would've missed. Squeeze. Slow."

"But what if somebody's attacking you?"

"Even slower then."

She focused on the earthly target. This time, even double action, the muzzle was steadier.

Again.

"Good."

"I want to try single action."

"Go ahead."

She cocked the gun with her thumb, mimicking Shaw. Aiming, then slowly pulling the trigger. The muzzle was solid on target. And the gun itself didn't waver. She was strong. It's not easy to hold a gun that size motionless for very long.

He asked, "You have a sport?"

"Volleyball."

So, arm strength.

Keeping the muzzle down, she looked up into Shaw's eyes and whispered, "I want to shoot a bullet."

His momentary debate ended with a harsh voice behind them. "Absolutely not."

Allison Parker was walking up fast. "Give that back to him."

"Mom . . ."

"Now."

A defiant sigh. Hannah handed the weapon to Shaw, keeping the muzzle pointed down. He reloaded the Colt and slipped it into his waistband. He told Hannah, "Get a box for the pans and lids. Put it on the top of that." He pointed to a gardening shed on the side of the house near where the camper was parked. "Tie the line to it. Make sure it's taut."

"All right." The girl was moody. She walked into the cabin.

"Basic safety instruction," Shaw said. "There're a lot of guns in this country—"

"Too damn many."

"—and she'll probably come across one in her life."

"No guns," Parker said emphatically. "I will not expose my daughter to firearms. She's a child."

Shaw didn't mention the age he'd been when his first lesson occurred.

Icily she said, "And I'd appreciate it if you'd keep them out of sight when she's around."

"If I can."

She stared at the lake for a moment, as that subject was put to rest.

But then it was time for another to surface.

Colter Shaw said to Parker, "Tell me."

"What?"

"I need to know."

Parker looked at him briefly, then back to the lake. "What do you mean?"

"I need to know why. The truth about what's going on. I've heard a couple of reasons why he's coming for you. But I haven't heard anything from *you*. If we're going to control this, keep you and your daughter safe, I need to know why."

Another duck glided over the mirrored surface and touched down, sending a V of ripples toward the distant shores. They traveled far.

Allison Parker stared at the idyllic image for a moment. She was absolutely frozen in place. Then: "Let's go inside."

64

Why are you doing this to me . . . ?

She and this curious man, this adventurer, were in the living room of the cabin. The scent was of must and some pungent cleanser.

Allison Parker found herself touching her cheek yet again. As for the ridge from the break, her doctor was wrong. It was as prominent and sharp as a knife blade.

Was she really going to tell this man, a stranger, the truth?

He'd clearly already guessed something. He was tough and blunt but those qualities weren't inconsistent with smart and perceptive.

But there was something beyond just his likely familiarity of domestic battling from his reward business that encouraged her to go ahead. It was the quality of his listening. When she spoke, or Hannah spoke, or Frank Villaine spoke, Colter listened. He wasn't waiting for a moment to jump in with a comment about himself or offer unnecessary advice. The speaker was the center of his universe.

Now he waited, leaning back against the fireplace and watching Hannah dig in the kitchen for the cooking implements that would be their ADT alarm.

Speaking softly, Parker said, "Jon and I were good for years. Oh, how I loved him. He was smart. He was funny. Hard to believe now, but he was. He never smiled much but he'd get off some hilarious one-liners. A good father. He helped Hannah with her schoolwork. He used most of his vacation time for parental leave with her, when I had to work.

"Ah, but then the drinking. When we met, were first married, he didn't drink much, but when he had more than one or two, he went into a different place. There were two of him. And the drinking Jon would get mad. Not just your pissed-off mad. It was in a different dimension."

The pale seahorse, with its smile or sneer or sensuous gaze, rose into her thoughts.

Allison Parker didn't bother to tell herself: Do. Not. Think. About. It.

Shaw said, "Jekyll and Hyde?"

A nod. "It came from his father. Being emotionally changed by liquor, I mean. A therapist told me about that. Mood can be passed down. But his dad, he got laid off from a factory on Manufacturers Row and started drinking in earnest. Drank himself to sleep almost every night until the end. But when *he* drank he mellowed out. Without the booze Harold was a prick, short-tempered, violent. Jon told me the family used to get him drunk so he'd stop insulting people and embarrassing them, whipping Jon and hitting his wife. Jon got the gene in reverse, I guess you could say."

The coming narrative was as complicated as it was difficult to speak of, but she'd recited it to herself so often, like a journeyman Shakespearean actor, she knew the tale cold. "About three years ago, he was in the field with his partner. He was working a big corruption case. He gets a call that there've been shots fired in a house a block from them. This father's gone on meth and threatening his family and shooting up the place. Jon and Danny were the only ones around. They suit up with body armor and go in."

She found her throat thick. She could picture the incident clearly, as if she herself had been there.

"The minute they walked in, the father shot Jon's partner in the head, then killed his own daughter. Danny wasn't dead and the father kept shooting. Jon knelt in front of Danny, you know, like a human shield, protecting him. He took four or five shots in the chest—they hit the plate, broke ribs, but didn't get through. One was low. Hit his leg. Jon killed the father and saved the rest of the family."

Shaw asked, "And Danny?"

"He lived. Retired, of course. And Jon recovered well enough. The wound healed but there was a lot of pain. He tried everything. TENS, codeine, Tylenol. Nothing worked, so they went to Oxy. Finally, it helped. But . . . Well, you get what happened next."

"Addicted?"

"Finally he got off the pills. And the pain came back, big-time. Stayed clear of the drugs. But he found a substitute."

"The drinking."

She lowered her head. Repeated in a whisper, "The drinking. The word should come with a capital 'D' . . . I suppose it numbs pain, if you drink enough. But it had that other effect on him. Anger, bullying, sarcasm, physical fights."

"Programs?"

"They worked for a while. Then they didn't. He had good sponsors, but he still slipped. I went to Al-Anon, Hannah tried Alateen. Pointless. He couldn't, or wouldn't, change. I had the police out a dozen times, but he always seemed to sober up just enough to convince them I was exaggerating."

Shaw said, "And they cut him slack. He was the cop who'd saved his partner."

A sad smile. "The Hero of Beacon Hill, they called him—the neighborhood where it happened. I . . ."

Control it, she told herself. And kept the tears away, though her voice clutched and she had to start her sentence again. "I thought about leaving him. Like my mother left my father. He was a serial philanderer. I made plans to get away but then he'd come around. He'd take Hannah to her events, he'd bring us presents. It was all back to normal—until out came the bottle. And it was coming out more and more."

Inhale, exhale . . .

"Then, November, last year, Jon was helping Hannah with a project for class. They were building something, soldering, bolting it together. Having a great time. Then, all of a sudden, like a switch got flipped, he stands up. I know he's going out. And I know what that means. I tried to stop him. Begging."

She could picture it so clearly. Her hand on his denim shirt, gripping the cloth. But he just kept going, into the snow.

"When he comes back, he stinks of whisky, he can hardly walk. And then, ten minutes later I'm on the ground, a broken cheekbone, blood everywhere." Parker looked out the window and took in her daughter's earnest job of setting up their security system. "The police couldn't let that one go. Attempted murder, a firearm, me in the hospital. They had to arrest him. And I pressed charges. His lawyer and the prosecutor cut a plea deal. They dropped the attempted murder and gave him thirty-six months."

She scoffed. "Except apparently in his case that meant *ten* months." She lifted her hands, a gesture that silently repeated the mantra "Hero Cop."

And the man who listened well listened now. He nodded, his face suggesting he was taking it all in. But then he looked her over closely and said, "Aren't there a few gaps you want to fill in?"

Allison Parker stared briefly, then could only laugh.

She thought: As a matter of fact . . .

But the coming narrative was interrupted at that moment by a loud repeating blaring from the field in front of the house. Frowning, Hannah walked inside quickly from the back porch, and the three of them looked up the drive.

"It's Frank," Parker said.

Villaine's silver Mercedes SUV rocked slowly up the driveway.

They walked outside to greet him.

The vehicle pulled to a stop about fifteen feet away.

The man who stepped out of the vehicle, though, was not Frank Villaine, but a hulk of a creature in a black suit and tie. His unsmiling face was ruddy with a rash. He leveled a pistol at the trio. He uttered an odd word. Parker wasn't certain, but it sounded like "Dawn-doo . . ."

His black eyes scanned them all quickly, then settled on Colter Shaw. The faintest of smiles, then he shook his head.

65

Shaw didn't bother to judge sites of cover and shooting preference-point angles and distance. At the smallest defensive movement, one—or all—of them would die.

He was just wondering about the second man from the motel when he heard behind him, "Hey, there. Be smart, be smart."

The man in the tan jacket had dirty blond hair, severely parted at the side and slicked back. He too held a Glock.

Shaw looked at Hannah's face, less scared than defiant.

The thirty percent chance had come to pass.

It happens. Thirty is not zero.

Parker raged, "Where's Frank? What'd you do to him?"

Jacket said, "Shh there, pretty lady."

"No," Hannah whispered, understanding Villaine's fate. "No! You asshole!"

Jacket smiled.

People give up information eventually. Everyone does. Pain is one of the most powerful forces on earth. Shaw hoped Frank gave up the address fast, and the Twins ended his agony: both the physical pain, and the psychic, from betraying them.

Toward the front of the property the alarm in Parker's car shut itself off.

Eyeing Shaw, Suit said, "I know you are of a certain sort. That is clearly on the table. And you have a weapon."

How did they know that? Both of his guns were hidden from sight. Then Shaw remembered that Merritt had seen him at Parker's house and must've noticed the Glock before he slipped into the garage and escaped. He would have told the Twins about it.

Suit continued, "You do this for a living, I have no doubt. But here." He aimed the muzzle at Hannah's neck. The girl gasped and Parker started forward. She stopped when Suit moved the weapon closer.

Shaw said calmly, "I'm taking you seriously. Just move your aim aside."

The men eyed each other for a moment, then Suit eased the gun to the side. He nodded to Tan Jacket, who handed his pistol over to his partner and stepped forward. Pulling on blue gloves, he frisked Shaw expertly, and relieved him of the Glock, the extra mags, the Colt and the phone. He unloaded the weapons and tossed the ammo into the lake. The guns and phone, he dropped into a fire pit filled with ashes and half-burnt logs.

He then searched Parker; his hand started slowly

down her spine. Fury on her face, she elbowed his arm back.

Eyes on his partner, Suit said, "Let us just move along here."

Tan Jacket gave a laugh. He took her phone and Hannah's from Parker's pockets. She muttered, "My daughter doesn't have anything. Don't touch her."

Suit nodded.

Tan Jacket shrugged and tossed the two phones into the pit, along with another one, taken from his pocket—probably a burner they had no use for.

And a burner it turned out to be. Tan Jacket had brought with him from the woods—where Shaw could see the white Transit parked—a large red can of gas. He poured a good amount into the pit. With a lighter, he set fire to the contents. Shaw watched his father's gift, the Colt, burn.

Suit stepped back, keeping the gun in Hannah's direction. He said to his partner, "The camper."

Jacket took back his own gun and walked to the Winnebago. He stepped inside.

Hannah was staring at Suit. While her mother was livid, the girl was not. Her face was a mask of calm.

She'd be thinking:

Never fight from emotion.

Shaw would have to watch her. Now was not the time for bold moves.

"Where's my husband?" Parker asked angrily.

"On his way."

She said bitterly, "He's paying you. How much?"

"Just hush . . . Better for everybody."

She continued, "He's poor. Whatever he told you, he's lying. I have money. I have a lot of money. I'll pay you more."

"That hush thing."

"Mr. Shaw," Hannah whispered.

He saw her eyes were swiveling slowly from him to Suit. The muzzle of the gun had drooped as he glanced toward the Winnebago.

The girl would be suggesting that they take him together.

Fifteen seconds, on his back.

Shaw shook his head firmly.

Her mother perhaps mistook her calm focused eyes for paralyzing trauma. She walked to Hannah, embraced her, glaring and defying Suit to stop her.

Tan Jacket emerged. He was carrying Shaw's laptop and a handful of burner phones. These went into the pit, and black smoke, astringent, rose as the plastic burned.

"Now," Suit said, "you all. Into the camper."

Hannah shot a look toward Shaw once more. He said, "We'll do what they say."

Parker, her arm around Hannah's shoulders, walked to the Winnebago and climbed inside. Shaw looked over the men closely, then he too walked up the stairs and pulled the door shut after him.

66

Moll announced, "I do not like the looks of that man. Worse than I thought."

"Worse?"

"Dangerous is what I mean. I did not like his eyeballing us. That was not comforting."

Desmond grunted. Moll guessed this meant he agreed. His flute tunes were more expressive than what came out of his mouth.

Moll was looking over the lake. "Wonder what they catch here." Avid outdoorsman though he was, Moll didn't fish. Hooking something was different from shooting it.

"Bass."

"You know that from looking at the water?"

Desmond said, "No. But anybody asks what do you catch in this lake or that lake, just say 'bass.' Who's to know different?" He'd replaced his gun and took out the flute. Blew a note, then another. Lowered it away from his mouth. "That girl. She was downright hostile. And she thinks more of herself than she is."

Moll's eyes went to the camper. He said slowly, "That alarm thing he rigged?" Nodding toward the Kia half hidden in the bushes. "If we'd rolled up the Transit, he would have got a half-dozen rounds off with that Dirty Harry gun of his. And he shoots tight groups, I do not doubt."

Desmond nodded.

Moll continued, "He might be in there right now making a gun out of a pipe and shotgun shell hidden somewhere."

"Don't disagree. I'm not in this to get blasted like a wild boar."

"Do you know what I am thinking?"

"Hm . . . ?"

"Not to wait for Merritt. Is there any downside to not waiting?"

Desmond's face suggested he was pondering.

Moll answered his own question. "Do not see much of one."

"Granted that. And I am more than a little choked that this has turned into ten times what it was supposed to be. So?"

Moll looked to the fire pit.

His partner's eyes grew rounder. Hungrier. "Hell, we're going to burn everything up, let me have at her."

"And get past Motorcycle Man? I'll pay for your next two visits to the truck stop."

Desmond said, "Three."

Moll sighed. Were they really negotiating over this? "Okay."

Desmond lugged the gas can to the Winnebago and poured the contents on the ground under the engine compartment. The two had burned vehicles before and learned that flames could not breach the tank, but would quickly melt fuel lines under the motor, and fuel would gush out, spurring the fire on. Even diesel would go if the temperature was high enough.

When he finished, he turned to Moll. "Might be more, you know, humane to shoot. We could leave the door open. Get 'em as they come out."

Moll shook his head. "Motorcycle comes out, with a bow and arrow and pipe bomb. No, they stay nice and tight inside. You know how it goes, a place small as that? The fumes will knock them out before the fire gets them. Be like going to sleep."

Desmond noted a gardening shed. He opened it up and extracted a flat-head shovel. He carried it to the Winnebago and wedged the tool between the ground and the door latch. He tested it; the door wouldn't open.

Desmond collected a broom from the shed and lit the bristles from the dwindling fire-pit flames. He carefully touched the burning end to the fuel.

With a muted hush, a bed of blue and orange flame rolled under the camper.

Desmond danced back, and Moll smiled at the sight.

The men sat down on chairs on the porch—like they were buddies sipping whisky and telling tall tales after a day in the field taking their quota of bobwhites or pheasant. They watched the relentless progress of the flames, the torrent of black smoke.

A few minutes later the screams began.

Desmond looked at his partner with a raised eyebrow and muttered, "Fumes my ass."

Moll stood still, listening to the cries. He looked at the cabin. "Probably some things in there we should take care of. Computers. More phones."

"Probably."

The men walked inside. Moll shut the door behind them. He wondered if that would mute the shrieks of agony.

It didn't.

67

Colter Shaw said to Hannah Merritt, "You scream like a pro. You ever do any acting?"

The girl shrugged. "Like, not really. Middle school I was in *Pippin*."

She seemed unfazed by what had just happened. Unlike her mother, who was stunned.

The three were lying on the ground fifty feet inside the thirty percent forest. They'd made their way here after Shaw had popped the escape hatch in the floor of the camper under the bed. He'd cut and installed it himself and had had the suspension of the Winnebago raised to allow for such an exit.

When the pair had finished dousing the ground under the camper with gasoline, he'd raised the hinged bed and pulled open the hatch. "We'll wait for a few minutes. The more smoke the better. When you're out, crawl to the left. Stay low. They'll be expecting us to try to climb out a window. And I want somebody to scream."

Which Hannah had, at an ear-piercing volume.

Parker tried too, but it came out a squawk. Shaw had actually smiled. Partly to calm them, partly because of the sound.

When flames had been visible in the front window and smoke had breached the interior, Shaw decided that whatever cover there was would have to be enough. "Go," he whispered.

Shaw went last in case one of them panicked and froze. Hannah first. Then Parker. Once outside, they had crawled through the grass until they were well into the woods, where they now lay.

He saw the Transit, not far away—parked on a logging trail Shaw hadn't known about. Could he use the van in any way? Twenty percent yes, eighty percent he'd be spotted. Not worth it.

Parker now whispered, "They . . . They were trying to burn us to death. Why?"

Shaw had no answer to that. The Twins had the opportunity to shoot the three of them, which would at least be merciful. Merritt probably hadn't wished that level of excruciating pain on them, though he couldn't be sure. He had undoubtedly tortured Parker's lawyer to find out where they were headed before he killed the man. And he would have known about the torture of Frank Villaine.

"It was your home," Hannah said, looking at his stoic face. "It's gone."

True. But the vehicle was now a thing of the past.

Never let sentiment affect your decisions . . .

Parker asked, "We wait for the fire department? We can't call, but somebody probably saw the smoke."

Hannah said, "They might not come. Remember we saw those farmers burning the fields."

Shaw: "And when they don't find our bodies, those two'll start searching. We leave." He glanced up a path that led through the dense green and brown and gray woods, crowned by dark oaks and dotted with pine, brilliant green in the places were the sun lay upon them.

Thinking of what the Marshall County deputy, Kristi Donahue, had told him about this part of the state, he asked, "How far is Millton?"

Parker considered. "Ten miles, I'd guess. North. Whichever way that is."

Shaw pointed. "We'll head there. Get to a phone. I think we can trust those police. They won't have any connection to Ferrington PD. I have a friend, former FBI. I'll call him too."

Parker said, "The highway we were on? Route Eighty-four? It leads right there. We can follow that. Maybe we could get a ride. At least we can use somebody's phone."

It was Hannah who said what Shaw was thinking: "I think we have to stay in the woods. They'll expect us to hitch." She sighed and her lips were tight as she said, "And when he gets here they'll have two cars to search for us."

The singular third-person pronoun was uttered with a punch of disgust. Jon Merritt was no longer "Dad" to her.

68

No one was answering.

Sonja Nilsson—the former first lieutenant and decorated sniper born Beatrice Anne Gould—was walking from her rental car to Ferrington police headquarters on Abbott Street.

Colter Shaw wasn't answering. And Frank Villaine wasn't answering. Allison Parker had sent one email to her mother but was no longer responding to Ruth's, Marty's or Nilsson's own.

The woman was so damn paranoid that she wouldn't even tell her mother where she was.

At the front desk, Nilsson asked for Dunfry Kemp, and was told he was presently unavailable.

In her best military voice she said, "If you could tell him I'm head of security at Harmon Energy."

Four minutes later she was being ushered into one of

the most cluttered offices she'd ever seen. The huge officer—a bodybuilder, maybe—was more than a little rumpled himself. How long without sleep? She bet twenty, twenty-two hours. She had much experience with the condition herself and could assess it in others.

"Detective. Sonja Nilsson."

"Wait. You're the lady who was almost blown up."

She had called the sunburnt detective from the scene of the blast about the forensic analysis of the explosives. He'd reported they weren't ready yet. But he'd send them when they were. He absolutely would.

ASAP...

"I'm not here about that. You've been working with Colter Shaw on the Allison Parker disappearance."

"Yes, that's right. We have been. Sure have." His eyes went to a stack of folders, as if asking, where did those come from?

"Mr. Shaw's found her."

Relief edged into his face. "So all is good."

"No, not good," she said. "They've vanished again. They were in Marshall County but went north. The last we knew they were right near the border, so we think they're in Everett now. I want to get some deputies involved, looking for them. Will you help me with that?"

Never say: I hope you can help. Never ask: Can you help? Always hit them with a direct question: Will you? No way to wiggle out. Either agree or refuse.

She could have phoned Kemp, of course, but Sonja Nilsson had learned an in-person visit by a six-foot blonde, built like the soldier that she'd been, fixing the subject with her piercing green eyes, usually got better results.

"Fact is . . . I'm pretty busy here."

She just looked at him. This technique worked too.

Kemp's expression finally limped to: I guess. He picked up the phone. He wasn't disgruntled, she sensed, he wasn't irritated or resentful. He was just damn tired.

Welcome to the club.

Was it good for you?

Thinking of Colter Shaw.

Thinking of the kiss.

She forced herself to put that memory aside. Not easy.

As he was bounced around, telephonically, from one office of the Everett County Sheriff's Department to another, Nilsson looked around the office. How many cases was he juggling? Dozens, at least. She noted a memo about the Street Cleaner, a briefing from last year. Was the poor detective on that one too? After all this time, it fell into the category of cold case, the hardest to solve.

The detective turned back to her, hand over the mouthpiece of the landline. "I've got a Corporal Shepherd on the line."

She held her hand out and took the phone. Nilsson identified herself and explained briefly about the situation: A former cop had been released from prison after a domestic battery and was pursuing his wife. Two men were helping him. There's already one homicide. The wife and daughter and a couple of others with them have disappeared. "And we're dark on coms."

"Ah. I see."

She'd used the military expression, thinking he might be a vet himself; many sheriff's deputies were. His reaction suggested this was the case, and therefore he was more inclined to help her.

"The latest is they probably crossed into your county in the last few hours. Probably on Fifty-five or Eighty-four, maybe a smaller road. Any cameras up that way?"

"None of ours. Maybe a town or two have one for speeding. We're not linked into that. Let me ask, Miss Nilsson, what's Ferrington PD doing, or Trevor County? Or Marshall?"

"You know how it is, fugitives out of their jurisdiction. Not that motivated. And they're slammed to start. Will you get it out and free up a car to search?"

"Give me the particulars."

"You're looking for a Winnebago camper, beige and brown. A silver Mercedes SUV and a gold Kia." She gave him the tags for the first two. She had none for Allison's rental. "The suspects're in a white Ford Transit. No known tag number. And they're armed."

"This's a kettle of fish," he said, sighing. "I'll send it out on the wire. Now, as for a cruiser, I can assign one, but we're a big county. Can you narrow it down?"

"Hold on."

There was a map of this quadrant of the state on Kemp's wall, partially obscured by folders. To the detective she said, "I'm moving these." She gave him the phone and then removed the folders and set them on the floor.

Nilsson took the handset back. "I'm looking at a map. You have one?"

Shepherd chuckled. "I live here, miss. Forty-six years."

She scanned the map. From Frank Villaine's there were two towns they might go to, northwest to Millton, or due east to Stanton.

She mentioned these options to the deputy.

"Let me ponder."

Nilsson studied the map. The first alternative, the route to Millton, would take them through a cluster of lakes. The bodies of water had colorful names: Crimson Rock, Snowshoe, Timberwolf, Halfmoon.

This put her in mind of her conversation with Colter about fishing.

Then the corporal was back on the line. He said, "Okay, what I'd do, I was them, I'd stick the cars in a garage and park the Winnebago in a big RV campsite. Needle in a haystack. And there's only one place they could do both of those: Stanton. I can have a cruiser there in fifteen minutes."

"I'll rely on your expertise, Corporal. Appreciate the help."

69

D awndue . . ."

Thinking of the first time the singsong mantra had wormed itself into his mind.

The melodious birdcall came from when Moll was sighting down the barrel of a Colt. The man, on his knees, looking back at Moll, crying, "Don't do it, please! Don't do it! Don't do it. Don't do—"

Dawndue . . .

That'd been a happy job, a good one, a fast one. A pull of the trigger and he had gotten $10K in his pocket and an infectious expression to carry about for the rest of his days.

This job was not like that one. Not at all.

This "Dawndue" was the obscenity version.

Moll rose on his thick haunches from where he'd been looking down at the grass, near the rear of the smoldering Winnebago. The men had found two computers in the non-soundproofed cabin and stepped outside to add them to the fire pit. Then Moll had squinted and walked to where he now stood.

The *bent* grass.

The *scuffed* dirt.

He scanned the woods and, seeing nothing, turned to the cabin. "Problem."

"What?"

"They got away."

Desmond scoffed. "Not likely that." He rose and jumped off the deck, walked to the back of the smoldering ruins of the camper, regarding the tamped-down grass, the marks in the dirt. "We heard screaming."

"Because somebody screamed."

"You let me have at mom, we wouldn't be in this situation."

"Just do not," Moll snapped. He squinted through the smoke at what seemed to be a trapdoor in the bottom of the camper. Grimaced.

Desmond poked at the ash with a stick. "He's not going to be happy."

"No, he is not." Moll stared at the dense woods. "You were them, where would you go?"

Desmond considered this. "Only one place. Millton. Ten miles, little less."

"It's Everett County. No friendlies in the sheriff's office." Moll looked around, squinting through the smoke. "What did we leave behind that could be a problem?"

Desmond nodded toward the forest, where he'd hidden the Transit. "Tread marks from the Ford."

Moll scoffed. "Here? I do not think cops here even know what *fingerprints* are. Tread marks are in a different dimension to them." He gazed at the daunting woods once again. Where are you, Motorcycle Man? He felt a wave of anger, which seemed to make his skin itch even more. He didn't bother to fish out the spray. He was tired of both the sensation and trying to ease it.

"I'll take care of the Merc."

Desmond poured the remaining gas under Frank Villaine's SUV and touched it off. He tossed the can in after. A tiny flame became a major flame. Then a torrent of flame that swept away all trace of the two men. "What about the Kia?"

"We didn't touch it. And we wore gloves in the cabin. Anyway, no time now."

They walked through a stand of trees to the path where Desmond had parked the white Ford van. They climbed in, Moll behind the wheel. In ten minutes they were cruising slowly along Route 84, the road that led to Millton.

"They won't be hitching," Desmond said.

"No. But they will stay close to the highway. Use it to guide them. Not like they have their GPS anymore."

Moll hit the hazards and he drove slowly northwest, half on the shoulder when he could. Both men were scanning, Moll left, Desmond right, for any clue that gave away their prey. They knew what to look for. They'd done this before.

70

This is called a loaded march," Ashton Shaw is saying to his three children. "Or a forced march. As in you'd rather be doing something else." He chuckles and continues to stride along a mountainside path on the outskirts of the Compound.

Colter, Dorion and Russell are behind him, in that order.

On their backs are packs weighing thirty pounds or so. He had tried to give Dorion a lighter one, but she wouldn't hear of it.

Their passage is fast, and the children are keeping up, though breathing hard. Their father is not. Ashton Shaw, an academic by training and in practice, had to be the most fit professor on earth.

Over his shoulder he calls, "Roman soldiers learned loaded marches before they ever touched a weapon. To become legionnaires they had to hike twenty miles in five *hours, with a forty-five-pound pack, and carrying a sudis. Who knows what a sudis is?"*

Colter reads more than his siblings and he particularly likes history. "A sharpened stake they used to build night-time defenses with."

"Good," Ashton says. Russell seems irritated his younger brother could answer.

"Hey, I know!" Dorion calls enthusiastically. "Let's make some sudes and we can carry them like the Romans!"

Both Colter and Russell tell her to be quiet.

Shaw, Parker and her daughter were on their own forced march, in the woods north of the cabin on Timberwolf Lake. They were burdened by no packs but they were plenty challenged: the uphill terrain was dense with thick briars and brush, roots, rocks and trees—standing and fallen. The survivalist, the swimmer and the volleyball player were, however, making good progress.

The scorched skeleton of the Winnebago was now several miles behind them. Hannah was on point, a spot she'd seized. There was no reason for her not to be in the lead. Both Shaw and her mother had a good eye on the girl and any potential threats ahead.

They continued their hike in silence. Over them were branches and boughs of oak and pine, yew, beech, box elder and hemlock. Beneath, ground cover of eastern hay-scented fern, aster and ragwort. Moss everywhere. These were old forests. Damp and rainy Middle America rarely saw the purge of cleansing forest fires, and trees grew and grew until the stronger choked the weak.

Coming to a particularly formidable wall of greenery,

Colter pointed to the left and they continued onward. Ashton Shaw had taught his children how to navigate by the sun and stars, ever challenging, as the earth had the inconvenient habit of spinning.

Never assume the sun and stars are your only source of nav. Use whatever works . . .

The words were probably a paraphrase of his father's, but the point was clear, and today Shaw was not using celestial navigation but dependable Route 84, from which the occasional hiss of cars and of a tractor-trailer's engine brake guided them north, to the safety of Millton.

They made better time once they moved into a forest that was mostly pine, with little tangled ground cover they had to work their way around.

Hannah said, "I'm thirsty."

Shaw was too. He knew a dozen rules for finding and drinking water in the wilderness—such as, look for animal tracks around ponds because if it's safe for other creatures it's probably safe for you, and never drink from clear ponds because there's a reason nothing's living in them—but said, "We'll wait. Don't have time to find a safe source." The day was moderate of temperature and the air humid. There'd be no danger of dehydration before they finished the trek. Thirst was an irritation, not a danger.

Never let discomfort trick you into taking a risk . . .

And few things were more devastating and dangerous than waterborne illnesses.

After forty minutes, they broke from the trees and

found themselves on a riverbank over a wide, slow-moving river. There'd be a bridge nearby but Shaw hoped they could ford; he wanted to avoid any roads the Twins and Merritt might be on.

It didn't seem that deep. The surface color told Shaw this.

The sound of a clearing throat startled them, and they turned to see, on the other side of a dense growth of brush, a gaunt and sallow-faced young man. He was hunched over, looking at the phone he held in his left hand and frowning in concentration. His right gripped a short spade, with which he'd just dug a small hole in the mossy earth. He wore sweats, a stocking cap not unlike Hannah's.

He was suddenly aware of the trio and, as he gasped, his eyes first widened, then pinched into a frown.

"Hey," Shaw said amiably.

No response.

Shaw looked down. "Sorry."

Now confused.

"Lost a cat or dog? You're burying it."

"Uhm. Yeah. That's right."

But of course the truth was that what he'd dug was a meth or opioid dead drop. He was screenshotting the GPS coordinates of the location and would later text them to a buyer once the money was received. Shaw had heard that Bitcoin was all the rage for even the most backwoods of transactions.

He guessed it was a family business, given his youth. How many kin were nearby?

Parker frowned. "That's sad."

Hannah offered, "Yeah, sorry, dude." Shaw could see from the tension in the girl's shoulders she understood exactly what was going on.

Parker said, "Our camper, it burned up. We lost everything. Can we borrow your phone?"

Mistake.

He'd think they were either undercover narcs or, more likely, competitors, trying to get his cell away from him. Shaw's plan had been to act casual and get close to the kid, then take him down and grab the phone from his hand. Parker had killed their advantage.

No one moved.

The quiet was broken by crow caws, the wind switchbacking through the dry, clicking autumn leaves, a jet's faint engines, miles aloft.

The boy stirred. Thinking hard.

At least he wasn't armed, or he would've drawn.

Another moment passed.

Then, fast, he lifted the device to his ear, commanding Siri or whoever the goddess of his phone was to "Call Dad!"

Hell . . .

Shaw charged forward. The boy was shouting, "It's Bee. I'm at the place. There're people. I need help!" He dropped the phone and took the shovel in both hands and started to swing. His face was desperate and terrified.

Shaw easily dodged and kept moving forward, driving the young man back.

After one fierce swing—Bee nearly stumbled—Shaw twisted the tool from his hands and the boy turned and took off in a panicked run.

There'd be company soon, but Shaw concentrated on the phone. He lifted and disconnected the call. Before it locked, he fished Deputy Kristi Donahue's card from his pocket and dialed.

As it rang, he pointed north again and the three started moving quickly toward the river.

The call went to voice mail and he left a message about their general position and that they were heading north toward Millton, just west of 84. They were being pursued by the men from the Sunny Acres attack.

He'd decided that no one in this county likely owed anything to the Hero of Beacon Hill and was starting to dial 911 when he heard, almost simultaneously, the gunshot and the snap of the slug that hissed a foot over his head.

71

Jon Merritt was wrong.

There is one similarity between Dr. Evans and an outside-the-prison shrink.

They each have a large clock on the wall. The business of therapizing must fit tidily into the magic interval. It's fifty minutes on the outside. Here, forty-five.

Every time he sits across from the doctor, safe in his personness, he thinks of the clock on the Carnegie Building, sitting just over the surface of the Kenoah.

The clock that stopped running and transformed its hands to angel wings.

The Water Clock . . .

"Let's talk about your drinking, Jon."

So he's not picking up where they left off last week. He doesn't remember—or care about—the insight Jon had started to tell him. But Jon the Charmer says amiably, "Sure, Doctor."

Dr. Evans says, "You're doing well in the program."

There is an active twelve-step here. The majority of in-mates have substance issues.

"Okay." Merritt attends, he talks. He lies. It's all good.

"You said that drinking makes you angry, Jon. Is that fair?"

Merritt doesn't like the doctor using his given name. He's heard about transference—a connection between doctor and patient. That's the last thing he wants.

When you have a secret like the Truth, you don't want to connect with anybody. Confessions sometimes happen.

But he nods agreeably. "Oh, that's true."

Watch the word . . .

"You mean you get mad at them."

"I guess. At them, at everybody." He shakes his head. "I don't want to. It just happens."

Then the doctor does the looking-off thing once again.

The light filters through the barred and thick-glass windows.

Dr. Evans returns. "When did you start drinking?"

"A kid. My dad's bar. It wasn't a bar. He called it that. Just a shelf in the kitchen."

"He let you have some?"

"God no. Too stingy for that. I snuck it."

"And replaced it with water, so he never noticed?"

"No."

Tuna Doc lifts an eyebrow. "So maybe he knew. Maybe you wanted him to know."

This sounds shrinky. Jon doesn't want to keep going with it. But he says, "That's good, Doctor. I think you might be right."

And for half an hour, they run through the timeline of alcohol: When Merritt felt the problem got to be a problem, embarrassing or dangerous incidents caused by intoxication, putting people at risk, missed opportunities to turn his life around, what does he miss about drinking the most, now that he's been in prison?

Jon the Charmer is a talented narrator.

Then Dr. Evans sails in a different direction. "You said your father was better when he drank. What did you mean by that?"

"It was so weird. Sober, he was a terror. Drunk, he was fine. He'd never beat me or hit my mother. We wanted him to drink. Then he was nice."

"And you're nice when you don't drink, but bad when you do."

"Yeah. What's that called? Ironic?" *Merritt smiles at this, but inside he is cautious. He has no idea where the doctor is going and needs to keep his arms wrapped protectively around the Truth, keeping it tucked out of sight.*

"Did you and your mother try to get him drunk?"

"We had to. If he wasn't . . . numb, I guess you'd say, if he wasn't numb he could snap. That story I started to tell you—" *Merritt says this before thinking. The doctor looks at him. He doesn't know how to retreat.* "I was nineteen. At Henderson Fabrications. I'd worked overtime."

The doctor is frowning, like this is somewhat familiar.

Merritt grins and nods, fixing up the narrative for the doctor, but within him he boils. The one thing he's telling the doctor that's true and important, and goddamn Sigmund Freud here just doesn't get it.

"I'd work overtime. I was putting myself through college and needed the shift differential. He thinks I've been screwing around and he's going to whip me." He doesn't bother with explaining his father's odd term, "crowning about." He keeps the smile stoked up. "Nineteen! And he takes his belt off." Merritt fixes up an astonished voice. "And you know what his concession to kindness was? To use the end without the buckle. He tells me to turn around. He's going to whip me on the ass."

"Nineteen, really?" Then Dr. Evans looks at the clock that is not the Water Clock; these hands never stop moving. And then back to Merritt. "Ah, but I see our time is up, Jon. Hold on to that memory. It might be a good one to explore."

Without a thought, Merritt snaps like a tensioned wire. He rises fast and grabs his chair and flings it against the wall. He lunges forward, well within the doctor's sphere of personness, and leans toward him screaming, "Fuck you, fuck you, fuck you!"

And Jon Merritt realizes he's about to find out what happens when the panic button gets slapped.

72

They were fording the river.

The bottom was sandy and firm, and treading forward they moved as quickly as one could through the stubborn aquatic resistance. They were about halfway to the other shore when Shaw looked back. A trio broke from the woods behind them. It was Bee and probably Dad. With them was a skinny woman of about thirty, haggard, with a ponytail, shiny from the long absence of shampoo. She wore gray sweats and a Santa Claus T-shirt. All held pistols. They were moving cautiously to the riverbank.

Noticing Shaw, Parker and Hannah, they began shooting as they pressed forward, bullets flying mostly into the woods and water. None was trained, and helping the inaccuracy, they'd probably been indulging in their own product.

Shaw, Parker and Hannah dropped below the surface.

Gripping their arms, Shaw muscled them toward the far shore, now about forty feet away.

Then thirty . . .

The tweakers were firing randomly, generally near the place where their prey had submerged, though one bullet shot through the water near Shaw's head and the shock wave slapped hard.

Twenty . . .

The riverbed began to rise and soon they were on the muddy shore. "Stay low!" Shaw was dragging them with him. Hannah gave a yelp at his tight grip. He didn't release it.

On this side of the river there was a low bank, which they had to climb, exposing them to more gunfire, but the shots continued to land short or long. Beyond the bank's crest was a tall wall of marsh grass, white, beige and pale green. They pushed through it and stumbled into the soupy ground.

The gunfire ceased.

Shaw looked back and saw the tweakers standing in a circle talking among themselves. Another woman, older, fifties, approached. She was in a red-and-white gingham blouse and bulky jeans. She strode from the woods, carrying a long gun. The matriarch of the family, her angry lope suggested.

Bee was pointing toward the woods where Shaw and the other two now hid. One word from Gingham Woman shut him up. She spoke to Dad and the younger woman, maybe her daughter, and together they turned away and vanished into the forest, headed to their trailers or shacks, and the lab.

Hannah said, "You called the deputy. Let's wait here."

"No. We can't risk it. I told her we're going to Mill-ton. We can meet her there." He gestured around him. "This terrain, we can get there in three, four hours."

He looked at Bee's phone. The screen was blank. The unit might dry out and power up, though his experience was that, despite what YouTubers promised, mobiles rarely worked after a dunking. Besides, he was sure that even if the cell revived, it would be locked.

"Let's get going."

As he and Hannah started forward, Parker muttered something Shaw didn't catch. He turned back. The woman said in a weak voice, "I don't think I can."

Hannah gasped, "Mom!"

"I mean," Parker whispered, "I can try. But . . ." She held up a hand covered in blood.

One of the tweakers had shot accurately after all.

73

Yet again his ex and daughter had gotten away.

As the two triggermen burned the camper of the private eye, or whatever the man with the motorcycle was, the three had escaped north on foot, through the woods. The two pursuers would be searching the surface roads to Millton. Merritt himself was following on foot, trying to pick up their trail in the forest.

Where are you?

Goddamn it, Allison!

He found he was moving quickly, not paying attention to the noise he was making. He supposed that stalking your prey required silence. But he didn't care. He had a gun, he had ammunition and he was mad.

No sin is worse than betrayal.

Looking at the ground, he saw no sign of anyone having passed by. Maybe there were broken branches and overturned stones that were a road map pointing him to where they were. But he'd been a city detective. He could read concrete and asphalt and hardwood and carpet and smears revealed by alternative light sources. Not this, not here.

Still, there could be little doubt where they were heading—north to Millton. Any other destination would have meant a trek of twenty, thirty miles. And the path he was on was the straightest line to that dingy town.

Where was it exactly from here? He pulled out his phone and loaded the map.

It was because he was looking down that, as he walked out of a stand of pine saplings, he nearly ran into a pale young man hugging a garbage bag in his skinny arms.

Both stopped fast.

Merritt moved first, drawing the pistol and aiming.

"No!" the kid cried. "Not again."

No idea what that meant.

"Drop the bag."

He complied, looking around. A desperate gaze in his eyes.

It meant he'd have kin or friends nearby.

Keeping that in mind.

"Turn. Your back to me."

He did and Merritt pulled a gun from the kid's back pocket. A revolver. An old Colt. Embarrassing for a drug runner, having a piece like this. Any cooker or supplier worth his salt would have at least a Glock, if not a big showy chrome SIG.

"Walk forward. The bushes."

He headed into a cul-de-sac of foliage.

"Stop."

He stopped.

"Can I turn around?"

"Why not? If you want to."

The boy had the wild eyes of a sometimes user. "It's my daddy's property you're on. Private."

Merritt laughed. "Your daddy doesn't own shit." He was glancing back at three shallow holes he'd dug and the cheap shovel he'd dug them with. "You're collecting product fast as a squirrel at first frost."

He wondered: Did it have anything to do with some distant shots he'd heard earlier?

"Now, need to know: Some people came this way. In the last half hour. Three of 'em."

"I don't know."

Merritt lifted the gun.

"Come on, man, okay, okay, yeah. Man, woman, a girl. Went over the Rapahan."

"That river?"

"Yessir."

"They have a run-in with you? I heard shots."

"I don't know."

Merritt sighed long.

The boy whined, "They started it. This guy did. He was shooting at us! Just started for no reason."

"With what?"

"Huh?"

"What kind of gun did he have?"

"I don't know. A big one."

"Funny since all the guns they had are burnt up,

smoldering in a fire pit. And if there's a Dick's Sporting Goods 'round here, I missed it."

The kid was looking at the ground.

No need to hassle him further. And the clock was running. "You traded shots. You and who else with you?"

"My sister, my aunt, my dad."

"You hit any of them?"

"Believe so, yessir. The woman."

"How bad?"

"Her leg, I think."

Merritt turned and looked north. You could just see the flicker of lowering sun on the river. Wounded, she couldn't move fast. Dusk would be coming soon, and they'd have to shelter.

"What's between here and Millton?"

"Not much, sir. No towns."

"Anything?"

"Few hunting cabins."

"People in 'em?"

"I don't know."

Probably not. Deer season didn't open till next month.

Merritt picked up the garbage bag. Inside were a half-dozen others, clear plastic. They contained packets of meth and opioids.

"This's mine now." Merritt stepped back, to put more distance between him and the tweaker, and slipped the bag into his backpack.

"Oh, man . . ."

"The minute I leave, you going to go running to daddy?"

The kid's eyes were disks. "No, sir. No, sir! I promise. I'll just stay here. An hour. Two, you tell me. I don't want to do this shit. My aunt makes us. You can't cross her. I want to be a mechanic. It's a righteous skill and one I'm good at. I'm leaving this behind soon as I get a real job."

Ramble, ramble, ramble . . .

The kid eyed Merritt's gun, which was waving back and forth like wheat in a soft summer breeze.

"Oh, Lord, man, I got a girlfriend. She's gonna have a baby. I think it's mine."

What Merritt was wondering: Would a gunshot give away his position or would the sound bounce around confusingly on the nearby rocks?

The second one, he decided, and pulled the trigger.

The young man cried out briefly as the slug tore through flesh and bone. His limp body dropped hard to the ground, on a pile of leaves that represented all the colors of autumn.

74

A gunshot.

Shaw waited.

No others.

How far away? A mile or two.

Had the Twins had a run-in with the tweaker family? Or had the shooter been Jon Merritt?

The shot was something to be aware of. But another priority loomed.

Allison Parker's wound.

She lay on a bed of pine needles as Shaw examined it and Hannah held her hand.

The slug had missed the femoral vessels. Hitting one would have been fatal by now. He improvised a tourniquet with a strip of lining torn from his jacket. But they were always a stopgap; constant pressure, then surgery, were preferred to field tourniquets. Not options now.

He used a branch to tighten the strip and helped her

to her feet. He found a larger length of wood to use as a crutch and handed it to her.

She winced but said, "Okay. I've got it."

"Look," Hannah said. She'd found what seemed to be a logging trail, running north. If the mills that gave the town its name were for sawing and not grain, maybe it ran all the way there. They couldn't make it by nightfall but he wanted to narrow the distance to the town as much as they could.

Shaw glanced behind them. No pursuit that he could see.

They started along the wide path, Parker relying on the oak staff and her daughter. She asked, "Did it go through? The bullet?"

"No, it's still in there." This was good and bad. Bullets leave the muzzle of a pistol at over 400 degrees Fahrenheit. By the time they strike flesh, they're cooler but they still cauterize many blood vessels. The large hunk of lead and copper also puts pressure on the arteries and veins. The bad part was that the tweakers' guns and ammunition probably were not very clean, which upped the risk of infection.

"So." Hannah was looking down, partly to check their route for roots and rocks, partly to avoid looking her mother's way, it seemed. "I kinda was wrong. About Dad. I was a shit. Sorry."

Parker glanced toward her daughter, and it seemed to Shaw that her face tightened in pain, not because of the wound but from seeing the girl's expression.

"It's nothing, Han." The woman's face seemed as troubled as Hannah's.

"Yeah. But . . ."

They fell silent as the three kept pushing forward.

Surrounding the dirt route were more of the tall pines—here some green, some dead and bleached to bone. Deciduous too, oak and walnut and maple. There was deer sign and bear, a small one, but it wouldn't be a cub; they're born in January. So there would be no protective mothers around.

Hannah was vigilant, Shaw noted. She looked around as often as he did.

Shaw heard a clicking and a rustle of leaves. He was almost amused when Hannah, not shifting her gaze from the woods, reassured him and her mother. "It's okay. Only the wind."

They made it another mile—farther than Shaw had thought—before Parker pulled up, breathing hard.

"It's hurting more."

"The shock's wearing off."

Some people who were shot feel merely a tug or tap, nearly painless. That goes away soon and the ache begins to grow.

The woman sagged.

"Mom!" Hannah got her mother around the waist.

"I'm sorry," she said. "I really can't . . . It's too much."

Looking around, Shaw spotted a hollow. "Get down in there." He and the girl helped Parker into the shallow dip and eased her onto a bed of leaves.

Shaw climbed out and studied the surroundings. He noticed the disturbed ground of a path left by the regular transit of animals—beavers, he decided. These would lead to a stream or lake and, now that it was clear the three would have to be in the woods longer than planned, he wanted a source of water. Choosing at random, he turned left and followed the trail. Only thirty or forty yards away he came to a ridge. He looked down and saw a large, dark lake. On the shore, not far away, was a cabin. In front of it was a grass-filled parking area, which was overgrown—no cars had been here for months. The exterior of the structure was faded and the porch leaf-covered but otherwise in good shape. Maybe they'd find medical gear inside.

And weapons.

He spotted no telephone line, though it could be underground.

Another meth lab?

Probably not, given the unoccupied appearance of the place.

Part of him, though, hoped it was.

As for any tweakers inside—Shaw's surprise appearance would be *their* problem. He noticed a number of good-size rocks on the ground.

He made his way down the hill and, silently, up to a side wall. The drapes and shades were drawn open. Inside, the place was dark and dusty. No sign of any recent inhabitants, though it was furnished. And he could see animal heads on the wall.

He returned to the hollow.

As he relaxed the tourniquet, he told them, "There's a cabin. Not far. Deserted. Doubt there's a phone, but maybe medical supplies. We need to get that leg cleaned."

He tightened the binding again and, with Hannah's help, he got Parker to her feet.

Shaw said, "I can carry you."

"No." This was uttered defiantly. "I'll walk."

In fifteen minutes, they were at the structure, which he estimated was a little over a thousand square feet. A sagging covered porch extended across the entire front, a swinging bench on the right side. It swayed. There were two small windows in the front. As they approached from a shallow angle—it was easier on Parker than a straight climb down the steep hill—Shaw caught sight of a dock extending into the lake. It listed dramatically to the left and the wood was rotten. No boats. Nor were there any other visible houses around the lake, which he put at four hundred acres.

One problem was apparent: the driveway would lead to a larger road, which had probably been mapped on GPS; the Twins and Merritt could find their way here.

The good side to this was that Deputy Kristi Donahue might do the same.

Parker set one foot on the sagging first step, paused and said, "I think I'm going to . . ." She completed the sentence in silent pantomime, losing consciousness and sagging. Shaw caught her before she dropped more than a few inches.

"Mr. Shaw!"

"She just fainted. Pain probably, not blood loss."

Shaw hefted her in both arms and nodded toward the cabin. "Try the door."

She gripped the knob and turned. "Locked. Can you pick it? Did your father teach you how to do that?"

Ashton had, yes.

But now Shaw simply reared back and kicked hard—aiming for an imaginary target about six inches on the other side of the door, to give himself extra drive.

It slammed inward with a crack that was oddly similar to a gunshot.

75

The last abode they'd escaped from had been devoted to fishing.

This was a hunting lodge. Shaw got a better view of the dozens of deer and elk heads he'd seen from outside. The glazed button eyes gazed just past them.

Weapons? He guessed no, eighty percent. The overgrown parking area suggested the place hadn't been used for a while, and hunters would not be inclined to leave armament for any length of time in a cabin easily broken into.

A living room spanned the front of the structure. A parlor was to the right, bedrooms behind that. To the left was a dining room and, beyond that, the kitchen.

Nothing contemporary or chic about it. A 1950s bungalow.

Shaw laid Parker on the sofa in the parlor and lifted her legs. She remained passed out.

"Mr. Shaw . . ."

He examined Parker's color, checked her pulse and assessed her temperature. "She's all right. But she's dehydrated. See if the water runs."

As the girl left, he tried two light switches. Nothing. The place probably had a well, which would be inoperative if there was no power. He looked at Bee's phone once again. Still gone.

Parker came to, sweating, looking around as she tried to orient herself. "Hannah . . ."

"She'll be back in a minute."

Shaw was surprised to hear water running.

So, city supply. Maybe they were closer to Millton than they'd thought.

The girl carried three glasses into the parlor. "Is it okay? I let it run, but . . ."

The water had a brown tint. Shaw took a glass and smelled it. He sipped some. "It's just rust. Not like the Kenoah." Hannah helped her mother sit up and the woman drank. So did her daughter. Shaw too.

"Ick," Hannah said.

"Iron's good for you." Shaw's face was deadpan.

The girl rolled her eyes as she laughed.

He walked to a front window and looked out. No sign anyone was in the woods. He said to Hannah, "First aid kits and weapons. Guns preferably. A hunting bow'll do."

"You can shoot one?"

I can *make* them, Shaw thought. If he had time he'd do so now.

"Look everywhere. You take the kitchen. And dining

room. All the closets and pantries. Oh, liquor too. It's an antiseptic."

She walked off to start the search. Shaw stepped into the nearest bedroom.

After a few minutes she called, "Got something here maybe you can use. Like, a weapon."

"All right. Keep looking."

In the two bedrooms all Shaw found was bar soap and washcloths.

He called again to Hannah, "The stove work?"

A clank, then a gasp. "Spiders!" After a moment: "No gas."

So he couldn't boil and sterilize bandages. He'd make do with soap. After running the water in the bathroom for a few minutes to clear the impurities, he soaked the washcloths. On one he rubbed the bar, creating a good lather.

In the parlor he called to Hannah, "Any knives?"

"A couple."

"Bring me the smallest, a kitchen knife, not dinner."

She appeared with a paring blade.

Shaw helped Parker roll over. He asked, "Aren't ripped jeans in now?"

She offered a tepid laugh.

He undid the tourniquet and tossed it aside.

Starting at the bullet hole, he cut a long slit in the jeans and pulled the two sides open wide. He looked over the wound. The round had been clean enough so that no serious infection had set in. Nor had the bleeding increased. She was stable for now.

He gripped the soapy cloth.

She said, "This where you tell me it's going to hurt?"

"Take a deep breath."

She did, and as he washed the wound, she said, "Oh, well. My . . . Oh, shit."

He then rinsed the leg with the water-saturated cloth and patted the skin dry. He cut a long strip of cotton from a sheet, about six inches wide, and, after pressing a dry terry-cloth square over the wound, bound her leg tightly.

"Okay?" he asked.

"As can be expected," Parker whispered. She blinked away tears and took a clean washcloth to wipe sweat from her forehead. A feeble smile. "Guess you turned the heat up."

Smiling too, he rose. The patient was taken care of, as best he could do. Now it was time for weapons.

He walked into the kitchen. "You said you had something we could use?"

She lifted a plug-in air freshener.

He frowned.

She asked, "Like can't you make it into a bomb, or something?"

"Glade?"

"MacGyver."

"What?"

She said, "It was a TV show. This guy I went out with for a while? He liked it. So we binged. The hero made these things, like bombs, out of everyday stuff."

"Not air freshener."

"Oh." She gave a shrug and returned to searching.

Shaw wedged a kitchen chair under the back door-knob and took its mate to the front, did the same. Off the dining room he looked through a utility closet. He found a canoe paddle. It would make a functional club. He set it on the kitchen table, along with two butcher knives, one ten inches, the other twelve.

"What about this?" Hannah asked, pulling a plastic bag from under the sink.

He smelled naphtha.

"Mothballs. If we had any quicklime we could make Greek fire."

"What's that?"

"The ancient Greeks used it like a flamethrower. You study history?"

"Yeah, some. It's cool up to the Roman Empire, then it gets complicated. And boring."

Colter Shaw couldn't disagree.

"Can you make some?"

"No lime. It's only good against moths."

"Oh, there's this." Hannah held up a jar of cayenne pepper. "I got some in my eye once and it was like it was on fire. Can we make pepper spray out of it?"

"Is there a spray bottle?"

There wasn't.

"Are we going to do a security thing, like with the fishing line?"

"No. We'd be too exposed."

And what would they do anyway if the Twins tripped an alarm? At Timberwolf, they had real weapons.

Then something across the kitchen caught his eye.

He walked to the sink, where sat a large box of Tide detergent. He picked it up. Thought for a minute. He pulled a juice glass from a cabinet. Then he yanked down a curtain rod, bare of drapery, from above the window in the back door. He said to the girl, "Now I need a pen."

She ripped through kitchen drawers. "Here's one."

"And one last thing. Any rubber bands?"

They found none.

He asked, "How 'bout that thing in your hair?"

"The scrunchy?"

"That'll do."

She tugged it off and handed it to him.

Hannah turned and looked at the detergent, pen, glasses and hair tie. "You sure you never saw *MacGyver*?"

76

They are inside."

Desmond asked, "How do you know?"

"Window, right. Curtain moved."

The man leaned forward, stuck his head out of the bushes.

"Could be."

"No, it is." Moll went back to cover. Desmond too.

The men were across a weedy parking area from a brown clapboard cabin. Not having any luck in their search along Route 84, they'd pulled over and checked real estate records. They'd found this cabin on Deep Woods Lake. They had parked a half mile away, off an old logging road on the other side of the hill that faced the place. Moll, an expert at deer and elk sign, had spotted footprints, which led to the cabin.

One foot—Allison's, Moll thought, by the size, was

shuffling. It appeared her daughter was helping her. And he'd spotted blood. Those gunshots earlier.

"They armed?"

Moll shrugged. "Doubt it. Maybe found one inside there. Then again, I would not leave a weapon in a place like that. Too easy to break into."

The broad, calm lake behind the cabin was dark blue. No other properties were visible around it.

"A trapdoor in the bottom of a Winnebago?" Moll's voice was rich with disgust. He had no problem assigning blame to Desmond, or anyone else, but he wasn't above taking responsibility himself. "I should have checked that."

Desmond was still for a moment. "Who'd know? How could you know?"

Which Moll appreciated.

"So? What do we do?"

"As far as they know, we are somewhere else, probably on the highway. Has to be a back door. Leads to that dock." Another glance at the complex green and brown surroundings. Thinking where he would set up the blind, if this was a recreational outing. At least on this hunt, he did not have to worry about upwind, downwind. Human noses were useless, unless a triggerman was wearing too much Paco Rabanne.

Desmond asked, "Where the hell is Merritt?"

Moll had checked texts. "On his way."

"I feel like we're doing all the work here."

"Are we getting paid or not?"

Desmond's lips grew tight in concession.

Moll said, "You circle around, to the back. I go through the front."

A nod in reply. They drew their pistols and moved out, side by side, crouching, while they used the tall brush for cover. Moll smelled a sour aroma. Stinkweed. A memory from his youth arose, though it attached to nothing more concrete than simply being in the woods.

"Goddamn," Desmond whispered.

"What?"

"Two grasshoppers spit tobacco on me."

"I would focus. Can we?"

They paused behind an overgrown hedge.

"Give it five minutes, then pound on the back door. Call 'Police' or something. When they turn that way, I can get them from the window. You take anybody who tries to come toward you."

"I like it," Desmond said.

"And, remember, we should do Motorcycle Man first."

77

Once again, Shaw's percentages didn't hold up.

The Twins had found the place.

He and Hannah were staring through the curtain in the front window as the pair slowly moved from cover and started toward the cabin, pistols in their hands.

They were approaching through the brush to the right of the house as you faced it. Suit paused and crouched, Jacket continuing on. They were going front and back.

Guns against a canoe paddle, kitchen knives and the latest weapon Shaw had found, a claw hammer.

Suit was going to take the front door, Tan Jacket the rear.

Hannah looked his way and he nodded. She moved aside the curtain over the right front window.

Then:

"Look!" Hannah whispered.

Suit glanced at the tree he was approaching, then the window where the curtain had moved. He froze and dropped quickly, prone, powdering his suit with dirt. In a harsh whisper he called out to his partner, who was about twenty feet in front of him. Jacket seemed confused but then he also dropped to the ground.

Suit glanced again to the window. Hannah moved the curtain again. And the two men quickly crawled back in the direction they'd come until they were under cover of the brush on the other side of the parking lot. From there, they hurried up the hill, using trees for cover and disappearing into the shadows of the late fall afternoon.

"It worked," Hannah said, peering out and laughing. She squeezed Shaw's arm.

Tide laundry detergent comes in a distinctive box. With its red-and-yellow concentric circle logo, it could easily be used as a firearm target by people who'd live in a cabin just like this and not have disposable money for commercial targets or the inclination to drive to a sporting goods store to pick some up.

So when Suit began making his way forward, he noticed the front of the Tide carton Shaw had mounted on the oak. He also would have seen the dozen holes tightly grouped in the center of the "bullseye"—holes that Shaw had made with the pen Hannah had found.

Then Suit's glance at the house when the curtain moved revealed something else—what could be taken as a rifle mounted with a scope aimed his way from inside the darkened living room through the parted curtain.

So they'd fled—from a gun that was really the kitchen

curtain rod on top of which was the juice cup mounted backward with Hannah's scrunchy, looking for all the world like a rifle barrel and telescopic sight.

The *belief* that your opponent has weapons can be as effective as weapons themselves.

Hannah had pulled the curtain aside to better watch the retreat.

Shaw said, "No. Back from the window. Never present unless you've got to."

"'Present'?"

"Present yourself as a target."

"What're we going to do?"

A careful look out the windows. No sign of the enemy in all the places an enemy would be. "If the deputy doesn't find us before dark, I'm going to start a fire at the end of the dock. There'll be patrols for brush fires. They'll see it. Send somebody."

"Won't those two assholes shoot them?"

"No. They'll know that if the responders don't call in, there'll be police and the area'll be sealed. They'll figure it's smarter to leave. Come up with another plan."

She frowned. "But, we don't have matches. Like, can you start a fire?"

He nearly smiled. "I can."

Her look said, I should have known.

Shaw cut small holes in the curtain at one of the front windows. And one at each side. "Your peepholes. You're in charge of surveillance."

She seemed pleased he'd given her the assignment.

He added, "Don't touch the curtains."

"Never present," she replied.

A nod.

Hannah said, "What about the back?"

"Maybe. But that'd expose them to our imaginary rifle."

She looked out the kitchen window, nodding. "I'd make it a five percent possibility."

"I think five percent is just about right."

78

As the cabin's interior grew dimmer with the lowering sun, Shaw assembled the meager weapons—the knives, the hammer and the paddle. He set them on the coffee table in the living room.

Using the tool, he pounded several bricks from the fireplace. He placed each into a separate pillowcase and tied it closed just beneath the stone. Crude bolos, the Argentinian weighted lasso. He could fling one fairly accurately, making an armed attacker dodge, giving him a chance to get within hand-to-hand combat distance.

Knife-fighting distance too.

He examined the ten-inch blade. The stainless steel was not high carbon. It was cheap and dull.

He pounded another brick out of the fireplace and began whetting the knife.

Hannah glanced back from her surveillance station at

the broken fireplace. "Hm. Second house we've screwed up today."

He lifted an amused eyebrow and continued honing. Shaw had always enjoyed sharpening blades. He liked the sound of steel against stone, he liked rendering dull into keen. He finished one and had just started on the second, when he heard Parker's voice from the parlor. Soft.

"Colter? Can I talk to you?"

He said to Hannah, "Keep watch."

"Got it."

Shaw walked into the parlor. "You all right?"

"Feeling better. Something to say."

He pulled a chair close.

"You asked me about November, if there were some gaps I wanted to fill in."

"You don't need—"

"I do." She adjusted the cushion she was using as a pillow to sit up slightly higher. "That night. Jon's back at the house. Drunk. I'm bloody, lying in the snow beside the pool, my cheek is cracked."

"I remember."

Another hesitation. She inhaled deeply, and this was not from the pain in her leg. Then: "Colter? Jon never touched me that night. November. He never touched me." Her voice caught. She controlled it and continued, "I got his gun. I hit myself in the face a dozen times. Hard. Really hard. I crawled inside the house—left a trail of blood. I called nine-one-one and said he beat me and said he was going to kill me. Two squad cars came right away. Jon had passed out, and I was a bloody mess. They cuffed him and recovered the gun. I told them I got it away and threw it into the bushes."

"Explaining why your prints were on it."

She wiped a tear. "A wife of a cop knows cop things."

"Was he so drunk he thought he'd actually hit you?"

"No. He knew I was setting him up. But his lawyer said the jury would never buy it. My word against his, and I would win. He could get twenty years for attempted. They worked out a plea for the thirty-six months.

"Oh, God, I didn't want to do it. I tried everything I could not to. I got him into therapy, into programs, but none of it worked. If I brought up divorce, that only made him angrier. I knew some night he was going to hurt me or Hannah, bad. Maybe accidentally, thinking we were intruders. But it was going to happen. And then there was the psychic toll on her. I could see her declining. I wasn't going to let that happen. When he left that night I decided: I had to sacrifice my husband for my child.

"So, in answer to your question, back at the fishing lodge: *that's* why he's after me. Every night I hear his voice as the cops led him off. Looking back at me and saying, 'Why are you doing this to me? Why are you doing this to me?'"

"So, he never hurt you?"

"No."

Shaw recalled that the only other person who'd said Jon had hurt her was her mother, Ruth. And she'd been referring to the attack he now knew was staged. "You haven't told anyone else?"

She shook her head. "You're easy to confess to, Colter."

He heard that a lot.

"Hannah?" he asked.

"She suspects. It just sits there between us. It never goes away." A sigh. "A thousand times I thought about confessing. But then I'd go to jail for perjury, and Hannah'd be raised by a dangerous, angry drunk. And my daughter would know what I did. No, I had to stick to my decision." Her eyes looked around the parlor. "Now, Colter. One more thing."

"Go ahead."

"If anything happens here, get Hannah out. Leave me. Promise." Her tone said that this was inflexible.

"All right." No point arguing at a moment like this.

"Now, the Kia, at Timberwolf Lake, the glove compartment. You'll find an envelope. Black. Fireproof. If I'm not around, I want you to get it to my mother. There're instructions inside."

A will? he wondered.

"It's got blueprints and diagrams of a dozen inventions of mine. Technical things, control systems, industrial mechanics . . . I did them on my own time. They're mine, legally. Not HEP's. They're not all finished, but I've got the names of some patent lawyers who can find some people to help. I've left notes, explaining everything." She glanced toward where Hannah stood, peering out the front window. "She doesn't know about it. I've kept it from her. I don't need to freak her out with endgame strategies now. She's been through enough."

Shaw had a sense that the girl would be fine with endgame strategies. But he said, "I'll take care of it."

She squeezed his hand, a weaker gesture than he'd hoped. They'd need that hospital soon.

Parker closed her eyes and lay back.

He returned to the living room and finished sharpening the second blade. Good, not great. Sharp is a function of the quality of the metal, and this knife might cut paper once or twice but would need steeling right after. How would it do on flesh?

Well enough.

Then Hannah cocked her head. Shaw heard it too, the sound of tires in brush and on gravel. He gestured her back and looked carefully through the curtain.

A dark sedan rocked over the uneven, overgrown drive. It pulled into the parking area in front of the cabin. Though dusk was descending, it was still light enough to see the driver.

Sheriff's deputy Kristi Donahue.

Shaw called, "Our ride is here."

"Dope!"

The deputy climbed out, hitched up her service belt and, after looking around, started toward the cabin.

Shaw opened the door. "Deputy!"

"Colter! You're here."

"Keep down. Two hostiles, the high ground behind you. The pair from the hotel."

She stepped back to the car, crouching, using it as cover. She scanned the forest, her hand on her gun. "You're with Ms. Parker and her daughter?"

"They're here. Allison's hurt. Bullet wound. Missed the vitals but we need to get her to surgery."

"There's a hospital twenty minutes away. I'll help you." Staying low, Donahue started toward the cabin.

She got only halfway.

Jon Merritt burst from the brush beside the driveway, a backpack over his shoulder, a pistol in his hand. He leveled the revolver at the woman and before Shaw could bark a word of warning, he fired two rounds, striking her in the head.

The deputy fell like a discarded doll to the grass, which was by then already dotted with her blood.

79

Hannah screamed.

Allison Parker called from the parlor, "Han! What?"

Mouth open, eyes wide, the girl stared out the window.

Shaw watched Jon pocket the dead deputy's pistol, her two extra mags and phone. He pulled the girl away from the windows and closed the drapes again, then he slammed the door and wedged the chair back under the knob.

Hannah was sobbing. "No . . ."

When Shaw looked again, Merritt was gone.

Shaw turned toward Parker. "It was Jon. He killed her. The deputy."

"Jesus, no . . ."

It was then that Shaw noticed that the woman's car was still idling.

Kristi Donahue hadn't shut the engine off when she'd arrived. Merritt hadn't noted this. He'd neutralized a threat and, in a hurry to rendezvous with his hitmen, he'd forgotten about the vehicle.

Scanning the forest. No threat from him or the Twins. Not yet.

How long would it take Shaw, Parker and Hannah to get to the sedan? Twenty seconds.

While the short move would be painful for the woman, there was no other choice. He'd carry her to the car and, basically, shove her into the back. They'd speed away before the three hostiles, hearing her scream, could arrive and start firing.

He called to Hannah, "We're going to the car." She was staring toward the window, not seeing a thing. He said firmly, "You with me? Hannah. I need you with me."

And like flipping a switch her eyes came to life. She inhaled, wiped tears away with her fingers and nodded.

"Get your mother up."

She vanished into the parlor. Shaw looked again outside. Still clear.

He joined the girl and they helped Parker into the living room. "Oh, no," she whispered, looking through a gap in the curtain. The pool of blood was slowly growing.

Shaw got his arm around her shoulders and helped her to the front door.

Hannah glanced at her feet and saw a bolo. She picked it up. Hefted its weight.

Shaw started to open the door.

Just as a human form appeared in the woods, pushing through the brush.

Crouching, Jon Merritt hurried to the car once again. He stepped unceremoniously over Kristi's body, reached into the passenger compartment, shut the engine off and pocketed the keys. He started to leave but noted something in the backseat. Opening the door, he took out a short black pump shotgun on a strap and a green and yellow box of shells.

He turned toward the forest to meet his triggermen, who would be easing carefully through the woods for the final attack.

Hannah exhaled slowly, her face a mask without expression.

She was no longer crying, though her mother was. "No, no," Parker said breathlessly, wincing. She was leaning against the parlor doorjamb.

They would probably know by now the detergent box target was a trick—otherwise one of the occupants would've fired when Merritt came back to snatch the keys and scattergun.

"What now?" Hannah asked coolly.

It had come down to the twenty percent option.

Shaw pointed from one side window to the other. "Escape routes. Before they come, they'll fire into the cabin. I'll be watching. That'll give me their positions. There'll be a lull before they come in. They'll be worried about cross fire, hitting each other. I'll tell you which window's best to go out of. Get into the brush and just keep going as fast as you can. Follow the shore. Circle around to the far side of the lake. It's not that far to the highway, the one that leads to Millton. Flag down somebody."

The girl nodded.

The twenty percent referred to the success of getting out of the cabin. Once they were in the bush their chances increased dramatically. The woodland was dense and the sun was nearly down; covering darkness was spreading.

But getting over the twenty percent hump was going to be tough. Would one or all of them be hit when the three men peppered the cabin? And if they did make it out, would they be picked off in the yard before they made it to the relative safety of the woods?

Parker said, "The lake . . . Swim?"

"Too cold and not with your leg."

A scan of the grounds. Nothing out the front or the other side window.

Where were they?

The snake you can't see is worse . . .

Hannah was studying the side yard, east, then west.

He saw her focused eyes, her stance.

This took him back to the Compound, when he was her age.

Sixteen. Stalking through woods similar to the ones surrounding them now, armed with the Colt Python, following two sets of tracks—his father's, and those of the man who was hunting him.

Sixteen. Rappelling down a hundred-foot cliff to Ashton's body.

Sixteen. Resolving to find and kill that killer himself.

Hannah's voice was urgent. "Mr. Shaw, you made it sound like you're not coming too. Aren't you?"

"Not right away. I'm going to get one of their weapons."

"I'll help you." The words were crisp and unwavering. She lifted a bolo.

"No. Your mother'll need you."

She paused. Finally she whispered, "All right."

Shaw looked over the pathetic weapons they had: a kitchen knife and canoe paddle, bolos, a hammer.

MacGyver . . .

He was about to check the surroundings again. But just then Shaw's eyes cut to the girl's. He cocked his head. She nodded. Again, they'd heard something at the same time.

Footsteps were approaching the front door.

The attacker had come from one side yard while Hannah was checking out the other.

"Down." He gripped the knife in one hand, the hammer in the other and walked to the door. Hannah helped her mother to the floor and picked up one of the bolos again. She swung it ominously back and forth.

Volleyball . . .

A moment of howling silence, tension flooding the room.

And then:

"Alli, Hannah. It's me."

"Jon?" Parker gasped.

Shaw looked out briefly. Yes, there he stood alone. "Merritt, I'm armed."

A faint chuckle. "Armed? With a kitchen knife and some kind of slingshot."

Thuds sounded on the resonant porch.

"All my weapons. There they are. My hands are up."

Shaw glanced outside. Merritt stood at the bottom of the steps, wincing. He was in pain. His arms were skyward. On the porch were the deputy's Glock, two revolvers and the shotgun. The backpack too.

He said, "Just tugging up the clothes, giving you a look."

Shaw had, for no reason, expected a low, raspy voice. But Merritt's was soft and tenor.

With his left hand, Merritt lifted his windbreaker shirttail and jacket and turned slowly. No other weapons. Shaw noticed a massive bruise on his belly.

"I'd just as soon not stand out here much longer. I saw those two assholes in the woods and they're not very far away. Sorry, Han. Language."

80

First, Shaw secured the weapons.

This was not governed by a never rule. Though if there were one, it would read: Never be stupid.

He took the Glock, made sure it was loaded and a round chambered. It went into his waistband, right rear. An easy, practiced draw. Two mags in the left front pocket of his jeans.

The others—the two revolvers and the shotgun—he checked and set in the corner.

"Car keys?"

"Right pocket." A nod at the windbreaker. "Two sets. Mine and hers."

"Toss it. The whole jacket."

He did, wincing once more.

Shaw fished out and pocketed the keys.

"The wall."

Merritt knew what Shaw meant and he complied, feet

spread, palms flat against the ugly green wallpaper. Despite the lifted-shirt routine Shaw frisked him carefully, with his left hand, keeping the Glock muzzle near his neck. Shaw relieved him of a phone.

"PIN?" Shaw asked.

Merritt gave him the numbers. "But it's not working, hasn't been for a half hour."

Unlocking the unit, he saw that the screen didn't say NO SERVICE. It was simply blank, though the unit was powered on.

"The radio." He pointed outside to Kristi's sedan.

"It's not a sheriff's cruiser," Merritt said. "It's her private car."

Shaw said, "We drive out." He looked at Merritt. "With you restrained."

The man shook his head. "We wouldn't get fifty feet. They're up the ridge, those two, waiting for you. They've got long guns. With scopes. The Buick's a half mile up the road. After dark, I'm thinking we'll start the Chrysler." A nod toward Donahue's car. "Gun the engine. That'll distract them. Then hike north through the woods to the Buick. Get to Millton."

A look outside. Yes, if they were on the ridge—and it was a logical place to be—they could pepper the car with hunting rounds. Merritt's plan was not a bad one.

Parker asked, "How long till dark?"

Shaw glanced to the sky, a rich blue, bleeding to gray. "Forty, fifty minutes."

He then said, "Sit," and Merritt did.

He looked over to his ex-wife sitting on the floor.

"A.P., how is it, your leg?" Using what must have been a pet name from the old days.

She didn't answer. She seemed capable only of staring at the man.

Shaw answered for her. "It's not a bleeder. I've done what I can, but I want her in a hospital soon."

"In the backpack," Merritt said. "Pills. Painkillers. I took 'em off a tweaker about two miles from here. He told me you'd been hit."

The shot he'd heard. Was it Bee he'd had the run-in with? And was the young man no longer of this earth?

Shaw unzipped the backpack and pulled out a plastic bag, large, though it contained only one small bag of white pills.

"Oxy," Merritt said. "The real thing. Stolen from inventory. It's safe. No fent or anything else mixed in."

Parker said, "Not now. If I need it." Maybe thinking of her husband's addiction.

"No, A.P. You'll have to be able to move. And move fast. Take one. Hannah? There water here?"

The girl's cool façade had dissolved, and, uncertain, she glanced at Shaw, who nodded. She stepped into the kitchen, ran a glass and brought it to her mother, who took the pill that Shaw offered.

He looked at the larger bag, dusted with meth residue.

Noticing his eyes, Merritt said, "The kid had some deliveries of ice in there too. I dumped it." He shrugged. "Once a cop . . ." He examined Shaw. "I saw you on your cycle, at Alli's rental. I decided you weren't blue, but that pat down, maybe I was wrong. You've done this before. You ever law?"

Shaw didn't answer. He nodded to the backpack. He asked, "Other weapon?"

"Sort of." The men's eyes met and Merritt seemed almost amused at his own ambiguous response. "It's wrapped up in a towel."

Shaw dug through the bag. He found a bottle of Bulleit bourbon, what looked like an antique metal desk clock, food, papers, clothing and, at the bottom, something heavy wrapped up in terry cloth. He opened it. For a moment he didn't move.

No . . .

He was holding the scorched metal frame of his Colt Python, the grip burned away. The last Shaw had seen of the weapon it was in the fire pit at the lodge on Timberwolf Lake. Merritt said, "Had to be yours."

Shaw nodded.

"A fine weapon," Merritt continued. "Thought you wouldn't want to lose it. A gunsmith can fix it up. Good as new."

Shaw now studied Merritt and was aware that prison had not been kind. He was pale, and eyes sallow. The thinning hair added to this image. He'd lost muscle recently. He slouched.

Hannah spoke in a whisper of disbelief. "You shot her!"

It was Colter Shaw who responded. "I don't think Kristi was who she seemed to be."

Merritt added, "She *was* a Marshall County deputy,

that's true. But she was working with them, those two who burned up your camper."

"But," Parker whispered, "*you* hired them . . ."

Merritt appeared confused. "Me? Where'd you get that idea?"

"This's a trick," Hannah blurted. She turned her fierce eyes toward him. "You killed Mom's lawyer!"

"Oh, David? He's fine. Well, pissed off, I don't doubt. But fine. He's out by now."

"Out?" Parker asked.

"I thought he knew where you were hiding. He didn't. After we had a talk I was convinced of that. But I didn't know if I could trust him, so I taped him up in the basement of one of the old factories on Manufacturers Row. I mailed letters to the police and his paralegal telling them where he was. Mail, you know, with a stamp. I didn't want him out too soon.

"No, Han. I didn't hurt him. I didn't hurt anybody, the past couple days. Not seriously. Shot a clay pot of your friend Dorella's."

"What?"

"No danger. Just needed her and her shotgun back in the house. And I stole this woman's Buick. Mrs. Butler. Threatened her, scared her some. But I didn't hurt her. That tweaker I got the drugs from? I shot him, yeah, but only in the foot. I couldn't have him running back to his kin. I needed to get on your trail. He probably got a concussion when he fainted and hit the ground. Felt bad about it. But, then again, that boy did not make a very wise career decision."

Parker seemed to be wrestling with all this. Trying to decide whether or not to believe him.

Colter Shaw was inclined to. About seventy to eighty percent.

A chill voice, Hannah's, asked stridently, "And Mr. Villaine?"

"Villaine? What about him?" Merritt's pale brow furrowed. "Oh, no . . . is he?" His shoulders slumped farther.

"He's dead," Parker said angrily.

"Jesus Christ . . . No, no . . ." He looked in the direction of the hill in front of the cabin. "They found out about him because of me." Dismay flared. Merritt lowered his head to his hands. "I was so stupid . . ."

Parker said, "I don't understand . . . Any of this."

But Colter Shaw did. Finally. He looked over the former cop as he sat placidly in the stern wooden chair. "He hasn't been trying to kill you. He's been trying to save you."

"That's a fact, sir." Merritt directed a smile toward his daughter. "And what've you two been doing the whole time? Playing hide-and-seek."

81

Something about me being released from County was wrong from the start."

But then Merritt stopped talking, glanced at his daughter. "You colored it. Your hair. It's nice."

She gave no response, just looked back with a steady gaze, then returned to surveillance duty.

Shaw said, "You thought you were being set up."

He nodded. "Didn't make sense. Good behavior? Doesn't get you out earlier, not unless it's in the plea deal. And to free up beds? Since when does County give a shit about conditions in a fucking lockup?" To Hannah. "Sorry."

"Look around," the girl said. "Let's take language off the table."

"Somebody wanted you on the street," Shaw said.

"Yessir." He eyed the glass of rusty water sitting on the coffee table. "Can I?"

Shaw nodded. The man downed it in gulps, wiped his lips. He paused and lowered his head. Shaw wondered if he'd be sick. But he controlled the sensation. Breathing deep. Slowly.

"But who and why? One idea occurred to me. Yesterday, I went to see the head of one of the crews. Guy named Dom Ryan. The two of us, we had an arrangement a few years ago when I was running OC cases. He helped me take down a couple of the really bad crews. I looked the other way on a few of his deals. So yesterday I paid him to make some calls and find out if there'd been any special service orders involving me."

Parker frowned and Shaw said, "He means contracts. Professional killing."

Merritt continued, "Ryan found out that, yeah, somebody'd ordered a hit. My name was attached. But *I* couldn't've been the target."

Shaw said, "Nobody's easier to kill than a con in prison. You'd get shanked in the yard and that would be it. Questions wouldn't be asked."

"Exactly. The hit had to be you." He was looking at Allison.

"Me?" she gasped.

"Whoever got me released made sure I had a motive: I was supposed to be furious at you. The triggermen would make it look like a murder-suicide. I'd kill you, then myself."

Bewildered, Parker asked, "What do you mean 'furious'?"

"That was the other reason I knew my release was

bogus. The letter from you to the discharge board, telling them not to let me out, that I was dangerous."

"What letter?" Parker said. "I never wrote anything."

He glanced at Shaw again, then to the backpack. Shaw nodded and Merritt retrieved some sheets of paper. "The letters about my release. Look at the last one." He handed them to Parker and she flipped through them.

"This's forged," she whispered.

"I know." He said to Shaw, "It's all about how I hurt Alli and Hannah, was abusive all our marriage."

Parker stared at the letter. "No, no, no . . ."

"I was an asshole, sure, but only for the last couple of years."

Shaw remembered that Parker had said the marriage was good until the Beacon Hill shooting and his descent into drugs and drinking. And that he never physically hurt either of them.

"And that last paragraph."

Parker skipped to the end. She frowned. "What on earth is this?"

"It says how she knows some secrets of mine that I don't want revealed."

She gave a pallid laugh. "Secrets? You? Makes it sound like you were mixed up in the corruption scandals." She looked at Shaw. "He was the most honest cop on FPD. When he started, on Vice, on the riverfront? More pimps went to jail for trying to bribe him than running girls. Oh, and the day he was shot? He'd just found twenty thousand dollars of payoff money, skimmed from the cleanup fund. Hidden in a dead drop at a construction site. He could've pocketed it. But the first thing he did when he came out of surgery was tell his captain about the cash."

Merritt said, "And look at the bottom of the letter. The redaction?"

Shaw saw two thick lines under the woman's name.

"It's not very redacted."

She held it up. "You can see the address of our rental. Whoever did it *wanted* you to know where we lived."

"I was supposed to go there right after I got out. Didn't matter if I was going to warn you, or kill you myself, or just visit. The point was to get me to your rental house. The triggermen'd be waiting. They'd do the job." He shrugged. "I didn't know all this then. All I knew was: contract hit, you were the target, and I couldn't trust police or anyone else. I had to find you both, get you out of town, until I figured out who was behind it.

"I didn't have your new number, emails, social media. I couldn't find you anywhere online. I had no idea where you were. And who was there to help me? Marty Harmon, your mother? They wouldn't believe a word I told them."

"So that was a lie somebody told David: about the prisoners you'd told you wanted to kill me."

"What?" he scoffed. And didn't bother to state the obvious: that was part of the setup too. To support the claim that he was in fact murderous.

Merritt slicked back his thinning blond hair, and his face deflated. "Then I made my mistake. Oh, man, did I screw up. I paid Ryan again—this time to help me find you. He says sure. And what does that prick do?"

Shaw said, "Called up the triggermen and whoever hired them and cut a deal. You gave Ryan the leads you'd found, and he sent them right to the killers. And when *they* found a lead, Ryan sent it to you."

"That's right. He didn't have any quote 'contacts' in the county, like he promised me. It was those two." An angry nod toward where Suit and Jacket waited atop the hill in front of the cabin. "I thought you might go to a women's shelter. Ryan told them. They went to check it out. Thank God, you weren't at any of them. Who knows what they would have done to the staff?

"And they were the ones that saw Han's selfie and figured out about the motel. They told Ryan. He told me. I was heading up there when you got away."

Bitterness flooded his face. "I might as well've been texting the triggermen directly." Then a shake of the head. "I found the name Frank Villaine and thought that might be a lead. Could Ryan find the address? He did and gave it to those two, as well as me. He hoped the murders would go down there. But you were gone."

Hell of a coordinated plan, Shaw reflected, wondering again who was behind it.

Merritt gave a grim laugh. "And finally . . . finally, I got it that something was wrong. They needed to get me to where they'd tracked you down—for the murder-suicide—at Timberwolf. But how did Ryan's contacts know you were there?

"Just didn't seem right. I went up there but stayed out

of sight. I saw them burning the camper. And I saw you escape. And just after that, she got there." A nod toward the front, where Donohue's body lay. "The guy in the suit handed her an envelope. I went after you on foot. Then I got a text from Ryan, some bullshit about your being spotted in the cabin here by local police or somebody. Of course, the truth was the triggermen'd found you and told him where. I slipped around them and came through the woods from the north."

Shaw asked, "And no idea who put out the contract?"

"No. Ryan said he tried, but—bullshit. He lied and took my money." Merritt gazed toward his ex-wife. "So why? Why would somebody want you dead? All I could think was it was some project you're involved with at HEP."

Parker grew thoughtful. "Well, I'm the only one who could finish the fuel rod containment vessel on schedule. To find somebody else and bring them up to speed, the Pocket Suns'd be delayed at least a year. That might be the end of the company."

Colter Shaw, however, had another theory. He said to Merritt, "So. You go to Ryan and ask about a special services contract."

"Right."

"And word comes back there is one—and your name's attached."

He nodded.

"But Allison's not 'Merritt.' She kept her maiden name."

Silence for a moment. Then Parker gasped. Merritt whispered, "Hannah?"

The girl's eyes narrowed.

It was only a sixty, sixty-five percent hypothesis but it seemed logical.

"Why?" Merritt asked.

"I don't know. Not yet. Maybe you witnessed something . . ." A thought occurred. "Maybe you *photographed* something. One of your selfies. At the fishing lodge, they burned your phone and computer. Why go to the trouble unless they wanted your files destroyed?"

At this thought he upped the likelihood to seventy-five percent.

The girl lifted her palms. "But, I mean, which one? I've taken, like, thousands of pictures."

Jon Merritt pointed to the backpack. "The envelope?" Shaw handed it to him.

"I found these in your room. I thought they might have some clues about where you and your mother might go to."

Hannah, while obviously concerned with the direction of the conversation, continued scanning for threats. She met Shaw's eyes and he nodded. His encouragement clearly pleased her.

Shaw helped Parker onto the couch. He and Merritt sat beside her. Merritt began flipping slowly through the stack.

In the images, Hannah tended to assume the same expressions—cynical, doubtful, wryly amused, sardonic.

Similar poses too: cocked head and hip. Sometimes fingers making signs that teens would know. Her outfits were more or less the same too: stocking cap, sweats and jeans, all of dark hue. Gloves without fingertips.

She stood in front of car wrecks and buildings being demolished, over dead fish in the Kenoah, bleak winter landscapes, collapsed buildings, protests about climate change and about the decision of United Defense to back out of their plans to build in Ferrington, a street demonstration about the Tasing of a Black motorist by angry white officers, factory scenes, snide teenagers mocking a gay couple, a pickup with four hunters in the bed holding shotguns, one of them about fifty sticking his tongue out flirtatiously at her, a drunk passed out in front of a tavern.

Dozens flipped by.

"Stop," Shaw said.

"What is it?" Parker asked. "You see something?"

As he stared at the selfie in front of them, another theory arose—and if it panned out, it might possibly reveal the *why* of the hit.

And when you have the *why*, the *who* is often not far behind.

Shaw considered all the moving pieces as he stared at the dingy ceiling. He asked Merritt, "You got Frank Villaine's address from Dom Ryan?"

"That's right. I found a work email Frank sent you, A.P. I couldn't get a local address. Ryan did."

Shaw said, "Now, the question is, how did *I* get Frank's name?"

Parker and Merritt regarded each other. She said, "Marianne, didn't you say?"

"She gave it to me, yes. But she was only asking your coworkers about your old friends. Did you ever tell anyone in the office about Frank and where he lived?"

Shaking her head. "No. By the time I went to HEP, Frank and I had gone our separate ways."

And with this bit of information, hypothesis became proof.

"Where did Marianne Keller really get Frank's name and address? From Dom Ryan."

"But Marianne works—"

Shaw finished her sentence. "For the man who ordered the hit. Your boss, Marty Harmon."

82

Harmon put this all together—getting you released, forging the letter from Alli—because he couldn't let anyone see these."

He laid out several selfies before him. He tapped one.

The image depicted Hannah in the foreground, wearing a bulky sweatshirt and a stocking cap. Behind her was a gaping doorway, forty or so feet high, opening onto a gloomy and gray warehouse. Five men stood inside, at work. What was distinctive visually was that while the image was largely monochrome, the orange safety vests of the employees stood out boldly and formed a pentagram. It was a striking photo, well composed.

Two of the workers seemed to be looking the girl's way. One bore a troubled expression.

Inside, in the back, were hundreds of pallets of bottled water. And several tanker trucks.

Parker was squinting and sitting forward to see.

"That's HEP. Building Three. The warehouse near the river."

Hannah said, "I took it when I was staying after school with Mom. I was bored, so I walked around and took pictures."

"What're you thinking, Colter?" Parker asked.

He found another of their daughter's selfies. Two workers in Building Three were running a large rubber hose from one of the tanker trucks parked inside the cavernous building to a drain in the floor.

Shaw asked, "Does that drain lead to the river?"

"Probably. Building Three's over a hundred years old. Most of the drains lead to the river. I thought they were sealed. They should have been."

"They're open now. It's toxic waste. Harmon's intentionally polluting the Kenoah."

"Why the hell?" Merritt asked.

Shaw pointed to other pictures in front of him, selfies from the same series, taken at the company. He asked Parker, "Have you ever had a radiation leak at the plant?"

"No, never."

"Anywhere in the area? Any accidents at all?"

"No . . ." Then she frowned. "Well, there was a traffic crash a few miles east of there. About six weeks ago. One of our trucks taking spent fuel rods to a disposal site missed a turn and—"

Shaw said, "And went into the river."

"A tributary, I think. But, yes. Same thing."

"Upstream of downtown?"

"That's right. But there was no radioactive spill."

"How do you know?"

"Because a spill would have to be reported. Nuclear Regulatory Commission. The state too."

"That doesn't mean there wasn't a spill. It just means no one reported it."

"But . . ." Her voice faded.

Merritt was catching on. The former detective asked Parker, "How was the crash handled? Police called?"

"No police. No need. Single-vehicle accident. Marty took care of everything himself." Parker frowned. "You know, one thing was odd. The driver of the truck? He quit, just after the accident. Moved out West."

"No," Merritt muttered. "He didn't move anywhere."

Hannah turned away briefly from her watchman duties. "You mean, Mr. Harmon had him . . . killed?"

Her father nodded. "I'm afraid so, honey."

Shaw said, "Now look at this one." He tapped the image in front of him. Behind Hannah in this shot were pallets of chemical drums. One set of drums was stenciled with the letters KI, the others with DTPA.

Shaw said, "The first one's the symbol for potassium iodide."

"My God," Parker said. "But that's . . ."

"An antidote for radiation poisoning. The second one, DTPA's diethylenetriamine pentaacetic acid. It binds to particles of radioactive material in the bloodstream and they pass out of the body through urine."

A look to Parker. "There *was* a spill when that truck went into the river and it got into the Ferrington water supply. Then Harmon polluted the river intentionally with toxins, so everybody at risk would drink the bottled water he gave them—water laced with the antidote. He couldn't afford even the hint of a radiation leak."

"How do you know about this stuff?" Merritt asked.

Hannah answered. "Mr. Shaw, like, knows everything. His father was a survivalist."

Shaw, Russell and Dorion had had a hundred hours of training in toxins and antidotes, radiation included. His sister took a particular liking to all things nuclear.

Merritt scoffed. "The great benefactor of the city . . . Bullshit." Then he was frowning. "But he'd do all this, just to cover his own ass?"

Parker said, "Oh, nuclear's always controversial. We have to do everything right. The smallest accident, with any injuries? It could close down the company."

Hannah now asked, "What do you think, Mr. Shaw? How much time till it's dark enough to leave?"

He joined her and gazed up at the sky. "Twenty minutes."

Merritt, his eyes on Parker, said, "Shaw, Hannah, you two keep an eye out, would you? I want a word alone with my wife."

83

I n the parlor of the hunting lodge, door closed, Allison Parker sat slowly back on the couch that had been her hospital bed for the past few hours.

The pill had been humming like a quiet engine and she was nearly pain free. And not as groggy as she'd expected. It was one hell of a drug and she could see why Jon had fallen for it.

She watched her ex-husband pull up a chair and sit opposite her, the same chair, the same spot where Colter Shaw had just been.

Jon Merritt . . . the man who had once been her husband, the man with whom she'd shared so very much.

With whom she'd spent joyous and energetic and playful times in bed.

With whom she'd created a child, a beautiful and smart and unique child.

With whom she'd fought bitterly to save herself and that very daughter.

He sighed.

And as he did, Parker cocked her head and inhaled. She tried not to react but suspected the tiniest of frowns crossed her face.

Jon laughed. "Can't smell anything, can you?"

"I . . ." She was blushing.

"It's all right. No, I haven't had a drink since the day of my sentencing. And for the record, not a wise idea to show up drunk in front of a judge."

She glanced toward the door, referring, in silence, to the bottle of bourbon, which Colter Shaw had removed from the backpack.

"I bought it yesterday morning. I needed to see that I could handle it. Never even opened it. The most powerful stuff I've been drinking since I've been out's been Pepsi. Straight, no chaser."

She said, "I heard about that—in the Al-Anon meetings. People who were dry would sometimes get a bottle and keep it close. To test themselves."

He nodded. "You were in Al-Anon. Hannah Alateen. You did that for me."

Parker shrugged. "Didn't last long. For her. Me either."

He sighed. "That's not on you, A.P. The program only works if I meet you halfway. And I didn't get close." He rested his palm on her unwounded thigh, tentatively, as if prepared for her to whisk it off.

She didn't.

He said, "We don't have much time. Need to get a few things said."

"Jon."

"Need to."

This was his imploring self. From the old days. Dead serious and orbiting around the important.

But, my God, he was a man who would talk to you. And listen. How rare is that?

"Okay," she whispered.

"Beacon Hill."

This wasn't what she'd been expecting. She thought he would bring up her betrayal under the seahorse.

He spoke the next words slowly. "The Beacon Hill incident . . . Sounds kind of like a thriller novel, doesn't it?"

Allison Parker wouldn't know. *Advanced Semiconductor Applications in Radioactive Environments* was on her bedside table.

He said, "Truth's like a splinter, don't you think? That's what the doctor told me in County. Dr. Evans. Good man. A splinter. It's got to come out one way or the other."

She had no idea where he was going. But nodded encouragingly.

"Beacon Hill . . . Meth-head father, family, hostages, barricade, weapons. Gunshots reported. Danny and I armor up and go in, no time for SWAT. We get inside, and right off, Danny's hit. The shooter was in full body armor."

Jon was breathing hard now, as if he'd just run a race. "Son of a bitch keeps firing and firing . . . Christ, there were bullets everywhere. The only cover in the room was this bookcase. With all the books, the slugs weren't penetrating. Except there's somebody hiding there. It's his daughter, home from college."

"The only victim who died." She felt a chill within her. Was this going where she thought?

"And the father's getting closer, firing constantly. Must've had a twenty-round mag. I had to get to cover. One slug was an inch from my ear. I could hear it over the sound of the gunshot. They break the sound barrier. He aims again and—" His voice clenched. "And I know he's going to get me. So I just grabbed the daughter and pushed her out. I got behind the bookcase. She gets hit."

She recalled the girl was shot multiple times.

"Oh, Jon . . ."

His pallid face was a mask, maybe the most wrenching expression she'd ever seen on him. Worse even than on November 15 as he was led off in cuffs.

"Then, finally, there's a pause. He's reloading. I step out fast and take him down. I know he's gone. I call for medical and try to help the girl. But . . ."

Six shots, Parker was thinking. What could he do?

"She didn't die right away, A.P. She stared at me, looking confused, like she'd asked me an important question and was waiting for the answer. And then she was gone too."

Tears appeared in his eyes. She put her hand on his.

"But your leg . . . Oh . . ."

He nodded. Wiped his face. "I gloved up, finished reloading the perp's gun and hit myself in the body armor, and then parked one in my thigh. Make it look real.

I lay down in front of Danny, like I'd been hit, shielding him."

"Jon . . ."

"I killed her, A.P. I told myself I did it because he'd stop shooting when he saw his own daughter. Give me a chance to acquire. But that was bullshit. I might as well've just used my own piece on her. I should've gone down for second-degree murder or aggravated manslaughter. But, no, I ended up the Hero of Beacon Hill. The ceremony, the articles, the looks when I walked into the station . . . The more adoring they were, the more it stabbed me."

"So *that* was the pain you were trying to stop. The drugs, the drinking."

"Oh, the leg? That was nothing." He glanced at hers. "You'll find that out in a couple of weeks. No, it was the girl's eyes asking me that question. I saw her everywhere. I was lying in our bed, walking down the street, physical therapy, driving . . . doing *anything*. The drugs dulled it. After that the booze. But she kept coming back.

"Half the times I came home wasted? I'd been out to her grave in Forest Lawn. I'd buy a bottle before I went and finish it there or on the way home."

Parker frowned. "November fifteenth. The anniversary of Beacon Hill."

He nodded.

She touched the side of his head, the hair above his left ear. This was a place where she would seat her face when they made love, a connection that she found so very comforting and, when the moment arrived, electrical.

What plagued him wasn't psychosis. It was guilt.

"You didn't plan it," she whispered.

"I made the choice."

"Did you? Let the engineer have a word."

He looked into her eyes.

"It was action, reaction. You pick up a hot pan, pull back and smack your baby in the nose. Not for all the money on earth would you hurt her. But it happened. You do things automatically to survive."

Then her head was down and she felt tears. She whispered, "I did the same thing. I sent you to prison."

"To save yourself and Han." He shook his head. "Ain't we a pair, A.P.?"

"Hannah suspects I did it."

"Oh, her father can do no wrong in her eyes?"

Then his expression changed and another item on the agenda appeared.

"Have you noticed anything about my marvelous complexion? Don't have much of a tan."

She gave a laugh. "You've been in jail for nearly a year, Jon."

"I'd still be looking this way if I'd been sunbathing in the Bahamas."

He displayed some puncture wounds on his arm.

She frowned.

"Chemo."

She stared at the needle marks. "Oh, Jon, no!"

"Found out about two months ago. Been with me for a while, looks like. I knew I was feeling bad, but they don't have the best doctors in County. They had a good shrink, but the internist was a kid. Treating cons for practice. I had a session at Trevor County Med yesterday. Then went to my motel room and puked like I'd been drinking. Only, this time I was sober, so I could enjoy the lovely experience to its fullest."

She was about to ask about the prognosis, which she had always found an ugly word, fit only for medical pros, not to be used among those we loved.

But she didn't need to. He'd understand it was the next logical question. He said, "It's not looking too good. They don't tell you exactly, you know. But I got a little time left in me." A grin. Then he said briskly, "Enough of this, A.P. Right now we got work to do. Let's get to it."

He turned his hand over and pressed hers, palm to palm, and he helped her stand.

84

Colter Shaw said, "Dark enough."

The four were in the front room. Shaw and Hannah had been looking out the windows. He had seen nothing of the Twins. The girl confirmed that she hadn't either.

"Ah, Han," Merritt said to his daughter. "Something I brought for you."

The incongruity was almost funny. The man sounded as if he'd just arrived at a party with a gift for the birthday girl.

He took the backpack. "We had a metalworking shop in prison. For rehab. Somebody'd try to make a crossbow or knife sometimes, but what we were *supposed* to make were coatracks and boot scrapers. You remember our project? That we were working on when I went out—that night in November?"

"For class. We had to make some historical thing. Something to do with Ferrington."

"I said I'd be back and we'd finish it." He clicked his tongue. "And we know how that ended."

She nodded, her face solemn.

"Well, here it is."

He pulled out the clock that Shaw had seen earlier when he'd searched the bag.

Hannah actually gasped, looking at the thing. She whispered, "The Water Clock."

Shaw hadn't paid attention before but he now saw that it was a faithful reproduction of what he'd seen on the Carnegie Building beside the Kenoah.

The only difference was that the hands were not in the angel wings pose.

"It really works. Water drips from here." He tapped a reservoir in the top. "And turns the gears. Probably wouldn't want to run railroads according to it, or schedule airliners, but it's accurate enough. I tried it out."

She hugged him. "It's so cool! Bring it with." And held it out.

Merritt stood away from the girl. "You hold on to it."

She frowned. "But . . ."

He said, "You all go first." He picked up the keys to the deputy's car and handed the Buick's to Shaw. "A half mile up the road, on the right. I nosed her into some juniper and forsythia."

"No, Daddy, come with us!"

Merritt said, "We've gotta be smart about this. Trick 'em. You hike out through the woods. I'll start up the car, drive it back and forth, like it's stuck. You drive to Millton and send back the cavalry."

"Jon, no!" Parker said.

"It's all going to be fine. When I left prison yesterday, this guard, he said I was a lucky man. Well, he put it a little different. But he did say 'lucky.' And I am. Luckiest man in the world." He cast a look to his daughter. "Hey, Han, come here a minute."

Merritt stepped to the corner and Hannah joined him. He bent down, his mouth close to his daughter's ear. He whispered. As he did her face grew still. Then he stepped back and watched her, his own expression one of uncertainty. After a moment she hugged him and she too whispered words that were also inaudible to Shaw and Parker.

Merritt joined Shaw and they distributed weapons. Shaw took the Glock, Merritt the shotgun, and he placed the revolvers and extra ammunition into the backpack, which he slung over his shoulder.

The men shook hands.

Merritt walked to his former wife, hugged her and kissed her cheek.

"Daddy, please . . ." Hannah tried one more time.

"All good, Han." He laughed. "There're only two of 'em. Against me? They don't stand a chance."

85

Lying in a clearing on the hill overlooking the cabin, Moll wondered how long it would be until their reinforcements arrived. Three more men, three more guns.

He scanned the scene, the barrel of the long Winchester, the gun he loved like kin, easing back and forth as he sighted along the porch. The moon was low and lopped in half, but it provided some light. Enough to shoot by.

A glance down. His phone showed the time, but there was still no signal. That wouldn't last. Marty Harmon had told him the power to the local cell tower could only be cut for so long.

He let the gun sit on the sandbag he was using for a shooting rest and sprayed Benadryl on his arms and neck.

He scanned the cabin again, Kristi's car, her body . . .

A crack of twig behind him. He turned, pistol ready.

The men Harmon had sent to help finish the job.

Desmond had led them from where they'd parked, next to the Transit, on a nearby logging road. Beside his partner was a heavyset redhead of about fifty and, behind, two men who seemed to be in their late twenties. They were all dressed in dark clothing, jackets and chino-style pants, tactical gear lite. The younger ones toted long gray plastic cases.

Moll had known Dominic Ryan for years. The man had hired him and Desmond a few times to make some bodies and dispose of them. And he'd also hired them to dispose of bodies that Ryan's men themselves had made.

Crazy thing, this present job: Harmon hiring Moll and Desmond to kill the girl—along with her mother and Merritt himself, making it look like a revenge murder-suicide. Then, out of the blue, Merritt pays Ryan to find out if there was an open hit. Ryan jumped at the chance and called Moll, who put Ryan and Harmon together. It became a joint venture, which it needed to be because the missus and the kid took off. A four-hour job turned into this mess.

Moll stood, looked over the young coworkers. The bony pair had sneery faces, even when they weren't sneering, and Moll could imagine them looking forward to beating people for late vig payments and protection money.

Moll thought again about the Irish rebels in a past life.

"The Rising of the Moon." Ah, that was the song.

Moll and Harmon had decided that since the murder-suicide fiction would no longer work, they'd create a new scenario: the killing of the family would look like revenge for one of Merritt's past cases. Maybe one of those ganja crews, maybe one of the corrupt county officials he'd brought down. Ryan would get some confidential informants to leak the word. Maybe one of the Irish kids had some weed and they would plant it here. Point fingers at the Jamaicans. Shaw would die too.

Dawndue . . .

Ryan didn't introduce the skinny men who were with him but nodded them aside as he walked up to Moll, squatted in his sniper nest and looked over at the cabin.

"They're in there?" Ryan asked.

"That is correct."

"Who?"

"Merritt, his ex, the girl. And Motorcycle Man."

"Thoughts?" Ryan asked.

Desmond said, "Merritt's got a car somewhere, but it can't be that close and I don't think they'll hike to it. One of 'em's hurt. We saw blood, fresh."

"Which one?"

Moll said, "Woman, I think. So. They'll try and take Kristi's car."

"Where is she?"

"Can't you see?" Moll asked, suddenly irritated.

Squinting and scanning the area, Ryan grunted when he noted her body. "Shit. She was good. She drove getaway a couple jobs for me and lost investigation reports at the sheriff's office. That sucks."

It did. All the more because a couple of times she'd spent the night at Moll's house. It was after Chloe and before Jean. She'd been more interested in the faux furniture than the sex but that was more or less true for Moll himself. He said he'd paint her a piece but never got around to it.

The two kids removed Bushmaster M4s from the cases—short, black assault rifles. They went through the ritual of loading and charging. Moll had never understood the label, and the stigma attached to it. "Assault." They were no different from any other semiautomatic rifle—one finger pull, one shot. A deer did not care one bit if it was hit by a slug from a scary-looking soldier's gun or one from an elegant walnut-stock hunting rifle with an engraved, blued barrel and receiver.

Though, for his part, he would never own anything but the latter, like the Winchester he gripped now.

One sneery boy, the skinniest, said, "I'm a shot. Want me to take out a tire?"

Moll said, with a hint of exasperation, "Do you think it might be better to wait till they were all inside the vehicle? Or do you want to dig them out of the cabin?"

The kid said nothing, not appearing offended, and Moll supposed it was a helpful quality to be able to accept your own dimness.

The other sneerer asked, "What'd that kid do that Harmon wants her gone?"

"Do not know." When Marty Harmon had hired him and Desmond for the special services, the CEO had not shared. Fine with Moll.

He said to the newcomers, "They think it's only the two of us. No idea it's five, and that we've got those." A nod to the M4s. "They'll keep the car dark and hit the driveway as fast as they can. They'll think we'll have time to get off maybe two, three shots and then they'll be gone."

Desmond said, "But when they get to that spot—" He pointed to a patch of dirt and grass at the end of the parking area. It was an unobstructed view from the ridge here. "—we'll open up."

"Good kill zone," the chastised sneerer said approvingly, as if he spent a lot of time thinking about things like that.

Desmond led the two younger men down the ridge and positioned them with a good view of the clearing.

Ryan squinted once more. "Can't see in the cabin."

Allowing himself a contraction, Moll said, "We'll know. When we hear the engine."

Which, just at that moment, sparked to life.

86

When Jon Merritt started the deputy's sedan, Colter Shaw climbed from the side window of the cabin and dropped into the brush below the sill. He scanned the landscape, sweeping the Glock, two-handed, from right to left, back again.

"Clear," he whispered, then tucked the gun away, reached up and guided Allison Parker out and to the ground. She winced not a bit. The drugs that Jon had relieved the foot-shot tweaker of were doing their job.

Hannah climbed out after her mother, needing no assistance. She'd brought the brick bolo, which Shaw was ninety-five percent sure she'd never get a chance to use. With her too was the water clock. She had summarily rejected Shaw's suggestion to leave it behind.

The three now moved north into the brush and forest—mostly pine and hemlock—that filled the land between lake and road, which ran parallel to the water.

Across the overgrown driveway, to the right, the ground rose steeply to the hills where the Twins waited with their long guns.

They were about fifty feet into their escape when the sound of the engine revving hard reached them. This was followed by spinning tires. And then the grind of metal as Merritt would have driven the car onto a boulder, as if he hadn't seen it. The engine roared and more dirt scattered. Hanging the car up and making a commotion to free it was a solid idea.

Hannah turned and gazed back, slowing. In the duskiness, her expression couldn't be seen clearly. Was she alarmed? Proud? Worried?

Shaw touched her shoulder and nodded. She refocused on their transit. And on helping her mother, who might have been largely pain free for the moment, but was prone to stumbling, in her opioid haze.

Eighty, ninety yards from the cabin, a thick hedge of greenery arose on the right side of the road. No one on the hill would be able to see them, and Shaw directed the others onto the roadway itself, where they could make better time.

A snap. Another.

Like a soldier on point, Shaw held up a hand and they stopped. While it would have been impossible for a hillside sniper to target them, one of the Twins might have suspected an end run like this and come down here to see.

Shaw scanned around, peering into the dark. Two-handed again, he swept the ground with his pistol. No visual threat. He heard: wind, early autumn leaves rustling, the click of branches.

Another snap.

Then the intruder waddled past: the beaver that had led them to the cabin, or maybe its mate or sibling.

Offering an irritated glance toward the humans, it stalked on.

Shaw caught Hannah's eye and they shared a smile, then continued along the overgrown road that promised at least the hope of safety.

87

O n the ridge, the men looked down toward the grind and engine roar as those in the parking area below tried to dislodge the car from where it had beached on a rock.

Moll rose from his nest and joined Ryan. Together they walked into the trees just above the car.

"The hell," Ryan muttered. "Didn't they plan it out? Know where the rocks were? We don't have a shot."

Moll nodded. He wanted to pull the spray out and hit his arms and neck. But Ryan would see it as a sign of weakness. Later.

Now the sound of the car shifting: forward, reverse, forward, reverse. After a moment Moll could hear what sounded like a ratcheting jack. Tough to get a car free that way—the parking area was dirt and clay and the tool would sink under the big car's weight. But it might lift the front end high enough to roll it backward off the rock.

Come on. Get it done.

Moll heard a voice from below, half whispering as it called, "Not working."

Ryan said, "That's Merritt." After a moment: "We need to get this over with. We'll give it a few minutes, then move in."

"I do not want to do that," Moll whispered in a foreboding tone.

"What choice is there, they can't get that damn thing loose?"

Moll inhaled deeply, taking in the smell of tree bark and dirt and fragrance from petals brilliant during the day and colorless now. Soon, all scents would be hidden under the aroma of the chemical scent of burnt smokeless gunpowder.

What a few days this had been.

"See anything?" one of Ryan's men called.

"Quiet," Moll snapped in a whisper. You didn't telegraph your location to a deer; why do so when your prey were armed humans?

Ryan glanced his way, eyebrows raised. It was an apology of sorts for his man's carelessness. Moll wondered if either youngster was kin.

Kristi's car still idled, but the jack was now silent.

Had they given up that—

The faintest of crackles behind them. He glanced to Ryan, who was frowning. Their eyes met and they turned.

The light was almost completely gone but there was no missing Jon Merritt holding a shotgun aimed steadily at the two of them. The man's head was tilted slightly and his expression might have been one of surprise. Of course: He hadn't expected other shooters, much less Dom Ryan himself.

So the car had been a diversion.

Maybe Motorcycle Man had come up the other side and was aiming at the farthest sneery kid.

Goddamn . . .

A standoff.

Now would come the demand to toss down their weapons. Negotiations would begin to figure out some way to let those in the cabin get away safe.

Jon Merritt, though, had a different solution. In a calm voice, not a whisper, he said to Ryan, "I was just thinking about you, Dom. That there's no worse sin than betrayal."

Then fired a shotgun load into his throat.

Racking another shell, he swung the muzzle toward Moll's blood-flecked face.

88

His plan would have been good if, like he'd told his daughter, the only hostiles were the two trigger-men.

Jon Merritt supposed he should have figured they'd bring in more people. Though he'd never guess one of them would be the snake Dominic Ryan.

After shooting the mob boss, there was immediate return fire from along the ridge, and Merritt had had to crouch fast, missing the chance to take out the big man in the black suit. He had flung himself into the bushes beside Ryan's body and, though Merritt had fired, the load of pellets had missed.

He had slid and tumbled and run then slid some more down the hill, and when he hit level ground, he scrabbled back to the car.

There, crouching beside the driver's door, he assessed. He had eighteen shotgun shells. The tweaker's revolver had six in the cylinder. The other pistol—the one he'd bought from Ryan's man—had five in the wheel and he had fifteen .38s the man had "generously" thrown in for free.

Of course, fighting an enemy in a forest in the dark? Well, obviously a scattergun was the best tool for the job.

He gave a chuckle, thinking, Don't I sound like a combat veteran? Yet in his whole career as a police officer, even in the tough precincts of Ferrington, he'd fired his weapon but two times.

Not counting Beacon Hill.

They would regroup on the hilltop, trying to figure out the best way to come at him—well, *them*, since it seemed none of them had been tipped to the exodus by Allison, Hannah and Shaw.

They could easily flank him here. So he opened the door, which put on the dome light, and, staying down, pumped the accelerator by hand, the car now in neutral.

With their attention on the sedan, Merritt hustled back to the cabin, shotgun in one hand, backpack in the other, the pistols tucked into his belt like a righteous pirate. He eased through the front door. The maneuver sent another jolt of pain radiating through his body from the rubber-bullet-bruised regions. Another as well: from the scar of the bullet hole where he'd shot himself. The toughened circle of flesh throbbed on occasion. He sometimes felt it was God's way of reminding him of his sin.

He closed the door and wedged the chair under the knob.

Inside, the cabin was almost completely dark now but he recalled the location of every window and the back door.

He peered out. He thought he saw some forms moving cautiously through the forest toward the car.

Not worth the twelve-gauge pellets yet.

Merritt reached into the backpack and extracted the bourbon. He stared at it. Then, with a laugh, he ripped off the plastic seal, uncorked the bottle and took a sip, actually coughing, just like he did the first time he stole some of his father's bourbon, hoping the sting in his mouth would relieve the sting of the welts on his buttocks.

Another drink.

The second mouthful went down smoother.

Gripping the shotgun, looking out the right front window for a target.

Where were they?

A breeze came through the window, fragrant with some herbal smell. He'd learned something about horticulture helping his daughter in biology. He and Hannah were going to start another project. The water clock was for history. The new one would be for biology: hydroponic gardening.

One more sip.

And another after that.

"Nineteen, really?" Then Dr. Evans looks at the clock that is not the Water Clock; these hands never stop moving. And then back to Merritt. "Ah, but I see our time is up, Jon. Hold on to that memory. It might be a good one to explore."

Without a thought, Merritt snaps like a tensioned wire. He rises fast and grabs his chair and flings it against the wall. He lunges forward, well within the doctor's sphere of personness, and leans toward him screaming, "Fuck you, fuck you, fuck you!"

And Jon Merritt realizes he's about to find out what happens when the panic button gets slapped.

But the man doesn't summon help.

Dr. Tuna Sandwich is actually smiling. "But we're not going to worry about the clock today. Let's keep going. All right with you?"

Breathing hard, Jon stares.

Dr. Evans walks to the tossed chair, picks it up and replaces it. He gestures for his patient to sit.

He does.

"There's a famous psychiatrist. He had this theory I like. He said that everybody has a prime disconnect. He means a constant and essential problem. Most of our unhappiness flows from that. We've talked for months now. You're intelligent, fair, responsible . . . But you, like everybody else, have a prime disconnect. Yours is an addiction."

"The drinking, sure, well—"

"No, not *the drinking*."

This gets Jon's full attention.

"You were a police officer. You run drug cases?"

"Yeah. Sometimes."

"Then you know about precursor."

"Chemicals used in the early stages of cooking drugs."

"You have a precursor too. Alcohol. You're not addicted to that. You're addicted to what alcohol cooks."

"Which is?"

"Anger."

Jon gives one of his humorless laughs. "I'm addicted to anger? What does that mean?"

"We're addicted to behaviors that numb us from uneasiness, depression, anxiety. Lashing out does that for you. But you hold back, it builds up, builds up . . . And you start drinking. Then the barriers come down.

"Now that we know that, we have to look at where the anger comes from. That'll take some time to answer. Your father has something to do with it. A belt? At nineteen? Because you were working overtime? His reaction, his behavior were inexcusable. You were furious . . . But you didn't say anything."

"No."

"Because you were afraid he'd go away from you."

Jon says nothing.

"I think that's true. And something to think about. But that's only part of your disconnect. I've been thinking about this quite a lot."

Answering the persistent question: the doctor is an obsessive wrestler for his inmate patients, and not a morose-housewife daydreamer.

"I looked at your PD record. Not a single disciplinary problem in your career. No citizen complaints. Not one."

A certain resident of 8248 Homewood in Beacon Hill might have a say about that, but she's no longer able to fill out the paperwork.

"You saw terrible things in your job and you couldn't react. Abuse, murder, predators, cruelty, right?"

A shrug.

"Tell me about some."

"Of the cases?"

He nods.

Where to start?

"The father on Monroe Street who raped his daughter. The husband on Prescott I cuffed with his wife's blood still on his knuckles. The DUI'd businessman who'd been driving when he was 2.0 and knocked an elderly woman twenty yards into the middle of Ferris Street. The M.E. said she was dead before she hit the ground. The mother with a cigarette-burnt baby in the ER swearing to me that the daughter did it herself." His voice begins trembling, and by God, yes, he feels the anger now. *"And the pricks—the suspects—come into court, and they're: 'Oh, sorry, it's not my fault, you don't understand.'"*

He inhales to control the rage. *"They say you get used to it. No. Never, never, never, not for me. I was on fire the whole time, from the scene to the arrest to booking to court."*

"And you handled it the way you should have. Professional. But that meant you put it all away. And there it sits. That fury. Just waiting for you to take a drink so it can escape."

Jon barks the first laugh he's ever uttered here that isn't sarcastic or fake. *"You planned that. The our-time-is-up thing."*

Dr. Evans smiles. *"I had to see it. Had to see you angry. It didn't work the first couple times—when I said our time was up at a critical point. And when I kept staring out the window, like I was lost in the ozone. Well, finally you blew.*

And I got a good look at the dynamics of your anger. And there's more where that came from, a lot more."

Jon hunches forward, breathing hard. He's tired and he aches. He hasn't been feeling well lately. The chair incident, a small thing physically, has exhausted him. Is he sick? He'll check in to Med later.

The doctor continues. "Now, something else I've observed. You haven't had a drinking problem all your life. It's fairly recent. Something happened in the last few years to make it worse. A lot worse."

Ah, the crosshairs scanning for the Truth like a sniper on the battlefield.

And Jon says, "Maybe."

He is thinking the dots are connecting. The Truth—killing the meth head's daughter. Then the drinking, more and more. Then the anger pouring out.

And flooding his life, sweeping away his wife and daughter and profession.

The doctor is looking at him with staunch patience.

But Jon Merritt is not prepared to reveal the secret that he is a murderer, the man who substituted the life of that girl in a Beacon Hill bungalow for his own.

Not yet.

The doctor seems to understand that this will be a conversation for another day. Perhaps with him, perhaps with someone else. The man seems satisfied to have gotten where they are.

He looks Jon up and down. "I don't even think you like the taste of liquor."

"You know, I really never did."

Notes are tapped into the tablet.

"What have we learned today, Jon?"

"If I take a fucking drink, I'm going to get mad as shit."

The doctor smiles. "My psychiatrist's handbook couldn't've put it any better."

At this particular moment, however, in this backwoods cabin, what would soon be the bullseye of a deadly shooting gallery, it was the perfect time to take a fucking drink.

Which he now did again.

No, he didn't like the taste, but the enemy was coming.

And he needed to be filled with rage, not reason.

He squinted into the night, noting that beside the deputy's car a lush stand of brush that had not been moving a moment ago was moving now.

Jon Merritt aimed the shotgun at it and slowly squeezed the trigger.

89

All that shooting!" Allison Parker said.

"Mom, shhh," Hannah said, just as Shaw lifted his finger to his lips.

He motioned them along the road. He believed he'd counted four different weapons, in addition to the distinctive-sounding shotgun. So Marty Harmon had apparently called in additional guns. Shaw hadn't thought that a likelihood, given the cell outage, but maybe Jacket or Suit had driven into a different zone and called for help.

And where was Jon Merritt now, and how was he faring against that firepower?

As if in answer, there was a lull in the shooting.

Then two more pistol shots.

And silence.

Another hundred yards and they were at the Buick. Colter Shaw quickly cleared it and the surrounding brush. He returned and covered Parker and Hannah as they walked to the vehicle. They got into the backseat. Before starting the engine, Shaw hit the accessory function and when the dash came alive, he quickly dimmed all the lights.

"Belts," he said. It could be a rough ride, some possibly off road.

They all clicked in.

"Han," Shaw said, subconsciously using her nickname. "Watch the ridge to the right. That's where they'd be."

She pressed her face against the window.

"You see anyone, tell me and move to the left side. You and your mother keep down."

"Okay."

"We move fast once I hit the ignition. Ready?"

The girl nodded. Parker did too. She winced. The meds were wearing off. She'd refused to take another one. It was just as well. Shaw would need her to be alert too.

Shaw pressed the start button and immediately slammed the shifter into drive, speeding onto the rough surface of the road. He drove fast but slower than he could have in full light; to the left were steep drop-offs to the stream or river that fed the lake behind the cabin.

There was, at least, no issue with directions; the cabin lay at the end of this lengthy dirt road, which would take them straight to a highway. Once there they'd be in Millton in ten minutes.

He listened again for gunfire.

Still nothing.

The shotgun had been the first weapon fired; Shaw suspected—hoped—that Merritt had surprised the party and taken one of them out. Was it one of the Twins? A creepier pair of men Shaw had never met. Who were the others? Dom Ryan's crew, maybe.

"No one. So far," Hannah said. Then she added softly, "There's no more shooting."

"He's retreated," Shaw said.

Hannah: "Or he's killed all of them." Her voice faded toward the end of the sentence.

Or . . .

Another half mile.

They entered under a canopy of trees. It was darker now. Shaw had to slow down.

Hannah said to her mother, "Daddy was saying something to me, at the cabin? Just before he left?"

"I saw."

"About forgiveness."

Did this have to do, Shaw wondered, with the woman's keen fear: that Hannah would learn of what she'd done to her father?

"He wanted me to forgive him."

"For what?"

"For hitting you with his gun that night in November. He said drinking wasn't an excuse."

"Did you?" Parker asked in a soft voice.

After a pause, Hannah said, "I don't know what it

really means when you say you forgive somebody. It's, like, more complicated, isn't it?"

"It is, yes," Parker said.

"Well, I *told* him I forgave him." The girl sighed, Shaw believed. She added, "You know, I thought you might've done it to yourself. To get him arrested. I'm sorry I thought that."

Parker said nothing for a moment. Then: "It's behind us now."

Life gets by on ninety percent truth and ten percent deception. And not all of those lies are bad. Sometimes honesty derails a train bound for important destinations. In any event, this wasn't Colter Shaw's game. He was here to make sure they survived in body, not in heart and soul.

He gave the phone to Hannah. "Signal?"

"No. Still blank."

Shaw decided, to be safe, he'd use the navigation app in the car and find a circuitous route to get to Millton, back roads and neighborhoods exclusively.

The odds of pursuit?

If there was still gunfire, he'd say ten percent.

With the silence, he guessed sixty. No, Jon Merritt had not killed them all. But they might think that he, Allison and Hannah had fled on foot into the woods and be looking for them there.

They must be only—

Suddenly there was a flash of white to the right.

Parker screamed, Hannah said, "Mr.—!"

The Ford Transit thundered through the brush and broadsided the Buick hard.

The impact shoved the vehicle over the embankment. It rolled two and a half times, crushing emaciated pine saplings, and came to rest, upside down, in the middle of the steep hill.

90

Shaw smelled the sweet aroma of gasoline.

"Out!" he called, rolling down the windows, unlocking the doors. All of the airbags had blown. Parker and her daughter didn't seem badly hurt, though they were stunned. "Gas. Get out!"

He undid his belt, dropping to the ceiling. He turned and undid Parker's. She'd been fumbling with it. She landed in a pile, barking a muted scream of pain. Hannah hit her own harness and twisted as she fell, landing like a cat on all fours. They crawled out.

Hannah reached back for the water clock.

Shaw said firmly, "Han. No."

She looked toward him and nodded.

"Stay low. Move that way." He pointed downhill—and lateral. Not only was the sedan at risk of catching fire, but it teetered at a twenty-degree angle on soft earth. It wouldn't take much to start it tumbling.

Shaw stood and fired one round into the windshield of the Ford van. There was no human target; he wanted only to tell them he was armed, which would buy some distance and time, and allow them to set up a good defensive position. He heard shouting: directions given, possible sightings. It seemed to be only the Twins. Had Merritt gotten the others? Shaw had a feeling that he had.

Hannah was helping her mother.

As the three continued down the slope, Shaw glanced up the hill and saw the two forms coming after them. Yes, the Twins. They had drawn their handguns and were beginning to shoot in the direction of the ruined car. Their tactic with the van hadn't quite worked. They too had been slammed by the airbags and, still stunned, weren't firing accurately.

Still, a random bullet could be just as deadly as one fired with precision.

When they were about fifty feet below the Buick, Shaw noticed Parker slowing.

Looking back up the hill, he saw Tan Jacket standing to fire. The man dropped just as Shaw squeezed off a round.

A miss.

Thirteen shots left in the weapon, two fifteen-round mags in his pocket.

Never lose track of remaining ammunition . . .

Ahead of them, Shaw spotted a culvert about three feet deep. "There." He gestured them into it. Then he rolled in and peered over the top like a soldier in a trench, scanning with his weapon. He looked behind them. No escape that way. The hill, descending to the river, offered limited ground cover and the moon was up, its cool light bright enough to spot targets.

He looked back over the lip of their trench, scanning to the left.

"Mr. Shaw!" Hannah whispered. She'd ignored his order to stay low. "Right! Look!"

It was Suit.

Shaw acquired and was about to fire when the man vanished.

They'd be flanking, he assumed. And they'd need to finish up quickly. The highway wasn't far away, and on a pleasant night like this, car windows might be down, drivers and passengers would be wondering about the shots. No hunters at this hour, of course.

"What should we do, Mr. Shaw?"

He looked around the immediate area. "Cover yourselves up with leaves as much as you can."

She hesitated. The girl who wanted a gun didn't seem happy at the thought of hiding.

But then she got to work, piling leaves on her mother and then hunkering down and burrowing under the rustling blanket herself.

"I'm moving up there." He pointed to high ground. "I need to get into position."

She gave a smile. "That's what people like you say. They get into *position* to *engage*."

He nodded to her and went over the top of the ridge and began a soldier's prone shuffle to the left.

Where are you? Where?

The breeze was troubling dry leaves and branches, covering up the sound of his transit, but also making it difficult or impossible to hear the Twins' steps.

He rose and stood before a thick swath of tall grass. He couldn't see much: the top of the Transit, the inverted Buick.

Gazing from left to right, looking for any sign of movement that was not caused by the wind.

Left, right . . .

Except flanking was not their tactic.

Maybe assuming his attention would be to the sides, they went for a frontal assault.

One of them, high on the hill, began covering fire in Shaw's direction, while the second, hunched low, like a linebacker, rushed through the tall grass, directly toward him.

In a crouch, he aimed at where the man would be, judging from the sound and the disturbed greenery.

He inhaled, exhaled leisurely, holding the firearm out.

What if somebody's attacking you?

Even slower then . . .

Forty feet away, thirty-five, thirty . . .

Now.

Shaw fired. The Glock kicked.

The man kept coming.

Two more shots, slightly left and right of where he'd first aimed.

Neither did these hit him.

Impossible. Shaw hadn't missed. Body armor?

The man was now only twenty feet away. He'd break

from the grass into the clearing any minute. Shaw aimed at the spot where he'd exit.

By the time he realized that this wasn't the enemy at all but the spare tire from the Transit they'd rolled his way, the wheel sped from the grass and slammed into Shaw's chest, sending him tumbling down the hill.

91

The Twins charged forward in the wake of the tire.

Shaw had dropped the Glock under the impact. He rose to his knees, struggling to breathe and scanning for the weapon. Suit fired a shot his way and kept coming. Shaw rolled into a thicket of brush to take cover.

Jacket turned to his left, searching for Parker and Hannah. He was not far from the culvert where they lay, but with the darkness and under the camo, he was having no luck spotting them.

From his cover, Shaw scanned the ground and saw his own gun lying twenty feet away, directly in the path of cautiously approaching Suit.

Maybe he'd miss it . . .

But, no, the big man paused and then stepped forward fast, snagging the gun. He whispered, "Dawndue . . ." Like a weird birdcall. The man had said the same thing at the house just before they burned the camper to the ground.

Suit stood upright and looked around. He called, "Come on, Motorcycle Man. I have your six-shooter. Show yourself."

Shaw noted that he had another weapon. Something strapped behind his back. Maybe one of the .223 assault rifles.

After a moment Suit called, "You left those ladies alone for my friend to find. That is a shame on you. He is not a normal fellow when it comes to that topic. Come on out and we will make it quick. I will see to it my friend does not misbehave."

He somehow had the idea that Shaw had continued to the river. That was the direction in which he was scanning, trying to see through the tangles and shadows. He called, "Come on. Going once, going twice . . ."

Jacket yelled, "I got 'em." He was pointing toward the culvert. "Get up!" He fired a shot. Parker screamed but out of alarm. She wasn't hit. Neither was Hannah. "Come on, rise and shine. Up you go."

The two climbed from their nest. Leaves clung.

Suit kept scanning for Shaw.

Jacket said, "Where is he?"

"Down the hill. Maybe knocked out. Wheels can be formidable."

Jacket was looking over the landscape. "Don't see him." He turned to Parker but his eyes settled on Hannah. To his partner he called, "Listen. I've been patient.

You were right when we were going to do it the first way. Now things've changed."

"You think we have time here? *Really?*"

"'Course not. We've got the body-mobile. Let's take her with us."

Suit sighed, grimacing, a man finally worn down by a persistent argument. "All right, all right. Get her in there. Fast. Truss her up and then we'll find Motorcycle Man."

"No!" Hannah cried.

But this was not a reaction to Jacket's plans for her. She was staring at what Suit had unslung from behind his back.

The shotgun they'd last seen in her father's hands in the cabin.

Answering for certain the question that had been on all of their minds.

Hannah launched herself at Jacket.

"Whoa. Feisty." He sidestepped and grabbed her around the chest. To Suit he said, "Told you she was attitudinal."

Parker climbed to her feet, crying out against the pain in her leg and with fury at seeing the man grip her daughter. Jacket glanced at her, noted the wound and kicked her in the damaged leg. She screamed and fell back, clutching the limb, sobbing.

Jacket kissed the top of Hannah's head and laughed when she spit at him. "Come on, let's get you inside."

Shaw quietly moved ten feet to his right, keeping under

cover to pick up what he'd been looking for—a rock the size of an orange. He drew back and flung it as far as he could over Suit's head. When it landed, the man turned toward the sound, firing the shotgun. This deafened him, as Shaw had planned, so he couldn't hear the sprint behind him on the crisp leaves. When Suit saw there was no target, he started to turn. But too late. Shaw powered into him.

He had aimed low, his shoulder targeting the man's kidney. The blow, he knew, is nearly paralyzing from the pain it delivers, and Shaw followed up by simply gripping the man's pants cuffs and standing fast—the same maneuver he'd described to Hannah. The man went down on his face. Shaw stood and dropped a knee onto his other kidney. Suit screamed, releasing his grip on the shotgun. Shaw scooped it up, along with his Glock and Suit's pistol, which he pocketed.

Jacket aimed but didn't shoot. Shaw was kneeling beside his partner.

But he had a similar problem. He had no sight solution with Jacket holding Hannah. She was virtually a shield.

Shaw called to him, "We're near the highway. People've heard the shots. Marty Harmon has no pull in this county. Get on the ground, arms and feet spread."

Jacket said nothing, just continued to sweep his gun in Shaw's direction.

Suit stirred but he was no threat; enough pain was coursing through his body to keep him down for ten minutes.

Shaw said, "On the ground."

"Okay, tell you what. Help my buddy up and we'll just go our own way. Put this down to a bad coupla days all around. What do you say?"

The man was just buying time to find a target. And he would have a far easier shot than Shaw would, since Hannah was in front of most of his body. Shaw was an expert marksman but, in the dark, this was not a shot to attempt.

When would he point the gun toward Hannah and Parker and tell him to toss down his weapon? Surprised he hadn't already.

But of course Ashton Shaw had an answer for that.

Never surrender your weapon. There are no exceptions . . .

"You understand there are records leading to you and your friend. There's nowhere to hide. It's over with."

He didn't answer.

Silence.

Which was broken by Hannah's voice. The girl swiveled toward Jacket and said, with a calm that was unsettling, "Hey, mister. Look at me."

This was followed by a high-pitched scream.

Coming from Jacket's mouth. He released the girl, dropped his gun and began wiping at his eyes furiously. "Oh, Jesus, Jesus . . ."

Shaw looked at Hannah's hand. What was she holding? He realized it was the jar of cayenne pepper from the cabin.

The man was wailing. He dropped to his knees and

was wiping at his eyes with his sleeves and the tail of his jacket.

Hannah stepped away from him slowly, looked down at her feet and picked up his gun. She pointed it at him.

"Hannah!" Shaw called. "No."

Any death from this point on would be murder.

The girl didn't move. She kept the muzzle on the man as steadily as when she'd practiced with his Colt Python. "They killed him." A whisper.

Parker struggled to her feet. "I know, Han. But don't do it. Give me the gun."

The weapon was a Glock. Point and shoot. A five-year-old can fire a Glock.

It also has a light pull and her finger was on the trigger. Shaw was surprised it hadn't discharged yet.

"They killed him," the girl said again.

Parker hobbled closer. "Han, please?" Her mother wasn't ordering, she wasn't threatening. This was simply a request from one adult to another.

The girl didn't move.

Jacket cried, "We've got money! A lot of money." Still wiping. To no effect.

Hand out, Parker stepped closer yet.

Shaw said, "Remember our rule. Never engage unless you have to."

The gun remained where it was for a moment. Then she lowered it and her shoulders slumped. She handed the weapon to her mother, just as Shaw had taught her, the muzzle in neutral aim.

The woman put her left arm around her daughter's

shoulders and they stepped farther away from the sobbing man, who'd stripped off the jacket and was using it
to blot his eyes.

Parker lowered her head to her daughter and spoke—
words Shaw couldn't hear. Hannah frowned. Parker
spoke again, apparently repeating what she'd said. The
girl nodded and stepped back. She covered her ears.

No, Shaw thought. No . . .

Parker turned the weapon toward Jacket and, in a two-
handed combat shooting stance, shot him in the head.

He dropped. She walked up and fired a make-sure
round.

Wincing, breathing hard from the takedown, Suit
climbed to his feet. Parker turned the gun on him. Suit
stared not at the gun but at the body of his partner. He
seemed as paralyzed as when Shaw had taken him down
moments ago.

Parker studied the man closely.

Shaw stepped away.

Suit's shoulders lowered, hands drooping at his sides.
This was a man programmed never to beg. He was now
resigned to death.

But Parker didn't fire. The gun lowered.

She called to him, loudly because of the deafening
gunshots, "Month and a half ago you killed someone."

He tilted his head in cautious acknowledgment.

She continued, "Marty Harmon hired you to kill a
truck driver. There was an accident on the Hawkins
Road Bridge. A truck missed a turn. It went into a tributary near the Kenoah."

Suit nodded slowly, thinking maybe that honesty might be a way to survive.

So, this was the man who had killed the driver of the radioactive waste truck.

Suit looked toward Shaw. Then back to the woman who held his life in her hands, unfailing justice in the form of an efficient, mass-produced Austrian pistol.

Parker was nodding. "The driver was in the water trying to get the truck out. You went in too, to kill him. Your skin, it started right around then."

Suit's eyes narrowed.

"You've got radiation poisoning. It's advanced. There's nothing you can do about it now." She shrugged. "Except die. Slowly."

He was looking at his hands, then to her.

Parker said, "Get out of here." When he didn't move, she fired a shot at his feet. He jumped back. She raged, "Go!"

He looked around uncertainly, then backed away. He turned and began to jog into the darkness.

Shaw joined Parker and she offered him the pistol—just as carefully as her daughter had done. She said, "I don't *like* guns. That doesn't mean I don't know how to use them."

92

N o, it's all right. It's our time now. Little sooner than we'd planned is all."

"What're you thinking, Marty?" Marianne Keller's voice, through the phone, was subdued as she took all this in.

Marty Harmon was in his Maserati Quattroporte, in a tawdry truck-stop parking lot, thirty miles west of Ferrington. Overhead lights, green and fluorescent, lit the lovely camel-tan interior of the fine vehicle. Quite the contrast to the surroundings.

"We'll have to be smart. Two separate planes. I'm going now. Yours is booked for eleven tomorrow."

"Morning?"

"Morning."

"Marty . . ."

Marianne usually wore the supreme confidence of

beauty born. Now, though, her world was shaky. Still, while her voice hinted at concern, it wore a blush of pleasure. She'd be thinking of good outcomes looming. For two years she'd wanted him to leave his wife and be with her, and if it took the bottled water cover-up falling apart to move things along, well, okay. As long as she was . . . protected.

Harmon understood this about her.

"We're leaving from Granton Executive Airport, the private one. You know where?"

"Off Fifty-five north."

"I've got you a Learjet. The number is . . . Can you write it down?"

"Go ahead."

"The number is N94732. It'll take you to the fixed-base operator terminal in Atlanta. I'll meet you there."

"We can't go together?"

"No. Safer this way. I'm flying to Charlotte and then driving to Georgia. From there, St. Croix and eventually France."

There was a company in Paris that had an active small modular reactor operation. He and Marianne had talked about opening a joint venture between HEP and Fabrication de Systèmes Nucléaire de la Loire.

"You've been brushing up on your French, right?"

"*Oui*. Like you said."

"That's my girl. Now, there's a go-bag for you in the bottom of my office closet."

"You made one for me?" Her voice was now adoring.

"Of course I did." He gave a kind laugh. "There's

about two hundred thousand in it. Go into the office in the morning, act like nothing's happened. If anybody asks where I am, tell them I've gone to Washington for a meeting with the NRC."

"Marty, what do they know?" The adoration had slipped.

"I think we're safe. There's no evidence. No traceable phone calls, no emails, no paperwork. I've planted stories that those two men wanted to kill Allison because of her containment vessel. Sabotage. And the move overseas? I'd had enough. Armed spies stealing the S.I.T. trigger? Attempted murder of my engineer? Maybe I'd be next. And we left together . . . because we're in love."

"Oh, Marty . . ." The worship was back.

"I should go. Eleven tomorrow."

"N94732."

"Good, baby. I love you."

"Love you, Marty."

Harmon disconnected, started the car and drove to the edge of the truck stop, a particularly dingy area of crumbling asphalt, discarded truck parts, patches of grease and oil, sickly vegetation dying from spilled chemicals. He parked under a large, full beech tree—the species that loses its leaves last of all deciduous trees. He was next to a black Cadillac sedan, engine idling. The sedan was registered in the name of Harmon Energy.

He nodded to the sturdy driver, who rolled down the window. He was wearing latex gloves. Harmon handed him an envelope of ten thousand dollars and his phone. The man put the car in gear and sped from the lot. He had instructions to drive to an international airport a hundred miles away, where the car would be left in long-term parking, after imprinting its presence on a half-dozen video cameras.

Harmon opened the trunk of the Maserati and took from it a large backpack and his own go-bag, which contained several passports—his picture, but different names and dates of birth—and eight hundred thousand in cash. This was merely spending and bribe money for him. The bulk of his resources were in Bitcoin vaults.

He still resented that his coffers were diminished by the $200K he'd set aside for Marianne Keller. He had debated a figure. Then decided that a fifth of a million would make her believe that he was sincere and truly wanted her with him in his new life.

She'd never suspect what was really going to happen: that she'd be arrested as she left HEP to catch a private jet that didn't exist, carrying cash that Harmon's anonymous call would report she'd stolen from the company.

Then a police search of her computer would find it brimming with those very incriminating memos and emails that he claimed didn't exist—linking her to Moll and Desmond and the death of the truck driver and the cover-up of the spill.

They'd find emails too from Dom Ryan, who had—thank you, God—been killed up at that lake house. The best kind of witness.

Oh, everything would all lead back to Harmon ultimately. But the essence of escape is diversion and misdirection. By the time they tied the pieces together, he would be safely ensconced in his new home, immune from extradition.

A home that was not in the French Republic.

Leaving the lovely car unlocked, he tossed the keys on the floor. He smiled sadly in farewell; he had no idea what its fate would be. But in this part of the state it would disappear within the hour. What exactly a meth cooker would do with this masterpiece of a vehicle he had no idea. Probably he'd just change the plates and drive it; the market for chopped parts from an Italian supercar was somewhat limited.

A moment later a box truck drove slowly under the beech tree, its back door open.

The vehicle didn't stop but was going slowly enough that Harmon could easily toss in his bags and jump inside after them. He pulled the back panel down. Security cameras and any extremely unlikely drones would have seen zip.

Harmon slapped the front of the box and the driver began to accelerate.

Quite the elaborate plan.

But then it had to be.

The problem wasn't, of course, the Ferrington Police Department, which still employed a few men and women on his payroll—that was the advantage of committing crimes in a poor metropolis populated by the desperate.

No, the trouble was that the feds were involved now.

Thanks to the man that Harmon *himself* had hired to be yet another player in the death of Hannah and her mother: Colter Shaw.

Well, it had seemed like a fine idea at the time.

But that was, of course, just the nature of being a brilliant inventor. After all, Thomas Edison had as many failures as he'd had successes.

Very likely more.

93

The Kenoah River was tainted only in and around the city of Ferrington, where twentieth-century capitalism and, more recently, Marty Harmon himself had laced the broad waterway with exemplary toxins.

As the current flowed downstream and the chemicals dissipated, the river took on a different tone, the color mellowing from bile to gentle brown. Now here its banks grew lush with trees and plants that could never survive within the city limits. Thirty miles along, where the river broadened to a width of two hundred yards, waterfront development blossomed. Restaurants, shops and pleasure craft docks.

Also working piers, where transport ships were tied up. These weren't big oceangoing container ships or Ro-Ros—roll on, roll offs. They were old-style break-bulk vessels that carried not containers but pallets.

The ships were usually named after individuals; the

owners didn't paint on the stern clever phrases and puns like the ones doctors and lawyers with sailboats come up with after a martini or two. The ship Martin Harmon had chosen was the *Jon Doherty*—the first name ironic in the extreme.

Measuring one hundred and ten feet, stem to stern, she was sixty-two years old, abraded and rusty, aromatic of grease and diesel fuel, but she had one feature for which Marty Harmon had paid the captain a hundred thousand dollars: a scuffed but spacious stateroom for a passenger. It would be his home for the next week— which was as long as it took the *Jon Doherty* to travel west to, and then down, the Mississippi River, terminating in New Orleans.

There, another ship—this one a container vessel, with bigger and better accommodations—would take him to the Lagos Port Complex in Nigeria.

Africa . . .

The continent that was the future of the world.

The continent in which he would begin to seed his small modular reactors, once he got his new company up and running. He would be two years late, but no matter; the miraculous devices would see the light of day. He actually smiled at the clichéd thought.

A long voyage, and boring, though he would have his computer, a printer and reams upon reams of paper. Also, an encrypted satellite phone, on which he would spend the time laying the groundwork for his new life.

The truck turned off the highway and the ride grew rougher.

As he held tight to canvas tie-downs, Harmon thought of the incidents of the past six weeks: the radioactive spill, killing the driver, racing to find the toxic sludge to pump into the Kenoah and arranging for the iodide water to hand out to the good citizens of Ferrington.

A smart plan, constructed on the fly . . . and all brought down by a goddamn sixteen-year-old girl and her selfies.

Jesus Christ . . .

The truck squealed to a stop. The driver banged twice on the wall. They hadn't settled on a code, but it was obvious this meant they'd arrived at the pier where the *Jon Doherty* was docked.

He lifted the door and looked out. At 11 p.m. the area was deserted, except for a few workers loading boxes onto pallets and tying them down. Latin music played from a boom box.

He hopped out and grabbed his bags, then walked to the driver's side of the truck. Harmon handed him another $10K. "Thank you, Ramon Velasquez." A reference to the fact that he was undocumented and Harmon knew his full name and if he didn't keep quiet, he would be shipped back to Mexico by Customs and Border Protection in a lick.

"Is all good, Mr. Harmon."

The transmission clattered into gear and the truck drove off.

Smelling fuel and a faint but rich swamp scent, Harmon walked toward the pier where the ship was docked. A half-dozen lights were on inside the superstructure.

He'd been assured by the captain that he was welcome at any time.

A hundred K in small bills buys one an armful of hospitality.

The tied-up ship rocked gently. Low waves lapped. No spray. The night was sedate. Lewisport had once been a tribal village and later a trading post and way station for travelers. At this time of night, it probably looked much the same as it had then: a cluster of low, darkened structures, the river's rippling surface, on which moonlight danced, the silhouette of uneven and uninhabited swamp and forest on the far shore.

He was now feet away from the gangplank and he had a sense that when he set foot on board he would be immune. Of course, it wasn't as if he'd be in international waters. He would be subject to the laws of whatever state the ship was passing through. Still, the protection he was afforded was not of legality but of anonymity. Which was by far the better of the two.

And he had the added safety net that even if the hounds were focusing on him they would be pursuing hapless Marianne, the remnants of Dom Ryan's crew and a black Cadillac.

Ten feet, then five. His footsteps gritted on the asphalt.

The chunky pulse of marimbas and horns and guitar filled the air.

Then he heard:

"Martin Harmon! FBI! Drop the bags and put your hands up!"

"Hands up!"

"Now!"

He exhaled in disgust.

He turned. The three workers were not workers at all. And they were joined by a number of other men and women, wearing navy-blue windbreakers with the letters of their employer on the front and back. All had pistols in their hands and half were aiming directly at him. The others were scanning the dock for any hostiles Harmon might have invited along.

Jesus Lord . . .

"Drop the bags! Hands up!"

He complied.

Several charged forward, clicking on handcuffs and frisking, removing everything in his pockets, looking through the luggage and backpack.

"Weapon," one called.

Harmon had brought an old revolver and a box of ammunition. He hadn't fired a gun in years but he thought it might be helpful.

The gun was unloaded and sealed into an evidence bag.

The man who seemed to be the lead agent approached and formally arrested him on a blur of charges, flight to avoid prosecution, conspiracy to commit murder, wire fraud, battery . . . Harmon lost track. He did not waive his right to remain silent.

Another figure approached.

Ah, but who else could it possibly be?

The FBI agent looked to Colter Shaw. "You got it

right. What'd you say the odds were that he'd trick the drones at a truck stop and head here?"

The man said laconically, "I recall, it was about eighty-five percent."

The agent looked Harmon over. "Mr. Shaw had the idea that the only place you could hide is Africa and the only way you'd beat the watchlists was to take a cruise."

"What proof do you—"

Shaw interrupted. "Sonja matched the explosives in the bomb at her Range Rover to what was used in the Pocket Sun triggers. And she got you on tape going into the Secured Substances room at HEP an hour before the explosion. And before you ask how could a CEO like you make a bomb, remember that you're an engineer with a chemistry degree."

Shit . . .

An agent gripped the man's arm. "This way."

Harmon, though, turned and looked from Shaw to the agent. "You have to understand. I wanted to improve people's lives. Get them out of poverty. My Pocket Suns could do that! I did what I did to make the world a better place."

The look Shaw gave him seemed to say: Which is exactly what we're doing right now.

PART THREE

NEVER

FRIDAY, SEPTEMBER 23

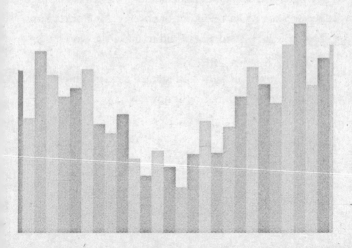

94

Colter Shaw was in the office of FPD detective Dunfry Kemp.

Significantly fewer file folders were present, with the result that more of the walls showed, and the many stains and scuffs on the brown and green surfaces were far more obvious. On the whole, the place looked better with the buffer of files.

Kemp was looking over his statement, nodding.

Shaw noted that the officer accepted the most important line of dialogue in his performance: "In my judgment, Ms. Parker used only the force necessary to protect her own life and the lives of her daughter and myself."

Always good to have a version of the script ready, in case a firearm and a body were involved.

The police had turned cooperative.

It seemed that the reluctance to pursue Jon Merritt was due not really to the reputation of the Hero of Beacon

Hill, but to the fact that Harmon had a captain and two detectives on his payroll. One of these was Dunfry Kemp's supervisor, who had assigned him the Merritt case, along with the numerous others to hamper the search for the former cop and his ex-wife and daughter. All with an eye to letting the Merritt murder-suicide proceed with as few glitches as possible.

With those on the take suspended, Kemp was unleashed and he'd turned into quite the efficient law enforcer.

"We'll need you to testify, Mr. Shaw."

He nodded.

"Bet you've done that before."

"I have."

"So you travel around the country looking for rewards, do you?"

"That's right."

Kemp seemed intrigued, and Shaw wondered if he was going to ask where to submit his resume. But he said, "You like doing that, why don't you just join up?"

Regulations and a dreaded desk.

"I like traveling."

"Well, keep it in mind, sir. Fact is, policing's the best job in the world."

"I've heard."

"Prosecutor'll be in touch." Kemp slid the statement forward to Shaw, who signed it.

The man then asked, "You heard how he's doing? Need to talk to him too."

"Better."

The individual they were referring to was a prior participant in the incident, someone not expected to make a reappearance.

Frank Villaine.

Who was not dead after all.

The Twins had arrived at the man's house just as he was leaving, intending to torture him into telling where Allison and Hannah had gone. They hadn't expected him to be armed and he let loose with his Glock and fled into the woods. One of the Twins caught him in the back with a slug and he went down. They assumed he was dead or soon would be, and then found that they didn't need his cooperation; they noticed that the GPS in the Mercedes was programmed with his destination: the cabin on Timberwolf Lake.

Villaine had been found by a neighbor that evening and rushed to a hospital. Allison Parker was presently with him.

Shaw rose. The men shook hands.

It was then that his phone hummed with a text. He read the words. Debated only a moment and replied.

He stood on the riverwalk, near the Fourth Street Bridge.

Beneath him the mustard-brown Kenoah muscled past.

Shaw inhaled. Harmon's toxic cocktails were no longer being dumped into the victimized body of water, and it seemed there'd been an improvement in the odor.

Imagination? Maybe.

He was looking across the river, at the famed tourist draw, the Water Clock—the inspiration for the project that father and daughter had tackled for history class. The model of the attraction that Jon Merritt had built in prison had been recovered from the wrecked Buick and returned to Parker and Hannah. It was still in working order and was now sitting on the mantelpiece of their rental home. He wondered what had become of the bolo.

"Hey there," came the melodic, Southern-laced voice.

Sonja Nilsson was climbing up a stone stairway from a dock twenty feet below. She'd been conferring with two men on a small craft fitted out with a bristle of scientific equipment.

Shaw nodded a greeting.

The woman was in jeans, a work shirt and a leather jacket, a far cry from the stylish outfit she'd worn when they'd first met in Harmon's office. An orange safety vest too. Her blond hair was done up in a braid that was then swirled into a careless bun and pinned firmly to the back of her head. Looking for all the world like a Saturday morning shopper in Stockholm, about to stop for a coffee. Minus the vest, of course.

"How's your Range Rover?"

"A couple of weeks. Quite the long pause when I told the insurance examiner that the cause of the damage was an improvised explosive device."

Shaw peered down at the Kenoah. "And the water quality?"

The workers had been wielding yellow Geiger counters.

"We're good. Negligible from the point of the spill to here. Downstream, it's negative."

So the radiation was no longer a threat.

He glanced at her face and noted her scanning about them. He had just done the same. Her jacket was partly open and he could see the grip of her weapon.

Their eyes met.

Ah, that green . . . Nature, or not?

He said, "Probably we're good." Referring to risk assessment.

True.

Nilsson would always be cautious about being on the watchlist, thanks to the larcenous government contractor. As for individuals involved in the HEP situation, though, there were none left to pose a threat.

At Deep Woods Lake, Jon Merritt had killed Dominic Ryan and one of his Irish crew. The other, wounded, was in jail and fully prepared to gab.

Tan Jacket—Desmond Sawicki—was gone, of course.

And so was his partner, Moll Frain, the man Allison Parker had set free. There was no danger of his making a shocking act-three appearance, like the supposedly dead henchman at the end of a bad movie. He was found this morning in his workshop on the outskirts of Ferrington, dead by his own hand. He was sitting in a chair made of aluminum but painted to look like rich wood. He himself had decorated it. Apparently he was quite the artist. Who would have thought?

"Is HEP shut down?" Shaw asked.

"For a spell."

The Mason-Dixon phrase, and appropriate accent, coming from the mouth of a Swedish fashion model both jarred and was oddly appealing.

She continued, "We've got EPA, NRC and AEC inspectors on the way. But—" She glanced down at the boat. "They'll find the same things we just did. And we'll get the green light to start up again."

Then Shaw told himself: Stop it.

Referring not to his government regulators or corporate operations but Shaw's own debate about her eye color.

"Who'll replace him?" he asked.

"The board'll be meeting to make a pick. There's talk that Allison Parker'd be a good choice. No management experience but she knows the product better than anybody. And"—a smile—"the business of atomic energy's been a man's world forever. It'd be good for a female to be the face of HEP. But nobody's asking my opinion. I'm like you, Colter. Just hired help."

Shaw noted, across the street, an FPD Crime Scene van parked in front of a gloomy alleyway on Manufacturers Row. A plain-clothed detective was interviewing some men who appeared to be homeless.

"What happened there?"

"Drug deal gone south, I heard."

Shaw said, "Thought maybe that serial killer resurfaced. The Street Cleaner."

"No, she's still at large."

Shaw's brows furrowed.

"Oh, didn't you know? It's a woman. So says the DNA. Rare. But we girls can get up to bad business too, you know."

Shaw laughed. For a brief time, he'd wondered if Jon Merritt himself might be the Street Cleaner, taking his job as Vice officer one step over the line. But he'd given the theory only thirty percent and then discarded it entirely.

"What about the bait?" he asked. "The fake S.I.T. trigger?"

"Went live last night. In Dubai. That's an international hub. It'll be going elsewhere. We'll find it."

Then Nilsson was saying, "Now. About my text."

He lifted an eyebrow.

"We owe you some money."

He'd forgotten that finding and guarding Allison Parker and her daughter was a job. The man hiring him was in jail, as was the keeper of the petty cash purse, Marianne Keller. Shaw supposed, though, that there was somebody in accounting who could arrange payment.

But Nilsson had another agenda.

"How'd you like to triple it?"

"Hm."

"I'm in touch with somebody in Interpol."

Shaw knew the organization. It was not, as many people thought, a law enforcement agency itself. It was an intelligence clearinghouse sharing information about crime and criminals among overseas law enforcement departments.

"They caught some intel from a source in Eastern Europe. Money went into a secret account in Siberia."

Though obviously not all that secret.

"The recipient was supposed to steal a proprietary component from a manufacturing company in the U.S. The Midwest."

"In the nuclear reactor business, by any chance?"

She continued, "The thief blew the job. But his bosses gave him a second chance. If he couldn't get the part this time, he was to—quote—'significantly disrupt' the company. He would not be given another opportunity."

"Abe Lincoln."

She frowned.

Shaw said, "Lemerov."

"Right."

He pictured the lanky man and recalled the meeting in the motel not far from where the two of them stood now.

But don't pat back too fast, Mr. Colter Shaw. More rounds to come. More rounds to come . . .

Tom Pepper had said that the Russian had been deported—put onto a plane bound for London—but had then disappeared.

She asked, "You read military history?"

"Some."

"I'm fascinated by tacticians. I think the top five are Stonewall Jackson, Erwin Rommel, Sun Tzu, Alexander the Great and Hannibal Barca—that's, yes, the Carthaginian Hannibal." She shook her head. "His command at the Battle of the Trebia? The Carthaginians lost a few thousand men, the Romans more than twenty thousand—half their army."

Both their eyes were on the Water Clock.

She said, "You strike me as a bit of one yourself. I'd like to hire you to step into the shoes of our Russian. Figure out how he'd strike the company. Where, when, how. And help me stop him." She cocked her head. "Legally, of course." Her smile appended the word *probably*.

"So what do you say, Shaw? Until you have to hit the road again?"

He turned to her, just as a cloud parted and her face was bathed in brilliance.

Suddenly, the answer was clear:

She wasn't wearing contacts.

95

C olter Shaw pulled his Avis sedan, a not-bad black Malibu, into the driveway of Allison Parker's rental house on Maple View Avenue.

Hannah was sitting cross-legged on the porch, rocking slowly in a hanging swing, wearing jeans, a pale green knit stocking cap and a bulky maroon sweatshirt whose sleeves were far too long. The girl was waving goodbye to a lanky teenage boy, who had lengthy blond hair and was dressed similarly to her. Like a natural athlete, he dropped his skateboard, hopped on and wove down the sidewalk balletically, then out of sight.

Kyle. Wasn't that the name? From the look he shot her upon departing, Shaw assigned him a slot far higher than ten percent.

He collected the bag beside him and climbed from the car.

"Hey, Mr. Shaw!" Hannah smiled. Then surprised him

by climbing from the swing, stepping forward and hugging him hard. He reciprocated gently.

"Mom's at the hospital. Think she'll be here soon."

Shaw said, "I know. You doing okay?"

"Yeah, it's cool." Spoken more like somebody who'd just dodged the flu, not been the target of professional killers.

They continued onto the porch.

He handed her the bag.

She extracted the slim book that was inside.

"Oh, hey. What you were telling me about."

Ralph Waldo Emerson's *Self-Reliance*.

"Dope! Thanks." Her face grew earnest. "I'll read it. Not like the way I tell my teachers I'll read something. I mean I'll really *read* it. Oh, hey, Mr. Shaw, there's something I want to show you." She picked up a notebook sitting on the swing. It was nearly identical to the ones that he used on his reward jobs. She offered it to him. "I wrote a poem."

He read the lines.

Colter Shaw, a man of percentages and careful assessments, not a man of the arts, nonetheless felt his pulse accelerate with every word. "It's good. Very good."

"Do you like it? Really?" It was clear his judgment was important.

He nodded.

"I've been working on it nonstop."

"The meter, it's good. The rhythm."

Her eyes shone. "I tried to get that down. I didn't want it to rhyme. That's lame. You know, singsongy."

"Like your selfies—unconventional."

Beneath her modest smile, the girl was beaming.

A car pulled to the curb. The brakes squealed.

Instinctively Shaw reached for his hip.

A pointless gesture as he had no weapon to reach for.

Pointless too because the driver was Allison Parker. She climbed from her 4Runner and walked toward Shaw and Hannah, limping only a little. She winced slightly as she climbed the stairs to the porch.

He lifted an eyebrow.

"It's good. Some physical therapy for a few weeks."

"How's Mr. Villaine?" Hannah asked.

"He'll be fine. They're discharging him tomorrow. I was thinking he should stay here, with us, for a few days, until he recuperates."

"Definitely," Hannah said.

Parker then told her, "Your grandmother Ruth's flying in soon. We'll go pick her up."

"And Noonie?"

Merritt's mother, Shaw guessed.

"She'll be here tonight. You'll have to sleep on the couch." A smile. "I saw that look."

But the girl did not appear seriously put out. And her face brightened when Shaw said to Parker, "You know, your daughter's quite the poet."

"Han's a woman of many talents: photography, poetry." She eyed the girl. "*And* differential equations."

"Mom . . ."

Parker nodded at the notebook in the girl's hand. Hannah started to show it to her, but Parker said, "No, Han. You read it. Out loud."

"Uhm, I don't know." Was the girl blushing?

"Please."

After a moment. "I guess." She bent to the notebook.

The Never Rule

Most people grow up and learn about life
    Every step of the way.
They learn how to do the things that are good,
    And change what they see that is not.

For some of us, though, things can go wrong.
    And we find we learned nothing at all.
The past is just lost in a dark, cloudy fog,
    And we can't see a way to escape.

But if we're lucky we find someone to help
    And they teach us just what we need.
Not by explaining or drawing a chart.
    But just by the way that they live.

How to be honest and how to be brave
    And how to be loyal and strong.
But that wouldn't have happened to me in my life.
    If it wasn't for you.

So I'm writing this poem to give you my thanks
    For making me who I am.
And I've made up a rule I'll recite every day:
    To never forget what you taught.

"Oh, my, Han. It rocks. Just beautiful."

"You like it?"

"Really." Parker hugged the girl.

Hannah stared at the page and then asked in a soft voice, nearly a whisper, "Do you think he'll hear it?"

Shaw asked, "'He'?"

"Yeah, my dad. You know, who I wrote it for."

Oh . . .

"I'm going to read it at his memorial service. You believe in that kind of stuff, Mr. Shaw?"

"What?"

"You know, that he might be there at the church? Like a ghost? I saw this show on TV, that spirits sometimes hang around after we pass. So we can say goodbye."

He said nothing about his views on the occult, which he'd spent virtually no time considering. The subject does not appear in the survivalist canon. He told her, "Some things we just can't know."

Hannah took this as validation and nodded.

She stuffed the notebook back into her book bag, along with the Emerson. Her eyes went wide suddenly. She said to him, "Oh, and I have something for *you*!" She bounded off the swing, leaving it to rock vigorously, and pushed inside, the screen door slamming loudly behind her.

Shaw said, "She's doing okay, it looks like."

But Parker didn't respond. Her eyes on him, she was offering a shallow smile. "I'm sorry."

He lifted an eyebrow.

"You thought the poem was about you?"

He was that transparent? "We connected at the lake house."

"A mom, a dad, they live in their children's souls. No one else admitted to the inner sanctum. Whatever the bullshit, the anger, the words between them, they finally let us come back in, for good or bad. And Freud got one thing right: the tug's just a bit stronger with mothers and sons, and fathers and daughters." Parker glanced at the bag, where the notebook containing the poem rested. She smiled. "I got snubbed too, you'll notice."

Then Parker said, with a schoolmarm's firm tone, "But don't think what you've got with her's superficial. It's real and important. You affected her. What you taught her, and showed her, that'll stick."

Before Shaw could respond, Hannah appeared, holding a small brown paper bag in her hand.

With a grin, she handed it to him. "Here."

He opened it. Inside was a jar of cayenne pepper.

"Until you get your gun fixed."

He laughed. He said goodbye to both of them and started for the car.

Hannah called, "Hey, Mr. Shaw, I thought up another rule."

He turned. "And what's that?"

"Never lose touch."

He gave her a nod and climbed into the rental, then pulled onto Maple View, the GPS directing him along the route that would take him eventually to the red-brick enclave of Harmon Energy Products.

Acknowledgments

Novels are not one-person endeavors. Creating them and getting them into the hands and hearts of readers is a team effort, and I am beyond lucky to have the best team in the world. My thanks to Sophie Baker, Felicity Blunt, Berit Böhm, Dominika Bojanowska, Penelope Burns, Lizz Burrell, Annie Chen, Sophie Churcher, Francesca Cinelli, Isabel Coburn, Luisa Collichio, Jane Davis, Liz Dawson, Julie Reece Deaver, Grace Dent, Danielle Dieterich, Jenna Dolan, Mira Droumeva, Jodi Fabbri, Cathy Gleason, Alice Gomer, Ivan Held, Ashley Hewlett, Aranya Jain, Sally Kim, Hamish Macaskill, Cristina Marino, Ashley McClay, Emily Mlynek, Nishtha Patel, Seba Pezzani, Rosie Pierce, Fliss Porter, Abbie Salter, Roberto Santachiara, Deborah Schneider, Sarah Shea, Mark Tavani, Lucy Upton, Madelyn Warcholik, Claire Ward, Alexis Welby, Julia Wisdom, Sue and Jackie Yang, and Kimberley Young. You're the best!

TURN THE PAGE FOR AN EXCERPT

When a New York City construction crane mysteriously collapses, causing mass destruction and killing an innocent person, Lincoln Rhyme and Amelia Sachs are on the case. A political group claims to be behind the sabotage and threatens another crane collapse in twenty-four hours, unless their demands are met. The clock is ticking.

With New York in a panic, the stakes are higher than ever for Rhyme and his team to unravel the plot before the timer runs out and the city and its people are reduced to rubble. Then Rhyme realizes that the mastermind behind the terror is his own nemesis—the Watchmaker.

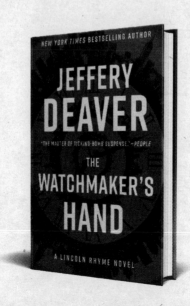

NEW YORK TIMES BESTSELLING AUTHOR

JEFFERY DEAVER

"THE MASTER OF TICKING-BOMB SUSPENSE." —PEOPLE

THE WATCHMAKER'S HAND

A LINCOLN RHYME NOVEL

1

His gaze over the majestic panorama of Manhattan, 218 feet below, was interrupted by the alarm.

He had never before heard the urgent electronic pulsing on the job.

He was familiar with the sound from training, while getting his Fall Protection Certificate, but never on shift. His level of skill and the sophistication of the million-dollar contraption beneath him were such that there had never been a reason for the high-pitched sound to fill the cab in which he sat.

Scanning the ten-by-eight-inch monitors in front of him . . . yes, a red light was now flashing.

But at the same time, apart from the urgency of the electronics, Garry Helprin knew that this was a mistake. A sensor problem.

And, yes, seconds later the light went away. The sound went away.

He nudged the control to raise the eighteen-ton load aloft, and his thoughts returned to where they had been just a moment ago.

The baby's name. While his father hoped for William, and his wife's mother for Natalia, neither of those was going to happen. Perfectly fine names. But not for Peggy and him, not for their son or daughter. He'd suggested they have some fun with their parents. What they'd decided at last: Kierkegaard if a boy. Bashilda if a girl.

When she first told him these, Garry had said, "Bathsheba, you mean. From the Bible."

"No. Bashilda. My imaginary pony when I was ten."

Kierkegaard and Bashilda, they would tell the parents, and then move on to another topic—quickly. What a reaction they'd—

The alarm began to blare again, the light to flash. They were joined by another excited box on the monitor: the load moment indicator. The needle was tilting to the left above the words: *Moment Imbalance.*

Impossible.

The computer had calculated the weight of the jib in front of him—extending the length of a Boeing 777—and the weight on the jib behind. It then factored into the balance game the weight of the load in front and the weight of the concrete counterweights behind. Finally, it measured their distance from the center, where he sat in the cab of the crane.

"Come on, Big Blue. Really?"

Garry tended to talk to the machines he was operating. Some seemed to respond. This particular Baylor HT-4200 was the most talkative of them all.

Today, though, she was silent, other than the warning sound.

If the alarm was blaring for him, it was blaring in the supervisor's trailer too.

The radio clattered, and he heard in his headset: "Garry, what?"

He replied into the stalk mike, "Gotta be an LMI sensor problem. If there was moment five minutes ago, there's moment now. Nothing's changed."

"Wind?"

"None. Sensor, I'm . . ." He fell silent.

Feeling the tilt.

"Hell," he said quickly. "It *is* a moment fault. Forward jib is point three nine degrees down. Wait, now point four."

Was the load creeping toward the end of the blue latticed jib on its own? Had the trolley become detached from the drive cables?

Garry had never heard of that happening.

He looked forward. Saw nothing irregular.

Now: −.5

Nothing is more regulated and inspected on a construction site than the stability of a tower crane, especially one that soars this high into the sky and has within its perimeter a half-dozen structures—and hundreds, perhaps thousands, of human souls. Meticulous calculations are made of the load—in this case, 36,000 pounds of six-by-four-inch flange beams—and the counterweights, the rectangular blocks of cement, to make sure this particular crane can lift and swing the payload. Once that's signed off on, the info goes into the computer and the magic balance is maintained—moving the counterweights behind him back and forth ever so slightly to keep the needle at zero.

Moment . . .

−.51

He looked back at the counterweights. This was instinctive; he didn't know what he might see.

Nothing was visible.

−.52

The blaring continued.

−.54

He shut the alarm switch off. The accompanying indicator flashed *Warning* and the *Moment Imbalance* messages continued.

−.55

The super said, "We've hit diagnostics and don't see a sensor issue."

"Forget sensors," Garry said. "We're tilting."

−.58

"I'm going to manual." He shut off the controller. He'd been riding tower cranes for the past fifteen years, since he signed up with Moynahan Construction, after his stint as an engineer in the army. Digital controls made the job easier and safer, but he'd cut his teeth operating towers by hand, using charts and graphs and a pad attached to his thigh for calculations—and, of course, a needle balance indicator to get the moment just right. He now tugged on the joystick to draw the load trolley closer to center.

Then, switching to the counterweight control, he moved those away from the tower.

His eyes were fixed on the LMI, which still indicated moment imbalance forward.

He moved the weights, totaling a hundred tons, farther back.

This *had* to achieve moment.

It was impossible for it not to.

But it did not.

Back to the front jib.

He cranked the trolley closer to him. The flanges swung. He'd moved more quickly than he'd meant to.

He was looking at his coffee cup.

The chair—padded, comfortable—did not come factory-equipped with a cup holder. But Garry, an afficionado of any and all brews, had mounted one on the wall—far away from the electronics, of course.

The brown liquid was level; the cup was not.

Another glance at the LMI indicator.

A full −2 percent down in the front.

He worked the trolley control and brought the load of flanges closer yet.

Ah, yes, that did it.

The alarm light went out as the balance indicator now moved slowly back to −.5 and then 0, then 1, and kept rising. This was because the counterweights were so far back. Garry now reeled them in until they were as far forward as they could go.

It brought the LMI needle to 1.2.

This was normal. Cranes are made to lean backward slightly when there is no weight of a load on the front jib, which should, at rest, be about one degree. The main stability comes from the massive concrete base—that's what holds it upright when there's no balancing act going on.

"Got it, Danny," he radioed. "Stable. But I'll need maintenance. Got to be some counterweight issue."

"K. I think Will's off break."

Garry sat back and sipped his coffee, replaced the cup, listened to the wind. It would be some minutes before the mechanic arrived. To get to the cab from the ground, there was one way and one way only.

You climbed the mast.

But the cab was twenty-two stories above the ground. Which meant at least one, maybe two five-minute rest stops on the way up.

Guys on the site sometimes thought if you were a crane operator you were in lousy shape, sitting on your ass all day long. They forgot about the climb.

With no load to deliver, no hook block to steer carefully to the ground, he could sit back and enjoy the indescribable view. If Garry wanted, he could put a name to what he was looking at: the five boroughs of the city, a huge parcel of New Jersey, a thin band of Westchester, one of Long Island too.

But he wasn't interested in GPS information.

He was thrilled by the browns and grays and greens and white clouds and the endless blue—every shade far richer and bolder than when viewed by landlocked pedestrians below.

From a young age, Garry had known he wanted to build skyscrapers. That's what he had made with his Legos. That's what he had begged his parents to take him to visit, even when his mother and father blanched at the idea of standing on observation decks. He only liked the open ones. "You know," his father had said, "sometimes people go crazy and throw themselves off the edge of high places. The fear takes them."

Naw, probably not. There was nothing to fear from heights. The higher he got, the calmer he became. Whether it was rock climbing, mountaineering, or building skyscrapers, heights comforted him.

He was, he told Peggy, "in heaven" when he was far, far aboveground.

Back to baby names.

Kierkegaard, Bashilda . . .

What would they really pick? Neither wanted a Junior. And they didn't want any names currently in vogue, which you could find easily in the tiny booklets on the Gristedes checkout lane.

He reached for his coffee cup.

No!

The level had changed again. The front jib was dipping once more.

−.4

A moment later, the duo of warning signs burst on again, and the alarm, which had defaulted back on, blared.

The balance indicator jumped to −1.2.

He hit Transmit. "Dan. She's moving again. Big-time."

"Shit. What's going on?"

"Can't reel the load any farther. I'm dropping it. Clear the zone. Tell me when."

"Yeah, okay."

He couldn't hear the command from here, but he had a view through the Plexiglas straight down between his legs and saw the workers scatter quickly as the ground foreman told them to get out of the way.

Of course, "dropping" the load didn't mean that literally—yanking the release and letting the seventeen tons of steel free-fall to the ground. He eased the down lever and the bundle dropped fast. He could see, on his indicators and visually through the Plexiglas, exactly where it was on descent. At about thirty feet above the ground, he braked, and the bundle settled onto the concrete. Maybe some damage.

Too bad.

He adjusted the counterweights, hit the hook release and detached the load.

But this had no effect.

The word "impossible" came to his mind yet again.

He cranked the counterweights backward once more.

This *had* to arrest the forward tilt.

No load and the counterweights were at the far end of the back jib.

And still . . .

"Dan," he radioed, "we're five degrees down, forward jib. Counterweights're back."

−6.1

A crane is not meant to lean more than five degrees. Beyond that, the complicated skeletons of steel tubes and rods and plates begin to buckle and bend. The slewing plate—the huge turntable that swung the jib horizontally—was groaning.

He heard a distant but loud crack. Then another.

−7

Into the radio: "I'm losing it, Dan. Hit the siren."

Just moments later came the piercing emergency cry. This was not associated with a crane disaster specifically. It just meant some bad shit was going to happen. Instructions would be coming from the loudspeaker and on the radio.

"Garry, get out. Down the mast."

"In a minute . . ."

If Big Blue was going down, he was going to make sure she landed with as few injuries to those on the ground as possible.

He scanned the surroundings. There were buildings almost everywhere.

But fifty feet to the right of the jib was a gap between the office building in front of him and an apartment complex. Through the gap, he could see a street and a park. On this temperate day, there would be people outside, but they had most likely heard the siren and would be looking toward the akilter crane.

Cars and trucks, with windows rolled up?

"I'm aiming away from the buildings. Have somebody clear that park on Eighty-Ninth. And get a flagman into the street, stop traffic."

"Garry, get outta there while you can!"

"The park! Clear it!"

Creaking, groaning, the wind . . .

Another explosive snap.

He operated the swivel control and the slewing plate cried from binding against the bearings. The electric motor was laboring. Then, slowly, the jib responded.

"Come on, come on . . ."

Thirty feet from the gap.

Any minute now. He could feel it. Any minute she was going to drop.

Cars continued to stream past.

His decision was logical, but nonetheless stabbed his heart.

People were about to die because of him. Maybe fewer than if he didn't move the jib, but still . . .

The numbers rolled through his frantic mind.

Distance to the gap: twenty feet.

LMI: −8.2

"Come on," he whispered.

"Garry . . ."

"Clear the goddamn park! The street!" He tore the

headset off as if the distraction of transmissions was gumming the mechanism further.

Twelve feet from the gap, nine degrees down.

The joystick was all the way to the right and the jib should have been swinging madly. But the binding metal of the slewing plate had slowed it to a crawl.

Slowed, but not stopped.

A sudden squeal. Nails on a chalkboard . . .

He jammed his teeth together at the sound.

Ten feet, ten degrees down.

Eight feet from the gap.

Please . . . A little farther . . .

Close. But if Big Blue failed now, the jib would slice through four or five floors of offices, all open design, hundreds of workers at desks and in cubicles, at coffee stations, in conference rooms. He could see them. A few were on their feet, staring at the tilting mast. No one was running. They were taking videos. Jesus . . .

Seven feet.

The motion stalled momentarily, then resumed, with the squeal and grinding even louder.

He nudged the stick to the left and it responded, swinging back a foot or two, then he shoved it to the right. The plate resumed its rotation in that direction, past the sticking point.

Six feet from the gap, down twelve degrees . . .

Crack . . .

The loud sound from behind made him jump.

What was it?

Ah, of course.

The exit door in the floor that led down to the mast, to the ladder, to safety, had buckled. He climbed from his seat briefly and tugged. Useless.

There was only one other exit—above him. But that gave no access to the mast.

Forget it now. Just get another five feet and she'll be clear.

The jib was still tilting down, but the LMI indicator had stopped at −13. The engineers, of course, had known that there was no point in going farther. A jib would never tilt that far forward.

Six feet away from the lifesaving gap, the mast suddenly pitched forward a few feet. Garry slipped from the seat and fell. He landed face-first on the bulb of the window. From here, he found himself looking straight downward, twenty-two stories, to the jobsite. He inhaled and exhaled deeply, leaving a design of condensation on the glass in front of him. It was, curiously, almost in the shape of a heart.

He thought of his wife.

And of their child, soon to be born.

Kierkegaard or Bashilda . . .